BETTER THAN THIS

Stuart Harrison was born and grew up in England. He lived in New Zealand for many years before returning to England to write his first novel. He now lives in Sydney, Australia with his wife and their two young sons where he writes full time. He travels often to both New Zealand and England, both of which he misses. His website address is: www.stuartharrison.com

Stuart Harrison

BETTER THAN THIS

HarperCollins*Publishers*

This novel is entirely a work of fiction.
The names, characters and incidents portrayed in it are
the work of the author's imagination. Any resemblance to
actual persons, living or dead, events or localities is
entirely coincidental.

HarperCollins*Publishers*
77–85 Fulham Palace Road,
Hammersmith, London w6 8jb

www.**fire**and**water**.com

Special overseas edition 2002
1 3 5 7 9 8 6 4 2

First published in Great Britain by
HarperCollins*Publishers* 2001

ISBN 0 00 651457 X

Set in PostScript ITC New Baskerville by
Rowland Phototypesetting Ltd,
Bury St Edmunds, Suffolk

Printed and bound by
Clays Ltd, St Ives plc

This Is For My Mother

ACKNOWLEDGEMENTS

To Susan Opie, my editor at HarperCollins, Ilka Heinemann at List, and Stephanie and the team at William Morris: Thanks.

Part One

CHAPTER ONE

I woke suddenly, aware that I was alone in bed and certain that Sally had left me. My sleep had been troubled, and I lay in the darkness feeling my heart beating too fast, assailed by panic under which lay a melancholy loss.

How had it happened? When had we stopped being happy with one another? I tried to recall an incident, some defining moment but I couldn't settle on anything. We had been married for eight years. I had never screwed around, not even once during that time. I had been attracted to other women, sure, and perhaps once or twice I'd even been in situations where I was tempted to do something about it, but I loved Sally and that was more important to me than any one-off encounter I knew I'd end up regretting. But lately we'd been fighting more than usual, and talking less. There were problems with the bank and with the agency that my partner Marcus and I jointly owned which had taken its toll on my marriage. But what was wrong with us went deeper than that.

Gradually, as the boundary between sleep and wakefulness dissolved, I wondered if the images that lingered in my mind were real or imagined. Had I dreamt Sally was gone? She had left the house in the dead of night with a suitcase clutched in one hand, which she put in the trunk of her car. The next thing she was at the airport, where she caught a plane to her parents' house in Oregon. A vestige of bitterness remained when I imagined her mother comforting her, reminding Sally that she had always known this would happen.

I reached out, and beside me in the bed there was only an empty space. At that moment I heard the toilet flush, and a second later the bathroom door opened spilling a wedge of light across the floor. I feigned sleep as relief washed over me. Through half-closed eyes I watched as Sally appeared framed in the doorway. She wore a long pale cream nightgown through which, as she reached to turn out the light, her body was clearly delineated. I glimpsed an image of shadows and curves, the softness of her breasts, the slope of her belly. Then, with the light extinguished, she came ghost-like back to bed.

For a moment I didn't move, but I needed physical reassurance of her presence and I turned on my side and lay my hand on her shoulder. 'Sally.'

She had her back to me, and mumbled something I couldn't make out. When I tried to turn her towards me she grudgingly resisted, a reminder that all was not well between us. I tried to remember the last time we'd made love but all I knew was that it had been a long time.

I recalled an occasion several months earlier when Sally had announced that she needed to see her doctor because she was finishing up her supply of birth control pills.

'What do you think?' she asked.

'About what?'

She fixed me with her steady gaze. 'Should I renew my prescription?'

I knew what she was getting at but I pretended not to. 'I guess,' I said abstractedly. 'Have you seen my keys?'

Sally, though, wasn't going to let me off that easily. 'So, you think I should?' she insisted, an edge of warning in her voice I knew better than to ignore. I paused and reluctantly met her eye.

'Why wouldn't you?'

'Because taking the pill over long periods can affect a woman's ability to conceive. It might be a good idea if I stopped and gave my body time to adjust.'

The unspoken but clear purpose of this conversation hung poised in the air between us. It had been a while since we'd last had a discussion like this. I searched for the right note of understanding when I replied. 'Sally, I really don't think this is a good time. Maybe if you wait a little while. You know how things are at the agency.'

Her mouth tightened just perceptibly. 'It isn't as if I would fall pregnant right away.'

'I know that, but you can't be certain. Things are tough right now and what with the mortgage and everything else . . . I just think a little more time,' I finished lamely.

'Christ!' She got up and started clattering dishes as she emptied the dishwasher and banged them down on the counter.

I got up and went over to her. 'Sally . . .'

She shrugged me off angrily. 'Don't try to get around me. I'm tired of this, Nick. I'm tired of everything.' She whirled around to face me. 'It's never the right time.' She paused and I saw a resolve in her eye and I guessed what was coming even before she said it. 'I'm not going to take the pill any more. If you don't want me to get pregnant, then you take responsibility for a change.'

For a few days afterwards things were tense between us. One night I came home and found a packet of condoms on my night stand. I put them away in the drawer and though Sally must have noticed neither of us mentioned them. But gradually the incident was forgotten, or at least put aside. It must have been weeks later that I reached for her one night when we were in bed, and somehow all the friction and minor hurts that featured in our lives these days were forgotten as we tried to recapture a semblance of our former closeness. But in the height of passion, locked in a deep kiss as I moved to lay over her, and she shifted position to accommodate me I remembered the condoms. I broke off and fumbled for the drawer.

'What is it?' Sally asked, and then she realized what I was doing.

She watched me in recriminating silence and I could feel her mood change and when I kissed her again she was barely responsive. Our passion evaporated leaving only awkwardness in its place.

Now as I remembered that occasion I let my hand drop from her side. 'You okay?'

No answer, but I could tell she was either angry or upset, or both which puzzled me. True, we were going through a difficult time but I sensed a tension in her that was raw, as if from a fresh wound. We hadn't argued the night before, so it couldn't be that. I'd arrived home late, which wasn't unusual. It must have been around nine-thirty or so. Sally was reading a magazine in the living room. She looked up and offered her cheek when I bent to kiss her, and said there was chicken salad in the refrigerator if I was hungry. Shortly afterwards she said she was tired and was going to bed. I stayed up alone.

I picked at the salad and drank a couple of glasses of wine, then, when the bottle was empty, rather than open another I poured a scotch and ice which I drank in front of the TV watching a rerun of *Seinfeld*. I wasn't paying attention so I turned it off. I was thinking instead about the meeting Marcus and I had with the bank in the morning which would determine the future of Carpe Diem, the advertising agency we had started together several years ago, but which I alone had brought to the brink of ruin. I sat there drinking scotch and brooding. My friend and partner was barely speaking to me, my life was collapsing, and there was no solace to be found in my marriage. It occurred to me that Sally and I probably hadn't spoken more than a dozen words to one another the whole of that day. When I went upstairs to bed it was after midnight and she was asleep.

Right now Sally remained unyielding and I needed to pee so I went to the bathroom, making sure I closed the door before I turned on the light. While I emptied my bladder I studied my reflection in the mirror. I've always had thick, dark brown hair which I wear short but I saw something that startled me, and leaning closer I examined the strands of white at my temples. I tried to tell myself it was the light but I knew it wasn't. My brow was creased in frown lines, and I noticed for the first time just how deep they ran, like furrows in a ploughed field, and the crow's feet around my eyes seemed more pronounced than I remembered. I was so absorbed with these unwelcome signs of aging that I splashed on my foot.

'Shit,' I muttered.

I finished up, then rinsed my foot off under the tap. I looked back at my reflection. I was thirty-four years old but I appeared older than that. My eyes weren't as clear as they should have been. Too many late nights pouring over market reports or preparing for meetings, too much booze in the process. I'd get home dead tired and knock back another couple of drinks, then sleep badly until dawn, if I was lucky. I stood back from the mirror. On the plus side, though I was a pound or two heavier than I ought to have been I was still in okay shape. I have the characteristic deep chest and wide shoulders of a swimmer. Ever since college I've hauled myself down to the pool at least three or four times a week. A hundred lengths without stopping. Smooth, even strokes, not hurrying but not slouching either. Lately I hadn't been going as often, but I was still making it when I could. The grey hairs still worried me. It wasn't vanity exactly. It was more like fear and mild panic. I'd be forty before I knew it, and then what? I had achieved very few of the things I wanted to in my life, and the clock was ticking. I could almost hear the soft trickle of the grains of sand falling through some cosmic hourglass that represented my allotted time on this earth.

My eye fell on a partially open pack of Carefree on the vanity top. The rows of smooth, white tampons in their clear glossy wrappers resembled, oddly I thought, virginal bullets. Beside the box a sliver of cellophane lay where it had fallen and suddenly I knew what was wrong with Sally. She'd been moody for a couple of days when I thought about it. She must have known, her body signalling the coming change. She always complained how her belly became swollen just before her period, not that I could see it. I stared at the open pack. It was a stark symbol of the discord between us.

By six-thirty I was showered and dressed and drinking my first cup of coffee in the kitchen. Sally sat at the bench wearing a big white fluffy robe which she seemed to shrink inside. She still looked half-asleep. Her big brown eyes were half-hooded, and her bee stung lips lent a pouting, almost sullen expression. She was thirty-one but looked younger, still girl/woman. Steam from her coffee cup drifted like mist before her face, and she appeared to gaze into the middle distance, her thoughts hidden. I glanced at the time.

'I should be going,' I said. 'I don't want to be late for the meeting.'

She cast me a brief accusing glance but didn't say anything. I thought about the traffic build-up on the freeway, but I had a little time and I was reluctant to leave just yet.

'Look, it's going to work out. Once they see our new projections the bank will give us a break.' I went over and put my hands on her shoulders, and bent to kiss her neck. Her skin was soft and warm and I breathed in the mingled scents of sleep and the hair shampoo she used. I wanted to put my arms around her, tell her I loved her, have her lean back against me the way she used to, her eyes closed, her lips a little parted as I murmured in her ear. But as if she sensed my intent she got up abruptly and went to put her cup in the dishwasher.

'You had your period didn't you?' I said to her back. Her shoulders stiffened slightly. 'That's what you're upset about isn't it?'

'Is it?' she said, refusing to face me.

'I think so, yes.' I hesitated, then I took a tentative step towards her and she must have heard me because she turned round. Her eyes were glistening, but I wasn't sure if she was angry or upset.

'You should go,' she said.

I glanced at the time, thinking she was right, but I couldn't leave her like this on this day of all days. I needed to know everything was okay between us. I needed to know she didn't hate me. I forced a note of optimism into my voice that I didn't really feel. 'When this is all over we can start trying . . .'

Sally shook her head violently. 'I don't want to hear this.'

'You're just . . .'

'What? I'm just what?'

'I don't know. I can guess what you're thinking, that's all.'

'Really?' she said. She was angry now. She wiped her

eyes with a vigorous gesture, like she meant business. 'So, what am I thinking, Nick? Tell me, I'd like to know.'

I wished suddenly that I had left when I had the chance, that I hadn't gotten into this, but I was committed now. 'I think you're afraid the bank will pull the plug on us this morning. And then we'll have to wait a while longer before we can think about starting a family.'

She uttered a short humourless laugh. 'Well, I should be used to that shouldn't I?'

Beneath her anger was a blunt edged blade of truth. 'It'll work out, Sally, I promise,' I said. Her shoulders sagged slightly in weary resignation.

'You know, I don't know if I care.'

I was a little shocked and I couldn't believe she meant it. 'How can you not care about our future?'

'Our future? I don't know what that is any more.'

This kind of talk bothered me deeply. The one thing I'd always held onto was my dream, my idea of what our lives would one day be like. But dreams need people to believe in them otherwise the colour begins to bleed out of them like an old painting and they begin to seem less real, taking on the mantle of wistful imaginings instead of something actually possible. I was suddenly aware of something I'd known for some time. Sally didn't believe any more. I tried to rally her.

'Our future is what it has always been. This house, a family. Isn't that what you want?'

'It doesn't matter what I want though does it, Nick. It's about what you want.'

'What I want is for you to be happy. For both of us to be happy together.'

She gave a little shake of her head. 'If that's true why have you never wanted me to get pregnant?'

'Come on. We've been all over this. I want kids as much as you do. I only ever wanted us to be ready. I want us to have all the things a child needs. For you to be able to stay home and not have to go to work. I just think it ought to be the right time, that's all.'

'The right time?' She gave me a cynical smile. 'Right. And when is that going to be?' She started ticking off the fingers of one hand. 'Let's see, first you wanted to wait until the agency was on its feet. Then we had to have the right kind of house, which you made damn sure it took for ever to find because there was always something not quite right. Wrong neighbourhood. Too far from the city. Too close to the city. Garden too big, garden too small . . .'

'This isn't fair,' I cut in.

'No! No it isn't fair, you're right. Because I've always gone along with you before. I went along with you when we finally found this house and you said we should wait awhile because we'd borrowed more than we could afford. So I waited. And then when the agency was doing okay, when everything was going along just fine, what happens then?'

I knew what was coming. A little over a year ago we had taken on a new client, a start-up dot.com company. They folded owing us a lot of money. 'OfficeLine was a calculated risk. Nobody could have predicted they wouldn't make it.'

'Marcus was always against it,' Sally countered.

'If it was left to Marcus we would never take any risks. You can't run a business that way.'

'Marcus wanted you to slow down. Take it a step at a time. But you wouldn't listen. You never listen to anyone.'

It's easy to argue your case in retrospect if your position was ultimately proven right, and in this case I didn't have a leg to stand on. It didn't matter that OfficeLine might have easily been a huge success, and made us all rich. It could have happened. It just didn't. I couldn't win this one so I gave in.

'I admit it didn't work out that time. I made some mistakes. But I was doing what I thought was best. For us.'

'For us, Nick? Really, it was for us?'

'Of course.'

'You almost ruined us. We nearly lost the house, we nearly lost everything.'

'But we didn't,' I pointed out. 'We're still here.'

'Today we are, but what about tomorrow? I waited, Nick. I waited again while we worked another year to pay off the debts.'

Her voice cracked and I thought she was going to cry. I could see the anguish in her expression and it pierced me to my core. I wanted to hold her, reassure her and I started a movement that would have encircled her in my arms and held her against me while she sobbed against my chest, but she flinched as if she'd been struck and anger flashed in her eyes.

'And now, dammit, when finally, finally I thought everything was supposed to be coming right, I find out the bank are threatening to close you down again.' She shook her head in disbelief. 'How could you do it, Nick? How could you take such a risk again? And without telling anybody. Not even Marcus, let alone me? How could you have done that?'

'Look, I know how you feel,' I said, avoiding the difficult part of her question and concentrating on justifying what I did rather than the way I did it. 'But Spectrum isn't OfficeLine. It's a different situation. Once the bank understand that if we get this account it'll put the agency in a whole different league they'll back off. A couple more months and this will all be behind us. You'll be able to quit work. A year from now we'll be parents. I swear to you. This time it's going to happen.'

For a moment we stared at each other. My expression appealing, Sally looking as if I'd uttered something completely incomprehensible to her. Once again I made a move towards her but she spun sideways to evade me.

'No!' She held up her hand. 'I've heard it all before, Nick. And you don't know how I feel. You don't! If you did, if you cared about me, about what I want we wouldn't be having this conversation.'

She peered at me intently, as if trying to see me through a thick fog. The anger seemed to drain out of her and her shoulders slumped a little, but I didn't like what replaced it in her eyes. When she spoke again her voice was heavy with resignation and weariness. 'I used to think I knew you.'

'What do you mean? Of course you know me.'

'Do I? Sometimes I don't recognize you. You don't listen to anyone any more. You're so obsessed with making the agency into a huge success, it seems as if you'd do anything to get what you want.'

'I work hard, and I know what I want, is that so bad?'

'It is when you start lying. When you keep things from me.'

'I didn't tell you about the bank because I didn't want to worry you.'

'I'm your wife, Nick. You've known for months that you were in trouble and you didn't say anything. You went on pretending nothing was happening. This is my life too. And what about Marcus? For God's sake he's supposed to be your friend, not just your partner! This could ruin him too. Don't you think he had a right to know?'

'It isn't as simple as that, Sally, you know that. Marcus is a terrifically talented guy. Creatively he's the best, I've always said that. But even he'd admit that if it wasn't for

13

me Carpe Diem would never get any bigger. We'd stay the way we are for ever.'

'So that makes it okay to go behind his back? Ignore everything he says?'

'It isn't like that.'

'It is, Nick. It's exactly like that, and you're the only one who can't see it.' She shook her head, still peering at me. 'You've changed.'

I didn't like the way she sounded, the way she was looking at me. I could see how things must look to her, but she was wrong about me. All I wanted was for us to be happy. 'Sally . . .' I said, making a final appeal.

'Don't,' she said, placing a hand against my chest. Then again quietly. 'Don't.'

CHAPTER TWO

The house we lived in was a three bedroom, two bath clapboard with a two car garage in the wooded hills of Hillsborough. All of the houses on our street were set back from the road behind neat front lawns and shady trees. It was a pleasant neighbourhood where the lot sizes ran to a third of an acre and on a good day the 280 freeway allowed me to be in downtown San Francisco in less than half an hour. We bought the house four years ago when already real estate in the Bay Area was shooting towards the stratosphere fuelled by Silicon Valley. It cost seven forty-five then, but now was worth somewhere around a million. From the end of the street I could look across the valley and see houses less than half a mile away nestled snugly among the trees worth eight, nine, ten million. Crazy.

Back when we found the house I'd balked at the price, but looking for a family home had been my idea in the first place and I'd stretched out the search for six months before we found this one. At the time we were renting an apartment in South Beach. Sally had been becoming impatient, and so we'd put in an offer, even though it meant stretching our borrowing to the limit and ensured that Sally couldn't contemplate quitting work for a while until I was making enough money to meet the mortgage payments. She had argued we could buy something cheaper, but in the end I had got my way. There was no denying that I'd seen buying the house partly as a means of delaying starting a family.

It wasn't that I didn't want Sally to have the baby she craved. We'd always talked about having a family and I knew the day we were married how important it was to her. The only discord between us was about when we should start. When we were younger we were happy to nominate some vague future time when we were 'settled'. It was only when Sally hit her mid-twenties and she saw friends and people at work start to have babies that we began debating in earnest what being settled really meant. That was when the cracks appeared. To Sally it meant having a decent place to live in and earning enough to maintain a pleasant lifestyle. To me it meant something else. It meant having security.

When I left the house that morning I put down the top of my Saab convertible which was on a two-year lease to the company. It was the kind of morning that we don't take for granted during May in the Bay Area. The sky was robin's egg blue promising a fine day. As I turned onto the freeway to join the San Francisco bound traffic I wondered how much longer we would be living in Hillsborough. The 280 runs along a high ridge on the peninsula bounded by hills and woods on the Pacific Ocean side and the expensive communities built on the wooded slopes on the Bay side. It feels like a thousand miles from anywhere, and is a warm and sheltered environment protected from the cool air and fog that haunts San Francisco and the coastal towns of Half Moon Bay and Pacifica. As the crow flows it's no more than a couple of miles to the Bayshore freeway that runs parallel and carries traffic from the south and the east across the San Mateo Bridge on towards the airport and San Francisco, but the contrast couldn't be more different. Down there the view is of endless ugly housing and commercial development that appears devoid of trees, a land packed beneath a for ever boiling sky of grey cloud. Up here there is the sun and the woods and hills and peace. A nice way to begin the day, and a nice place to come home to at the end of it.

As I drove I wondered how long it would last. The bank was threatening to shut us down. That would mean selling the house and losing everything. For once I didn't notice the view. My stomach churned and every now and then I broke out in a cold sweat of fear. By the end of the day Carpe Diem could be history.

It was Marcus who had come up with the name when we decided to start our own advertising agency. He had to explain to me what it meant.

'It's Latin,' he said. 'It means Seize The Day.'

I liked it. Advertising agencies typically have names that are derived directly from the partners, as in the Saatchi brothers, or else they're either corporate bland, such as KCM, one of the biggies in the Bay Area and one I'd once worked for, or they choose something obscure and cutting edge. Going the latter route made us sound upmarket and trendy, not a bad thing in the advertising business, and the name we chose reflected a basic truth about Marcus and I. The arty feel was Marcus in a nut-shell, he was the creative genius whereas the go-getting sentiment applied more to me. I've always been the talker, the deal maker, the one who handled the clients. To-gether we made a pretty good team.

We met at college and became friends when Marcus was majoring in art and graphic design and I was doing a business degree and neither of us had any idea what we wanted to do with our lives. I moved into a room in the house where Marcus lived and from the beginning we got on well, even though in many ways we weren't alike. I was in the swim team and I ran the fifteen hundred, so a lot of the people I knew were from athletic circles, but Marcus wasn't much interested in competitive sport. His interests revolved more around political issues and he was often involved in petitions and protest marches about things like the destruction of the environment or the exploitation of the third world. The first time I saw him he was wearing faded jeans and a T-shirt with a marijuana leaf printed on the front. He had dark brown hair which he wore longish so that it constantly fell over his glasses and he had a short beard.

'Glad to meet you,' he said and shook my hand. He was a head shorter than me and my instant impression was that he was the intelligent, serious type. I pigeonholed him as one of the kind who ran the student bodies and the radio station, who always made me feel slightly uncomfortable with their knowledge of what was going on in the world and their belief that they should and could contribute to change. He was with a Eurasian girl who had the most stunning eyes and skin. I saw him with a lot of girls after that, always young, always beautiful and intelligent. I would run into them coming from his room on the way to the bathroom wrapped in a towel, and sometimes we'd exchange a few words. I was used to hanging out with the girls who buzzed around the jocks. A lot of them were fun loving cheerleader types, and mostly gorgeous. I'd always assumed guys like Marcus had to make do with what was left over, but of course I was wrong about that and Marcus opened my eyes to that truth.

Our friendship grew slowly. I liked being with Marcus because we talked about all kind of things I never could discuss with my other friends. Around him I didn't feel as if I always had to be presenting some macho front, but I could be who I was. I realized eventually that was why girls liked him too. Maybe he wasn't classically good looking or particularly athletic, attributes often admired on university campuses, but he was a good listener, and he didn't judge people arbitrarily. I don't know what he saw in me, but somehow we ended up firm friends.

After we gained our degrees we both finished up in San Francisco working in the advertising business. Marcus in design. Me in account management. We were at separate agencies when we came up with the idea of starting up alone. We recognized that our individual strengths could suit a partnership. That is to say Marcus handled the creative side while I dealt with the clients. It worked well that way. Being likable is one thing, but our clients would never have entrusted their brands with somebody like Marcus. Even in the casual business environment of California he made them uncomfortable. They expected advertising people to be a little quirky but they were also entrusting us with a lot of money. They wanted reassurance. They didn't expect us to wear a suit and tie and behave like bankers, but neither did they want to hire somebody who wore faded jeans and a Chilli Peppers T-shirt and looked like he probably got high a lot, which is the impression Marcus managed to convey without trying. Even that could have been forgiven if he could talk the talk, but numbers and markets, demographic targets, reach percentages and all the other bullshit jargon that advertising is riddled with was all just so much cotton wool to Marcus. He couldn't make sense of it. Had no feel for, or even the faintest interest in it.

Advertising, like any business, has its own language, and like any business it was invented for a reason. The reason is to make the mundane and pedestrian sound impressive. It is meant to exclude those who don't speak the language, to make them part of the uninitiated, to imply they don't understand the complex nature and rhythm, the subtleties of the science of advertising. Even the clients aren't expected to understand. Nobody even wants them to. Not even themselves. People are impressed by the incomprehensible. It makes them feel they are in safe hands, that people who know more than they do are flying the plane.

And so we produce masses of documented research to define a target audience in such and such a demographic. People who read this magazine and watch that TV show and shop at a particular supermarket rather than the one along the street, and we talk about penetration and reach (with a straight face) and show the client a concept to sell their new formula shampoo which in the end boils down to this: We show some images of a gorgeous young woman with incredible hair and a terrific body who attracts good looking men like bees to honey. The message is: Buy my shampoo and this will be you. Period. And the more a client is able to spend, the more they will sell. And that's pretty well what all advertising comes down to in the end, with slight variations, and the only thing you really have to do is find a way to make your ads shine out from the rest. And nobody believes it anyway, though secretly a part of all of us wants to, which is why it works. Rocket science it ain't. But we make it sound as if it is, and the client wouldn't have it any other way. It fits in with all the other stuff to do with revenues and cash flows, above and below the line costs, forecasts and projections, and all the things Marcus simply wasn't good at.

He was an ideas man, a gifted conceptualist. He dreamed up wonderful, innovative and clever campaigns, but put him in front of a room full of people and give him a presentation to make and he would turn into a mumbling wreck. Words would lose their meaning, numbers would transform into hieroglyphics. He would lose his place, emphasize the wrong phrase, misquote a figure, and if asked a question would blink myopically behind his round Lennonesque glasses and freeze like a rabbit caught in headlights on a lonely highway. In short he was a disaster, and we both knew it, which was why that morning when we met with the bank I was going to be doing all the talking.

Traffic seemed to be sluggish. I checked the time. I was running late because of the argument I'd had with Sally. All being well it was a twenty-five, thirty minute run into town, on a bad day forty-five. It was seven-thirty and though the meeting wasn't until nine Marcus and I had arranged to meet at the office first for a quick cup of coffee and a final run through of the presentation, though as our entire future rested on this meeting I had made damn sure I knew every word by heart anyway.

The traffic began to slow, thickening through the lanes like a stodgy cake batter. I wondered what the hold-up was, and then to my dismay I found myself slowly coming to a halt. I sat in my car wondering what the hell was going on. Every lane was at a standstill stretching as far ahead as I could see, and it wasn't until I turned on the radio that I learned a truck carrying yogurt had over-turned on the freeway up ahead of me. There was no exit ramp between where I was stuck and the accident, so there was nothing to do but to sit it out. I checked the time again then I picked up my phone and called Marcus.

He answered on the second ring. 'Hey, it's me,' I said. 'Where are you?'

'Just hitting Bay Street,' he answered.

'Great.'

Marcus lived across the Bay in Sausalito and his journey took him over the Golden Gate Bridge every day. From Bay to the office in South Beach was a short drive. He was going to arrive early, as I should have.

'What's the problem?' Marcus said suspiciously.

'I might be a little late.' I told him where I was and was met with silence.

'Dammit, Nick! How late?'

'I don't know, nothing's moving right now.' I had the radio tuned to a local news station which had a traffic helicopter on the scene from which a reporter was describing the mayhem below, conjuring images of fire department personnel and police officers spread all around the cordoned off accident. It sounded like a mess.

'Christ,' Marcus muttered. 'Maybe I should call ahead. Tell the bank what's happened and postpone the meeting.'

I didn't think that was a good idea. In the bank's view I'd already dicked them around for long enough by avoiding their calls and repeated demands for a meeting. I'd realized too late that I was pushing my luck and in the end when our accountant had told me the bank was going to cut us off cold, I'd had to practically plead for a chance to put our case. I hadn't told Marcus things were this bad but I knew I'd used up all our chances at the bank and I needed whatever residue of goodwill might be left in their cold financiers' hearts. Asking for a postponement now wasn't going to wash, yogurt truck or no.

'No good,' I said. 'Besides they'll just want to start without me.'

'How can we start without you?' Marcus questioned, and then in the silence that followed, the answer dawned on him. The tone of his voice which until then had been laced with sullen resentment altered to one of panicked disbelief. 'You mean they'll want me to go along anyway?' He thought it through another step. 'You're not suggesting that I should do this presentation?'

'Maybe it would be a good idea to go over it.' I counted to three, waiting for his reaction.

'Are you serious? I can't do it. You know I'd screw it

up! Damn it, Nick, this is what you do. There's no way I can pull it off.'

If there had been another way I wouldn't have even suggested the idea, but unless we could persuade the bank not to pull the rug from under us we were finished. At least if Marcus made our case we'd have a chance, however slim, and there was always the hope that I could still arrive late and take over. It came down to the lesser of two evils.

'Listen, you're not used to this kind of thing that's all. But you can do it as well as I can,' I said.

'That's bullshit and we both know it.'

'All you have to do,' I said soothingly, 'is go over the material now and get it fixed in your mind. I'll probably be there anyway, this is only a precaution.'

He was quiet for a few seconds as he absorbed the knowledge that I was actually serious. 'I can't believe you're asking me to do this.'

'I didn't plan it this way, Marcus. I didn't make that truck crash.'

'The way you see it, Nick, you never plan any of the shit that happens, but somehow it still does.'

I heard the echo of Sally's recrimination in Marcus's tone. A mixture of anger and disappointment. It was the disappointment that got to me. We were in trouble because at my insistence we'd decided to pitch for a new client. Spectrum was a software company that had just been taken over. The injection of capital meant they were a prize in their own right, but if we won the account we'd have a foot into the parent company too. It was a dream opportunity, one that could make us serious money. In fact it was a lot like OfficeLine. Or at least that's how Marcus had viewed it. But sometimes you have to run with your gut feel, and that's what I did. Even when things started going wrong, and money became short I knew in my bones we were doing the right thing, so to make life easier I just didn't tell Marcus what was going on. I thought we would get the account and everything would be okay, but then the bank stepped in, and finally I had no choice but to admit what was happening. I can still see him blinking in disbelief, then hurt clouding his eyes as he took off his glasses to polish the lenses.

And now Marcus thought I was letting him down again, but there wasn't much I could do about that. If I didn't make it he had to do the presentation to the bank or we were finished. 'Look, I know how you feel, I got us into this situation and I should be the one to get us out, but I can't do anything about this. I don't know what else to say to you.'

'No,' he said heavily. 'I don't know either.'

'I might still get there,' I said, though ahead of me the traffic wasn't moving. 'But if I don't, stall as long as you can, take your time. Don't rush it. I'll call as soon as I know anything.'

He hung up, and in that moment I felt our friendship had slid a little further in its inexorable momentum downwards. I looked at my watch. It wasn't looking good. I was sitting motionless with the roof down, breathing in clouds of pollution with the sun beginning to bake the top of my head.

On the radio the woman reporter in the helicopter was still talking. I listened with growing impatience. I don't know how she did it. The facts were that the overturned truck had blocked every city-bound lane on the freeway and that emergency services were trying to clear a route through. Somehow she managed to transform what was pretty simple information into something approximating a Hollywood epic. With increasing melodrama she related the scene below, describing overworked police trying to hold back the crowd of onlookers who'd abandoned their

24

cars while desperate fire-fighters tried to contain the spread of the spilled load, which she made sound like a hazardous explosive chemical instead of raspberry yogurt.

'I think there's a real concern by the authorities that we could have a pollution issue here.' Her tone was deeply serious, fraught with tension.

'I guess that could cause real problems,' the studio guy pronounced solemnly.

'Well, I guess it could . . .'

We were left wondering what kind of problems? A bad smell perhaps?

She kept piling information I didn't need. All I wanted to know was how long I was going to be stuck there. Every time I glanced at the time another few minutes had dragged by bringing me ever closer to the most important meeting of my life which it seemed I would not be attending.

'It's just like a parking lot down there,' the reporter said cheerfully. 'Nothing's moving at all,' she added in case we had missed the point.

I prayed for God to intervene. She announced that a lane might be cleared for traffic soon but ten minutes later nothing had changed. I kept thinking about Marcus arriving at the bank. He would stammer and hesitate as he tried to make sense of the presentation I'd prepared. Everything I'd worked for so far in my life was in danger of disappearing down the toilet. As the minutes continued to tick past and nothing moved I felt trapped and helpless. Every fifteen seconds I glanced at the time. My heart was racing and my palms were sweating. I tapped my hands on the wheel and wished that I still smoked. I couldn't understand how it could take so long to clear at least one lousy lane. To focus on something constructive I started planning my route once I finally got off the damn freeway. I knew a parking building near the bank which

I traced a mental route to, figuring if I went there instead of to the office which was maybe a fifteen-block walk from the bank I could save time. Of course if this had been any other city but San Francisco I could have caught a cab, but I didn't even bother thinking about the impossible.

'So far there hasn't been any progress on moving that truck,' the reporter said. 'The tailback is getting longer by the minute. This is a real logjam we have here.' Then, sounding almost cheerful she said, 'A lot of people are going to be getting very frustrated.'

I rolled my eyes. Give the woman a prize for her penetrating insight! Still nothing was moving. At eight-fifteen I began to wonder about fate and the meaning of it all, at the insignificance and pointless stupidity of life when it can be so profoundly affected by something as dumb as an overturned yogurt truck. I'd heard everything the reporter had to say a dozen times already. The sound of her voice began to piss me off. I imagined some doe-eyed vacuous blonde with a bland smile who probably got paid too much for doing this crap, but I kept listening, frequently looking at my watch while I alternately cursed God who I knew didn't exist anyway and the reporter with the irritating voice who I hoped went down with her chopper in a flaming pyre because she was driving me FUCKING CRAZY.

But finally she announced that at long last a lane had been cleared, and then another. Incredibly the traffic started to move. As I began to crawl forward I decided guiltily that maybe she wasn't so bad after all and checking the time I nurtured a faint hope that I might make it on time. It was eight twenty-seven. The lanes ahead started merging, and then traffic was moving faster. I thanked God who I now believed in again, just to be on the safe side.

It took ten minutes to pass the truck, which was still

on its side surrounded by fire service crew and police cars with flashing lights. The reporter said a crane was being brought in to lift it but I didn't need to know any more so I turned off the radio. As I drove I picked up the phone and called Marcus.

'I'm on my way,' I said. 'When you get there stall as long as you can.'

Relief flooded his tone. 'How long do you think you'll be?'

It was eight forty-six. 'Twenty minutes,' I said, though I was being optimistic.

'Twenty minutes?'

'Maybe twenty-five,' I said, thinking maybe forty. Marcus sounded doubtful again.

'Maybe I should wait for you.'

'You have to go in there,' I told him. 'I'll be there.'

'Right.' He hung up, and I had the feeling he had little faith in me any more.

I got off the freeway by Bell Park and headed up 3rd past the Moscone Centre. Every light I hit was red as is always the way when you don't want it to be. Each time I stopped to wait, I had to draw deep calming breaths and force myself not to look at the clock as it inched past nine. It was practically gridlock around the Financial District. Everybody was late and even more ill-tempered than normal. In San Francisco there are never enough cabs and the BART trains don't reach the outlying areas around the Bay where people are forced to move because nobody can afford to live near the city any more. An incredible amount of people and cars pour over the bridges every morning from points north and east, and from the peninsula like myself, creating daily havoc. The air was ringing with the sound of honking cars and the clamour of streetcar bells and a couple of blocks over a fire department siren wailed, echoing among the glass and concrete canyons formed by the skyscrapers. That morning I wasn't the only one cursing officialdom at City Hall. I kept hoping though, that I'd still make it before the hammer fell. Jesus! Why did these lights take so long?

Then at last the parking building was ahead of me. I pulled in and stopped with a squeal of tyres. I could still make it by half past if I was lucky. I grabbed my laptop and ran for the street and at the end of the block I leapt recklessly into the streams of flowing traffic ignoring the honks and shouts around me. A cab almost bowled me over but I half rolled on the hood and was on my feet again, raising a hand of apology to the guy who yelled out that I was a dumb sonofabitch. And at nine twenty-eight I passed through the main entrance of the bank, panting heavily and looking an odd enough sight to earn me a suspicious stare from a security guard. It took three more minutes to get an elevator to the fifteenth floor, and then a receptionist picked up her phone and at nine-thirty-one I was shown into the room where Marcus appeared chastened and already beaten into submission.

One look and I knew that it was bad.

CHAPTER THREE

It was a small nondescript room that contained a table and some chairs and a cheap print on the wall. There were two guys from the bank present, both wearing dark suits, both with their jackets hung on the backs of their chairs to signal they meant to get down to it. I knew one of them. His name was John Flynn. He was the officer who'd approved our original loan and with whom we'd had contact over the years. The other I didn't know. I guessed the reports spread out on the table related to our business.

Marcus almost sighed with relief when he saw me, though the look he shot my way was laced with a good dose of resentment too. A sticky sheen of perspiration stuck to his forehead. I made my apologies for arriving late and Flynn did the introductions. 'This is Scott Douglas, head of business loans.'

An unsmiling Douglas rose and we shook hands briefly before he got straight down to it. He gestured towards the set of figures our accountant had prepared which Marcus had let them see. It was a tactical mistake, since they had immediately focused on the bottom line, though on the positive side it meant Marcus hadn't even had a chance to make our presentation.

'As we've been discussing with your partner, your current position falls considerably short of your forecast,' Douglas said. He settled a grim look on me. 'You are of course aware that you had an obligation to inform the bank of any serious change in the circumstances affecting your business.'

'Those figures shouldn't really be considered in isolation,' I began. I opened my laptop and started to bring up the first screen of my presentation. I wanted to get them away from the nuts and bolts which I had to admit didn't look very good. 'There are other factors that . . .'

'We're not interested in any other factors,' Douglas cut in. 'We're a bank, Mr Weston. We like to do business the old-fashioned way. Statements and balance sheets are what we understand.'

His tone was curt, and was meant to shake me, which it did. But I recovered a little and tried to go on. 'I understand that. But what you're looking at is just a snapshot view of how we stand right now, it might be helpful to put that into some kind of context . . .'

Douglas cut in again impatiently. 'Maybe I should make something clear. You're in advertising. In your business you deal with concepts. Your role if I understand it at all is to make people act on their emotions. You present a thing in such a way that people suddenly imagine they have to have it to make their lives complete. Am I right?'

I resented his patronizing tone and it was a crude summing up of what we were about, but I didn't think this was an appropriate time to give a lecture on the finer points of advertising. 'Broadly speaking,' I agreed.

He smiled thinly. 'Well, in our business we like to deal with what we can see and touch. What's real. We're more comfortable that way. And right now all I can see is that you owe this bank a lot of money. The purpose of this meeting is to determine how you plan to repay that debt. That, Mr Weston, is the only context in which we are interested. Is that clear?'

I saw why Marcus looked as if he'd been taken into a

back room and worked over. I'd been expecting the bank to take a tough stance, but this was worse than I'd imagined. The message was loud and clear. Sit quietly, answer questions and don't try to give us any bull because you are already in deep enough as it is. Having felt he'd made his point Douglas went on.

'What we don't have here is a detailed breakdown of your company assets.' He shuffled through some papers. 'Your cars are leased, as is the office space you occupy.'

'The assets on the balance sheet are the office furniture and our computers,' I pointed out, which Douglas already knew.

He punched some numbers into a calculator. 'Let's say all up they would fetch ten thousand. That's quite a shortfall.'

'What do you mean they'd fetch ten thousand?'

Douglas looked up. 'I mean that's what the bank could sell them for.' He allowed a few moments for that to sink in before he went on. 'You both signed personal guarantees when you took out this loan originally, putting up your houses as collateral. Of course we all know how values have risen over recent years, but you both have substantial mortgages. We're going to need some current valuations on those.' He made a note on a sheet of paper and punched some more numbers into his calculator.

'Wait a minute,' I said.

'Yes?'

'You're talking about shutting us down?'

'You sound aggrieved,' Douglas said with a thin smile. 'What were you expecting? You currently owe the bank almost one million dollars and your cash flow is negative and has been for months. You're spending more than you're making, Mr Weston. Your revenues are falling. What did you think was going to happen here today?'

'I thought we'd get a fair hearing,' I said.

'A fair hearing?' Douglas repeated my words and let them hang in the air. 'Your current level of debt exceeds the agreed limit by almost a quarter of a million dollars, which it may surprise you to know we take a pretty dim view of. But perhaps you can explain how you consider your actions have been fair towards this bank?'

'I thought that's why we were here, so that we could explain our situation.'

'You seem to be forgetting something, Mr Weston. We've been trying to get you to do that for several weeks now.' He opened a page in a file and scanned its contents. 'Daily phone calls to your accountant, and then to you personally. Faxes. E-mails. None of which were answered satisfactorily.'

I could feel the weight of Marcus staring at me though I didn't look at him.

'I think you've brought this situation on yourself,' Douglas said.

There was brief silence while he waited for my reaction. I could get up and walk out, I thought. The hell with them. I had the feeling Douglas and Flynn were enjoying this. It seemed like they had made up their minds before either of us had even arrived and there was nothing I could do about it. I could feel Marcus silently telling me to do something. Get us out of this mess. I imagined going home to break the news to Sally that we were broke. No baby. No house or job. My dreams all fading, my whole life crumbling before my eyes. I figured I had nothing to lose so I may as well go down fighting.

'Fine,' I said. 'Go ahead and shut us down. But that isn't going to get the bank back its money. We're an advertising agency. We are the assets. Us and the people who work for us. You can have a fire sale with the god-damn furniture and take our houses, but like you said, we both have heavy mortgages. What will you clear? Five hundred thousand maybe? That's still half a million short of what we owe. But if that's what you want, go ahead. We can't stop you.'

'Fifty per cent is better than nothing at all,' Douglas said, unimpressed.

'How do you know you have to settle for fifty per cent?'

'Judging by your recent history I'd say we're lucky to get that.'

I shook my head and spread my hands. 'I don't know why you needed us here for this. You're not even prepared to listen.'

'Perhaps, Mr Weston, that's something you should have thought about before you put yourself in this position.'

He looked at me, and though his tone appeared unrelenting, I thought I detected a subtle expectation in his expression. I had the feeling he was waiting for something. But what? And suddenly I saw what it was. The bank was pissed off with us, and before anything else could happen we had to show that we were suitably contrite. He was waiting for me to eat some humble pie, which I instantly recalled was my favourite dish. I fixed a contrite, beaten down look on my face.

'I guess you're right,' I said heavily. 'It is entirely our own fault that we're in this position, and we realize that.'

I could almost feel Marcus bristle at the term 'we'. As far as he was concerned we were here because of me. Period. Douglas, however, made the merest inclination of his head which I took as an invitation to continue.

'We made some mistakes, and the biggest of those was not admitting we were in trouble before now. What we should have done is come right to the bank before things got out of hand. I guess we thought we could trade our way out of it.' I paused. 'Actually the shame of it is I still think we could.'

A muscle twitched in Douglas's cheek. He was weighing

me up, trying to decide if my humility was genuine or if I was just spinning a line. Perhaps the faint possibility that the bank might get all of its money back was too big a lure to let go without hearing me out, but he laid down the ground rules first.

'Okay, we'll listen to what you have to say. But let's be clear about a couple of things. This meeting was arranged at our insistence because you have repeatedly given this bank the run around. You owe us a lot of money. What we want to hear is how you intend to pay it back. If you have a proposal we're going to want to see detailed forecasts and we're going to go over them with due diligence.'

I resented his moralizing tone, and couldn't resist a comeback, though I disguised it with a smile. 'It's funny how things change, there have been times when I've sat in this room and you people have practically begged us to extend our borrowing.' I looked at Flynn who at least dropped his gaze momentarily because he knew that in our early days when things were going well what I was saying was true.

Douglas wasn't impressed. 'That's what banks do, Mr Weston. We lend our money to people who need it, so long as they can afford to repay it. It's what makes the world go around. It's the repayment part that is at issue here.'

Of course he was right and I knew it. It's one of life's ironies that banks are willing to throw vast amounts of money at you when you need it least, when business is good, but when you run into trouble and need it most, they have a knack of making you feel like a bum begging for nickels and dimes on street corners. What's more, the money Douglas referred to as belonging to the bank in fact, more accurately, belonged to their depositors. The bank simply took it in with one hand and lent it out with the other and along the way they charged in interest more than they paid out and garnered a fortune for themselves. I thought about the fifty-floor marble-clad building I was currently sitting in that bore the bank's name, an imposing and opulent edifice by anybody's standard, and how over the years Carpe Diem had played a small part in contributing to the cost of it.

'The point I'm making is that we have a good record with this bank,' I said. 'Since we first started our growth has been steady and consistent.'

Douglas flipped through his records. 'I'll agree that was true until last year. But this isn't the first time you've run into financial difficulties.'

'You're referring to a situation last year that was beyond our control. We took on a client that went under owing us a lot of money.'

'But bad debts are a fact of life. The trick is limiting your exposure to them.'

'When OfficeLine failed it was at a time when any dot.-com company had to practically fight off the investors who wanted to sink money into them. Winning that account was a big step up for us,' I argued, just as I had with Marcus when he'd been reluctant to commit so much of our resources into one account. 'We should have made six hundred thousand in fees during the first year alone.'

'It's not what should happen that counts, Mr Weston. It's what actually does. Otherwise we'd all be rich,' Douglas said with heavy condescension.

Fuck you, I thought, but I said, 'Nobody could have predicted that the market would crash,' hearing again the echo of a thousand arguments I'd had with Marcus over the same subject.

Douglas said, 'Whatever the cause, that setback almost ruined you. For a while you appeared to be recovering, but then we see this steady decrease in revenue. Lately it seems to be getting worse.'

'It's a phasing problem,' I said.

'Phasing? Maybe you'd like to explain that.'

'The truth is five or six months ago we stumbled over the chance to pitch for a new account. Perhaps we weren't in the best position to take it up.' I avoided looking at Marcus, who had argued so strongly at the time that we couldn't afford the investment. 'Have you heard of Morgan Industries?' Douglas and Flynn looked at each other and shook their heads. 'Maybe the name doesn't mean anything, it wouldn't to most people, but Morgan Industries is a half-billion-dollar-a-year company with an advertising budget that runs into tens of millions.'

'And you're pitching for their business?' Douglas asked, sounding sceptical.

I shook my head. 'We're not in that league. Not yet anyway. But Morgan Industries is made up of a number of companies who operate in technology associated markets. Their account is handled by KCM, but earlier this year Morgan bought a company called Spectrum Software, who for reasons of their own didn't want KCM as their agent, so we were given a chance along with some other agencies to pitch. It's a dream opportunity. Right now there's only KCM and us left in the race, and Sam Mendez who heads Spectrum isn't keen on KCM. If we win this one it would be a real coup. We'd have a foot in the door. From there the sky is the limit. Give us a year or two and we might have a shot for the rest of Morgan Industries' business.'

Douglas absorbed the implications of what I was telling him. I'd said all the things any banker in this city loves to hear. Technology, software, billion-dollar parent company. Music to their ears. But Douglas retained a banker's natural caution. 'But competing for this account presumably incurs a cost.'

'Significantly. A pitch like this can take months, as this one has. It means people are diverted from existing work, and if we get the business there's a period where the cash flow impact is negative. We have to work up briefs, design campaigns and pay for media and there's going to be a lag between money going out and money coming in from the client.'

'But you believe the benefit outweighs the cost?'

'That's putting it mildly. If we win Spectrum we'll be taken seriously as a contender for other big accounts. We specialize in technology and e-commerce, areas where these companies are spending tens of millions to create their brands. If we eventually took over all of Morgan Industries' business it would make us one of the biggest advertising firms in California inside five years, working in the biggest growth area the world has seen since The Industrial Revolution.'

He knew what that meant, we were suddenly talking about becoming a firm with a turnover of tens of millions. He took a few seconds to absorb these facts and it was clear he was interested now, but then he frowned when he looked back at the figures.

'And this explains your decline in revenue?' Douglas said.

'Like I said. It's phasing and it's temporary. We didn't really have the resources to make this pitch as well as take proper care of our existing clients. The truth is we took our eye off the ball and allowed our normal work to dry up a little. We thought we could ride it out, but the whole process has taken longer than we thought.'

'But you're still in the running?'

'We're not just in the running, we're almost home. It's almost certain that we're going to win the Spectrum account.'

Douglas stared at me intently. I knew what he was

thinking. He was trying to decide if he believed me. When I'd walked through the door he'd been planning to shut us down, and now he was faced with the prospect that if he did he could be losing the bank a lot of future business. If the scenario I'd laid before him came to fruition Carpe Diem would become a major client, and the bank would be there all the way to finance our expansion. He glanced at Flynn, and at Marcus. I silently prayed that he wouldn't ask Marcus if he shared my optimism. Marcus had never been in favour of this pitch, and I knew he wouldn't be able to conceal his doubts and resentments, but Douglas had already surmised that of the two of us when it came to business I did the talking.

'We're going to need to see detail,' he said cautiously, but sounding a hell of a lot friendlier than he had thirty minutes earlier. 'A lot of detail.' He smiled a little but he wasn't kidding.

'No problem.' I swung around my laptop and showed them the first screen of my presentation. 'This is how we expect things to go over the next two years. If we get the finance we need.'

I started doing my thing, and as they watched and listened I knew that I had them on the line. Now I had to make sure I didn't try to reel them in too quickly.

Two and half hours later, Marcus and I stood in the elevator as the doors slid closed. I exhaled and leaned back against the wall feeling like I'd just gone ten rounds with Lennox Lewis. Douglas and Flynn had gone over my plan with a fine tooth comb, critical of every detail, questioning my logic every step of the way. Every answer I gave they noted down and then five minutes later they would come back at the same issue from another angle. They were looking for weaknesses, searching for poorly thought out strategy or financial projections based on a shaky premise and the more they put the pressure on the more likely it was the cracks would appear if they were there. But gradually they'd been convinced, and by the time we left their attitudes had undergone a complete turnaround. When they saw us out they were wreathed in smiles and it was handshakes all round.

I loosened the tie I'd put on for the occasion and looked at Marcus. 'For a while there, I was worried.'

He took off his glasses and started polishing the lenses to avoid looking at me.

'You could look happier about this,' I said lightly.

'What exactly am I supposed to be happy about?' he said, meeting my eye at last. 'You heard what that guy Douglas said. They were going to shut us down. We would have lost everything.'

'I think they were trying to scare us. Anyway they're going to give us the money, Marcus. Two hundred thousand to tide us through the next few months.'

'That isn't what they said.'

'Well, as good as.'

In fact it wasn't as simple as that. The bank were going to monitor our situation closely and they wanted more information from our accountant. They intended to watch us every step of the way, and if anything went wrong they would pull the plug. But the point was that for now, at least, we had a reprieve. I was beginning to feel elated and I wanted Marcus to feel that way too.

'And if we don't get the Spectrum account?' Marcus said.

'We will.'

He was silent for a minute in the face of my refusal to contemplate the alternative. 'You got us a breathing space, Nick. That's all. If we don't get that account we're finished.'

I was saved from answering when the elevator came to

the ground floor and the doors slid open. We crossed the vast airy lobby featuring a huge modern sculpture in the centre that looked like a tangle of abstractly put together metal parts to me, but probably cost several hundred thousand dollars. Outside Marcus stopped on the sidewalk and started looking for a cab, always a fruitless exercise.

'Let's walk,' I suggested. It was still sunny, remarkably enough. The blue skies above the towers around us, the warmth of the sun, the reprieve we had just won all conspired to fill me with vigour and good feelings. I figured it was time I tried to put things right between Marcus and me, and I decided to fetch my car later. 'Come on, we'll get a sandwich and sit by the water.'

He agreed though he didn't look too happy about it. We headed towards our office in South Beach, not far from the new Giants stadium, Bell Park. For a while I talked about baseball, trying to engage him, but mostly he answered in monosyllables. We used to go to games regularly, though not this season. There was a good feeling about the Giants this year. Their first season since moving from Candlestick Park. Barry Bond was still the number one hitter and though some of the players weren't exactly getting any younger there was hope they would take the National Championship this year. I thought of all the times we'd sat in the stands, just the two of us. We'd eat hot dogs, have a couple of beers and hang out together. Guys' stuff. I missed that.

There's a place near Pier 38 where you can get a pretty good chicken sandwich and a coffee and sit and watch the world go by. The bay looks beautiful on a sunny day, even the Oakland Bay Bridge is something to look at. Maybe it isn't as striking as the Golden Gate, which is definitely more graceful in its design. But the Bay Bridge to me is just as impressive in its own way by virtue of its size. Thirteen kilometres and double-deck to boot.

I brought the drinks and food over to the table where Marcus was sitting. The Embercadero that skirts the waterfront has been turned into a nice place to sit and walk since the earthquake in eighty-nine. They tore down the freeway and planted a double avenue of huge palms and now there are apartment buildings springing up (great if you can afford a seven-hundred-thousand-dollar two-bedroom condo) and all kinds of businesses moving into renovated warehouses and the piers. It's hard to bear a grudge sitting in such a place. I hoped.

I sat down and said, 'Listen, I know I should've told you about the bank sooner.'

Marcus looked at me, the light glinting on his glasses so I couldn't see his eyes. 'Why didn't you?'

'I don't know. I guess I thought I could take care of it before you needed to know. I was hoping we'd get the Spectrum account then I'd talk to the bank . . .' My voice trailed off. The truth was I'd avoided thinking about the how. 'I'm trying to say I'm sorry.'

Marcus studied me. 'Are you, Nick?'

'You don't believe me?'

He started to answer then stopped and shrugged. 'It doesn't matter.'

'No, it does matter. It matters to me. I shouldn't have kept it from you and I wish I hadn't. But it isn't only the bank you're bothered about is it?'

His eye slid away and I knew I was right. 'Maybe we shouldn't get into this,' he said.

'How can we not get into it? We're supposed to be friends as well as partners. Don't you think it would be better if we cleared the air. I know you didn't want us to pitch for Spectrum, and I know why. But this isn't the same as OfficeLine.'

'Isn't it?' Marcus shot back unexpectedly. 'The way I

remember it you almost ruined us then too, which makes it pretty similar to me. But that isn't the point is it, Nick? I was against OfficeLine because I thought it was too risky ploughing so much into a single account, but you were so damn sure you were right you went ahead anyway.'

'You agreed, Marcus.'

'No, I gave in. There's a difference.'

'Maybe I did pressure you. But we were unlucky. If OfficeLine had started six months later with a more realistic plan it might have been a different story. Instead of ending up broke those guys that got it up and running would probably have ended up with more money than they knew what to do with. For chrissakes, Marcus, they were still in their twenties! And we wouldn't be sitting here having this conversation now. It was just bad timing. Could've happened to anyone. But Spectrum is a solid company and Morgan Industries isn't about to go broke.'

'But we almost did.'

'Almost. But we're still here aren't we?'

'Except that I never thought we should pitch for this account in the first place. We couldn't afford it. We didn't have the people or the time. We should've concentrated on hanging onto what we had.' His voice had been rising, now he paused. 'That's the whole point, Nick. We're here, but we almost lost it all and I didn't even know what was going on.'

'I apologized for that. Tell me what you want me to do and I'll do it.'

'What I want is for you to start treating me like an equal partner for once.'

'You think I don't do that?'

He uttered a short barking derisory laugh. 'Do you? I tell you what. How about if I said we pull out of the Spectrum pitch now. Would you do it?'

I stared at him, uncertain if he meant what he was suggesting, unable to believe that he could be though he met my gaze with unflinching seriousness. 'How could we pull out? After everything we've put into it. Even if we did it wouldn't do any good now. Without that account we're finished.'

'We could go back to the bank. Put together a revised plan and work our way out of this mess with the clients we already have.'

'It would take years, even if they went along with it. Which they wouldn't.'

'So, the answer's no,' Marcus said.

'It isn't a fair question. This is the biggest chance we're ever going to have. Ever. If we win this account we get everything we always wanted.'

'No, Nick, we get everything you ever wanted. You're the one that's always chasing the rainbow, you're the one that wants us to be another KCM. I was happy the way things used to be. We had a good client base, we were expanding slowly, and we were making a good living doing what we wanted to do. That's what I always wanted.'

'So, maybe I'm a little more ambitious,' I argued. 'Is that a crime? Is it going to break your heart if we make a lot more money. You still get to do what you want, Marcus.'

'But aren't we supposed to make these decisions together? Right now it feels like it doesn't matter what I say or think any more. You're in such a damn hurry to get wherever it is you're going.' He shook his head. 'You've changed. Sometimes I don't recognize you.' He looked at his sandwich, which he'd taken only one bite from and put it down. 'I'm not hungry. I think I'm going to go back to the office.'

I watched him leave and I kept thinking about what

he'd said, his words merging in my mind with the accusation Sally had made that morning. It seemed that suddenly nobody knew me any more.

CHAPTER FOUR

The decision to quit my well paid job with an established agency to go it alone with Marcus had not been easily taken. We were talking it over one night over beers and clam linguine at a place in the old cannery across the road from Fisherman's Wharf. It was early in October, which for me is the best time in San Francisco. The summer fogs have gone, the days are often sunny and warm, and with the return of school the tourist crowds have diminished to a tolerable level.

'Look at us,' I said. 'We're sitting here with a view like that right in front of us.' I gestured towards the glittering bay which was turning from deep blue to beaten copper in the setting sun. A ferry full of commuters heading home for the evening was making its way towards Sausalito. 'We're lucky. We live in one of the greatest cities on this planet. We're blessed with a good climate, we have great jobs, nice cars, pleasant places to live, and what are we doing? We're sitting here moaning about our lot.' I shook my head.

Marcus grinned wryly. 'It's the human condition. We strive for something more than we have.'

'You think so? That's why we want to quit our nice comfortable safe jobs so we can weigh ourselves down with debt? Can you imagine the stress we're letting ourselves in for if we do this? Running our own agency means we start from nothing. We'll face uncertainty every day.

We have no clients, no money. We'll need offices, cars, someone to answer the phone . . . we must be crazy.' I threw up my hands. 'I think we ought to have another beer.'

Marcus shrugged. 'Well, I don't know about you, but there's only so much longer I can go on figuring out new ways to make chocolate chip cookies sound interesting.'

I smiled. 'That's it for you isn't it? I mean it's about choosing what you work on. For that you'd give it all up.'

'I guess. That's a precondition by the way. If we do this, no food accounts. I have done my last campaign for processed cheese.' He pulled a face.

'That's what you're working on?'

'It is. And this is not how I wish to spend the rest of my life.'

'I'll drink to that.' We touched glasses and drank solemnly.

'So, why would you do it?' Marcus asked. 'Really?'

'Quit my job, my decent salary, my BMW three series with all the toys, my top-line health plan?'

'Those things are meaningless to you, right?'

I grinned. 'Right. Who needs them anyway?' But I ate the last of my linguine and played with my fork reflectively while Marcus waited for me to give him a real answer. 'You know what it is, really? I'd do it for the same reason that you would, in a way. It's about control. You want control over your work, I want control over my life.'

'Explain,' Marcus said. We were both getting a little drunk, but that's how it often was when we got onto this subject. When we were sober we talked about the nuts and bolts of where we'd get the finance, how we'd position ourselves in the market, all that good stuff. After a few beers we were into the big questions. Why? And what's it all about anyway?

'Control. Security. Call it what you like. It's the same thing,' I said. 'Why else do people go to work? I mean if it isn't for fulfilment, and for most people it definitely isn't, then it's to earn money. We have to have it, to pay for the food we eat, the houses we live in, for the education and health of ourselves and our families. We need to know those basic needs are taken care of. Security.'

'You want security?' Marcus said.

'Everyone does. Why else the world over do so many people buy into the lottery even though the odds against winning are practically fucking impossible. There are people out there who would spend absolutely their last buck on a ticket. Even ahead of food for themselves.'

'Isn't that because they want to get rich?'

'But what is rich? For most people winning the lottery is the only chance they are ever going to have to get real security. And security means control. That's what it's all about. Control. It isn't about houses and yachts and fancy cars. That's all just gloss. It's fuck-you money. That's what people want. They don't want to be at the mercy of some corporate asshole in an office tower somewhere, who decides one day that he's going to shut down a plant in Michigan or someplace where people have worked all their lives. They don't want to be afraid of losing it all. Their house, health plan, car, the works. Where does that lead? Some family is forced to move to another neighbourhood where they don't know anybody. There's not enough money coming in. Maybe the guy can't take it and he gets sick or takes off and leaves his kids so they don't have a father any more. It all falls apart. The whole fucking thing.'

Marcus looked at me in surprise at my unexpected and sudden passion. 'I never picked you as a champion for the common man.'

I shrugged self-consciously. I hadn't meant to get so

worked up. 'I'm just saying. It isn't money for its own sake that people want, it's about security.'

'You already have that,' Marcus said. 'You make a hundred and fifty plus a year. You're young, the people you work for like you. You're a high flyer at KCM.'

'But in the end, I'm just an employee. I have to watch my back all the time because there's always someone ready and willing to knife me right between the shoulder blades. Like that prick Larry Dexter for instance. That guy would cheerfully kill me if he thought he could get away with it and it'd get him an inch further up the ladder. I don't need that. I don't need to know that someday I might screw up, or somebody decides they don't like my face or the colour of my shirt. I could get fired and lose it all anyway.'

Marcus thought about that, hunched over his beer with his glasses slipping down his nose. After a while he grinned a little lopsidedly. 'You see the irony don't you? You're prepared to give up what you have now, which is your job, the salary, the car, in short your security. For what? Security!' He chuckled then cocked his head thoughtfully. 'Did that come out the way it was meant to or am I drunk?'

'You're drunk,' I said. 'But you're right. And you know what, I think we should do it.'

Marcus saw that I was serious and hesitated. Then he picked up his glass. 'The hell with it. To us.'

'To us.'

Four years had elapsed since then. Now here I sat, at my desk in my office in the agency we had started. Carpe Diem occupied space in a restored brick building that had once been a bond warehouse. It is tucked away in a little street which is surrounded by new apartment complexes which front the Embercadero near Pier 38. The apartments have views across the bay to Oakland and lots of small bars and restaurants have sprung up in the area serving all kinds of food from Korean to burgers to sushi. For years the bond warehouse had fallen into crumbling disrepair until a developer had recognized its potential and bought it for a song. Now it was home to a dozen exclusive boutique stores on the ground floor, and on the floors above a collection of trendy businesses that included a freelance graphics designer, an art gallery and an office design company which sold incredibly expensive minimalist furniture. And us.

The designer we'd hired to outfit our offices had given us a thirty-six-thousand-dollar curving glass wall that extended around the perimeter of what had begun as an empty space, and formed the front wall of the various individual offices which looked out over the central work area. It stood for transparency, he said. He'd also given us blonde wooden floors (symbolic of the purity of pine forests) and what appeared to be a partially dismantled scaffolding made out of chrome piping which stood against the west wall. Some of the plaster had been removed to expose the brick underneath, which created the effect of a job incomplete and hurriedly abandoned. The designer claimed this made a symbolic statement in keeping with our name; that we were too busy seizing the day to concern ourselves with unimportant incidentals such as the décor. There was a certain irony in that, given that the scaffolding sculpture, as he called it, had cost us twenty-seven thousand dollars.

That designer and his rabid symbolism had cost us a fortune, but the sad fact is it had been money well spent. Advertising is a reflection of an idealized life. It's about image and gloss. No matter how good or bad we were, once we had them through the door most potential clients made up seventy per cent of their minds about whether or not to hire us based on how we met their expectations of what an advertising agency should look like. The fact that we'd had to spend so much to create nothing more than a slick office might at first seem wasteful, but without it we'd have died on the day we opened.

Several days had passed since our meeting with the bank and I was busy preparing for a meeting with the marketing people at Spectrum Software. I was weary, and I took a break, leaning back and rubbing my eyes. My gaze fell on a couple of framed pictures on the bookcase in my office. One was of Sally and I just after we were married, a couple of months before we moved to San Francisco. We had flown down from Oregon for a job interview I had with Campbell Armstrong, one of the biggest agencies on the coast with offices across the country. I got the job and to celebrate we drove up the coast for the weekend. The picture had been taken outside the inn where we stayed. I tried to recall the name of it, but it eluded me. I was struck by how much younger I looked then, though Sally didn't seem to have changed so much. We looked happy. Only the young ever look that happy. It's because they don't know what's ahead of them.

The other picture was of me again, but much younger, nine years old in fact. I was standing next to my dad, both of us smiling at the camera. I went over and picked it up to look more closely. It was something I did now and then, trying to detect anything in my dad's eyes that might have forewarned of what would happen three months after the picture was taken. There were shadows, which might have hinted of the things that troubled him, but it was probably just the way the light fell on the camera lens.

I closed my office blinds and opened a locked drawer where I kept an old cigar box. Inside was a pistol which had belonged to my dad. It was a .38, hardly used, the grip cool and unfamiliar when I picked it up. Twenty-six years ago my dad had put the barrel against his head then pulled the trigger. It was depression, they said afterwards. I remember standing with my mom and my brother and sister beside his grave on the day of the funeral. I was the eldest of us three kids, and closer to our dad so maybe it affected me more than them. It seems that way now anyway. They're both happily married, one in Washington State the other in Georgia where my mother also lives. They have decent jobs, families. They seem untroubled by the past.

I put the gun down, and took a letter from the bottom of the box. I knew every word of each line by heart, but I read it anyway. The paper was getting fragile, almost torn at the folds, the ink smeared and faded from the amount of times I'd handled it. My dad wrote it the day he shot himself. He talked about his business failing, about the unfairness of life, about his childhood, fishing with his own father who'd died young, about the world being full of sonsofbitches. It didn't really sound a lot like him, except in places. It was a rant, and clearly that of a sick mind. The writing was spidery as if he'd written it in feverish bursts. The sentences were disjointed, flipping from subject to unrelated subject and back again without connective thought. But at the bottom was one final sentence. The writing was firm and legible and appeared to have represented at least one clear idea.

There must be something better than this

I carefully folded the letter away, and locked the gun in its box back in the drawer.

I was too tired to do any more work. My in-tray was overflowing with client folders and unanswered mail.

When we'd started the work to secure the Spectrum account I hadn't expected so much to be involved, but KCM were fighting hard and Sam Mendez and his team at Spectrum were taking inordinate care over their decision. I didn't know if that was because they were bucking the system within the group by considering a switch of agency, or whether they were just exercising extreme caution. Occasionally when I took the time to think about it I was puzzled. The Spectrum account was sizable for us, perhaps worth half a million or so annually in fees, but that wouldn't normally warrant a process that had taken this long or involved so much effort. I kept telling myself that Morgan Industries, the real prize, made it worthwhile.

Sometimes that wasn't easy. I picked up an envelope that had arrived a week earlier. Inside was a letter from WebLink, one of our better accounts. It was signed by Jerry Parker, the guy who owned the company, and who I'd dealt with for three years. The wording was terse and to the point. 'Due to late delivery and poor execution . . . despite repeated expressions of concern . . . the situation has become untenable . . . no alternative but to advise you that from this date forward the services of Carpe Diem are no longer required.' I read it through with a mixture of feelings. The shock I'd felt when I first opened it had been replaced with anger at myself for allowing this to happen, but also at Parker for not calling me and laying his concerns out straight on the line. When I had called him to try and talk him round he was almost hostile.

'I'm running a business here, Nick. We gave you plenty of warning that we weren't happy with the attention we were getting. You just weren't listening.'

He was probably right, I admitted to myself. I'd involved so much of my time on the Spectrum project, and everybody else's time too, that everything else was on the back burner. WebLink wasn't our only unhappy client. I felt like a juggler who had too many balls in the air, with sweat on my brow as I desperately tried to keep track of them all, but even though my hands were moving in a blur of speed I couldn't keep up. One slip, one tiny fractional loss of concentration and I'd drop them all. I told myself again, as I had with increasing frequency of late, that it would be worth it in the end. We were going to win that account.

I contemplated the letter in my hand. Marcus didn't know about this. I'd put off breaking the news to him until after the bank meeting, but I still hadn't found the right moment. I knew he'd see it as vindication of everything he'd said. I was tempted to toss it in the waste bin, but it seemed that if I did I'd once again be hiding things from him he had a right to know. As I had hidden the trouble we were in with the bank. On the other hand what difference did it make? There was nothing he could do, and if we won the Spectrum account . . . correction, *when* we won the Spectrum account, losing WebLink wouldn't be such a big deal. I hesitated, torn between conflicting arguments. Logic overruled emotion and finally I crumpled the letter and threw it in the bin.

I shut down the file I was working on and the Spectrum logo which I'd put on my desktop winked on and off. Before I closed down the screen I checked my schedule. I'd made a note months ago to remind me of an exhibition that Alice was holding the following night which until then I had totally forgotten about. Marcus and Alice had been living together for the past two years. She was an artist who worked from a studio he had built for her at the back of the cottage they shared in Sausalito. The idea of going to one of Alice's exhibitions wouldn't normally rate highly on a list of fun things to do but I thought maybe this was a chance to start mending fences. It had been a while since the four of us had done anything together, though there had been a time when we'd all go to a restaurant maybe once a month or so, or spend the occasional day out on the launch that Marcus owned. He'd always liked boats. In college he had a kayak. Sometimes he'd persuade me to go out with him and we'd paddle for miles on the grey Pacific in all kinds of weather, the sea sometimes choppy, the wind throwing spray in our faces, in winter the cold turning my hands blue. It didn't matter to Marcus, he liked to be out on the water.

After he bought the launch, Sally and I used to spend weekends away with him and whoever was his girlfriend of the moment. We'd cruise down the coast and find some secluded bay to anchor where we'd swim and barbecue on the beach in the evening. When Alice came along we didn't go so often. She and I had rubbed each other up the wrong way from the beginning. No question that she was a looker. Heads turned when she entered a room, and I was as struck with her Nordic beauty as the next guy would be. The problem was that I saw something in her eye the first time we met, and I soon realized it was a kind of disdain. It became apparent she considered herself unappreciated as far as her art was concerned. She thought the world turned on commerce and thought too highly of those who had the ability to make a buck, that people like herself were undervalued. That meant me. Forty-eight hours confined on a boat together was more than either of us could stand. Usually we ended up in some kind of argument that left Sally and Marcus looking on uncomfortably from the sidelines.

I went in search of Marcus. The office was deserted and I realized it was later than I'd thought, but I found Marcus still at his desk. He looked up when he sensed me in the doorway, and when he saw who it was he frowned a little.

'I just saw a note about Alice's exhibition,' I said. 'I thought we might come along.'

He looked surprised. 'You don't need to do that.'

'I'd like to.'

'I thought you didn't enjoy that kind of thing?'

It was true I didn't, but I figured I could keep the peace for an evening. 'It's never too late to change is it?' I quipped. I don't think he was sure what I intended him to read into that.

'I suppose,' he agreed uncertainly.

'Why don't we have dinner afterwards, the four of us?'

I could see he was less than enthusiastic about the idea, but he thought it over and it was clear he couldn't think of a way to turn me down. 'I'll mention it to Alice.'

'Great. It'll be good to see her again.'

I went back to my desk and about ten minutes after that I saw him leave, and a half-hour later I decided to call it a day myself. I thought I was alone but when I turned out the lights at reception I saw a light was still on in the office so I went back to switch it off. It turned out that it was coming from Karen's room, who besides myself was our only account manager. She was typing into her laptop, her expression concentrated, illuminated by her desk lamp.

'Working late?' I said.

She looked up with a start. 'I didn't hear you.'

'Sorry.' I gestured to the clock on the wall. 'It's not that I don't appreciate your dedication, but don't you have somewhere else you could be?'

She sat back in her chair and rubbed her neck. 'I didn't realize the time. I needed to get this done before to-morrow.'

I went over and looked at her screen. She was putting

together a costing projection for a print ad campaign for one of our clients, along with reach and frequency rates for the target audience. All the usual stuff. Karen had worked for us for eighteen months. She was smart, good with people and pretty as well, but right then she looked tired.

'Why don't you finish it in the morning,' I said. 'Go home, have a glass of wine, put your feet up.'

She shook her head. 'Can't. I have a meeting at eight. Anyway it's almost done.'

I felt guilty because for months now she'd been snowed under with extra work I'd pushed onto her to lighten my own load.

She looked at me as if she'd guessed what I was thinking. 'If I was home I'd probably be working anyway. I didn't have any plans. I'll just be a little longer.'

'I'll make it up to you, Karen.'

'I'll hold you to that.' She smiled and went back to her laptop. It seemed like the list of people I had to make things up to was growing longer by the day.

Traffic was light on the freeway, and I was home by nine, which had to be the earliest in a long time. I could hear Sally's voice from the kitchen so I went on through. At the door I paused when I realized she was talking on the phone and I caught the tail end of a conversation.

'. . . guess people change,' she said heavily, then silence as whoever she was talking to replied.

'I don't know. I don't know what I'm going to do. It isn't easy.'

More silence.

'I'm not sure it's a good idea. I don't know right now. Everything's kind of confused.'

I froze with my hand on the door. Something about Sally's tone struck a discordant note. Though I could only hear one side of the conversation and it could all have been perfectly innocent, I just knew that something wasn't right. It was more the way Sally sounded than what she said, which was weary with resignation, as if she was at the end of the road, but there was a certain intimacy implied by what I'd heard as well. The way people sound when they're speaking to somebody they're close to. I wondered what wasn't a good idea? And what was confused?

'I better go now. Yes. Okay, 'bye.'

She hung up, and a second later I pasted a smile on my face and went into the room. Sally was standing by the counter, wearing a thoughtful, indefinable expression and biting her bottom lip the way she did when she had something important on her mind.

'Hi,' I said.

She did a double take. 'I didn't hear you come in.'

I went over and kissed her cheek, then I went to the refrigerator and took out a bottle of white Zinfandel. I held up a glass. 'You want one of these?'

She shook her head. 'If you're hungry I can make you something.'

'I already ate,' I said, which wasn't true, but I had no appetite. 'What did you have?'

'Oh, just a sandwich.'

I poured a glass of wine. 'So who was that?'

'Who was what?'

'On the phone.'

'Oh. It was my mom.'

'How is she?'

Sally went over to the dishwasher and started unloading it. 'She's fine,' she answered with her back to me.

I kept watching her, wondering if I was imagining it or was she avoiding my eye. 'So what else did she have to say?'

Sally threw me a quick glance. Normally if she'd told me her mother had called I could be expected to instantly lose interest. 'Not much.'

'How's your dad?'

She paused in the act of putting away a stack of plates. 'He's fine, Nick.'

I tried to remember exactly what Sally had said. It could have been her mother. They were close and always had been, though totally unlike one another, I was happy to say. Who else could it have been anyway? I asked myself.

Sally finished putting away the plates and faced me. 'They want to come down for the weekend next week.'

I couldn't disguise the sudden unpleasant surprise I experienced. We had lived almost our entire married lives in the Bay Area and in all that time Sally's parents had never once visited us. It was an unwritten rule that Sally went to Oregon and stayed with them, which she did regularly, even frequently this last six or nine months. Very occasionally I went with her. But rarely, and usually only for a day or two. It was better for everyone that way.

'It's only for a couple of days Nick,' she said tightly.

'Why are they coming?' I asked.

'Do they have to have a reason?'

'It's just that they never have before.' I was getting on shaky ground here and I was well aware of it.

'Why are you always like this with my parents?' she demanded.

'It isn't your parents.'

She glared at me. 'Meaning?'

'Come on, Sally, I don't have a problem with your dad, but you know as well as I do that your mother and I don't exactly get on.'

'Well maybe it's time you tried a little harder.'

'Well that's great. Are you going to tell her that too?'

'I should have known this is how you'd react. You can't even make an effort for once can you?'

'*I* can't make an effort?' I said in disbelief. 'For Christ's sake, Sally, your mother can't stand me. I don't ever remember her making any kind of effort unless it was to try and stop you from marrying me.'

'Can't you ever forget that? It was all a long time ago.' Grimly she turned and strode from the room.

Nothing could be guaranteed to start a fight quicker in our house than the subject of Sally's mother. It was the one constant disharmony we'd always had to live with, and I knew well enough after all the time we'd been together that it was a fight I couldn't win. No matter how justified I was in resenting the woman, no matter how much Sally had fought with Ellen herself, they were still mother and daughter. Over the years Ellen had gained the upper hand. Sally was like a prize, something we both coveted. In the beginning Ellen's opposition to my relationship with her daughter had only driven Sally closer to me, but after we were married she subtly changed tack. She never pretended to like me, because Sally would have seen through that, but she made sure she kept her barbed comments and put downs mostly out of Sally's earshot. I guess I'd never been as duplicitous and slowly Sally had come to believe that I was the bad guy. I went after her, adjusting my tone, talking to the back of her head.

'Look, you just took me by surprise. You have to admit they've never wanted to come here before.'

'Maybe that's because they know they're not welcome,' she snapped as she turned to face me.

I sensed there was more to it than Sally was letting on. She hadn't been up there for a month or so and now the sudden turnaround.

'Did you have a fight with your mother?' I asked.

She gave a quick impatient shake of her head. 'No. I'm going to take a bath.'

She started up the stairs, a flush of anger creeping up the back of her neck. I didn't want her to go, for us to be like this again but I couldn't think of anything to say to stop her.

I went back to the kitchen and poured myself another glass of wine. I was mulling over the impending joy of Sally's parents visit, which made me think about the phone conversation I'd overheard. If Sally had been talking to her mother it hadn't sounded as if they'd had a fight. She hadn't been angry, more uncertain, or saddened. Maybe she was talking to her father, I reasoned, but that was unlikely. Frank didn't get involved in emotional issues. He left family matters to his wife and the only thing he ever really talked about was his garden. Why wasn't Sally going up to Oregon as usual? I kept seeing her expression when I'd asked who was on the phone, the quick, guarded flash in her eye, like somebody with a guilty secret.

When I went upstairs I hung up my trousers and sat on the bed to unbutton my shirt. The pillow was inviting. I wanted to lie down and close my eyes. Sally emerged from the bathroom in a cloud of steam. She opened her closet door, then with her back to me she unfastened her robe before bending over and stepping into a pair of panties. She let the robe fall to the ground and reached for a nightdress. At the brief sight of her partial nakedness I felt a twitch in my loins. The curve of her spine formed a hollow in the small of her back above her buttocks. She was in good shape, her body taut from the rigorous programme of Pilates exercises she'd begun almost a year ago, in preparation for when she had a baby, she told me at the time, adding pointedly under her breath, if she ever did. When she turned in profile I glimpsed the upward tilt of her breast, the pink tip of a nipple.

A fleeting vision of an occasion when we'd once made love in a wood on vacation several years back flashed before me. The sun was slanting down through the high green canopy, like columns of light in a vast airy cathedral. The warmth of the ground rose up to us carrying with it the sweet loamy smell of earth and leaves which was somehow seductive. I remembered it was warm and the feeling of damp hair, and a trickle of moisture running between Sally's shoulder blades which tasted salty on my tongue.

Just then Sally glanced over and caught me watching her. She couldn't miss the erection in my shorts, and for about a millisecond she hesitated, unsure how to react. Then she looked away.

I was nervous the first time Sally took me home to meet her parents. I knew her grandfather had made a fortune in lumber, and that she had grown up in a large white three-storey house surrounded by six acres of grounds that was a far cry from the city neighbourhood I called home. Her grandfather, however, made a series of bad investments, a trend continued by her father in his younger years before he'd married Ellen. By the time I met Sally her parents were no longer rich, though that had never stopped Ellen from harbouring hopes that her daughter might be the one to restore the family fortune.

I was in my final year at college when we drove through the gates and along the drive that led to her family home. We'd been dating for six months by then, and the view I had of the house matched with the impressions I'd formed listening to Sally's stories about her childhood growing up in the small town she was from. I'd conjured an image of slightly decayed grandeur, which was borne out by signs that the cost of upkeep had become too steep. The house needed painting, and some repointing work on the chimneys needed doing, the grounds were unkempt except where the lawns were maintained. Sally grinned.

'I told you we're just regular folks.'

'Yeah, right. And your grandfather was just a lumberjack.'

It was a joke between us. I'd always said her parents would be horrified if she brought somebody from the wrong side of the tracks home, like me. To which she'd always said she was going through a rebellious stage and she liked a bit of rough. In fact it was secretly less of a joke to me than it was to her. I hadn't exactly been brought up in a slum but sometimes I felt as if I had.

'Remember,' Sally reminded me when we arrived. 'My mom can be difficult until you get to know her.'

Her mother came out to meet us. She would have been in her mid-forties then and I remember thinking that if it was true that daughters end up looking like their mothers then I was in luck. Her hair showed no trace of grey, though she probably coloured it, but her skin still retained a youthful freshness, and she was as slim as her daughter. Sally introduced us and as we shook hands, though she smiled, her eyes remained cool as she silently appraised me. Sally looked on with what I realized was an expression of slight apprehension and it occurred to me she was hoping for her mother's approval. All at once I was aware of subtle tensions in the air between mother and daughter. Uncertainly I made some remark about what a nice house they lived in. Ellen agreed that it was though a subtle undertone seemed to warn me that I shouldn't get any ideas about getting comfortable.

Later that day she contrived to talk to me alone on the pretext of us getting to know one another.

'You must get Sally to introduce you to her friends while you're here,' she said. We were in the sitting room which had large windows looking out the back where Sally's father had his glasshouses. Frank had made a brief appearance before disappearing outside where I could now see him planting something. Sally had told me he was a lawyer with a practice in town, though his passion was growing exotic plants.

'Has she mentioned Garrison?' Ellen asked me.

'Garrison? I don't think so,' I said.

'Really? I'm surprised. They were always such good friends.' She suggested we sit down and she asked if I would like tea. 'Garrison's father is Tom Hunt. Their family has lived in the area for generations,' she added.

'Maybe she mentioned him and I forgot.'

'He would be around your age. Aren't you in your final year?'

'That's right.'

'I'm right then. So is Garrison. He's going to be helping his father after he graduates. They have a lot of business interests in this area. Real estate, land and so on.' She poured tea for us and passed me a cup. 'He's a very good skier. Sally and he went together one year. A whole crowd of them went. One of the boy's fathers has a lodge at Lake Tahoe. Do you ski, Nick?'

The smile she gave me was as pointed as a knife.

'No, I never have,' I said.

'Really? You're from Portland didn't Sally tell me?'

'That's right.'

'And what do your parents do?'

'My mother works as a personal assistant. My dad died when I was young.'

'I'm sorry to hear that,' she murmured.

It went on like that for a while. She quizzed me about my background while offering snippets of insight into

Sally's own life, subtly making a point about our differences it seemed to me. Later I asked Sally about Garrison Hunt whose name kept cropping up.

'He's just somebody I know,' she said. 'Why?'

'Because your mother keeps talking about him like he's Mr Fucking Perfect that's why. Did you date this guy or something?'

She admitted that she had for a while, though it wasn't serious. I got the impression that nevertheless her mother had decided he was the right one for her.

'She can be a bit of a snob sometimes,' Sally said with gross understatement.

She herself thought Garrison was pleasant, charming, and reasonably good looking, but he didn't flip her switch.

We ate dinner with Sally's parents that night. Her father didn't say a lot. He was pleasant, but I got the impression his mind was elsewhere a lot of the time. I thought Sally was being particularly attentive to me. She made a point of holding my arm when we went through to the dining room. The room was large and obviously little used. The table was enormous, a heavily polished antique with twelve high-backed chairs placed around it which seemed ridiculous for the four of us. I didn't know why we didn't eat in the kitchen, which was large and comfortable, instead of in this cavernous room where by the time the food reached the table it was cold. Frank sat at one end, with Ellen on his right and Sally on his left with me beside her. Sally chattered with uncharacteristic nervousness, telling funny stories that presented me in a flattering light while her mother smiled with forced politeness.

'More potatoes, Nick?' Sally asked. 'More wine?'

'Don't you think he's good looking?' I remember she asked her mother once, and kissed me quickly.

Her mother looked on with grim disapproval. I found Sally's behaviour forced and unnatural, and wondered what point she was trying to make, and whether to me or her mother?

Later, when Sally was helping clear away, Ellen took the opportunity to collar me alone again.

'You and Sally have been seeing quite a lot of each other, haven't you?' she said.

'I suppose we have.'

'You know, I married when I was quite young, Nick. Of course I've been very fortunate and I've been happy, but I've always hoped Sally would experience more of life before she settled down. I'd like her to travel, to experience things.'

I wasn't certain what she was getting at, but I was surprised at the inference. 'Sally and I are dating,' I said. 'We haven't talked about anything like marriage.'

'No of course not,' she said with a laugh. She paused for a moment. 'You'll be finishing college next year you said? What will you do then?'

'I don't know yet,' I admitted. 'I haven't any firm plans.'

'You're taking a business degree aren't you? If you like I might be able to introduce you to some people who could help you. I have some friends in Chicago.'

'Chicago?'

She smiled. 'I know people there who run very large companies. I'm certain they're always on the lookout for bright young people.'

I didn't know whether to believe my ears. It seemed she was offering me a kind of unsubtle bribe to make sure I moved somewhere a long way away from her daughter. I said something to the effect that I would certainly remember her offer if I ever thought I was interested in moving to Chicago, and I think in that moment we understood each other.

That night as I lay awake in the dark there was a tap at my door. Before we'd arrived Sally had warned me we would have to sleep in separate rooms, which of course I'd expected, but when she crept down and slipped into bed with me I was glad to see her. I'd been thinking about her mother's offer, smarting from the insult it implied that I wasn't good enough for her daughter. When I told Sally she thought I must have misunderstood.

'Then what the hell was that performance over dinner all about?'

'I don't know what you mean.'

'Bullshit. I suppose I misunderstood when she kept talking about that Hunt guy you used to see and how he's been asking after you.'

'Don't tell me you're jealous.'

'This isn't about jealousy, Sally.'

She must have realized then how I felt. 'I'm sorry,' she whispered in my ear. 'She'll come around.'

'She's not going to come around,' I told her.

'She will once she gets to know you properly. I warned you about her before we arrived.'

'You said she could be difficult to get along with. You didn't tell me she was a class A bitch.'

'She just wants the best for me,' Sally said, a little hurt.

'The best being somebody else, like Garrison Hunt for instance.'

'It doesn't matter what she wants. This is my life remember, and it's you I'm here with now isn't it?'

To make her point she slipped her hand down across my stomach and took hold of my flaccid penis. She pressed her body against me and whispered in my ear.

'I don't want us to fight. Make love to me.'

I said, 'Did you ever fuck this guy Hunt?'

'What?'

'You heard.'

Her hand retreated. 'Do I ask about who you've slept with?'

I felt bad and wished I hadn't asked. But some things we have little control over. 'Did you?' I insisted.

She hesitated. 'No. Satisfied?'

'Yes,' I answered, but in fact I knew she was lying. She couldn't meet my eye, and to change the subject she took hold of me again.

The blind needs of the flesh, preprogrammed with a one track mind took precedence over quibbling issues of wounded pride. Sally squatted over me and lifted her nightdress over her head. Her body was pale in the darkness, the smooth curve of her hips drawing my eye to the plane of her stomach. She settled over me, drawing me into the folds of her flesh, then leaned forward to support herself, with her hair brushing my cheek.

'Forget about my mother,' she whispered.

I reached around and in one swift motion rolled her over. She looked up at me, startled by our sudden exchange of position, then she grinned. We began making love. Sally closed her eyes, and a soft breath of air escaped her mouth. I whispered in her ear that she was beautiful, that I loved being with her like this.

She clung to me and softly moaned and I looked into her face at her closed eyes, the smile that played on her lips and I thought of her mother lying in bed somewhere on the floor above us who didn't think I was good enough to be with her daughter, and I thought about Garrison Hunt too. A lot of old feelings welled up in me, things I hadn't felt for a long time since we'd had to move from our old neighbourhood after my dad had died because we couldn't afford to live there any more, and I'd slowly lost all my old friends. Sally moved beneath me, our bodies in rhythm. She rose towards a climax, arching her back a little and thrusting her hips, her arms tightening around me. The bed-head banged against the wall.

I whispered what I wanted her to say to me, but she

shook her head, her eyes screwed tightly closed, so I stopped moving and withdrew from her a little. Her eyes flew open and she locked her thighs so tightly around me I thought she'd snap my spine like a stick. She dug her nails into my back.

'No,' she commanded.

'Say it then.'

She hesitated, then whispered, 'Fuck me.'

I had an agenda here, but I had to admit that it was kind of exciting hearing her speak like that. Sally wasn't ever a prude, but she wouldn't normally talk that way. 'I can't hear you.'

I was straining against the pressure of her legs to keep myself apart from her.

'No don't,' she said.

'Say it then.'

'I told you.'

'Louder.'

Suddenly with unexpected power she thrust her hips violently upwards.

'FUCK ME.'

It probably seemed louder than it actually was. Her voice reverberated through the silent house.

The next day at breakfast her mother fixed me with a withering stare and when it came time for us to leave she was nowhere to be seen. Sally was unusually quiet, and wouldn't meet my eye. I regretted making her say what she did. It was childish and reeked of insecurity, and I knew Sally's mother must have said something to her. She eventually admitted her mother had taken her aside and they had argued, but she would never tell me what had been said.

Perhaps Ellen had hoped our relationship would run its course, but after I'd gained my degree and started working she must have decided to leave nothing to chance. I found out that sometimes when Sally went home she went out with Garrison Hunt. She claimed it was to keep her mother off her back, and I could imagine there was some truth in that. Nevertheless we argued furiously about it, and when Sally claimed there was nothing I needed to be jealous about, I asked why she had kept it from me. She stopped seeing him after that, but once we met him when he was in Portland and she introduced us. Sally had always claimed he knew how things stood, and he was doing her a favour by taking her out sometimes, but I saw the look in his eye and recognized competition when I saw it. The guy was just waiting for his chance.

The year Sally graduated, we decided to get married. The ceremony was held in Sally's home town. At the reception Ellen sat at the top table, her expression grim. A year after that, we moved to San Francisco.

CHAPTER FIVE

The night of Alice's exhibition Sally and I drove across the bridge to Sausalito. The exhibition was being held in a building that had once housed a boat building company, but no more apparently. It was at the far northern extreme of the town, away from the hugely expensive real estate that clings to the hillsides above the town, where in the evening the people who live there sit on their decks drinking martinis and admiring one of the most famous views in the world, of the Golden Gate Bridge and the forty-two hills of the San Francisco skyline. It's a fact that in the Bay Area the wealthy live high up and breathe air often rarefied by the scent of obscene fortunes made in Silicon Valley. Whether Sausalito or Pacific Heights, Nob Hill, the slopes of Cow Hollow or the hills above Palo Alto at the beginning of the valley, nowhere else is the notion of getting to the top more literally interpreted. In these areas a modest three-bedroom home can set you back five million. Even across the bay the hills above Berkeley and Oakland reflect the same trend. Only options in a dot.com fortune will buy you entry to these suburbs nowadays.

Marcus and Alice lived in the less fashionable part of Sausalito, on the flat, tucked around the corner without a view, far from the pretty painted Victorians that house the waterfront restaurants and boutiques. The exhibition was held only a few minutes from their tiny cottage so I found it easily enough. A kid, no more than nineteen or so stood at the door self-importantly checking invitations, and by the time we arrived a small line had formed.

'Christ you'd think it was the city gallery,' I observed. Someone in front looked round.

'Keep your voice down,' Sally hissed.

There was a time she would have smothered a grin but these days it seemed like I couldn't do anything right. Her admonition put me in a sour mood. I didn't care if anybody heard me or not.

We finally reached the door and I handed the kid our tickets which he scrutinized in case they were forgeries. I found this irritating. The artists inside all wanted to sell their work, hence this exhibition, but they often limited these shows to a select few in the belief that this would somehow induce a competitive bout of cheque book waving. It might work for the uptown galleries and artists whose work is known, but down here in a converted warehouse it simply smacked of pretension.

The ticket checker had long hair tied back in a ponytail. He wore battered leather sandals and a short-sleeved shirt unbuttoned to show the leather necklace around his neck. Everything about him, right down to the packet of Gauloise in his breast pocket was carefully cultivated to be anti-mainstream, anti-fashion, anti-bourgeois, anti-fucking-everything, but in fact it looked as if he'd bought his image off the rack in Gap under 'Artist', right next to 'Rebel'. A girl stood close by, dressed in what looked like a muslin sheet, but she was stunningly pretty. He kept looking over at her hoping she would notice how important he was. When he handed back our tickets, his gaze flicked over us, and a faint smirk curled his mouth. It was clear he had us pegged as Mr and Mrs Suburban Couple. Capitalist pigs shackled to the yoke of commerce, unlike himself who was an ARTIST.

His face was marked with that curse of adolescent youth, pimples, and I leaned in close and whispered to him quietly.

'There's a big yellow one right on your nose that needs squeezing, buddy.'

His smirk vanished, replaced with an expression of deep mortification, his eyes darting automatically to the stunning girl. I grinned to myself as I walked away.

'That was childish,' Sally told me.

'I don't care,' I said.

We were in a large open space with perhaps a hundred other people. A girl in tight jeans with a bare midriff and rings through just about every part of her exposed anatomy offered us a glass of something that turned out to be warm, cheap fizz. The invitation named three artists so we wandered around looking for Alice, passing among groups of serious types deep in discussion, and others like me whose expressions betrayed their wish to be someplace else where they could get a beer.

'Why did you want to come?' Sally said, catching my expression. 'You hate these things.'

'I hate the phoniness.'

'Then why are we here?'

'Because we were invited.'

'Nobody expected you to turn up.'

'I thought it would be a nice thing to do. And we're having dinner later, we haven't done that for a long time.'

Sally stopped suddenly, her expression at once serious. 'This isn't the answer, Nick.'

'The answer to what?'

'You're here because you think you can fix things with Marcus this way. But it isn't going to be that easy.'

Before I had a chance to reply somebody called Sally's name and we turned to see Marcus threading his way towards us. He and Sally smiled at one another as he kissed her cheek.

'You look terrific.'

'Thanks,' she said.

'Glad you could make it,' he said, though his smile slipped a fraction as he glanced at me.

'Pretty good turnout,' I remarked.

'Yes.' He looked around as an awkward moment descended over us, and then Sally asked where Alice was. 'She's over there,' he said, and began leading the way.

I followed them as we made our way through the crowd. Despite the differences Marcus and I currently had, at least he and Sally weren't affected. They'd always liked each other. She laughed at something he said, her eyes sparkling merrily. Christ, when was the last time I'd seen her laugh like that? Marcus had a way of putting women at ease. He hadn't altered the way he dressed for twenty years, he still wore jeans and a T-shirt pretty well all of the time. With his glasses and longish hair he didn't look much different from the way he had at college, but I think that was part of his charm. He was kind of ageless, like somebody who'd just decided not to grow up, in some ways.

Back at college I'd asked Sally once why she thought women were attracted to him. At the time I'd just bumped into a girl with striking almond shaped eyes who'd emerged from his room wearing only a T-shirt that barely covered her butt.

'Wish you were in his shoes?' Sally teased.

I denied it, and it was true, but I was curious. Sally said she thought women felt safe around Marcus because he was non-threatening and they instinctively knew they could talk to him as they would their best friend. He listened. He was genuinely interested in what they had to say.

'I don't think guys know how unintentionally seductive that can be,' she remarked.

Years later I asked Sally if she found Marcus attractive and she looked at me in surprise, but then after a moment's thought she'd answered yes, she supposed she did. I didn't mind. A funny thing about guys is that we want our best friends to think our wives are pretty, and our wives to be attracted to our best friend. It's a kind of validation of our choice of partner. I think Marcus had always wanted me to like Alice too, and vice versa, and the fact that we plainly didn't get on had always been a source of regret to him.

We found Alice, who was deep in discussion with somebody on the subject of a framed canvas bearing a splatter of vivid red paint. I read the card underneath. The title of the piece was *Rage*.

'I was going through a very tough emotional time then,' Alice was saying. 'I felt I needed to express something almost . . .' she searched for a word. 'Well, violent!'

The earnest woman with her nodded in empathy, then Alice saw us and said something and the woman melted away.

I experienced the same conflicting sensations I always did when I laid eyes on Alice. An instant dislike at her phoniness teamed with a gut appreciation of how physically arresting she was. Over the years Marcus had dated some pretty attractive women, most of whom I'd liked. Though he usually went for arty types, they had their feet on the ground. Often they worked as designers or copy-writers, people he met through work. None of that for Alice though. Physically she was in a class of her own. She was tall, almost five eleven, and had long dark blonde hair and pale green eyes. I thought she looked Nordic, though she claimed her ancestors came from Chile. Her eyes were the most startling I'd ever seen. They were so pale, like emeralds buried in ice. She and Marcus had been living together for two years by this time, and still I sometimes had to look twice.

She and Sally kissed and told each other how great they looked, though there was a certain coolness from Alice. They had never hit it off as the best of friends, partly because they were quite different, but also purely because Sally and I were married which made Sally suspect right from the start in Alice's view.

I cast my eye over the pictures on the wall, which to me were indistinguishable from something a four-year-old might have done, except Alice gave all hers a fancy title. She finally acknowledged me, and I kissed the smooth cheek she offered.

'How are you, Alice?' I asked.

'Fine. I was surprised to hear you were coming, Nick.'

She made surprised sound the same as disappointed. Despite myself I acknowledged silently that she looked sensational. Unlike a lot of her artist friends she dressed normally, and that night she had on pale khaki pants that rode on her hips and a black figure hugging top. An artist she might be, a starving one she wasn't. I think Alice had made up her mind a long time ago that being poor was neither romantic nor fun.

'So what do you think, Nick?' she asked, seeing me looking at her paintings. She made no attempt to hide her sarcasm, as if we all knew what my opinion would be and that it was worthless anyway.

The truth was I thought what I always had, that giving a splatter of paint a fancy name doesn't change the fact it's still a splatter of paint, but I wasn't looking for a fight. I fixed my eye on a canvas of muted blues, painted in a swirling seamless pattern. The card underneath said the piece was called *Blue*.

'I like this,' I said.

'Really?' Then her momentary surprise became suspicion. 'Why?'

'I like the colours I guess.'

She fixed me with a condescending look which annoyed the hell out of me but I tried not to let it show.

'You like the colours? What do they say to you?'

They say it's a nice blue painting, what the fuck else should they say? I thought. To me this kind of stuff was just wall decoration. You hung it because it looked good and it matched a rug or whatever. But I kept my feelings to myself and a pleasant smile on my face.

'It's kind of soothing,' I replied, knowing that was what she wanted to hear.

She indicated the next one, which was a square of warm yellow bleeding out to orange at the edge. It was called *Daybreak*. 'What does this one say to you?'

I didn't like it because I don't much like yellow, and I resented the hell out of her patronizing tone. She seemed to be in even more of a mood for needling me than normal. 'Reminds me of sunrise on a summer's morning.'

'Creation,' she said.

Whatever, I thought.

She smiled thinly, and wasn't, I think, taken in at all. We moved along the wall past her other works. She kept asking me what I thought of each one, and whatever I said the look in her eye told me she thought I was full of it. But it wasn't that I didn't like them, I just couldn't stomach all the bullshit she liked to wrap them in. All that representative analysis that I always thought was apparent only to her. They were all variations on the same theme. Colours, abstract patterns. The fact was, if Alice thought splashing haphazard colours on a canvas was a fulfilling way to pass her life, that was fine by me, so long as I didn't have to agree with everything she said. For her part she'd always made it clear she thought I was at best

a philistine, at worst a moron. Marcus and Sally had somehow melted back as if to give us space and they looked
on with nervous smiles waiting for the inevitable fight to
erupt. Then the last of Alice's paintings caught my eye.

'What's that?'

I went to take a closer look. The card underneath read
simply *Spring Meadow*. In the foreground a sea of green
spread across the canvas beneath a grey/blue sky. Beyond
it was a simple farmhouse, and on the porch a figure
stood gazing at the vista before him. The grass was dotted
with sparks of red and orange, and when I looked closer
I saw there were other colours too. Lilac, purple, blue
and yellow. It was a meadow lit with wildflowers. Wild
poppy, paintbrush, daisies. A wind was blowing, making
wave-like patterns of changing shades of green. The
figure on the porch stared out at his land in the early
evening.

All of this detail was represented by deft smudges of
colour and shape. The grass and flowers, the house and
the figure were suggestions rather than literal interpret-
ations of those things. Maybe it wasn't even a house, and
the figure wasn't somebody standing on a porch but that's
what I saw. I could almost imagine the way the house
would look inside. Plain but comfortable, the guy going
to help his wife bring in groceries from an old station
wagon out front, talking about a friend she hadn't seen
in a long time as he helped her put things away.

'I like this. How much do you want for it?' I asked.

She was taken aback and unsure if I was serious. 'That's
just something I was trying out. I wasn't even going to
hang it.'

'Where is it?'

She looked away. 'Nowhere. From memory. I don't
know where I saw it.'

For some reason I didn't believe her. I felt that there

was a story behind the picture, that it was in fact a very real place, that she even knew the figure on the porch. I'd often wondered what Marcus saw in her. Incredibly good looking though she was, Marcus wasn't the kind of guy to stay with somebody for that reason alone. Maybe there was a side of her that only he got to see. A real person behind all the bullshit.

'I'll take it,' I said impulsively.

'You want to buy it? But I haven't even told you how much it is.'

'So tell me now.'

She hesitated, then overcoming her surprise she met my eye challengingly. 'Seven hundred dollars.'

I knew Alice had never sold anything for seven hundred dollars in her life. 'That's a little steep isn't it?'

'I thought you said you liked it, Nick. Don't you think it's worth that much?'

I think she believed I was somehow making fun of her, and that I didn't really want the picture, so she was going to make me pay for it. She knew I could hardly tell her that no, I didn't think it was worth it without exposing myself, in her eyes anyway.

'Okay I'll take it.' It was reckless. Even though I did like the picture I couldn't afford to go throwing that kind of money around right then. Alice, however, seemed less than pleased. A glint of malice flashed in her eye. I wrote out a cheque there and then, and while I was doing it she wandered off so she wouldn't have to soil her hands with my filthy money. I gave it to Marcus and asked him to bring the picture into the office.

'You didn't have to do that,' he said.

'I like it,' I insisted. 'Why doesn't anyone believe that.'

A little while later Sally and I moved on to look at the work of the other artists. One of them was a sculptor, if that's the right term, who made incomprehensible shapes out of junk metal. The other made devices to produce effects of flickering light projected against a whole lot of different surfaces. We stood and watched one that changed from red to green to blue and then red again, a circle against a smooth plastic surface. It was called *Change*.

'What a genius,' I said under my breath.

Sally threw me a look. 'Why did you buy Alice's picture?' she asked.

'I liked it.'

'Seven hundred dollars is a lot of money. Are you sure it was the picture you were buying?'

I didn't reply.

After the exhibition was over, the four of us went to a nearby café to celebrate. Alice had sold two other pictures and at the table she proposed a toast.

'To success!' She looked at me. 'I suppose by your standards you think that's pretty funny. Eleven hundred dollars isn't exactly retirement money is it?'

'Success is a relative concept,' I said while I mentally did the maths and figured I'd paid more than three times what I should have for the picture I'd bought.

It was clear that Alice had already drunk a few glasses of wine at the show, and there was a belligerent glitter in her eye. 'Oh come on, Nick, don't be coy. Success isn't relative to you, it's measured in dollars and cents.'

'Why don't we order some food?' Marcus said.

Alice lit a cigarette. 'Not yet. I want to hear what Nick has to say. Be honest, you think eleven hundred dollars is nothing.'

'Actually I don't think that at all.'

She made a face to show she didn't believe me. The rest of us studied the menu and Marcus asked Alice what she was going to have.

'Just order me anything.' She poured herself another glass of wine as Marcus looked on with faint concern. 'It's all right, you don't have to worry, I'm not going to get drunk.' She smiled crookedly at me and raised her glass. 'Truce.'

'Truce.'

'I'm getting used to the idea that art isn't painting any more. People buy prints to colour coordinate a room. It's all billboards and pictures of girls in shampoo ads. Nobody wants to pay for real art. The truth is the money I made tonight is nothing. I could make a lot more doing something else with my life.' She took another drink. 'How much does a graphic artist in an advertising agency make, Nick?'

'I don't know, maybe fifty or sixty thousand,' I said.

'There you go. I made a lousy eleven hundred tonight. I might make ten thousand in a year if I'm lucky, when I could be making five times that. But at least I get paid for doing what I want to do, right? For expressing what I feel.'

'Money isn't everything,' I said in agreement.

Alice snorted her derision. 'Oh please. Spare me the cliché's. Money shows how we value things and nobody values real art any more. Take that picture you bought tonight. You didn't really want to pay seven hundred dollars. You didn't think it was worth it. Admit it. I could see it in your face.'

'I was surprised that's all.'

'Exactly! And why? How much did you expect to pay for something that I created from nothing? For an original piece of art that took days and weeks of work?'

'I was happy to pay the seven hundred.'

'You paid it. I don't know if you were happy about it. What I want to know is what you really thought it was worth?'

I spread my hands. 'I don't know what you want me to say,' I answered helplessly.

'The truth, or is that asking too much?'

Marcus flashed her a warning look and as Alice reached for the wine bottle again he said, 'Maybe you shouldn't have any more.'

She ignored him. 'We're waiting, Nick.'

'All right. Maybe I was surprised at how much you wanted for the picture. But I paid it didn't I?'

'Right,' she said triumphantly. 'But I wonder why?'

'Because, as I keep telling you all, I like it.'

'I don't believe you.'

'Fine. Whatever you say. I think it's great that you sold some pictures, and I think we should all have a nice dinner. Nobody ever bought anything from me that I created myself. You should be proud of yourself.'

She looked at me as if I'd told her she was a hypocritical cunt. 'The great Nick Weston says I can feel proud of myself, how about that? You're such an asshole.'

I'd had enough. I knew she was drunk, but I was sick and tired of this. 'You know I'd like to know what your problem is, Alice. I bought the picture, I gave you what you asked for it and still that isn't good enough. What is it? Do you think it's my fault you don't make as much money as you think you should? Are you blaming me because the world doesn't value what you do?'

'Oh, you'd like to think that wouldn't you, because you have all the answers. But you're wrong.'

'Am I? I think you're just bitter. I think you hate it that some people go out into the real world and do what they have to do to make a living and you think you're somehow better than everyone else and you resent the hell out of the fact the rest of the world doesn't recognize your talent.'

'Perhaps money doesn't mean as much to me as it does to you. I don't deny I think I'm worth more than I get, but that isn't what's important to me. Deep down it isn't what I'm all about. I'd prefer to make the little I do and still be painting the pictures I want to, expressing how I feel, rather than living a life that doesn't mean anything to me.'

'Oh please, don't give me that suffering for your art crap. It doesn't suit you.'

'What the hell does that mean?' Alice demanded.

We had both raised our voices. Sally and Marcus were watching us with a kind of fascinated horror and I saw all my good intentions going out of the window.

'Forget it,' I said.

Marcus put a tentative hand on Alice's arm. 'Maybe we should go.'

She shook him off and glared at me. 'I want to know what you meant by that remark.'

I shook my head. 'I think we should drop it.'

'Alice . . .' Marcus began but she cut him off.

'Don't try to shut me up as if this was my fault. You know the only reason he bought that picture was because he thinks he can wave his goddamn cheque book around and you'll suddenly forget what kind of a terrific friend he's been to you,' she said with deep sarcasm.

'Oh shit, I've had enough of this,' I said. 'I'll tell you what your problem is, Alice. You like to come on with this holy self-righteous fucking attitude and you look down on all us mere mortals trying to make a living while you stay pure to your faith, but I don't see you starving in a garret, I don't see your friends dressed in the kind of clothes you wear. But I guess it's okay to spend the money isn't it? So long as you don't have to actually soil your hands making it. Isn't that the way it goes?'

She sneered at me. 'You have the nerve to criticize me.

Better whatever I am than somebody like you. Somebody who lies and does whatever it takes to get what you want even if it means walking all over somebody who is supposed to be your friend.'

There was a brief uncomfortable silence, and after a moment Alice laughed.

'What's the matter? We're all friends here aren't we? Surely we can speak the truth amongst ourselves.'

'Let it go, Alice,' Marcus said wearily.

But she was beyond the point of letting anything go. She went on in a quiet but cutting tone. 'That's your trouble, Marcus, you don't say what you feel. You knew after the last time he almost ruined you it would happen again. You should have told him what you told me then. Maybe you wouldn't be in this position now.'

'That's enough!' Marcus warned.

'You see?' She looked at me. 'He couldn't do it in the end. Because you were friends.' She laughed.

'What is she talking about?' I said bewildered. Marcus appeared deeply uncomfortable.

'I'm talking about when Marcus was thinking about getting out. Selling his share of the agency and starting again. On his own, Nick.'

She could see that I was surprised and a little shocked. At first I didn't believe her, but when I looked at Marcus his expression was riddled with guilt.

'It was after OfficeLine went broke. Remember that, Nick?' Alice said.

I ignored her. 'Is that true, Marcus? Is that still what you want?'

'It doesn't matter now, does it?' Alice answered for him. 'There's nothing to sell, is there?'

Abruptly she stubbed out her cigarette and got up to leave and a second later Marcus said he should go after her and Sally and I were left alone. After a moment or two I said, 'Well, that worked out pretty well I thought.'

She tried to respond with a smile, but she only looked sorry for me.

CHAPTER SIX

I had a meeting scheduled with some of the marketing team at Spectrum Software, during which we talked about their positioning and overall strategy. Bev Jones, the head of marketing, ran the discussion, and her product managers came and went throughout the morning as we covered their individual areas. It went well. I had prepared for it as I had for every discussion I'd had with them, which is to say exhaustively. Sam Mendez appeared for the last half-hour, and took a chair against the wall, listening without comment as I ran through a summation of my thoughts. When I was done everyone drifted back to their offices until I was left with only Sam and Bev.

'That was a well thought out presentation, Nick,' Mendez said, getting up from his chair. He was a big guy, grizzled features, white hair, an ex-college football player who'd started this company twenty-five years earlier.

'Glad you thought so, Sam.' I sensed he was there for a reason, and hadn't stopped by to pass the time. He glanced at Bev, and they seemed to share a knowing look.

'In fact,' Sam went on, 'everything we've seen of you and your firm has been pretty impressive. We like your ideas.' He gestured towards the screen where a few moments ago I'd been running through some creative concepts Marcus and his team had come up with.

'I can't take credit for that part,' I said. 'I'm just the mouthpiece.'

'I don't know about that,' he chuckled, as if between us it was understood that really I was being overly modest.

'Your creative people only get a fair shot at it if you give them the tools to work with,' Bev said. 'That means you have to get the brief right.'

'Which means you have to understand our business,' Sam said. 'And I don't think there's any doubt about that.'

'I like to think I do,' I said. Privately I thought it was the understatement of the year. I had spent countless hours over the months researching Spectrum from top to bottom. I'd spent a lot of time talking to their people, not just the marketing team, but people in design, sales, distribution, and then others outside these four walls, the stores who distributed the products Spectrum sold, and ultimately put into the hands of consumers. I'd known right from the start that because I was up against a big outfit like KCM I couldn't leave anything to chance, because I knew they wouldn't.

'We know how much effort you've put into this,' Mendez said. 'It hasn't gone unnoticed, I wanted to tell you that personally.'

'I appreciate it, Sam.' I smiled, wondering again what this was leading up to.

'I'm going to put you out of your misery, Nick. The reason I came by today is to tell you we're just about ready to make our decision, and appoint the firm who'll be our advertising agency for the next five years.'

'Five years?' I echoed.

'Thought that would surprise you. That's why we've taken so long over this whole process. We want a five-year contract with the firm that wins.' He all but winked at me then before he went on. 'We have our reasons for that. Very good ones I'm sure you'll agree when you hear what they are.' Again the almost wink. 'What we'd like to do now is set a date for your final presentation. Are you in a position to do that?'

'Anytime,' I said without hesitation. We'd been working on it for months, putting together all we knew about Spectrum and what we thought we could offer them in a final package, constantly tweaking it as the weeks went by.

'I think Bev has explained how it will work,' Sam said, to which she nodded. 'Both you and the KCM people will present on the same day, then we'll talk it over amongst ourselves and come up with a decision about who gets the contract. Sound fair to you?'

'Sounds fine, Sam.'

'Good. Then let's set a date. How about the twenty-third?'

It was less than two weeks away, but again I didn't hesitate. 'The twenty-third it is.'

He held out his hand which engulfed mine. 'I'll look forward to seeing you then, Nick.' He pumped my hand vigorously. 'You've worked hard for this. I know that, and I respect it. Everybody here likes you and we like your work. See you on the twenty-third.'

With that he left us. When he was gone Bev smiled at me.

'You've won him over. If it was up to him you'd have the contract.'

'You think so?'

'I'm sure of it. But Morgan Industries really wanted to use KCM. They didn't see any reason to change. There will be someone from Morgan at the presentation, so make sure you're prepared.'

'You don't have to worry on that score.'

Bev held out her hand and smiled. 'I never thought I did.'

*   *   *

87

It didn't really hit me until I was in the car. Before that meeting our financial position with the bank had hung over me like an ever threatening cloud. Everything depended on winning the Spectrum account. And I mean everything. Not just my livelihood and my house, but also any hope of getting my marriage back on track, and of building bridges with Marcus. I didn't doubt that going after Spectrum was the right thing to do, but it would be hard to argue that position if it all blew up in my face. Suddenly it seemed everything had turned around. The world was turning the way it was meant to again. The constant churning in my stomach that I'd become accustomed to these last months abated some.

On the way back to the office I decided I needed a drink to celebrate, so I dropped in at a restaurant in North Beach which was the current hotspot for people in the advertising business. I like this district. It has a few sophisticated eating places, like Jo Jo's where I was going, back from Columbus and Broadway, but there are also a lot of mid-range restaurants where the food is great, but the atmosphere is better. It's the lively bustle of the pizza joints and the bars that attracts people. It's primarily Italian, and the Italians have always known how to have a good time with food and are less pretentious about it than the French, but the neighbouring Chinatown has leaked noodle houses in amongst the pasta places, and where Columbus and Broadway meet there are a few strip clubs that help give the area its flavour. They aren't too sleazy because they're mixed in with everything else, unlike say South Market Street and the Tenderloin where the bums and the hustlers make people uneasy walking the streets.

I parked, and walked a couple of blocks up from Washington Square, where in fact the bums were snoozing on the grass after a hard morning panhandling and waltzed into Jo Jo's. The place was full of people taking late lunches who weren't planning to go back to the office. The constant background of ringing cell phones was like the chirruping of electronic cicadas. I ordered a drink at the bar and cast my eye around the room to see if there was anyone there I wanted to talk to. A couple having lunch caught my attention. The woman was a very made-up blonde and her companion had a deep tan. I noticed something odd about their conversation. They appeared to be out of synch, nodding or gesticulating at inappropriate moments and sometimes speaking at the same time apparently oblivious to one another. It was only when I saw the wires leading from the phones on the table to the discreet ear pieces they wore that I realized that they weren't in fact talking to each other at all. I was fascinated, and kept looking over now and then and throughout the entire meal I don't think they exchanged a single word. It used to be when you saw somebody talking to themselves as they wandered the streets it was a sure thing they were schizophrenic or something. These days you never know.

The bar was busy. I took my bourbon and ice and drifted to one end away from the general hubbub. Somebody came up behind me.

'Nick, I haven't seen you here for a while.'

I recognized the smoothly oiled voice and turned to find Larry Dexter clutching a mineral water with a slice of lemon floating in it. Larry's drink of choice.

'Larry,' I said with little enthusiasm. 'Always a pleasure. What are you doing here?'

'Actually I'm having lunch with a client.' He shot his cuff to look at his watch making sure that I got an eyeful of the fact it was a gold Rolex. 'Should be here anytime.'

He smiled, flashing perfect white teeth that must have cost him a fortune. It was an expression he used to convey anything but humour, and on this occasion it made him appear mocking. It was as if he knew something which privately amused him.

'Don't let me hold you up.'

'No hurry, Nick. We don't often get a chance to talk after all, do we?'

He was, as ever, immaculately dressed. Dexter was the only person I knew in our industry who always wore a suit. Nothing overly flashy. They were always dark coloured, plain three-buttoned single breasted and tailored for a perfect fit. He teamed them with grey, mostly Italian, designer shirts and pure silk ties. With his black swept back hair and penetratingly humourless blue eyes he looked like an emissary from the Devil dressed to kill for the new millennium.

'I don't recall that we've ever had much to talk about,' I said. I finished my drink and signalled to the bartender for another. 'How about you, Larry. Get you one?'

'Thanks, but I'm fine,' he said without looking at his glass.

Still the same old Dexter, I thought. I raised my glass. 'Good health,' and sipped the bourbon through clinking ice. Dexter wore an expression of smug satisfaction as he touched his water to his thin bloodless lips. Somehow he always managed to make me feel as if I was but a step away from the gutter and a brown paper bag holding a bottle of cheap liquor.

We'd met when I had gone to work for KCM as one of a team of account managers, which had included Dexter. He'd been with the company for five or six years at that point, having started in the mail room and worked his way up. From the outset he viewed me as unwelcome competition. In fact he saw everyone the same way, only to varying degrees. He was good at his job but it was clear that Dexter had his sights set on bigger things. Though the clients he dealt with thought highly of him because he was efficient, and the company liked him because he brought in results, the rest of us recognized Dexter for what he was, which was a man with chilling ambition. He didn't fit in socially, even though on a Friday he'd go along when the rest of us hit a local bar to unwind from the rigours of the week. He'd hover on the fringes, sipping his mineral water and watching us get drunk with a faintly superior smile. People would turn around and find him at their shoulder while they were grouching about somebody higher up the food chain they thought was a pain in the ass. Dexter stored all this stuff away in case he could use it sometime in the future to enhance his position in the intricate manoeuvres of office politics.

KCM was like any big company in that regard. There were only so many promotions and plenty of people chasing them. Competition was fierce and you had to be able to play the game if you wanted to get ahead. Being good at your job only gave you an entry ticket to the race, the real test then was to align yourself with the right people. The people ahead of you who had already garnered a little power and were on the way up. Your name had to be heard in the right places, and the price for that was to be somebody's flunky, prepared to root around in the dirt for morsels of information your mentor could use to put some rival down. A word here, an insinuation there about drinking or unsavoury habits, rumours started with a seemingly casual remark, these were the guns and bullets of the corporate game. But you had to be careful, attach yourself to the wrong person and if they crashed and burned you could rapidly find yourself on the way out. I hated it all. There were too many factors beyond my control and there'd always be someone ready to knife me in the back at the first opportunity. I was happy to leave and let Dexter have the field. He was a dedicated player.

'It's ironic, don't you think, the way things have turned out,' Dexter commented.

'What's ironic about it?' I said.

'Both of us pitching for the Spectrum account I mean. It's like old days. Rivals again.'

'We both worked for the same company, Larry, that didn't make us rivals.'

'Competitors then. You have to admit that much. It's only natural after all. We both wanted to get ahead.'

I shook my head. 'You always assumed that I wanted what you did. But I was never competing with you.'

'Please. You mean to tell me you wouldn't have taken a promotion if you were offered one when you were with KCM?'

'Why do you find that so hard to believe?'

'You know I got Anderson's job just after you left.'

'I heard.' Anderson had been the senior account manager, about whom it was rumoured that he was getting a sideways move in a power shuffle taking place above him. Dexter had been smugly sure that he was in line for the job.

'I always wondered,' Dexter mused. 'If that had anything to do with you deciding to leave.'

'I quit to start my own company, Larry.'

'Yes. But the timing struck me as, well, a coincidence.'

I wondered why he was bringing all this up now. When I thought back I seemed to remember that when I'd announced my resignation Dexter had been subtly scathing about my intentions. It was almost as if he resented me leaving, which I hadn't understood. I'd expected him to be pleased to see the back of someone he regarded as a threat.

'Does it bother you that I left when I did, Larry? Did

you want me to be there when you got Anderson's job, so you could lord it over me?' I laughed. 'That's it isn't it? I can't believe you're still carrying that around.'

'You can laugh, Nick. But I think that's why you chose to leave when you did. I think you knew I would get that job over you.'

'Larry, it was years ago. And I hate to rain on your parade, but I didn't even want the job.'

'No of course you didn't,' he said scathingly. 'You wanted to set up your own company and make a fortune. Well, that hasn't worked out too well, has it?'

'We're no KCM if that's what you mean. Of course, if we win the Spectrum account things could change,' I added innocently. It was hard not to feel smug given my conversation with Sam Mendez earlier. I wondered how Dexter would feel if he knew about that.

He laughed. 'You don't seriously think that's a possibility.'

'Got you worried, Larry?'

He didn't react, but I wondered if I'd struck a nerve. I imagined he would have been highly pissed when he discovered that an upstart little agency was challenging KCM for a slice of their very lucrative pie. Especially when he found out who that upstart agency was.

'Let's be honest here, Nick. We handle the rest of Morgan Industries and it makes sense both for them and us to keep it in the family.'

'Obviously Sam Mendez doesn't see it that way. Maybe he didn't hit it off with your people.'

I wasn't sure why Sam had invited other agencies to pitch for his business, but there was a rumour doing the rounds that one of the chief reasons was that he didn't like either Sarah Miles, the account manager Dexter had assigned to Spectrum, or Dexter himself. He was meant to be a very upright moral type in his private life, and

Sarah Miles was known to be a person of ruthless ambition, quite willing to go the distance to get what she wanted. Speculation was she'd made some kind of a pass at Sam.

Dexter's smile vanished and to cover his irritation he took a sip of his drink. 'It's no secret that Sarah made an error of judgment,' he said tightly. 'But that problem has been taken care of.'

'So I heard,' I said. Dexter had fired her, even though he was probably the one who put her up to whatever it was she'd done in the first place. Currently she was telling anyone who would listen that she was happy to be out of it, claiming that part of her job had involved getting down on her knees behind the boss's desk on a regular basis. The way she told it, Dexter would carry right on with whatever he was doing while she was busy below, and when she was finished he liked her to leave the room without a word as if in pretence that nothing had happened. Takes all kinds, I thought.

Dexter recovered his poise. 'Sam will come around in the end. No offence, Nick, but this is kind of a David and Goliath situation here. KCM is a hundred million dollar company. Carpe Diem is what? Two million?' He smiled mockingly.

'You know what they say about size, Larry. Besides, if I remember my bible rightly, didn't David win when he came up against Goliath?' I finished my bourbon and rattled the ice cubes in the glass. 'You know I think you really are worried. What are you now anyway, a vice president of something? I guess you have your eye on the next step. Losing Spectrum would be a black mark wouldn't it? Sometimes you don't recover from that kind of thing.'

'Oh, I don't think I need to worry about that,' Dexter said confidently and again he smiled with that mocking look in his eye that was beginning to irritate me. 'Here, let me get you another drink.' He signalled the bartender, pointing to my glass. 'Must be stressful for you right now. How long has this been going on for? Four months, five? I've had an entire team dedicated to this one pitch full time. Creative people, two account people, my own input of course. That costs a lot of money even for us. Must have been a hell of a strain on your resources.'

'Well, don't lose any sleep over it, Larry, we've managed.'

'Have you?' His expression suggested he knew better.

'Oh I know you'd like to think we haven't and you've just got us beat with all that firepower and money you've put into this. But the fact is, Larry, it's almost over now and we're still here.' I grinned. 'You know what I think? I think you're worried I'm going to beat you. You take this personally don't you? Of course if I win I guess it won't look too good with the board at KCM either. One little independent agency kicking your butt.' I clucked my tongue. 'Heads are going to roll, Larry. Heads are going to roll.'

He fixed me with a cold stare, and just then the bartender brought me the drink Larry had ordered.

'Chin chin,' I said.

He grimaced, but though I'd touched a nerve he kept his poise. Then something caught his eye as he glanced towards the door, and he smiled, though the effect was unsettling more than anything.

'Here's my client.' He put his mineral water down and raised a hand to someone among the crowd, then he did a bad impression of something having just occurred to him. 'You know now I think of it you two must know each other. You'll probably want to say hello.'

There was no mistaking the look of sly triumph that spread like an oil slick across his features. A figure emerged heading towards us and I recognized the fair hair and stooped shoulders of Jerry Parker from Web-Link. He hesitated when he saw me, then regained his composure and came over. Dexter shook his hand.

'Jerry, glad you could make it. Look who I ran into. I was just saying to Nick that you know each other, don't you?' He looked at me with amusement.

'How are you, Nick?' Parker said with slight discomfort.

We shook hands civilly even though this was an awkward situation for both of us.

'Jerry and I are having lunch, Nick, so you'll have to excuse us.' Dexter was obviously enjoying himself. 'Good to catch up with you.' He started to turn away then checked himself. 'By the way. Good luck with that other matter.'

He was openly mocking, and for the first time I felt a vague unease. I watched them go, unsettled and worried. What the hell was Dexter doing taking on a client like Parker? KCM handled the really big accounts, the ones that spent millions on advertising, not little pissant companies like WebLink who might be important to us but wouldn't ordinarily have warranted a moment of Dexter's time.

Suddenly my confidence and good spirits evaporated. I was reminded of that old saying. It isn't over until the fat lady sings. I looked at the drink Dexter had bought me which stood barely touched on the bar. I wanted to leave it there, but I changed my mind and knocked it back in a single swallow.

Sally was out when I got home. She left a message saying she'd gone to visit a friend. It was eight-thirty and I was beat. I made a sandwich and poured myself a stiff drink which vanished without me noticing, so I poured another and ate my solitary dinner at the kitchen table. Sally had left some magazines out, the sort bought by new mothers that feature all kinds of articles about raising children and babies and so forth. I flicked through one looking at the pictures of round rosy mothers and their newborn children. At nine the phone rang and I thought it might be Sally but when I picked up there was nobody there. I could sense someone on the line though.

'Who is this?' I said. No answer. 'I'm going to hang up if you don't say something.' Still no answer.

'Sally? Is that you?'

Whoever was there finally hung up. I waited for the phone to ring again, but it didn't even though I must have stood there for ten minutes.

Sally came home about an hour later. I was still thinking about the phone call because though I kept telling myself it was somebody playing a random prank, I didn't really believe that. I'd had an odd sense about whoever was at the other end of the line. I didn't mention it to Sally. She came into the kitchen, glanced at my drink and asked about my day.

'It was fine.' I decided not to mention either the meeting or my encounter with Dexter. 'So, who'd you see?' I asked.

'Just somebody who used to work at the office.'

Sally worked for a chain of clothing retailers on the buying team. She was good at her job, but had never been ambitious. Her plan was always to quit working when we started a family.

'Who's that?' I was pouring another drink, making conversation.

'The one who had the baby.'

'Linda? I thought she moved away.' I was sure I remembered Sally saying her husband got a transfer to somewhere out west. Phoenix I thought. At the time I was vaguely relieved because Linda's pregnancy and the birth of her daughter had made Sally broody.

'It was someone else. You don't know her. Liz Herman. She was in accounts.'

I didn't recognize the name and I was struck by something off-key in Sally's tone. She poured herself a glass of water and drank it down, then put the glass on the bench.

'So how was she?'

'Fine.'

'What'd she have?'

'A girl.'

'That's great.'

'Yes. It is.'

'What's her name?'

'Her name? Anna.'

'Nice name.' I took a sip of my drink.

'Yes it is,' Sally agreed. 'Well, I'm tired. I think I'll go upstairs,' she said.

'Okay. I'll be up soon.'

I stood at the bench drinking my scotch, wondering about our conversation. Something hadn't seemed right. Sally had seemed nervous or jumpy or something and she'd been reluctant to meet my eye. Anna was a name I remembered she had once said she would like to call our own child if we had a daughter. Was that coincidence or was it the first thing that came into her head? Her purse was on the bench. After a while I opened it and found her address book, but when I turned to the page with entries beginning L, I couldn't find a Liz. Neither was there a Herman. I told myself it didn't mean anything.

A few minutes later I went up to our room and sat on the bed pretending to watch TV while Sally sat in front of the mirror to remove her make-up. Her blouse was undone and I could see the swell of her breasts beneath the white lace of her bra. The contrast of lightly tanned flesh against the pure whiteness of lace was sensual, given some added dimension by the careless manner in which it was exposed. She put a band in her hair to hold it back from her face while she used cotton wool and a cleanser to take off her eye shadow and lipstick. When she was done she used her fingers to massage in moisturizing lotion. She began to brush her hair, and appeared absorbed in the task, taking long slow strokes. Our eyes collided in the mirror and she faltered, surprised to find me watching her. Some quick shadow of expression passed over her eyes.

'You're not working tonight,' she commented.

'No.' I thought about telling her about my meeting at Spectrum, but then I remembered Dexter and I decided not to.

She resumed brushing her hair. I'd forgotten how much I liked watching her at times like this. I'd always found Sally at her loveliest when she was engaged in some everyday routine and was unaware of my interest, utterly unself-conscious. I used to watch her sometimes when she read a novel and I could always tell if she was enjoying the story. Small lines of concentration appeared on her brow and her lips might twitch in a smile at something she read, or clamp tightly shut if some terrible fate were about to befall the protagonist. If on the other hand she was bored her eyes would dart restlessly over the text and as she turned a page she would frown. But mostly I liked to watch her as she got herself ready for bed. The ritual of cleaning her skin and brushing her hair provoked all kinds of feelings in me. She could be unintentionally erotic just by leaning to one side so her hair fell away from her neck as she brushed from the base of her scalp outwards. A glimpse of bare flesh, the ridge of her spine could make me desire her more than when she was being deliberately sexy. It was partly because she drifted, without being aware of it, into a world of her own. Her expression became dreamlike as she pampered herself, and she became unaware of her surroundings. While some part of her conscious brain controlled her actions, another, the emotive part, swept her thoughts elsewhere like windblown leaves in the fall. I once asked her what she was thinking about, and she smiled and said she was thinking of us.

Now, though she was as lovely as ever, I was reminded of how long it had been since I had watched her this way. I couldn't help thinking there was something troubled in her expression.

'What are you thinking about?' I asked her.

She snapped from her reverie. 'Nothing.'

Abruptly as if uncomfortable at being caught in an unguarded moment she went into the bathroom and closed the door behind her. When she reappeared she was ready for bed. She tossed her underwear in the laundry basket and went to the door.

'Are you going downstairs again?' she asked.

I shook my head and she went to turn out the lights and check the doors were locked. After a moment I got up and went to the laundry hamper to retrieve her underwear. Her panties were white lace, to match the bra, in a G-string style with a delicate transparent see through panel at the front. I couldn't remember seeing them before, though I was sure I would have remembered. The brand was some French sounding name and when I looked in the waste bin I found the snipped off labels. I didn't know why I should be bothered that my wife had bought new underwear, but I was.

When Sally came back I went to the bathroom to brush my teeth and when I came out she was already in bed, reading a book. She looked up. 'My parents are coming this weekend,' she reminded me.

'That's right. I forgot.' Terrific, I thought sourly,

contemplating a weekend with Sally's mother, though outwardly my expression remained neutral. 'I should book a restaurant. Maybe Marios.'

A little while later Sally turned out the light. I lay there in the dark listening to the sound of her breathing. I thought about those baby magazines downstairs, the phone call earlier and Sally saying she'd been to see Liz Herman who I'd never heard her mention before. Then Dexter popped into my mind, and I kept seeing him as he went into the restaurant with Jerry Parker, that mocking secret smile. Two hours later I was still awake.

CHAPTER SEVEN

I had until the twenty-third to work on my final presentation to Spectrum, and I resolved to use every moment of that time to make sure I left nothing to chance. At my insistence everything else at the agency took second place, this had total priority, which didn't sit well with Marcus.

'This isn't our only account, dammit!' he argued in his office. 'In fact it isn't an account at all. We can't just shove everything else aside. We have deadlines to meet, not to mention people to pay. Or had you forgotten about that?'

'The bank are covering us, Marcus,' I pointed out. 'This is it. Less than two weeks.'

He stared at me, knowing it was pointless to argue. 'I hope you know what you're doing.'

So did I, though I didn't say as much. I had been over everything a thousand times. I couldn't shift the sense of unease that had lodged in my gut after meeting Dexter, but Sam Mendez had all but promised me the contract. One thing I was certain of, there was no going back now. The bank had us on a very tight leash, and our cash flow continued to fall. It was all or nothing.

I worked late every night and left the house early in the morning, snatching sandwiches when I could, drinking coffee and scotch to keep me going, hardly even seeing Sally. One day I called her at work just to say hi, but the woman I spoke to came back on the line and said she was at lunch.

'Was it important?' she asked. 'I can take a message.'

'No that's fine,' I told her, and was getting ready to hang up when she asked if I was sure nobody else could help. I hesitated, then I said, 'Well, actually I guess Liz Herman could, but she doesn't work there any more does she?'

'Liz Herman? I never heard of anyone by that name. She worked here you say? What department was that?'

'Accounts.'

There was a pause while she checked then she said, 'No, definitely nobody by that name.'

I thanked her and told her it didn't matter. For some time I pondered what this meant, but in the end I told myself there could be a hundred explanations. Maybe I heard the name wrong or I misunderstood, or the woman I spoke to was mistaken. I wasn't convinced by any of this of course, not really, but I chose to put it aside because I didn't know what I should do about it. Whatever 'it' was.

I barely spoke to Sally all week. We came and went and occupied the same space but not much beyond that. I was completely absorbed with preparing for my presentation. I knew that my marriage was drifting like a boat with nobody at the helm. On Wednesday we snatched some moments over coffee and I tried to tell Sally that once I had Spectrum in the bag I would slow down and we would spend more time together. It was kind of a holding action, my way of trying to make sure things didn't get any worse but she didn't want to hear about it.

'Have you ever considered that you might not get the account?'

'You sound like Marcus. Doesn't anybody have any faith in me?'

She looked at her watch and avoided answering me. 'I have to go. I'll be late.'

On Friday we caught a few minutes at breakfast. 'You look exhausted,' Sally commented.

'I'm fine,' I said, but I saw her eye drift to the empty scotch bottle I'd left by the trash bin. I was surprised myself when I finished it the night before, it seemed like just the other day when I'd bought it.

'You need to slow down.'

I shook my head and gulped my coffee. 'Can't. I've only got another week.'

'Are you working tonight?'

'Sorry.'

'You know my parents arrive this morning.'

'I know.' I would have worked over the weekend too if it hadn't been for her parents' visit but I compromised by promising I'd leave the rest of the weekend free. In fact I thought it was probably a good thing. I could use a break, and maybe a couple of days together would do us good, even with her parents tagging along. 'I booked a table at Marios for tomorrow night,' I said. This was a favourite restaurant of ours situated in the hills above Half Moon Bay where we used to go regularly. I knew Sally liked it and I thought she'd get a kick out of taking her parents there. She made no comment, however.

I went around to kiss her goodbye. 'Say hi to your folks, and don't wait up if I'm late.'

She didn't say anything. I left her staring into her coffee.

I didn't get home until midnight. The house was silent, though Sally had left a light on for me in the hall. I went through to the kitchen where an unfamiliar bag which I assumed belonged to Ellen sat on the bench. There was an empty wine bottle on the counter and the debris from a meal which I guessed Sally had left until morning to clear up. I decided to do her a favour, and so I loaded the dishwasher and wiped the pots and pans and left them to drain. When I was finished I went to the cupboard and fetched a new bottle of scotch which I opened. I was tired, my eyes were sore and I needed to go to sleep. Just a small one I thought, and dropped some ice into a glass. I took a sip, not really enjoying the taste but the burn of the liquor seemed to ease some of the tension from my neck. Distractedly I reached around and kneaded my spine. I let my eyes close and for a second I was almost asleep on my feet.

The harsh jangle of the phone disturbed me and I snapped to and snatched it off the hook before the whole house woke up.

'Yes?' I glanced at my watch wondering who the hell was calling at this time of night.

There was no reply.

'Who is this?' I demanded. Again, silence.

I got angry. 'Listen, I don't know who you are but I want you to stop calling here. Can you hear me?' I could feel someone on the other end of the line. I knew this had something to do with Sally. I'd been trying to think if she was seeing somebody, who it could be. A guy at work? She'd never mentioned anybody and I'd met a few of them at Christmas parties. I didn't think any of them were her type. A neighbour? Again I couldn't think of anyone.

'Who are you? Don't you have the balls to say something?' It was frustrating talking into space, to some insubstantial entity. 'Fuck you!' I said. 'Stay the hell away from my wife!'

I slammed down the phone. I still felt stupid. There was probably no guy. More likely it was kids playing a prank or a wrong number or whatever. Probably.

*   *   *

In the morning I woke early from habit, feeling lousy. Sally was still sleeping and the rest of the house was quiet so I slipped out of bed and crept downstairs. I needed to clear my head, make myself human again, so I got my things together and drove to the Peninsula Club on the way to San Mateo which has a gym and pool. That early on a Saturday there were only a handful of other swimmers, mostly the older contingent who always seemed to be there ploughing back and forth in the slow lanes with their steady unchanging rhythm, looking for all the world as if they could go on for ever. I chose a medium pace lane which I had to myself, and after I'd done some stretches I slid into the water and did a couple of warm-up lengths. My body creaked and protested, and my head throbbed, but after a couple of lengths I wasn't aware of the effort any more. The flow of water around me eased the tension in my muscles. I felt the build up of toxins in my body from too much booze and bad food rise to the surface where I sloughed it off the way a snake sheds its skin. Even so I couldn't manage more than twenty lengths, after which I sat on the side with a towel wrapped around me watching the old people in the slow lanes chugging along at the same steady, inexorable pace.

When I arrived home again it was mid-morning and Frank told me that Sally and her mother had gone to Palo Alto to go shopping. I found him in the garden where it was warm, the sun already high in a clear sky, but the light softened by a whitish haze in the air. In the hills the shades of green blurred in soft focus. We shook hands.

'Good to see you again, Frank.'

'You too.'

'How was your flight?'

'It was fine. Sorry we missed you last night. We would've waited up but Sally said you might be late.'

'I was, and I should be the one apologizing. Things have been kind of busy lately.'

He nodded. 'Sally said something about that.' He looked around the garden, and for a moment I thought I'd lost him. He seemed to have switched off, as was his habit. But after a while he said thoughtfully, 'Needs a little work out here.'

True enough, I thought. I hadn't taken the time to notice lately but the yard was a tangle of bushes and plants. I'd never had green fingers, it was as much as I could do to keep the grass mown, but I hadn't noticed how bad it had gotten out there. To my untrained eye it was hard to tell where the woods ended and our garden began. My eye wandered out over the view. There was a large white house on a hillside half a mile away which had been built a year or so earlier. It was secluded in the woods, high up with panoramic views. The guy who owned it, I heard, had started a dot.com company three years ago and when it had gone public he had made three hundred million dollars. Three hundred million! He was thirty-one.

I turned my attention back to Frank, who was bent over examining a dusky coloured rose bush that had grown into a thorny mess.

'Sally planted that when we bought this place,' I said. 'I haven't spent much time out here lately.'

'You need to cut it back. That way you'll get better blooms. And you need to get some of these weeds out or they're going to choke it.'

'There's a lot needs doing,' I agreed, looking around.

Frank indicated another plant that I didn't know the name of. 'Aphids. You need to spray or they're going to kill it.'

'I should get around to it,' I agreed. The plant did look pretty sad.

'You'll get beautiful flowers in spring if you look after it.'

He moved on, looking at different plants, stopping to examine their leaves. There had been a time when I'd wondered if Frank was a little simple minded. Even though he'd been a lawyer before he retired I didn't think his small-town practice would have been too demanding. As long as I'd known him his absorbing interest had been the plants he reared in the giant glasshouses behind his house, which he planted out to see if they would survive the heavy soil and cold Oregon winters. According to Sally he'd always left everything to do with home and family to Ellen. He never got involved in disagreements, instead when trouble brewed he retreated to the peace and calm of the world he'd created outside.

I walked around with him as he kept talking about what I should do in the garden, though I was only half listening. I had too many other things on my mind like late night phone calls when nobody is on the line, and non-existent coworkers.

'You have to nurture beauty, Nick,' Frank said.

I stopped, realizing that he wasn't beside me any more and I turned around. He was watching me with a curious kind of smile.

'Sorry, Frank. What did you say?'

'You can't just take it for granted, otherwise you might look around one day and it isn't there any more.'

'What isn't?'

'Beauty, Nick. I was saying you have to nurture it.'

He held my gaze for a second longer, then he sort of smiled and the moment was gone. As we moved on and mooched around the garden I kept thinking about what he'd said and the way he looked at me. I had the odd feeling that he was trying to tell me something. I was still thinking about it when he got my attention again.

'What was that?'

'I said we ran into that friend of Sally's who used to come around. The Hunt boy. Course, he's not a boy now. You remember him.'

'Garrison Hunt?' The name seemed to reverberate across the years, unearthing a lot of old feelings. I recalled the first night I'd spent in Sally's parents' house, how her mother had kept telling me what a great guy Garrison was.

'Yes. You met him didn't you?'

'Once or twice. Doesn't he still live in White Falls?' I asked. I was confused. It was a small town. I thought Frank probably ran into Garrison Hunt all the time.

'Oh yes. Still there. Sally sees him now and then when she comes home.'

I stared at Frank. This was news to me. He gazed back at me, his expression completely unreadable.

'Anyway we ran into him yesterday,' he said.

'Wait a minute. Yesterday? You mean in San Francisco?'

'That's right. He was just walking along the street minding his own business. Almost bumped into him. We had a cup of coffee. He was down here on business.'

'Quite a coincidence,' I remarked.

Frank smiled. 'Yes. I suppose it was.'

Which was an understatement I thought. In a city this size, they just happened to run into Garrison Hunt from White Falls, who just happened to be in town on the same day. I didn't think so.

'So how is he?' I asked.

'Seemed fine,' Frank said.

I was still trying to deal with this piece of news, and work out what it meant when I realized that Frank had moved on, and was talking gardens again. I remembered what he'd said before, about taking care of beautiful things, and now this about Garrison Hunt. Like a child's puzzle all the pieces that had been jostling around in my head, bumping into each other and not making sense all tumbled and clicked neatly into place. The phone calls. Sally's behaviour.

Sally and Garrison Hunt. It hit me like a hammer and the blood drained out of my face. Frank looked back at me.

'You okay, Nick?' he asked, his voice tinged with concern.

CHAPTER EIGHT

I left Frank in the garden, claiming I needed to take care of a couple of things, and I retreated into my office where I closed the door and took care of half a bottle of scotch. When I heard Sally's car it was around mid-afternoon. She and her mother were talking as they approached the front door, then I heard the rattle of Sally's key in the lock and the door swung open. Frank said they had gone shopping, but I couldn't see any packages other than a bag from the bakery. I guessed they'd spent the day talking, perhaps in some restaurant where they had gone for lunch. I had it all figured out. The way I saw it, Sally had met up with Garrison Hunt again on one of her trips home. I could see them bumping into each other outside the post office in White Falls, the laughs and apologies as he helped her pick up the letters Sally had been on her way to post for her mother. Maybe they'd gone for a cup of coffee and spent a cozy hour or two reminiscing. Next time Sally was in town they probably had lunch or dinner, and then it became a regular thing. One night he ordered an expensive bottle of wine and confessed to Sally in the romantic flickering candlelight how he'd always loved her and that was why he'd never married. I could see his self-conscious, half apologetic grin, the hint of nervousness in his eye because he was unsure how she would respond, and Sally looking down at her hands because she couldn't meet his eye, the colour rising in her cheeks.

'So how's Nick?' he probably asked.

'Oh.' She'd kind of smile but it would become a frown. No doubt she'd confide that things hadn't been going so well for her at home.

'Sorry to hear that,' he'd say, all understanding. The prick.

Those kind of secrets don't remain secret for long in small towns, and whether Sally had told Ellen herself, or Ellen had simply heard on the local rumour mill how her daughter and Garrison Hunt were seeing a lot of each other, it would have been an opportunity she couldn't let pass by. But I knew Sally well enough to know she wouldn't have taken something like this lightly. I hoped I hadn't come to mean that little to her. Maybe she had found events moving too fast, she didn't know how she felt any more, and so she'd decided to call time out. That would explain why she hadn't been up to visit her parents for a while, and it also explained why Ellen had thought it necessary to come to San Francisco. It was suddenly clear as day. Ellen intended to persuade Sally to return with her to Oregon. The encounter with Garrison Hunt that Frank had told me about was no accident, but undoubtedly had been well planned. All part of Ellen's campaign.

I met them on the doorstep. 'There you are. I was wondering how long you'd be. You have a good day shopping? I guess you didn't buy much though, did you?'

A flicker of uncertainty crossed Sally's expression as she registered both my sarcasm and the fact that I'd been drinking. I fixed her with an accusing stare, then turned my attention to her mother.

'Aren't you going to say hello, Ellen? It's quite a while since we saw each other isn't it? How is my favourite mother-in-law?' I lurched towards her and kissed her on the cheek, managing to stumble off balance in the act and bang our heads a little. She withdrew as if I'd shoved my hand up her skirt and her expression wrinkled in distaste.

'You two must have had a lot to catch up on I guess,' I said, grinning malevolently at them.

'You've been drinking,' Sally accused, her cheeks flushed with embarrassment.

'We all have our weaknesses. Temptations of the flesh. You know how that is, Sally.'

Her eyes narrowed suspiciously, wondering what I meant by my loaded remark.

'So, where have you been all day? Not shopping obviously. Bump into anyone I know?'

'Nick, what is this all about?' Sally demanded.

'How about yesterday. What did you do? See the sights? Have lunch? Slip into a hotel for a quickie?'

Uncertainty. Shock. Guilt. They all passed in turn across Sally's eyes. I'd hoped that somehow I had this all wrong, but one look at her and I knew that I didn't. I was struck with a sudden piercing pain which it took me a moment to recognize as grief.

Ellen began to squeeze past, and being reminded of her presence transformed my pain into rage. 'You two obviously have things to discuss. I think I'll go upstairs,' she said. But I wasn't about to let her off so lightly.

'What's the hurry? We haven't had a chance to have a chat yet. After all this does concern you doesn't it?'

She ignored me and said to Sally, 'I'll be in my room if you need me.'

'While you're up there you can pack your bags.'

Sally stared at me, the blood draining from her face. 'Nick . . .'

'What? What is it, Sally? You think I'm being a poor host. Maybe you're right. Forget that last remark, Ellen. I tell you what I'll pack them for you. How's that. I'll even drive you to the airport. What the hell, I'll drive you all the way to fucking Oregon. At least that way I'll know you're out of the state.'

'Dammit, Nick, that's enough!' Sally cut in.

'Enough? I haven't even started.'

'You're drunk!'

'Absolutely.' My voice had been rising, but now I was shouting. I knew if I looked in the mirror my face would be red and my eyes would be popping. 'I think every man has a right to get drunk when he hears his wife has been fucking some guy she knew in high school, don't you?'

There was a moment of shocked silence. Sally opened her mouth as if to say something but no sound escaped her.

'Don't,' I said wearily. 'If you're going to deny it, please don't.'

'I wasn't going to deny it,' she said quietly, sorrowfully.

'Then don't explain it either,' I said, but in my heart I was crying out for her to do just that because no matter the troubles we'd had I never thought it would come to this.

That was one scenario of events that passed through my mind anyway as I sat in my study after leaving Frank in the garden. I imagined it all, every word and gesture in vivid detail. It ended with Sally leaving me, fulfilling the premonition of the dream I'd woken from the morning of my meeting with the bank. It was the memory of that dream, and the sharp, painful realization that I might actually lose Sally that stayed my hand. The scotch bottle was already open and I fully intended to use the liquor to dull the shock of my discovery, but in the end I didn't take a drink. Instead I screwed the cap back on the bottle, and through my anger and pain I tried to understand what had happened.

You have to nurture beautiful things, so Frank had told me. I wondered if his comment had been advice in vague metaphor. Despite my instinctive desire to confront Sally with what I knew, wasn't that about exposing my pain, voicing my hurt so that I could see her guilt reflected as her own kind of pain? Didn't I want to show her how agonizing this was for me, and spear her heart the way mine had been? It was all about turning my feelings around, transforming them into a weapon with which I could blindly hit back. It was about me. Me, me, me. And I suppose in the back of my mind was the hope that I could shame her into seeing how wrong she had been, to make her fall on her knees and beg me to forgive her. But what if she didn't? What if amid her regret and sorrow I glimpsed something else, a glimmer of relief that it was at last out in the open. If she had begun an affair with Garrison Hunt, I believed that it had not been planned. Sally wouldn't do that. She would have left me first. That she hadn't done so after the fact suggested that she still had feelings for me, that she hadn't entirely written off our marriage. The more I considered it the more I saw that whatever happened had begun as a weak moment, an expression of her unhappiness, but once she had time to think things over she had ended the affair. Hence the end of her visits to Oregon, and Ellen's decision to come to San Francisco.

What I saw finally was that Sally hadn't been ready to leave me, but if I confronted her with what I knew I might well drive her away. I had a clear choice. Did I want that? Or did I want to fight for her? Painful as it was, I had to accept that if Sally had been so unhappy as to seek solace with another man, then I couldn't escape my share of responsibility for that.

By the time Sally and her mother arrived home I'd reached some conclusions. I loved Sally. I always had, and there was no question in my mind that I didn't want to lose her, but I didn't know either if I could keep secret what I knew. Garrison Hunt insinuated himself into my mind, derailing my train of thought. It was a long time since I'd last seen him, and I had no idea how much he'd changed. In fact I remembered him indistinctly. His features were vague. Brown hair, thinnish face, tallish and lean build. It was his demeanour I recalled more clearly. He possessed the innate inner confidence that you often find in the children of the wealthy. All his life he had been made to feel special. He went to a good school where athletic and intellectual ability were discovered and honed by well paid teachers who instilled in their pupils high expectations of themselves and what their futures might bring, and reminded them they had the means to meet those expectations. That is partly the inheritance passed down among the rich, and it's worth more than mere money.

If I'd learned that Sally had met somebody, a guy at work perhaps, with whom she'd somehow begun an affair, I would have found it easier to bear. The fact that it was Garrison Hunt made it harder. Not because he had money, although that was tied up in it, but because of who he was, what he represented. When I thought of him all my old feelings resurfaced. I remembered how Ellen had talked about him the first time I'd met her, making her unsubtle point about the kind of person she wanted her daughter to one day marry. Jealousy. Hurt. Wounded pride. And I allowed myself to imagine what Sally's life would have been like if she had married him instead of me. I saw them in their big house outside White Falls, which I had never actually seen in real life, but I envisaged a sprawling place on a grand scale, with horses and three or four children and Sally rosy cheeked and healthy in the Oregon snow, curled up with her husband in front of a roaring fire at night with a big dog lying at their feet on an expensive rug that took some tribes-people in a mountainous region on the other side of the earth ten years to knot by hand.

And so because and despite of everything that I felt, when Sally and her mother came in the front door I went out to meet them, and I kissed Ellen on her cheek and told her I was pleased to see her, and I must have sounded as if I meant it because Sally looked the slightest bit surprised as I kissed her too and asked if they'd had a good day, and I said nothing about the fact that they weren't carrying any packages and I didn't let on that inside my heart was breaking.

Marios was situated high in the hills. It was a place that Sally and I had found by chance not long after we'd moved into our house, and had been to regularly ever since, though the last time must have been six months or so ago. The view at night over the twinkling lights of Half Moon Bay far below, and the Pacific ocean, immense and awe inspiring when the sun sets, casting flames over the water like liquid gold from the hand of God, made for a romantic setting. I took the scenic route leaving 280 at Woodside and doubling back along Skyline Boulevard. The road twists and turns, dips and rises among wooded hills and valleys and the broad vistas of corn yellow grass of the Santa Cruz mountains. Sally's parents sat in the back, Frank gazing out of the window placidly, Ellen tight lipped and silent. I knew she was suspicious. I was being relentlessly pleasant, which even Sally had commented on when we were getting ready.

'You said you'd like it if we got on a little better didn't you?' I said. 'Well, I'm trying.'

Since that afternoon Ellen had been cool towards me. Polite but reserved, and I gathered from this that if she had been attempting to persuade Sally to leave me, so far at least she had not succeeded. Sally was wearing a simple black dress with a scooped back and neck, with silver earrings and a fine silver chain around her neck. She looked beautiful. She was preoccupied, and gazed out of the windshield lost in her own thoughts.

We reached the turnoff that led up through the trees to the restaurant, the lights glimpsed through the woods in the fading evening light.

'Looks like a nice place,' Frank commented.

'I think you'll like it,' I said. 'Sally and I used to come here often.'

I parked in the lot, which was planted with rhododendron and bougainvillea. The air was laced with their scent, and as we approached the terrace the bougainvillea that grew entwined in the railing was lit with the glow from the lamps placed all along the front. Each plant had flowers of a different colour, from dark purple through lilac through to blood red and orange, and many of the limbs had twisted in among each other so that it seemed as if it was all one plant producing a wall of impossible colour. In fact it reminded me of a splatter painting *à la* Alice. Without the deeply meaningful title.

At the entrance Mario was hovering as usual. He liked to greet diners personally and then hand them onto his maître d'. Throughout the evening he would pass unobtrusively among the tables making sure that everything was okay. If there was a complaint it was attended to without demur. He loved to see his customers enjoying themselves. They came to eat good food and drink fine wine and he made sure everybody had a good time so that when the bill came at the end of the evening they hardly even noticed the amount before they signed their credit card slip.

I had called the restaurant that afternoon and asked

to speak to Mario himself. When I'd explained that I needed to make a good impression he'd told me to leave it to him. Now when he saw us he approached with outstretched arms, beaming a smile of welcome.

'My friends, it is so good to see you!' He stopped and took both Sally's hands, and kissed her cheeks. His eyes drank her in. 'Sally, you look beautiful. Nick, you are a very lucky man.'

'I know it.'

When he turned to Ellen he took her hand and bent to place a formal kiss. 'No need to tell me who this lady is. I see where your daughter gets her beauty.'

I made the introductions and Mario shook Frank's hand. 'It is an honour to meet you, sir.' With a flourish he led us towards our table, dismissing the maître d' who hovered in the background. 'I will attend to these people myself,' he said.

He'd put us in the corner of the room, by the window where we had both space and uninterrupted views. The tablecloth was almost impossibly white, the places laid out with gleaming cutlery and glasses that shone in the soft light.

'After you called this afternoon, Nick, I took the liberty of choosing a wine for you,' Mario said. 'It is a Valpolicella, from a very famous estate. This vintage was the best they have produced in the last twenty years. I think you will like it, it is very special. I have only six bottles left.'

I murmured my approval when he showed me the bottle, and he produced a wine knife and removed the cork. I dreaded to think what all this attention was going to cost, but I was willing to go to any lengths to create the atmosphere for a pleasant evening.

The meal went as well as I could have hoped for. The food and wine were good enough to thaw even Ellen out a little, and afterwards Mario appeared and offered to show Sally's parents the house at the back of the property, part of which he had converted into a kind of museum of traditional Italian cooking.

When Sally and I were alone at last I poured the last of the wine into our glasses. Sally had been a little quiet during dinner.

'You okay?' I asked her.

'Yes. I'm fine.'

'You seem a little distracted.'

'Sorry. This has been nice. Thank you.'

'For dinner?'

'For making an effort with my mother.'

I grinned. 'She's not so bad.' In fact I'd enjoyed a degree of malicious satisfaction being attentive to Ellen, in the knowledge that I was subtly undermining her efforts to persuade Sally to leave me. We fell silent for a moment or two.

'Nick . . .' Sally said tentatively. 'I want to ask you something. Are you happy?'

I experienced a sense of dread. Conversations that began with such questions inevitably led somewhere I didn't think I wanted to go. I wondered if Ellen had been making headway, that Sally was about to drop the bombshell. I tried not to let any of what I was thinking show when I answered her. 'Define happy,' I said, and regretted it as sounding glib.

'I mean happy with me. Us. Our marriage.'

'Of course,' I replied as if the answer was obvious, but I saw that Sally was serious, and that trying to pretend otherwise was only burying my head in the sand even though I was afraid of where it would lead us. I reached across the table and took her hand. 'Nobody is happy for every minute of every day, Sally. At least not outwardly.'

She peered questioningly at me. 'But deep down?'

'Deep down I love you, just the same as I always have. That's what's important isn't it?'

'I guess,' she agreed. 'But you know that? Really? I mean you never have a moment of doubt?'

'Never.' I knew we weren't talking about me. She wasn't looking for reassurance, these were questions she was asking of herself.

'Maybe I don't always show it. I can't deny that things haven't been perfect between us lately. I've had a lot on my mind, but underneath it all there's nothing in my life that's more important than you.'

She dropped her gaze, with a sad kind of wry smile. 'I used to know you felt that way.'

'You don't any more?'

'I don't know. You say the words, but lately . . .' she gave a little shrug of helplessness.

I could let it go, I thought. Make some reassuring comment. I couldn't fix what was wrong in our marriage over one dinner, especially when any minute her parents would be back. I had to take this a step at a time, not push forward and spill all of my feelings in a rush. I sensed how confused she was, and I knew Sally well enough to know that right now she wouldn't be feeling good about herself. She was the kind of person who was likely to confess cleanly, but I wasn't ready for that. I knew I may never be ready.

But I also knew we had to make a start. 'But what?' I asked gently.

She met my look again, and it could have been the light but her eyes seemed to be shining unnaturally. 'This last year or so I've sometimes felt that what's important to you is your work. Making the agency a big success. Important to the point that's all you really care about.'

'That's crazy. Yes I care about it. I care about this deal

with Spectrum because it could change everything for us, but that doesn't mean I feel any less about you.'

'But you're obsessed with it. You work so hard, you're drinking too much, you're tired. We never talk any more. It's changed you.'

'It's an important deal, Sally.'

'That's what I'm saying. How important is it? Is it more important than your friendship with Marcus? Our marriage?'

'No, of course it isn't. Look I've made mistakes, I admit that and I can't change them, but once we have that account everything will work out.'

'Maybe that's partly what worries me,' she said quietly. 'You always say that, as if Spectrum is a fix all. I just don't think that it is. I didn't ever think we'd live like this.'

'You want a family, Sally. I know that. In a couple of months we can start trying for a baby. You'll feel differently then.'

'Will I?'

'Why not? Isn't that what you've always wanted.'

'Yes. But what about you, Nick? What is it you want?'

'The same as you. I want us to be secure first that's all.'

She gave a little shake of her head. 'Look around in the world. People start families all the time. Look where we live, the house we have, the cars we drive. How secure do we have to be? I think that's an excuse you use that I've never understood.'

It was hard to explain. I didn't even know if I could explain it. It was all tied up with my dad and my childhood and the way I'd felt when I was growing up, but these were things I'd never really talked about. Not even with Sally. It was a Pandora's box of emotions that I didn't want to open up. Some things we keep locked away, deep inside where the light never touches them, and though we know they affect everything we do, that they are a part of who we are we're reluctant to look at them too closely. But of course I'd thought about all of this. Why it was so important to me to be successful, to make a lot of money. The easy answer was because I didn't want to lose everything one day the way my dad did, because he was at the mercy of a big company with the muscle to put him under. But it wasn't that simple. There were other issues, that were deeper and confusing and I hadn't ever learned how to untangle them. I looked at Sally across the table and I wanted to try and tell her about the things I felt, but this wasn't something I could do in five minutes. Even as I thought about it I could see her parents coming back.

I squeezed her hand. 'Give me time.' Perhaps it was my expression, the nuance of my tone, but she appeared puzzled for a moment. Perhaps she half guessed that I knew she was thinking about leaving me. But then her parents returned and there was no time to talk any more.

I stood up, smiling. 'How was it?'

'Fascinating,' Ellen said, smiling at Mario. He was pleased I could tell, though something in Ellen's tone made me think he shouldn't take her compliment too seriously. We ordered coffee before I asked for the bill. I think Ellen sensed that something had happened while they'd been gone. She kept glancing at Sally thoughtfully.

When we left, Mario wished us goodnight at the door. 'I hope we will see you again next time you're in San Francisco,' he told Sally's parents, and again he kissed Ellen's hand.

I hung back to thank Mario for his trouble, and when I went down the steps Sally and her father had been sidetracked across the parking lot and were admiring a rhododendron, but Ellen was waiting for me and together we began walking towards the car.

'I hope you enjoyed yourself tonight, Ellen,' I said.

She turned to me and smiled coldly. 'I hope you realize, Nick, that I'm not taken in by any of this.'

'I don't follow.'

She continued to smile and spoke quietly so that we appeared to be having a civil conversation, though her eyes glittered with malice. 'Oh, I think you do. Did you imagine you could charm me with a meal at an Italian restaurant run by that obsequious little man? You didn't really believe that I could be swayed so easily did you?'

'I don't know what you're talking about, Ellen.'

'I mean this sudden outbreak of pleasantness, Nick. We can speak honestly, Sally can't hear us, and this has all been for her benefit hasn't it?'

'I know she'd like it if we got on a little better,' I said with an air of innocence. 'What other motive would I have?'

She regarded me with suspicion, but she didn't say anything. I figured she had an idea that I knew. Perhaps Frank had said something about our conversation. I took perverse pleasure in the understanding that she desperately wanted to throw Garrison Hunt in my face but couldn't. Sally would have sworn her to secrecy, and if Ellen said anything she risked the chance that Sally would never forgive her.

'I really hope we can get to know each other better in the future. We should learn to understand one another, Ellen.'

She threw me a look that could have reduced rock to ashes. 'Let's be clear. I don't know what game you're playing, Nick, but the only reason that I'm going along with this charade is that for some unfathomable reason Sally still seems to think there's something in your relationship worth salvaging.'

Despite our long history I was still surprised at her enmity and I shook my head. 'You still can't accept that

Sally married me can you? Even now it sticks in your throat.'

'I told Sally that I believed she was making a mistake when she first told me she intended marrying you, and I've never seen any reason to change that view,' Ellen said.

'Why, because my family didn't have money? Is that all that mattered to you?'

Across the lot Sally glanced our way, but Ellen smiled and spoke as if we were discussing the weather. 'I wanted Sally to have opportunities. I wanted her to do something with her life.'

'You mean you wanted her to live the life you never had,' I said. 'Did you know that Frank's family fortune was about used up when you married him, Ellen, or did that come as an unpleasant surprise?'

She flashed me a look of such vehemence that I thought for a second she would hit me. 'All I ever wanted was the best for my children. Sally was too young when she married you. I told her that. I said she ought to wait until she at least had some idea of what she was giving up.'

'What *was* she giving up? We're not exactly living in a trailer park in case you haven't noticed.'

'Perhaps not. But she certainly isn't happy.'

'Jesus, Ellen, we're not the first couple to have a bumpy patch in our relationship. It happens to everyone. What are you going to tell me? You and Frank never had a fight?'

'Oh, I think this goes a lot deeper than that.'

I hated the knowing edge in her tone. I thought if I pushed her hard enough she'd tell me about Garrison, and for a second I was almost tempted. Maybe it would be better anyway, and at least Sally would see her for the meddlesome crow she always had been. But the moment passed and then Ellen's expression abruptly changed and disconcertingly she laughed as if I'd said something funny. The effect was surreal until I turned and saw Sally and her father coming towards us.

'What are you two plotting?' she asked, looking at us both with vague unease.

'We've been learning to understand each other,' Ellen smiled. 'Haven't we, Nick?'

'That's right, we have,' I said, smiling with what felt like patent insincerity.

I put a disc on for the drive home, and when we reached the house I let everyone out while I put the car in the garage. When I went inside Sally's parents had gone to their room. Sally was in the bathroom, with the door closed. I heard the sound of running water and the toilet flush. I started to take off my shirt, entertaining the pleasing idea of wrapping it around Ellen's throat and throttling her. I had a vision of her with her tongue bulging and her eyes popping.

Sally came out of the bathroom. She had taken off her shoes and was in her stocking feet. Her head was down as she reached around to the back of her dress for the zipper.

'Nick, can you help me?' she asked. 'It's stuck.'

I went over, and saw that she'd caught her hair in it. 'Hold on.' I carefully separated the strands until I was able to release the teeth. Her hair smelled faintly of apple blossom, and the feel of it trickling through my hands reminded me of fine powdery sand.

'There.'

'Thanks.' She started to step away.

I put my hand lightly on her shoulder. 'Sally . . .' I began.

She turned around, her eyes clouded with unspoken

thoughts. I felt a great and sudden need for her, but not just physically. I wanted to hold her, feel close to her again, but when I put my arms around her and held her I felt her hesitation. She rested her head against my shoulder and for a while we remained that way. I kept thinking about Garrison Hunt, and an unwelcome image of them together kept insinuating itself into my mind. We parted awkwardly, and when we were in bed I kissed Sally's cheek, and with what felt like mutual relief we kept to our own sides of the bed and eventually fell asleep.

CHAPTER NINE

Sally's parents left early the following morning, thankfully sparing me from having to endure a day maintaining the pretence that Ellen and I were becoming the best of friends. I was hugely relieved when the taxi finally arrived to take them to the airport.

Once we'd put the bags in the trunk Frank and I hung around in the garden, waiting for Ellen and Sally to say their goodbyes. We said all the things people do in those situations which nobody takes seriously. I hoped they'd have a good flight, it was good to see them again, we'd try and get up to Oregon before long. It soon petered out. The way these things should be done is you just shake hands, say thanks for everything and you're gone. Everybody would really prefer it that way. But Sally and Ellen were still talking just inside the door, and Frank and I were left to endure a long uncomfortable silence.

I kept looking over towards the house, willing them to appear. Frank did too, and once or twice our looks collided. He rolled his eyes. We smiled. He looked at his watch.

'You should be okay on a Sunday, the traffic's light.'

'I expect the flight will be late anyway,' he said.

'They always are aren't they?' I seized on his opening. 'I remember once I was on a flight from New York, got delayed six hours.'

'Six hours?' He shook his head in wonder. 'That's a long time.'

'It was American I think. Or maybe United. Who're you flying with?'

'American.'

'I think it was United. You should be okay.'

'I think so.'

I nodded, and looked back towards the house, the possibilities of that topic exhausted. I prayed for an end to this torture. How much did Frank know I wondered? I thought I should thank him for warning me about Garrison Hunt, but then I figured if he'd wanted to get involved any further, he would've just said what he had to say directly rather than via his cryptic gardening metaphor. All the same I wanted to let him know I was grateful.

I stuck out my hand. 'I want to thank you for your advice yesterday, Frank.' He looked at my hand in vague surprise. 'The aphids.'

'Oh yes. The aphids.' He smiled and we shook. 'You should spray them.'

'Don't worry,' I assured him. 'I will.'

I looked over at the house again. I would have given a lot to be a fly on the wall so I could hear what final entreaties Ellen was making. When they appeared I studied them both for some clue as to what had passed between them. Sally seemed a little annoyed and I sensed a little friction. I opened the door for Ellen, and as she got in our eyes met briefly, a silent acknowledgment of our mutual dislike. Then Sally kissed her father and at last they were leaving. We stood in the driveway and waved them off until the taxi vanished around the next corner, then we dropped our arms and looked at one another. Suddenly alone.

As we started back towards the house it was impossible to ignore the eddies and subtle unspoken tensions between us. Sometime during the night I'd woken feeling thirsty, and on the way to fetch a glass of water I'd had an idea. Lately I'd taken to picking up the picture of Sally and me that had been taken years ago in Mendocino. I was struck by how happy we looked then. During the night I'd thought of that picture and it prompted an idea which at the time I wasn't sure was a good one, but now I thought it was. I loved Sally. I thought she loved me, and somehow we needed to start again from that point.

'You remember that inn where we stayed once up around Mendocino?' I said to Sally. 'It was after I got offered a job in San Francisco.'

'Yes,' she said, puzzled.

'I think we should go there.'

'What?'

'Right now. We should get in the car and drive up there. We could take the coast road. It's a nice day, we'd be there this afternoon.'

'Go all the way up to Mendocino. Now? Why?'

'Because we need to.' I stopped, and faced her. 'I haven't had a chance to think this through, but we both know we have to talk.' I reached for her hand and took it in my own. 'I feel like I'm losing you, Sally, and I don't want that to happen. I want us to go somewhere, away from here. I don't know, a change of scenery, maybe it'll do us good. It's just that I know I don't want to stay here and tiptoe around each other like people walking on eggshells. Like strangers.'

'But why Mendocino?' she said, trying to accommodate my train of thought.

'Why not? We were happy there once.'

'What about your presentation? My job?'

In truth that weighed heavily on my mind too, but some things shouldn't be put off. I shook my head. 'We can be back tomorrow. I'll make up the time and you can call your office in the morning.'

'I don't know, Nick.'

'Sally, please. We need to do this.'

She was silent for a minute. I didn't know what things she was weighing in her mind. 'It seems such a crazy thing to do,' she said, which I knew was no objection. She was halfway convinced. She looked at the house, and I think perhaps the idea of the two of us banging around together in there for the rest of the day made up her mind and at last she nodded her agreement, albeit uncertainly.

'Great. Go pack a bag.' As she went I banished the lingering doubts I had about this myself, aware that as well as saving my marriage I could be hastening the end.

We took the Saab and drove with the top down. It was a beautiful day, the kind that makes you want to get out on the road and drive for ever. We crossed the Golden Gate Bridge and took the old route one coast road that meanders north with the ocean on one side and hills and farmland meadows on the other.

At Bodega Bay we stopped at a store on the side of the road to buy a milkshake which we drank sitting on a bench overlooking the ocean watching the breakers roll in. We were talking, making jokes, trying to be natural with each other and doing a lousy job of it. Everything we did or said seemed forced and I couldn't help wondering if I had made a mistake. They say you can never go back somewhere to recapture a time of happiness, because our memories are idealist. We take snapshots of laughter and happiness and store them away, conveniently forgetting about the bad or the mundane.

As we went back to the car the wind caught Sally's hair and whipped it around her face. She swept it away and tossed her head and some loose strands caught in her milkshake, and for a second we both laughed. It was a tiny moment, but it was like a shaft of bright sunlight breaking through cloud, to remind you that it's there. I knew then I needed no reassurance to myself that I loved her as much as I always had. I couldn't imagine being without her.

When we started north again I rummaged through my CDs and found a drive compilation which I'd bought on impulse from a bargain bin on a market stall. At the time I'd pictured myself on the open road with the sun at my back, music playing and a long empty stretch of desert highway ahead. An escapist moment that was all imagery and vague longing, but completely lacking in substance. I couldn't remember ever playing the disc in its entirety. If I played it on the freeway headed for work the old songs only sounded corny and I couldn't think why I'd bought it.

Now, however, as the first track started playing, the music quickened my blood.

'Remember this?'

Sally listened. 'REO Speedwagon.'

'"Keep on Lovin' You".'

The verse built to the chorus, that whole wall of sound thing reminiscent of Phil Specter, with the echo effect in the vocals and the layers of instruments behind. There's something about certain songs that are perfect for driving. The sun was shining, we were cruising along the highway in no great hurry, and perhaps we were eager to seize on something that took us out of ourselves. We started to sing together, harmonizing badly at the top of our lungs.

It became a spontaneous competition to see who could get the most lyrics right, and to see who could sing the loudest and remain vaguely in the right key. I turned the volume up to full, and as that song ended and another began we were laughing. We passed a house back from the road, and in the garden a woman stopped to watch us go by. I don't know what she made of us. Perhaps she thought we were rowdy and ought to know better at our age, but then maybe not. I like to think she smiled indulgently as we went by.

When the album finished I dug around for a Simon and Garfunkel Greatest Hits disc I knew I had and we sung along to all those great tracks like 'The Boxer', 'Feelin' Groovy', and my all time favourite, 'Mrs Robinson', which was from *The Graduate*, a movie that Sally and I both loved and had watched together a dozen times on video. The songs were great. They captured some essence of time and place that was gone, but which lingered in hearts and minds. Like 'Mrs Robinson' they evoked a sense of lost innocence, and I suppose the sentiment and nostalgia reflected things we were feeling too.

At some point along the way to Point Arena the disc ended and I turned it off. We exchanged looks. How long had it been since we'd laughed that way, since we'd really had a good time? Sally looked away, as the music ended and the moment faded.

We arrived at Mendocino and drove through the quaint town and on to the inn where we'd stayed seven years ago. From the road it was suddenly familiar again. Little appeared to have changed, and a sign announced there was a vacancy. I made the turn and followed the curve of the approach road through a belt of silvery elms. The place was called The Lookout Inn, which we both remembered as soon as we saw the sign. More mansion than house, though there had been additions to the original construction, it was perched on top of a cliff on a promontory that was known locally as Lookout Point, though it didn't appear on any map. Built by a sea captain, the main house complete with an observation turret and a widow's walk, the story went that he had been a whaler out of Nantucket before he'd retired to California, where perhaps he preferred to gaze on the Pacific ocean rather than the cold Atlantic and the memories it held for him.

We checked in and were shown to a room on the third floor, the chief feature of which was a large four-poster bed. The prominence of it, and the connotations it evoked made us briefly awkward. Sally went over and sat down to test the mattress. She surveyed the expanse of the white bedspread, and when our eyes met she smiled uncertainly.

'Let's go for a walk, work up an appetite for dinner,' I suggested, to which she gratefully agreed.

At the end of the long sloping lawn, steps had been carved into the cliff that led down to the cove below. A crescent of dark yellow sand was flanked by black rocks on either side, the protesting ocean squeezed into the space between them. In the middle of the cove incoming waves boiled on underwater rocks out from the shore and by the time the breakers reached the sand they were short and messy. From the top of the cliff we stopped to watch. The cove was choppy, the water flecked with white, land and sea locked in a perpetual struggle.

'What are you thinking?' Sally asked me.

'Nothing,' I said, though I was thinking about us. It occurred to me that we were like the sea down there.

We climbed down the steps, and sat on the rocks. I skimmed a couple of smooth stones across the water but they were quickly lost in the chop.

I threw a last pebble. 'You look cold,' I said. The breeze coming off the ocean felt cooler down there. I took off my jacket and put it around her shoulders.

'Do you remember the last time we were here on this beach?' Sally asked. 'We were just starting out. We talked about the life we would have together. It never entered our heads that anything could go wrong.'

She was right. Back then we'd had the invincible optimism of youth. She hunched down, wrapping her arms around her knees.

'I've been thinking a lot lately. I used to think we wanted the same things, but now I realize that was never true.'

'In what way?'

'You know what I was thinking on the way up here? I started to remember what it was like, what we were like, back then. You think of those few days as a happy time, and they were, but I see now that all our problems started right here when we sat on this beach and talked about our plans and the fact is we weren't really listening to each other. You used to talk about starting your own company one day, being successful and I was talking about the house where we'd live and the kids we'd have and we thought they were all parts of the same ideal. But they weren't, not really. We said all the right things, made the responses, but I don't think we understood the importance of what the other wanted. Over the last few years I've come to realize how much success means to you, and that your definition of it is different from mine. In the same way I don't think you've ever really understood what having a family means to me. It was never something you felt passionate about. It was my dream and you just went along with it.'

'Maybe you're right,' I said.

She looked surprised. 'I didn't think you'd agree with me.'

'Let me ask you something, Sally. What is it you want? Not then, but now. Right now. What would make you happy? Tell me and this time I'm listening properly. Tell me and I'll understand.'

She thought for a long time before she answered. I didn't push her. The breakers rolled in and threw surf down on the sand, sucking the beach back to the ocean before another came in and threw it all back again. I could hear the draw and rattle of tiny pebbles being worn smooth, and pieces of rock being ground down to make more of the fine yellow sand. Gulls wheeled and screeched overhead, their calls carried away on the wind. When Sally answered it was quietly, thoughtfully, every word considered and given weight according to her feeling.

'I'm a woman. Having children is the most basic instinct that drives me, it's what my body is designed for. Maybe there are other women who don't feel this way. Maybe career or travel or whatever is what's important to them. But I always wanted kids. I just always pictured myself that way. Sometimes I feel as if I'm kind of incomplete because I don't know what it's like to be pregnant, to give birth to my baby, another human being. I don't think you can ever really understand what that feels like. Maybe for you it would be like being impotent, or castrated. It cuts right to the core of your self-image. I should have said all this a long time ago, before I let you convince me we should wait. First one thing then another. I started resenting you.' She paused, and wiped away her tears. 'But I won't deny it any longer.'

'Deny what?'

'The truth. I want children, and I want to have them with somebody who wants them too. Really wants them. And that isn't you, Nick.'

I stared at her, unwilling to believe what she was saying.

'I see that now. This last year or so I've come to realize a lot of things. You're not the person I thought I was marrying, and that's not because you've changed so much, I think you were always this way. I just wasn't listening properly.' Her eyes were filling with tears again and her voice was catching in her throat. 'I'm not saying that it's your fault, or that you're a terrible person. You're not. I know you love me and a lot of the time you can be sweet and gentle and considerate, but there's another side to you as well. I've seen what you're prepared to do to be successful.' She paused. 'Marcus was your best friend as well as your partner, Nick, but you pushed him aside when he didn't agree with you. You made decisions you didn't have a right to make.' She shook her head. 'I didn't expect that.'

I experienced a flash of bitterness. She accused me of betraying Marcus's friendship and yet what about her own betrayal? Was she planning to go off and have a family with Garrison Hunt? A guy who was born into money, who'd never had to start from nothing. No doubt he'd assured her that he was ready and willing to give her the children she wanted. I bet the sonofabitch couldn't wait to prove how willing he was, starting with a practical demonstration.

But my anger subsided, because I recognized the truth in what she'd said. 'You're right,' I told her. 'You're right that being successful is important to me. Maybe in a way it's even been the most important thing in my life.'

She hadn't expected such an admission, and it showed. I guessed she'd been expecting me to deny it.

'I'm not proud of the things I've done,' I went on. 'But I've always loved you. I've never for even a second stopped loving you, and I want us to have children together as much as you do.'

'You say that . . .'

'Let me finish,' I said. 'You know that my dad killed himself when I was a kid?'

She nodded, puzzled that I'd brought it up but also taken aback since it was a subject I had rarely talked about.

'He did it because his company failed. He started that business himself and worked a good part of his life to build it up. What happened was another company that was in competition with him was bought out by a national outfit based on the east coast. What these people did was sit in their office in some downtown building and stick pins in the map where they thought they ought to be, then they bought some local outfit and went about expanding their share of the local market, which meant in effect that they cut their prices. They could afford to run at a loss for a while and it was all part of the big corporate game plan so it didn't matter to them much, but for people like my dad it meant losing customers and business until in the end he couldn't go on and he went broke.'

I sounded bitter, even after all the intervening years. Sally didn't say anything, just waited for me to go on, which after a little while I did.

'I'm not sure what to tell you exactly,' I said. 'My dad thought he was a failure and he'd let his family down. He was disillusioned by it all I guess. When he killed himself he left me a note. It was all jumbled up and confused, kind of a tirade. But he thought he was a helpless victim of big business. Faceless corporate executives with money and power stepping on the lives of the little people. Which maybe was true to some extent. But that kind of thing happens all the time. He warned me not to let the same thing happen to me. I've still got the note.'

Sally's eyes widened at that. 'I've never seen it.'

'I keep it in my office,' I said. 'The point I'm trying to make here is that I learned early that I needed money if I was ever going to get control of my life. But it's not just about that. What I'm trying to tell you is that I loved my dad, and after he died I missed him. It changed my life, not having him around. Not just because we had to move, and we didn't have as much money. I don't think that matters much to kids. But I didn't know who I was any more. People treated me differently, eventually even my friends, and I became a different person myself. It was all mixed up with not having my dad around. Suddenly there was no one to toss a ball with, to chew over problems I didn't feel comfortable talking about with my mom. There's a thousand different ways I missed him, and every one of them affected me and it all added up and made me want to be somebody. I always wanted us to have kids someday, but I wanted to be certain I'd be there for them in the way my dad wasn't for me.'

I could have gone on. I could have told her that having a mother-in-law like Ellen had never done a whole lot for my self esteem, I could have related stuff from when I was a kid that made me feel the way I did. But the truth was I didn't know exactly how to explain myself any better than I had. I couldn't say how it made me feel when I went with a friend one time to a ball game, and we were sitting eating hot dogs with his dad, and this kid's dad looked at his son and I caught that look as he smiled, and my friend didn't even see him do it. It doesn't sound like much, but at the time I felt a keen pain, and if you multiply that by enough times, and add to it a lot of insecurities about not knowing where I fitted in with my old friends any more, it all leaves its mark. And to her credit, Sally didn't need me to fill in all the blanks. She understood at least some of what I was saying, and the fact that all these years I'd had this note from my dad that she didn't even know about made an impression on her.

'The bottom line is I never wanted my own kids to go through what I did. I wanted them to have a perfect world, and so I wanted control of my life before we started a family so I could give them that.'

I spread my hands helplessly. Our past lives affect us, but the manner of it isn't always cut and dried.

She was silent for a long time, thinking about everything I had said. She knew me well enough to know I'd told her the truth about myself, as much of it as I could figure out anyway.

'The thing is, Sally, this deal with Spectrum is what I've always wanted. I know I haven't always done things the way I should have, but winning this account means a lot to me. But not as much as you do. Nothing like. I want us to start that family. Maybe that's something I didn't truly realize until now.'

'But what if something goes wrong with Spectrum, Nick? What then?'

'It won't. But even if it did, nothing will change. I mean what I say. I won't make the same mistakes again. You, Marcus, in the end you mean more to me than any account. Somehow we'll get by.'

She stared at me, deep into my eyes. Her brow was furrowed and I had the feeling she was trying to peer into my soul, as if she was trying to assure herself that I knew myself well enough to claim such control over what drives me.

'Nick,' she said at last. 'Even if you really mean what you say, and I believe you do, we're not the same people we were last time we were here.'

I thought I knew what was coming.

'There are things . . . about us . . . about me . . .'

I took her hand, I didn't want her to confess her affair because if she did I would have to know details. I wouldn't be able to avoid asking where they had gone together, how often, for how long. Some things are best left unsaid. Someday I would ask her, when I felt able to cope with it, but not now. 'Sally, all that matters is now. Right here. What's done is done, it's what we feel now that matters.

Just say we'll give it a chance. What's the alternative? I love you and I think you still love me. Can you just walk away?'

She gave me a quick questioning look, but it passed and I wondered if she suspected that I knew about Garrison Hunt.

The waves crashed on the shore, and it grew colder as the sun went down. I waited for Sally to decide what she would do, and after a long time she squeezed my hand with a tentative pressure. Love may wither if it isn't nurtured, but the roots of powerful emotions run deep and they don't die easily.

That night I planned a romantic dinner in the restaurant that overlooked the cliff and the ocean beyond. By the time I was changed and ready Sally was still in the shower, so I said that I'd see her downstairs in the bar.

'Okay, I won't be long,' she called back to me.

I smiled at the sound of her voice. We had gone for a long walk after our talk on the beach, and gradually our uncertainty with one another had melted away. We held hands, we started to let down our guard so that every comment every gesture didn't have to survive the mill of scrutiny to determine how it would be interpreted. Now Sally sounded happy. I sounded happy. Or perhaps it was more prosaic than that. We sounded normal again. I left her to it and went downstairs to the bar where I ordered a beer. I asked for it to be added to my room account, which made me realize I'd brought the room key with me and Sally wouldn't be able to lock the door. Maybe it wouldn't have mattered in a place like this, but when you live in the city old habits die hard so I went back upstairs. As I approached the door I heard Sally's voice from inside, and I paused even as I reached for the handle, wondering who she was talking to. Her voice was muffled, so I put my ear to the door and caught the tail end of something she was saying.

'. . . to try again. I think he really means it.'

There was a pause and then, 'I know I said that, but we talked and he explained a lot of things.'

I knew at once she was talking to Garrison Hunt, telling him it was over between them. That she should call him brought home to me how far things had developed, how close I'd come to losing her.

'I know you understand how I feel,' she said after a while, and then there was silence while he responded. 'You're a good person, you know that?' she said.

I imagined he was being understanding to the last, a thoroughly decent guy, which made me sick. He was probably telling her that he hoped she would be happy, the noble loser backing down for the love of a good woman, though I was sure he'd add the rider that of course if it didn't work out he would be waiting ever so fucking patiently in the wings. Well he was going to have a long wait. I really didn't want to hear any more. It was the way Sally sounded that really got to me. Her voice was intimate, riddled with subtle nuances of faint regret and sorrow. The voice of a lover.

I went back down to the bar and took my beer to a table in the corner and I resolved that this ought to be a closing. The residue of anger I still felt was the price I would have to pay for saving my marriage. By the time Sally appeared, smiling, looking happier than I had seen her in a long while, I knew it was a toll worth paying.

We ate dinner sitting at a table by the window as darkness fell outside. Time might have stood still, except that when I looked at Sally I thought she was even more beautiful than she had been when we were last at the inn. It came from within, maybe it had as much to do with experience and self-knowledge as it did with the way she looked.

There were only two other couples in the restaurant. One an older couple who had the appearance of people who'd been together a long time and wouldn't have it any other way. They carried an air of being supremely comfortable in each other's company. The other couple were younger, and reminded me of Sally and me the last time we were there.

'You think they'll ever come back one day to repair an ailing marriage,' I joked.

'If they do, I hope it works for them,' Sally said.

The food arrived, and was excellent, though I hardly noticed what I was eating. We talked a lot about the past, and we left the present and the future to take care of themselves. Afterwards we ordered coffee and a cognac each. The fire in the bar was lit and we sat on a couch there in comfort, happy to watch the flames and let the liquor spread its warm glow. After a while I put my arm around Sally and when she leaned against me I could smell the scent of her hair, and her perfumed skin.

The bartender came over to fetch our empty glasses. 'Anything else I can get for you folks?'

We had a couple more, and then a couple more after that, and when he asked us a fourth time I looked at Sally. 'I think we're fine, what do you say?'

She grinned a little drunkenly. 'I think so.'

'I think we're going to turn in.'

The bartender smiled. 'Sleep well.'

We went on up holding hands as we climbed the stairs, which was something we hadn't done in a long time.

'Was he being funny when he said that about sleeping well do you think?' I said.

'Why should he be? Did you have something else in mind?' Sally said with a lascivious grin.

As we reached the top of the stairs I leaned to kiss her. She closed her eyes and her mouth parted slightly. We were tentative at first, then the last remaining tension eased and Sally relaxed into my arms.

'It's a long time since we kissed like that,' I said.

'Mmm. Too long.'

In our room the cover had been turned back on the bed, and a single lamp in the corner cast a soft light. We kissed again. She arched her back a little, pressing herself against my erection, and I lifted the top she wore and raised it smoothly over her head with a fluid motion. I found the clasp of her bra and slid the straps across her shoulders until she shrugged it to the floor then I held her so that I could feel the softness of her naked breasts against my chest, and the smooth curve of her back beneath my hands. I stood back a little and while Sally undid my shirt I ran my thumbs over her hardening nipples.

I bent to kiss her neck, the hollow beneath her ear where her hair was so fine. Sally slipped her hand between us and undid my jeans and I moved to accommodate her as she pushed them over my hips, then I stood back to kick off shoes and socks while she watched me with a playful smile. I hopped on one foot.

'There's no way to look dignified at this point.'

'I don't want you to be dignified.'

She pulled me back to her, and lifted her face to be kissed while she reached inside my shorts and grasped my erection firmly with one hand and cupped my balls gently with the other. The coolness of her touch made me draw in my breath.

'I want you naked,' she said, and let me go.

I obliged, and she looked me over from head to toe. If she had been anyone else, I couldn't have stood there as I did without embarrassment. Even so, enough was enough and I led her towards the bed.

'My turn,' I told her.

I ran my hands across her hips and buttocks. She was wearing a G-string so I could feel the smoothness of naked flesh beneath her skirt. I found the clasp and zip and the skirt fell in a whisper to the ground, then I gently pushed her back onto the bed and removed her panties. Her hair was dark against the bedspread, her skin smooth across her belly to the shadowed cleft between her legs.

'I love you,' I told her.

'And I you.'

I kissed her breasts and travelled down her body. She raised her knees and parted her thighs a little and I kissed between the soft damp folds of her flesh inhaling her scent like a drug. She sighed, her hands playing through my hair.

'I've missed you,' she murmured.

She was wet with desire, and shortly she grew impatient and pulled me up to kiss her mouth again, parting her thighs as I lay over her and wrapping her arms around me. She yielded easily as I slipped inside her and for a few moments we lay together, hardly moving, absorbing the sensations of intimate closeness again. Then we began to rock with a smooth unhurried rhythm. We knew each other's bodies, and how to please each other. She raised her hips a fraction so that I could move against her most sensitive area and she gasped a little. Supporting my weight on my hands I looked down at her parted lips, her closed eyes. She breathed in time with our movements. I ran my hand over her breasts, her sides, then sank down to kiss her again and she reached around to feel me moving in and out of her. Her legs tightened and she clenched the muscles in her abdomen, and as she began to climax I released myself and we held onto one another tightly.

*　　*　　*

I slept a dreamless sleep and when I woke it was morning, and sunlight streamed through a gap in the curtain. Sally was still sleeping and I pulled back the cover to look at her. Her hands were loosely clasped over her belly and a faint contented smile lay softly on her face.

CHAPTER TEN

On the twenty-third, the morning I was due to make my final presentation at Spectrum, I woke at five-thirty with a start. The last image of a dream I'd been having was branded in my conscious mind. Larry Dexter stood grinning at me, holding out something in his arms. I moved closer with my heart pounding, sweat breaking out on my palms, my eye irresistibly drawn to the bundle he proffered. I couldn't make out what it was, except that it was wrapped in a blanket of some sort and that every now and then it moved. Dexter's grin grew wider and he urged me to go ahead, take it. I reached out nervously and drew back the blanket and underneath it was a newborn baby. It turned towards me and began to cry, a loud rising wail, and I stumbled back in surprise and horror. The baby's face was that of my father, with half his head shot away, streaked with blood. I cried out and Dexter's taunting laugh echoed around me but when I looked again it wasn't Dexter at all, but Sally.

'Jesus,' I said to myself. My heart was still beating too fast, my body was clammy from sweat and the duvet on my side of the bed was twisted and thrown back. I lay there for several minutes thinking about the dream, wondering what it meant.

When I got up I dressed in T-shirt and shorts. My clothes were hanging in the closet all ready in a suit bag. When I was ready to leave I went around to Sally's side of the bed. She was still asleep, her face half covered by her hair, and I bent and gently moved it from her cheek. She looked peaceful with her eyes closed, breathing gently and I didn't want to wake her, though it would have been nice to have her wish me luck. Since we'd returned from Mendocino we'd recaptured a little of the ease we'd once had with one another. Things weren't so good with Marcus. Everybody at the office was flat out on the Spectrum pitch and you could feel the tension in the air. Nobody was under any illusions as to what this would mean for each and every one of the people at Carpe Diem, win or lose. There was a sense of frenetic activity, of everybody holding their collective breaths as the day drew closer, and all of this only served to remind both Marcus and me of the bank's hovering presence, and the discord between us that had brought us to this point. I figured that explained his cool manner, the undercurrents of unspoken feelings and I decided that until we had the Spectrum account in the bag there wasn't much I could do about it.

All I needed was this one account.

Before I left I leaned down and kissed Sally's cheek softly. She stirred and mumbled something under her breath.

I was at the pool by six. The girl on the desk smiled a greeting when I swiped my membership card and she glanced at the screen in front of her where my details came up.

'Hi, Nick. Haven't seen you in a while,' she said.

'I've been kind of busy.'

'You swimming today?'

'I think so.' Sometimes I did a circuit class or worked in the gym for a change.

'We have a new step aerobics class starting next week. The instructor is awesome. You should check it out.'

'Maybe I will.'

'Okay, have a good swim.'

Nice girl. Pretty, maybe early twenties. Like all the staff at the health club she had the healthy glow of the young and fit. They rotated who was on the desk in the mornings, and I don't think I'd seen that particular girl for a month at least, but she greeted me by name and knew I didn't always hit the pool. She couldn't have done it if my card hadn't flashed all my details on the screen. They were probably using a fairly simple software package, but it was that kind of business application that was continuing to change the world. What made me smile, however, was the Spectrum logo I glimpsed in the corner of the screen. It seemed like a good omen.

The pool wasn't busy that morning. While I pulled on my cap and goggles I scanned the traffic trying to decide between fast and medium. There had been a time in the not too distant past when I could have done my hundred in the fast lane without too much trouble, but I wasn't as fit as I had been then and I didn't want to kill myself. A half-dozen or so older people were using the slow lanes, ploughing up and down like ships on a long voyage. I had the impression they could go on for ever and sometimes it seemed as if they did. Back and forth, back and forth, arms rising and dipping almost in slow motion, touching the end and turning in a fluid movement, on and on they went. A guy perhaps in his mid-seventies emerged from the changing rooms. His skin was wrinkled and a little loose, and he had the skinny legs and vanishing butt of the elderly, but he looked loose and limber and when he dived into the pool he could have been twenty years younger.

In the end I took one of the fast lanes and I powered through my first five lengths like a torpedo, until I started to feel the burn from muscles unused to this kind of punishment. After a few more I was gulping air into my lungs on every second stroke. I knew I should've opted for a medium lane, but I shut out the pain and waited for the rush that is the reward for pushing it out when you hit the barrier. After twenty lengths I was about ready to give up. Fatigue dragged at my arms and legs like heavy weights and my chest was aching. I struggled to keep up the pace but after a couple more lengths my fingers scraped the end of the pool and I didn't think I could go on.

It was only determination that overcame physical limitation. I heard the voice of a drill sergeant in my mind. I told myself I was a weakling.

You've let yourself get slack and sloppy! You swim like a drowning dog! Get that head down and kick those feet! What the hell do you think this is? You think life is a stroll in the country? You want those people to see a sissy when you walk in that room this morning? MOVEYOUR-FUCKINGSELF!

If nothing else I was distracted from the pain that was stretching hot fingers across my back and shoulders, and the burning sensation of lungs starved of oxygen. I hit the far end and did a rolling turn and when I came up endorphins burst into my brain, engulfing me in a natural high that was like strapping on a power pack. I did another five lengths at full speed, until even endorphins couldn't quell the signals my body was sending me and when I hit the home end again I put my hands on the edge and hauled myself from the water in one move and sat gasping on the edge, chest heaving, head down.

When I looked up a woman was resting her arms on the side in the lane next to me. I'd spoken to her a couple of times and I knew she had a high-powered job with a PR firm downtown. She grinned.

'Feel good?'

'I'm a little out of shape, but yes, it feels great,' I said.
'Big day?'

'Big day.' I got up and started for the changing rooms.

'Knock 'em dead,' the woman called after me.

I grinned to myself. As I passed the slow lanes the old people were still there, and still looking for all the world like they could go on for ever.

I drove to the office and parked in the basement in my usual slot. Breakfast was a blueberry muffin and double espresso from the coffee stand on the ground floor of our building. It was still only seven-thirty and the woman who ran the stand was just opening. When the building was converted only the shell of the old brick warehouse had been left intact. Now the central open space reached up three storeys and was filled with light from skylights that had been installed in the roof. Steel stairways linked the perimeter walkways of the upper floors. The intended effect was semi-industrial chic, though sometimes when I looked up at the metal grid of the walkways I was vaguely reminded of a prison.

I let myself in the office and disarmed the security alarm, then ate my muffin at my desk while I powered up my laptop and went through my presentation one more time.

I was still going over it when Marcus arrived. He started to walk past my office then changed his mind and doubled back.

'You're in early,' he commented. He glanced at my laptop screen. 'What time are you presenting?'

'Eleven. Take a look. I made a few changes.' I ran through it quickly, highlighting the parts I'd worked on over the past couple of days. Of course he was familiar with most of the creative input because it was he and his small team who'd worked it up. 'It's good, Marcus,' I said when I was finished.

'Yeah,' he agreed without enthusiasm.

'You could try to sound a little more positive.'

He looked at me searchingly. 'I wish I had your confidence.'

'Don't worry about it,' I said, though I suddenly thought of my dream and felt an echo of unease. 'How's Alice?' I asked, to change the subject. It was the first time her name had come up since her exhibition.

He appeared awkward at being reminded of that night. 'She's fine,' he said cautiously.

We were going to have to talk about where we went from here sooner or later, and we were both aware of it. Alice had said Marcus wanted out of our partnership. I wondered if he still felt that way. It seemed like right then was not the time to get into it, even though since that night it had felt like an ever present obstruction between us.

'Tell her I like the picture by the way. I hung it in my office at home.'

'Right. I'll tell her.'

I was picking up odd signals. His discomfort seemed to relate more to talking about Alice herself rather than any awkward memory her name prompted. 'Is everything okay?' I asked.

'Everything's fine,' he said quickly, and I knew even if it wasn't he wouldn't tell me. He glanced at his watch. 'I better get on.' At the door he paused. 'Good luck today.'

'Thanks.'

Spectrum Software was based in a business park on the southern limits of San Jose, where technology companies seemed to sprout like mushrooms overnight. A couple of billboards by the highway promoted one of their products which was a program called Home Finance. I'd heard a rumour it was about to be dumped, replaced with something new, but secrecy surrounded the project and that was as much as I knew. Whatever was planned, it was overdue. The billboard showed a guy in his shirtsleeves seated at a desk in what was meant to be his home, with his wife standing behind with her hands resting on his shoulders. They were both looking at a document he was holding with perplexed frowns. The tag line was: 'Take the worry out of monthly bills with Home Finance.' The entire concept was dated and had all the punch of a tapioca pudding. Underneath the ad in smaller print was the legend: A Morgan Industries Company.

I turned into the lot and found an empty slot. I was surrounded by an octagonal hub of buildings housing the companies located on the park. The offices were individually detailed, but the buildings shared a common cubist design and acres of mirrored glass so they conformed to an overall concept. All of the manufacturing and warehousing facilities were housed in rectangular barn-like structures out of sight behind the offices where there was a perimeter parking lot for the people who worked in dispatch and assembly. The centre lot was where the designers and software engineers parked their cars. I had never seen so many BMWs, Porsches and Mercedes in one place before, not to mention the fair sprinkling of Ferraris and other exotics among them.

When I reached the Spectrum building a smiling young woman behind a long curving desk directed me up the stairs. A Morgan Industries logo shared wall space over her head. The major shareholder of the group was Nelson Morgan, who was now in his mid-forties and had a personal worth numbered in hundreds of millions. The little I knew about him was gleaned from scant business magazine articles, but he was renowned for keeping a low profile so information was sketchy. He'd started out in his early twenties with a partner who he met at college, but the company they'd formed had gone bust, so Morgan had started again a year later on his own. From selling custom-made computers he'd branched out, making his mark by his apparent knack of being able to spot coming trends in the market place and then buying smallish often undervalued companies that were in a position to take advantage of them. He pumped in investment funds, the companies expanded rapidly and their value vastly increased, making Morgan incredibly wealthy along the way. The only other thing I knew was that he had a reputation for being ruthless in his business dealings.

At the reception desk upstairs another pretty young Californian blonde took my name and asked me to take a seat. I was a few minutes early, but I didn't have to wait long before Phil Bennet, one of the marketing people I'd been dealing with, appeared.

He shook my hand. 'Nick. How're you doing?'

'Fine, Phil.'

'Great.' He smiled broadly, but his eyes darted nervously back and forth. 'We're in the conference room today,' he said. 'Only place there's enough space to fit us all in.' He started leading the way. 'I think we've got everything you'll need.' He began checking things off on his fingers. 'Projector to hook up to your laptop. Screen of course. There's a desk for you to lay out anything else you're going to need. Water. Coffee. Anything else you can think of?'

'Sounds like you have it covered.'

'Whiteboard? Flip chart?'

'No need, it's all on my laptop.'

'Terrific.'

He beamed and nodded, and beamed some more but I could have sworn there was something desperate in his eye, like he would have given his right arm to be somewhere else right then. I was conscious of the sound of our footsteps on the wooden floor. Phil began talking as if the lull in our conversation made him uncomfortable.

'Have you been in the conference room before? It's laid out in a U shape for this kind of thing. I don't know why we do that. I guess it works though.' He glanced at his watch. 'Right on time. That's terrific.'

I thought he seemed edgy. He was talking too much and he avoided looking me in the eye. We reached the door and he paused.

'Well, good luck.'

Something about his tone seemed all wrong to me. I said, 'Phil, is there anything I should know about today?'

He looked startled. 'What do you mean?'

'I get the feeling you're nervous about something.'

'Nervous? Hell no, why should I be nervous?'

'I don't know. Maybe it's me.'

He laughed but it sounded hollow and devoid of humour. He slapped me on the back. 'You'll be fine.'

I started to say something else but he cut me off. 'We better go in.' Then he opened the door and there was no more time. The entire marketing team was assembled inside. Sam Mendez sat in the centre facing the screen, and on one side sat Bev Jones, on the other somebody I didn't recognize. Phil took his place on one of the side tables with the other product managers and immediately found something on a notepad deeply fascinating. Sam rose to meet me. He shook my hand and gestured around the room.

'Nick. You know most people here I think.'

'Sure.' I shook hands with Bev, and nodded to the others.

'And this is Dan Morris from Morgan Industries.'

I shook hands with him too. He was heavy set and unsmiling and he didn't say anything.

'Okay, let's get started,' Sam said, getting straight to the point. He seemed less genial than normal, but I told myself it was probably the occasion and maybe the Morris guy. I guessed as a Morgan man he favoured keeping KCM, so perhaps Sam was simply hoping I'd live up to the build up he'd given me.

I went to the front of the room and began setting up. When I was ready I glanced around. Sam was speaking quietly to Bev. The Morris guy was writing something on a pad, and Phil was determinedly looking at a spot on the opposite wall. It didn't take a genius to figure out that something wasn't right. People tend to mimic one another in unconscious ways when they're in a group. Wherever I looked everybody was busy talking quietly to their neighbour or else they were examining their pens and notebooks, looking anyplace but at me. There was an unnatural tension in the room and I suddenly felt like the accused man who looks at the jury for a clue to his fate and finds nobody will meet his eye.

'Good morning, everyone.'

Gradually they turned towards me, their expressions politely blank. I had no choice but to put my misgivings aside and get down to the reason I was there. An hour is a long time to hold the attention of a group of people. My job was to put together all the information I'd gathered over months of research into Spectrum's business, and use it to show what Carpe Diem could bring to their marketing mix. There was masses of information: Strategy, demographics, targets, reach and frequency rates for proposed media – a lot of charts and numbers. The kind of stuff that can easily be about as interesting as watching grass grow. I turned on my laptop and an image was projected onto the screen.

'This is Billy,' I said.

My delivery was deadpan droll. A cartoon figure looked

back at the audience. Billy wore baggy trousers that collected round his ankles and a baseball cap on backwards along with an oversize T-shirt. He was white, round shouldered and had perfected an expression of sullen boredom. In short he was instantly recognizable as a stereotypical teenager. Nobody had expected this, and after a moment's surprise they all smiled.

'Billy's going to come along for the ride while I talk to you, because he's kind of interested in getting into the software business himself one day.' I turned to address the screen. 'Right, Billy?'

'Hey, I saw the cars in the lot out there, man,' Billy replied in the laid back drawl of a Californian high school kid. 'Do I get to make enough money for a Porsche?'

'Sure, Billy. Of course you have to work hard. It might take a little while.'

'Jeez, I know that. Like, I didn't expect it to happen right away,' he answered with pained exaggeration as if he was addressing a simpleton. 'I mean it could probably take six months or something, right?'

There was a ripple of chuckles. They were enjoying the show. The whole thing was intricately scripted of course, and I'd had to practise hard to get my timing perfectly synchronized with what Billy said and did. But I'd put a lot of time into this and I was word perfect and I never missed a cue.

'Let's take a look at some of the areas Spectrum operates in,' I said.

A chart flashed up headed accounting software, one of their key markets. It was divided into coloured segments.

'We can see here your share has declined recently.' I went on to quickly outline who the other players were, and how they were performing. It was pretty routine stuff and there wasn't a lot I could do to jazz it up, but I wanted to make the point that there was an opportunity here that they were missing. Suddenly Billy appeared again. He slouched across the screen and kicked one of the chart segments into touch.

'Sooo boring, dude,' he said.

More laughter. Suddenly something that was normally incredibly dull was starting to be fun. The segment spun and opened into a cool graphic and showed a competitor's logo on a building outside of which was parked the most fantastic looking customized sports car.

'Holy shit!' exclaimed Billy.

'You like that, huh?' I said.

The shot became a close-up picture and Billy started reciting the car's features while he practically salivated with lust.

'Four litre, twelve cylinder turbo charged motor. Zero to sixty in five point eight seconds, top speed a hundred and eighty miles an hour.' He hopped in behind the wheel. 'Man, the babes are really gonna go for this.'

'The guy who owns it works for this company, Billy. Want to know how he got it?'

Billy looked back at me round eyed. 'How?'

And suddenly I was talking about opportunities, and Billy was interested and so was everyone else in the room.

And so it went on. Whenever things were in danger of getting a little tedious, there was Billy, and soon people were waiting for him to appear, just to see what he would do next. It was humorous and attention grabbing and it allowed me to deliver my message, which of course was the point. It was a brilliant gimmick, and it showed off the kind of conceptual thinking we were capable of. Though the idea had originally come from Marcus, he'd decided we couldn't do it because creating an animated character like Billy was hugely time consuming and expensive. But I had bulldozed him into it because I knew right away Billy would give us the final edge we needed.

He was proof we could deliver and I knew that if we had done everything else well this was going to blow KCM and Larry Dexter out of the water.

But something still wasn't right. Everybody was interested in Billy, no issue there. The problem was, they were a little *too* interested. They laughed in the right places and they were attentive but it was as if Billy gave them an excuse to pretend I'd ceased to exist. I felt like a ventriloquist whose dummy has stolen the show and as I neared the end of my pitch a deep foreboding was clutching at my insides. I glanced at Sam Mendez and he was staring almost grimly at the screen, while Morris didn't even appear to be watching at all.

It was midday when I wrapped it up. I ended on a little speech telling them all how much I'd enjoyed the last few months, how excited I and everyone else at Carpe Diem was at the prospect of working with them. People shifted position uncomfortably, gazed at me blankly. A guy somewhere cleared his throat.

When I was done Sam rose from his seat. 'Thank you, Nick. A very interesting presentation.'

Very interesting? That was it?

Still, I expected him to ask if anybody had any questions, the usual routine with these things, but instead he looked at his watch.

'I think we're going to break for lunch now and we'll come back later to discuss amongst ourselves what we've just heard.'

Suddenly the room was transformed. People pushed back their chairs and gathered up their things. They couldn't wait to get out of there. Morris got up and made a comment to Sam, then offered me a brief nod of acknowledgment before leaving the room. Phil appeared and hovered at my shoulder.

'Great job, Nick. Fantastic. That Billy, he was a hoot.

So listen, can I help you with anything?' Obviously it was his job to get rid of me.

Numbly I started packing away, wondering what had gone wrong. Out the corner of my eye I saw Sam and Bev heading for the door and I knew this was my last chance.

I called out, and hearing his name Sam paused. 'Can I have a word?'

He and Bev exchanged quick glances, then reluctantly, it seemed to me, he said, 'Sure.'

I didn't know quite what to say, so I decided to take the direct approach. 'I get the feeling something's going on here that I don't know about.'

A second passed, and I knew he was deciding whether to be straight with me or give me some false bullshit assurance, slap me on the back and send me on my way.

'I'm going to be frank with you,' he began at last. 'I don't think I need to tell you how impressed everyone here has been with both you personally and your company over the past months. That goes for me as much as anyone.'

I waited. I could sense the 'but' that was coming. And I was right.

'But you may as well know that we won't be going with Carpe Diem,' he said.

Despite everything, the shock of this pronouncement was total. The very air seemed to waver, then was still. I stared dumbly, feeling sick. A faint hope surfaced. Any second I'd wake up, but this was no dream. 'I don't understand,' I managed to say eventually.

'I guess the least I can do is give you some kind of reason,' Sam allowed, his tone softening fractionally now that the worst part was done. He gestured to a seat, and without thinking I sank into it and he sat opposite me. He folded his large hands in front of him, and I stared at his knuckles, noticing for the first time the liver spots on the backs of his hands. His skin was gnarled and weathered like old wood.

'You may know we have plans to release a new product to replace Home Finance.'

'I heard something about it,' I agreed, wondering what that had to do with anything.

'What you may not know is that product is the reason Morgan Industries bought my company. They've spent a lot of money developing it, and a lot more is going to be spent launching it to the market place. Right from the start I've been under pressure from some people in Morgan Industries to stay with KCM. It was felt a small agency like yours might not be up to a project of this size and importance.'

I thought of the guy Morris. Was Sam telling me that a decision had been made over his head? But I saw right away that didn't ring true. Something had altered in Sam himself, in his attitude towards me. He fixed me with his intelligent penetrating gaze and I had the feeling he knew what I was thinking.

'Frankly, Nick, I'm very disappointed in you,' he said. 'I believed yours was the best company for the job. I fought for you. But it turns out there were certain things I wasn't aware of.'

'I don't understand.'

'Isn't it true that you've lost some clients lately?'

All at once I detected the shadow of Larry Dexter lurking somewhere in all this. 'We've lost one or two,' I admitted. 'That happens with any agency. People come and go. Relationships change.'

'True. But that isn't the case here is it?' He didn't wait for me to answer. 'The fact is I already talked to some of those clients you lost. I heard things that disturbed me.' His craggy eyebrows bunched over his eyes.

'Let me guess, Jerry Parker.'

'It doesn't matter who. The fact is there's a lot of money at stake here, a lot more than you probably realize. Morgan Industries paid forty million dollars for my company, but that's only the start. There's too much at stake to risk having our advertising business handled by a firm that might prove to be unreliable. The people I talked to told me things that frankly unsettled me. They said they could never get hold of you. They complained you were late with briefing submissions, you missed meetings or arrived late, turned in second-rate campaign proposals. And this wasn't just from one person. It came as quite a shock to me if you want to know the truth.'

This last sentence was delivered with solemn moral weight and I saw that in Sam's eye deceit was my true crime here. I didn't know what to say. Strictly speaking it was all true.

'I understand you're also having some financial problems,' he went on. 'That alone changes our position. We simply couldn't afford the risk of working with somebody who might not even be around next week.'

I wondered how Dexter had found out about that, but when I thought about it I saw it wouldn't have been hard. People who worked for us must have had an idea. Office rumours start circulating over drinks in some bar where other advertising people hang out. Nothing stays secret for long.

It struck me that the work we'd done to win the Spectrum account was the very reason for our downfall. With a little help from Dexter. I wondered briefly whether Sam might change his mind if he knew the bank had agreed to support us if we had his account, but I saw it was too late. Sam would never trust me again. I could only manage a wry twisted smile at the irony.

'I can see you're amused,' Sam said affronted. 'In that

case I don't believe we have anything more to discuss.'

He rose to his feet and strode from the room without another word and Bev went hurrying in his wake. For a long time I sat there, waiting for the world to cave in the way I thought it surely would. Finally, though, I stood up and finished packing up, and Phil showed me back to reception where we shook hands. He shrugged helplessly.

'Sorry it worked out this way.'

'Me too,' I said.

With leaden steps I went back outside and stood in the parking lot blinking in the Californian sunshine, the light reflecting in brilliant shards off the ranks of expensive cars that so embodied the pursuit of the American dream.

Part Two

CHAPTER ELEVEN

I heard the phone ringing through a veil of sleep and a sizable hangover so I turned over and pulled the pillow over my head and pressed it to my ears. In a little while the ringing stopped, and when I took away the pillow I could hear Sally's muffled voice speaking from downstairs. A minute later she appeared in our bedroom.

'Somebody wants to speak to you,' she said.

'Who is it?'

'I didn't get his name. Gary I think, something like that?'

Reluctantly I sat up. The room was dim, but I could tell from the gauzy light beyond the curtains it was late. 'What time is it?' I asked.

'Eleven-thirty,' Sally said. She went to the wall and plugged in the phone I'd disconnected the night before. 'What shall I tell him?'

'Tell whoever it is I'm not here.'

Sally gave me a look that signalled both slight reproach and understanding at the same time. 'You can't shut yourself away, Nick.'

I had tried though. For the past four days I had taken to my bed, only rising to get drunk again. To her credit Sally had allowed me the space to wallow. I came home early on the Friday having broken the news to Marcus right after my meeting with Spectrum. Sally had listened while I told her what happened, and hadn't said I told you so, not even with a look, and she hadn't tried to stop me when I broke open the scotch, and neither had she complained over the last four days, perhaps understanding that I needed this time to myself. But now she was gently telling me I couldn't stay drunk for ever and I knew she was right. I sighed and held out my hand.

She gave me the phone and then bent to kiss my cheek. 'It isn't the end of the world. Come down afterwards, I'll make some coffee.'

What to do without Sally. She said it wasn't the end of the world, but if that was so, why did I feel as if it was? I picked up the receiver. 'Hello?'

'Nick. I thought I'd call and offer my commiserations.'

'Dexter,' I said, heavy with disbelief.

'Too bad about Spectrum. I warned you this one was out of your league.'

My grip tightened on the phone. I imagined him sitting somewhere wearing that familiar mocking smile, dressed and shaved, savouring his moment of triumph. I caught sight of my own unshaven and red-eyed reflection in the mirror, my hair sticking out, my shoulders slumped in weariness and defeat. For a moment I felt the return of the vivid anger I'd dwelt on during my bouts of drinking.

'You sonofabitch!'

He laughed. 'I didn't think you would take it so badly, Nick. Business is business after all. In fact, to show there's no hard feelings I wanted you to know there's a job here for you at KCM any time you want it.'

'Fuck you, Dexter!' I started to hang up but he must have expected that.

'Starting salary a hundred and fifty thousand,' he said quickly.

Despite myself I paused. 'You're serious aren't you? You really mean it?'

'Like I said, Nick, business is business. You're good. One of the best. Why should I wait for some other company to snap you up. That wouldn't be smart. One fifty, Nick. And that's just for starters. You can choose your car, generous expense account, health plan, and a bonus system on top. You could make two hundred thousand in your first year.'

I thought I must be dreaming. The idea of working for Dexter was surreal, but not as surreal as the fact that he thought he could tempt me, even with what was undoubtedly a top flight offer.

'Forget it,' I told him.

'Don't be so hasty,' he said, talking fast. 'If half of what I've heard is true Carpe Diem is finished. You lose it all, Nick. Everything. Not just your company, but your car, your house, the works. Think about it. You're upset now, but the offer stays open. Call me.'

When hell freezes over, I thought as I slammed the receiver down. I stared at myself, groggy, bleary eyed, my head pounding and my mouth tasting like I'd chewed sand mixed with tar. I was stupefied by Dexter's call. It wasn't until I was under the hot jets of the shower that I began to feel vaguely revived and it started to make any kind of sense. Of course Dexter wanted me to go and work for him. He would probably even put me in charge of the Spectrum account in time, to rub my nose in it. It was a power trip for him. He simply wanted the kick of controlling me. I had a quick vision of years hence when Dexter was running the whole company and I would still be in the same job he'd make certain I never got promoted from. When I was all washed up and burnt out he'd call me into his huge plush office so he could have the pleasure of firing me, face to face. The more I thought about it the madder I got. I think it was that call that rescued me from a continued descent into self-pitying hell and which made me start thinking for the first time about fighting back.

'Who was on the phone?' Sally asked when I appeared downstairs.

'Nobody important,' I said.

She looked me over, noting with approval the shaved jaw, the clean shirt and trousers. 'That's better. How's the head?'

'Fine,' I lied, to which she frowned in disbelief.

'Have some aspirin anyway.'

I took them gratefully and swallowed them with my coffee. We sat down at the bench and Sally studied me with a serious look.

'So, how do you really feel?'

I knew she wasn't referring to the state of my hangover. 'The truth? Terrible. I really didn't think we could lose.'

'Marcus has been calling,' Sally said hesitantly.

'How does he sound?'

'About what you'd expect.'

I figured that was a nice way of saying how the hell do you think he feels when you just ruined him, cost him everything he's ever worked for?

'He was asking after you though,' she added. 'There's a meeting scheduled with your accountant on Wednesday. He wanted to know if you'd be there.'

'What day is it today?' I asked, glancing automatically at the calendar.

'Tuesday.'

'Christ,' I said, and put my cup down, overcome by a sudden heaviness, which I was beginning to recognize as the weight of despair. The brief fighting optimism I'd experienced in the shower began to rapidly evaporate in the face of reality.

'It'll be okay, Nick,' Sally said. She came and wrapped

her arms around me and for a while I lay my head against her breast wanting to be held and comforted, to have someone murmur that everything would be fine when my world was coming down around my ears. I thought of Dexter's offer, and my eye fell on a baby magazine on a chair. For some reason a fragment of my childhood appeared like a flickering home movie in my mind. I saw myself riding a bike along a pavement in the sun in the street where we had lived. My dad ran along beside me, steadying me and then as I gathered pace he let me go and stood panting as I rode on two wheels for the first time. I remembered that day. His shouts of encouragement as I sped along the road, feeling the first real taste of freedom and the breeze in my five-year-old hair.

'You're on your own now, Nick,' he called after me. 'You're on your own.'

In the morning I left for the office at seven-thirty, which was too late. The midweek traffic was heavy. On Monday everybody begins the week with a burst of enthusiastic energy and the freeways are busy from five in the morning, though the traffic flows easily because the peak is spread over a longer period, but by Wednesday the enthusiasm has waned and people are again sick of their jobs and their boss, having to get up in the morning. They've had an argument with their partner and the kids are driving them crazy. Midweek the traffic peaks later because everyone leaves home as late as possible, and they're caught in a slow moving crawl that makes everyone irritable. By Thursday people are considering quitting, selling the house and moving to a beach somewhere where they will live on fish and coconuts. The traffic doesn't move at all. By the time they get to work they're running late and for the rest of the day they feel like they're playing catch-up. The pressure builds. More people get fired or quit their jobs on Thursdays than any other day of the week. By Friday, however, everyone is in a good mood again because they're looking forward to the weekend and the traffic flows from before dawn. People want to get to the office early so they can have a long lunch or a few drinks at the end of the day to get the weekend off to a great start. By Sunday it's a disaster. It's the worse day for domestic meltdowns because everyone is starting to dread the week ahead. The weekend everyone was so looking forward to seems to have passed by without them having done any of the things they really wanted to, which was to sit down and put up their feet with a cold beer or a glass of wine, to watch some sports, or read a magazine or a book in peace and solitude. Have a little time to themselves. Instead they spent the entire weekend ferrying the kids from one sports activity to another, or else taking them and their friends to the mall or the movies and in between times there's the shopping to be done, the lawn to mow, that door to fix that's been sticking for six months now, meals to prepare, and invariably some unexpected expense occurs that brings home the realization that no matter how hard they work for the rest of their lives they're never going to have any money to buy that little boat or convertible or whatever it is they always wanted, and frustration sets in until it explodes in a torrent of recrimination and abuse towards their partner BECAUSE THAT PERSON HAS RUINED THEIR FUCKING LIFE

At ten o'clock Marcus and I were looking at a cash flow forecast our accountant had produced using our known overheads and revenues from existing clients. When he was done he turned the screen around so we could see the result for ourselves.

'It's not good guys,' he said regretfully. 'The bottom line is that by the time you meet your overheads and interest payments you're slipping further into the red.' He paused, his heavy jowled face making him look sad like a bloodhound. 'There's worse to come as well I'm afraid.'

'Worse? What could be worse?' I said.

'The bank were in touch on Friday. They're worried that your cash flow isn't meeting the projections you gave them and they wanted an update on your position.'

'When they see this, what's going to happen?'

'My honest guess? I think they'll pull the plug.'

Marcus got up and went to stand at the window with his back to us. Recrimination came off him in waves. Our accountant looked from Marcus to me, and I wondered how much he knew.

'There must be something we can do,' I said.

He frowned glumly. 'Well, I guess you could show them you have a plan to severely cut back your overheads, so that your cash flow is positive. Maybe if you convince them your revenues will pick up . . .' He didn't sound hopeful, but I seized on the straw he was offering.

'How do we do that?'

'Well, you'd have to get less expensive office space for a start. Trade down your cars. Sell whatever you could from your current premises that you don't absolutely need. Let go of all your people.'

Marcus turned around from the window. 'Fire everybody?'

'I'm afraid so.'

Marcus stared at me accusingly. You see, his expression shouted. You see what you've done.

What we were talking about here was starting again, but from scratch, working out of a couple of rooms in a cheap building in the Mission with a view over an alley.

'Even then I think the bank would still want a lump sum of money. You'd have to sell your houses,' our accountant added.

Marcus turned away, his face white, his lips pressed tightly together as if he was afraid of what words would spill out if he let them. 'We might as well let them take it all,' I said, voicing what I knew Marcus felt.

It was clear our accountant agreed, but he was determined to offer a hopeful note. 'At least this way you'd still have a business which you could build back up over time. And you wouldn't be declared bankrupt. I'm sorry. I wish there was something else I could tell you.'

But I knew it wouldn't work. Nobody was going to hire an advertising agency that was tainted with the dismal reek of failure. Our remaining clients would desert us in a week.

'We'll get back to you,' I said.

We went outside on the street to look for a cab, and eventually we even found one. I caught Marcus's arm as he went to get in. He turned and met my eye.

'I'm sorry,' I said.

He stared at me and I could see the struggle for control that was going on behind his eyes. 'Are you?'

'Of course.'

'You mean if you had the chance to do this all again, that you wouldn't?'

'What kind of a question is that?' I asked.

'Would you?'

'Of course not, knowing what I do.'

'Then what would you do?'

'I don't know. Go to the bank earlier maybe, get their support. That way we could've hired more people, we wouldn't have lost people like Jerry Parker to Dexter.' Marcus didn't say anything. 'What? What do you want me to say?'

He shook his head. 'You don't get it, do you?' He started to turn away to get in the taxi but I stopped him.

'What do you mean?'

'I mean it's still about you. What you want. It doesn't matter about anyone else. Me. Sally. Anyone.'

'You want me to say we never should have pitched for Spectrum, is that it? Okay, if it'll make you happy, fine. We never should have pitched.'

'Sure.'

'Okay, so I don't believe that. I admit I didn't do things the way I should have, and I regret that. How many times do I have to say I'm sorry? But the truth is we wouldn't be having this conversation if we'd won the account. We'd still be popping champagne corks. Admit it, Marcus, you wouldn't be complaining then, and neither would Sally.'

He shrugged free of my grip. For a moment there was a blaze of something in his eye. 'You know something? You want to know something?'

He was trembling with pent up emotion, and suddenly for some reason I didn't want him to say whatever it was he had in mind. I had this idea that if he did there would be no going back, he would unleash something neither of us would ever be able to forget. Perhaps the same thing went through his mind, at any rate the cab driver broke the moment.

'Hey, you guys wanna go anywhere or what?'

Marcus hesitated then got in, and we rode back to the office in silence.

That evening I shut myself in my office after everyone had left and took the phone off the hook. My eye continually strayed to the two photographs on my bookcase, the one of Sally and me in happier times, and the one of me and my dad. I was acutely aware of the gun that lay locked in the cigar box in a drawer behind me, and I began entertaining fantasies that revolved around shooting Larry Dexter in a particularly bloody and satisfying scene that Scorsese would have been proud of. But an insistent voice kept telling me that Dexter wasn't really to blame for my problems, he had only taken advantage of a situation I had created. The real culprit had been my own ambition. Like Icarus I had tried to fly too close to the sun and now I was falling to the earth below with all the velocity of a Russian satellite.

A solution appeared in the form of the idea that I could take out my dad's gun and do what he had when it had all gotten too much. Press the cold steel gently against my temple, screw my eyes shut and squeeze the trigger. What would it feel like, I wondered, as a small lead projectile punched a hole in my skull and tore through my brain scattering tissue and neurons in all directions? Would my thoughts be cast on the wind, so to speak, sucked into the air conditioning system and spewed into the atmosphere to waft gently over the bay? Would I still exist in some more peaceful ethereal form? Or maybe there would be nothing. A flash of light and a loud noise and I would fall off my chair. Sally would have the insurance money, marry Garrison Hunt, have his children and be happy without me. I wondered if my dad had thought like that, imagining that he was doing us all a favour.

When I got home Sally took one look at me and didn't need to ask how it had gone with the accountant. She held my hand, and squeezed it, and when we went to bed I lay cocooned by the darkness and her comforting warmth.

CHAPTER TWELVE

'We have to tell everybody what's happening.'

I looked up from my desk at Marcus, who came in and shut the door. Beyond the glass wall everything appeared normal. Sue, one of our graphic artists, was talking with Neil, a copywriter. They were examining an ad mock-up. Sue pointed at something and shook her head, then sipped at the coffee she was holding, her expression concentrated as Neil made some comment.

'They know we didn't get the account?' I asked.

'I haven't said anything yet,' Marcus replied.

But of course they knew. By now it would be common knowledge all over town. They would have guessed when I came back to the office from the presentation. One look at my face would have told them everything.

'So, what do we tell them?'

Marcus regarded me steadily. 'The truth.'

The truth. That we were closing the doors and they were out of work. I nodded my acceptance of the inevitable. 'I'll call a meeting for this afternoon,' I said. Marcus waited, clearly expecting more, and then I saw what it was. 'Don't worry, I'll do the talking.'

He nodded. Clearly he thought it was my responsibility.

At lunch time I went out to get some air. Anything to escape the office for a while. I'd let everyone know there would be a meeting at four, and now every time I looked up I saw people gathered in small groups talking furtively. They would glance towards my office and look away when they met my eye. They were way ahead of us. I guessed they already had some idea of what to expect. I knew most of them would have no trouble getting hired by other agencies, but that wasn't the point and neither was it going to make firing them any easier.

It was a short walk to South Park, which is a block-long narrow oval between 2nd and 3rd streets around which runs a narrow avenue. It's a peculiar oasis of gum trees and maples ringed by a collection of Victorian converts alongside exposed brick and rendered buildings both new and old, housing trendy boutiques and small cafés which nestle cheek to jowl with furniture restorers and motorcycle workshops. You enter from either second or third, busy thoroughfares both, where the constant noise of building work, tram bells, honking horns and sirens assails you, and suddenly you feel like you're in some peaceful village in Sonoma county.

I bought a coffee and sat on the sidewalk listening to birds twittering in the trees. A young woman next to me said hi when our eyes collided.

'You from around here?' I asked, making conversation. She had a laptop bag at her feet and was wearing a suit. Her eyes were the palest blue flecked with traces of green, and her skin was luminous. I figured her to be around her early twenties.

'I'm from Minnesota,' she said.

I avoided making any cracks. People from Minnesota tend to be sensitive. 'Tourist?'

She shook her head. 'I'm interviewing with law firms in the Bay Area.'

It turned out she was at law school in North Carolina in her second year, and she was thinking about taking a job in California. She had to be smart, because from the way she was talking she had her pick of the top firms.

'Well, I hope they pay you well,' I remarked. We talked about property prices.

'I guess I'll start on one twenty-five,' she said.

A hundred and twenty-five thousand in her first year out of school. She asked what I did.

'I'm in advertising,' I answered. We chatted a little while longer until I couldn't avoid the knowledge that I ought to be getting back, so I stood and shook her hand and wished her good luck. 'What's your name?' I asked as an afterthought. Maybe one day I would need a good smart young lawyer.

'Lorrie.'

'Well, I hope it goes well.'

She smiled. 'Thanks.'

I didn't think she needed any luck. She was young and pretty, bursting with brains and full of the confidence of the favoured few. The epitome of the American dream.

I had just sat down back in my office when my phone rang and I picked it up. Stacey said there was somebody to see me.

'Who is it?' I had no appointments and I was in no mood to talk to anyone.

'A Mr Hoffman?'

The name meant nothing to me. 'Do I know him?'

'I don't think so.'

We had a lot of people calling in trying to sell us something or other, usually advertising space in some obscure magazine or journal. They were adept at disguising their real purpose, knowing if they did they would never make it past reception, but Stacey was equally adept at spotting them and we had devised a simple code. 'Should I see him?' I asked. If she thought the visitor was selling something she would answer no, and then I would tell her to ask them to make an appointment by phone.

She answered in a low voice, almost a whisper. 'I think you should come out here.'

'Is something wrong?'

'He looks sick.'

I envisaged some crazy person in reception. 'You mean as in mentally?'

'No, I mean like he's ill.'

I gave up and went out to reception, where a frail looking guy sat waiting on one of the leather couches. Stacey looked worried and I saw why. His pallor was grey and he really did look ill.

'Mr Hoffman?' I said as I went over. He looked up at me from the only eyes that I've ever seen in real life that fitted the description sunken. They appeared to be drawn back inside his skull, as did the flesh of his face, like it was collapsing inwards. His short grey hair was insubstantial as if a good gust of wind would blow it right from his head by the roots. With difficulty he rose and extended his hand which, when I shook it, felt as frail as he looked.

'I'm Nick Weston. You asked to see me?'

'Yes. I'm Leonard Hoffman.'

'Are you okay?' I asked. 'Can I get you something? Water maybe?' I looked over at Stacey who took my cue and fetched a cup from the cooler which Hoffman accepted gratefully. I watched him drink, his Adam's apple like a bony fist in the wasted flesh of his throat.

'Thank you,' he said and handed back the cup.

'Are you sure you're okay? Maybe we should call a doctor,' I suggested.

Hoffman smiled ironically. 'Too late for doctors, Mr Weston,' he said. 'There's nothing they can do for me now. I'm dying.'

He said it without melodrama, patently not seeking

pity, but more as a wry matter of fact. I believed him. In fact I had never seen anybody still walking around who looked closer to death than he did. Despite his matter of fact manner I was uncomfortable, embarrassed even, because what can you say to someone under those circumstances? My instinct was to laugh uncertainly, offer reassurance, deny the obvious. Surely not. You can't be. You'll be fine. All of which had nothing to do with offering comfort but was a natural reaction on my part. We all want to shield ourselves from the unpleasant reality of our own mortality. When faced with the terminally ill we see ourselves as we will surely one day be, a bag of bones, shrunken and hollow eyed taking painful wheezing breaths, and it's not an image we relish. Death makes us uncomfortable and we would rather we weren't confronted with it, so when we are we tend to deny it.

As a way of getting in to see me, I figured this was extreme, even for an advertising salesman, so after he had assured me that he hadn't meant his demise was immediately imminent, I took Hoffman back to my office where he sat down and looked around with interest. His gaze lingered on the pictures on my bookcase and I took a moment to observe him. He was shabbily dressed, the flesh on his bones wasted by whatever disease afflicted him. From the way he spoke, and his manner I figured he was educated. His age was hard to determine. I waited for him to explain why he had asked to see me, reluctant to press him.

'Carpe Diem,' he said eventually. 'Seize The Day.' The irony as it applied to him seemed to amuse him. Though he was ill there was nothing wrong with his mind. His eyes, though pained, shone with a clear intelligence. 'An interesting name for an advertising agency.'

'My partner's idea. He's the creative one. I'm just the mouthpiece.'

'More than that I think. I've heard that you're astute.'

'Depends who you talk to,' I replied. My eye flicked to the office outside, and all the people out there who would no doubt think of different ways to describe me after I'd delivered the good news later that day.

Hoffman smiled. 'I've talked to a lot of people.'

'Oh?'

'I know a lot about you.'

'Such as?'

'I know that your business is in some financial difficulty.'

Whether he was ill or not, I wasn't about to discuss the state of our finances with a total stranger. 'How can I help you, Mr Hoffman?' I asked.

'I have a proposition for you,' he replied. 'I would like to hire Carpe Diem.'

For a moment I wasn't sure that he was serious. He didn't look like the sort of person who had need of an advertising agency. He was wearing worn brown cord trousers that were at least a size too big for him, and the collar of his shirt was fraying a little at the neck line.

He gave me a wry smile. 'I can imagine what you're thinking.'

I was a little embarrassed that he had read me so easily so I sidestepped his observation by asking a question. 'What is it you need an advertising agency for, Mr Hoffman?'

'What else? I have something I wish to sell. That's what you do isn't it?' He paused, short of breath, air rattled in his throat and his chest heaved with a wheezing sound. 'Lung cancer,' he explained. He took a bottle of pills from his pocket and shook several into the palm of his hand which he quickly swallowed. 'For the pain.'

When he had recovered a little he began to explain himself. 'How old do you think I am, Mr Weston?'

It was impossible to say. He had the shrunken appearance of the elderly, but disease can ravage the human body. 'Early sixties,' I guessed, knocking a good ten years off the age he looked.

'I'm forty-eight,' he stated matter of factly.

I tried not to react, but I was surprised. 'I've never been good at that.'

He made a dismissive gesture. 'I don't tell you this because I want your sympathy, just so you might understand what I have to tell you. You've heard of a man called Nelson Morgan of course?'

'Yes,' I answered cautiously, my curiosity suddenly tweaked.

'Then you know he owns a company called Morgan Industries.'

'I've heard of it.'

He smiled. 'Nelson Morgan and I were once partners,' he went on. 'I see you're surprised by that. Of course it was a long time ago. We knew each other at college. We began a company together when we were in our early twenties. Our plan was to design and sell software for the computer industry which was beginning to really take off then. The designing part was where I came in. Nelson was the business brains. The company failed as it turned out, partly because of timing. We were probably a year or two ahead of our time. I got a job and Nelson and I went our separate ways. We'd had some disagreements over certain things and we weren't such good friends as we had been. Friendship and business often don't mix well I think.'

Amen to that, I thought wryly. Hoffman went on to tell me how the next time he'd heard about Morgan was a couple of years later when he read an article in a trade magazine. Morgan had started another company and was making a lot of money.

'I wondered at the time how he'd managed to get so far so quickly,' Hoffman said. 'When our company failed we were broke, and this was before the days when investors were falling over themselves to throw money at anything remotely to do with the technology industry. It wasn't until a couple of years later that I discovered how he'd done it.'

Apparently when their company had collapsed, Morgan had kept a business program that was designed and written by Hoffman. At the time they hadn't been able to interest anyone in buying it, but it turned out that not long afterwards Morgan had managed to sell the program to another company who had used it as the basis for their own business application software package.

'He used that money to start Morgan Industries,' Hoffman said. 'Money that was half mine. But I never saw a cent of it.'

I wasn't sure that I believed a word of this, but I was interested enough to want to know more. 'If you're saying he cheated you, why didn't you sue him when you found out?' I asked.

'I threatened to. By then he was already wealthy, but the money he got for the program amounted to only a few hundred thousand dollars. Nelson claimed it was his work and skill that had turned it into a fortune. I didn't deny that. I only wanted what was rightly mine. He could have easily afforded to pay me, but he chose not to. He was adamant that once our partnership was dissolved he didn't owe me anything. I spoke to a few lawyers but they advised me my chances of a successful suit were slim at best, and in the end I decided it really wasn't worth it.'

He went on to tell me that his life since then had not run smoothly. He didn't get into a lot of detail but he said he'd been married and divorced three times and that he'd lurched regularly from the brink of success to failure.

'I'm an alcoholic,' he confessed. 'I haven't had a drink for almost a year now, but before that drinking was always the single most important thing in my life. It was my life. I believed that without it there was nothing worth living for.' He paused reflectively for a moment. 'Much of it I can't even remember now. A waste.' He shook his head, then made a small weary gesture, as if there was no point in dwelling further on what was for ever lost. 'But that isn't what I came here to tell you. About two years ago I got a job with a company in the valley. I was working as a software design engineer. I was sober for the first time in years, doing what I do well, what I've always had a natural talent for, even though I squandered it. The company was Spectrum Software.'

He paused again, this time to allow me a moment to absorb what he'd told me, guessing correctly that my interest had suddenly deepened.

'Of course you're familiar with Spectrum,' he said.

I didn't reply, but made a vague gesture which could be interpreted anyway he liked, but mostly as an invitation to continue.

'While I was working for Spectrum I had an idea for a new product that I took to Sam Mendez. He liked it and put me in charge of developing it further. You're familiar with Home Finance?'

'Yes,' I admitted.

'Then you know it was never particularly successful. The concept was outmoded and too narrow. But it did spark my idea, which was for a program designed specifically for the person working at home. Do you have any idea how many people no longer work from a centralized office, Mr Weston?'

I shrugged. 'A lot.'

'There are millions, and the trend will continue. And it isn't only people who work for companies, there are many more who run small business from their homes. The big corporations have their own in-house software designed for communicating and networking, performing all the specialized tasks they require, but individuals and small companies who make up the bulk of home workers can't afford that. I saw an opportunity for a package that was easily adaptable but was much more than simply a spreadsheet and word processing package with various add-ons, which is primarily what's available now. My idea was for something that would combine the best elements of available business software, including accountancy and forecasting tools, but would also incorporate home management and entertainment programs, and above all would be simple to use and configure to individual situations. The potential is huge.'

He paused. As he'd talked about this idea of his, the light in his eyes had seemed to grow brighter, and for a few moments he'd transcended the illness that ravaged his body, but now he slumped in his seat, as if drained. His eyes were still bright, but the light seemed to burn with an altogether different intensity. I was fascinated by his story, even though I had never seen him at Spectrum, or heard of this idea of his.

'Mendez liked my idea,' Hoffman said eventually. 'The problem was that Spectrum didn't have the finance to develop it properly. Something like this costs a lot of money to develop and market effectively, as I'm sure you're aware.'

That much was true. If the potential for such a program was as big as Hoffman claimed, and from what he'd told me I didn't have any reason to doubt it, then it could cost a great deal of money to launch it properly.

'So Mendez started looking for an investor,' Hoffman said and I began to see where this was leading.

'Which was Morgan Industries?'

'Yes. Nelson recognized the potential, though of course he didn't know I had anything to do with it, and instead of investing he did what he specializes in. He started negotiating to buy Spectrum. As soon as I realized what was happening I quit,' Hoffman said. He became subdued for a moment.

'For a while I started drinking again. Drinking a lot. That's always been my answer and my weakness whenever things didn't go the way I expected. All I could think of was the fact that Nelson Morgan was going to make a lot of money from something that had begun as my idea.'

I began to wonder again how much of this was true. With the kind of money Hoffman would have been paid, plus stock options which were the norm for a design engineer as good as he seemed to be claiming he was, he would have made millions himself if the value of the company increased because of his idea. He saw my doubt.

'You think I should have stayed,' he said.

'It isn't for me to say.'

'But you think it,' he insisted. 'I can see it in your face. You see me sitting here looking as if I probably haven't got a dime to my name and you think if it had been you, you would have stayed.' He sounded deeply bitter all of a sudden. 'You don't know what it feels like to have been cheated by somebody who was once your friend. He could have paid me what he rightfully owed me years ago. He wouldn't even have noticed it. But Nelson was always a cold hearted sonofabitch. Maybe it wasn't a hell of a lot of money, but it could have made a difference to me. My whole life might have been different.'

He stared at me with a slightly wild, unreasoning gleam in his eye and I understood how much this had eaten away at him over the years. Perhaps he believed it was this early disappointment that had started him drinking, and because of that all the accumulated failures and humiliations in his life were at least partly Morgan's fault.

'Besides,' he said after a few moments, in a more reasonable tone. 'What use is money to me now?'

He told me that after he left Spectrum and Morgan had completed the buy out, Mendez hired a whole team of designers to work on the project that Hoffman had begun.

'I still have friends at Spectrum and when I realized what was happening I decided to do something about it. I decided I didn't have to sit by and let Morgan cheat me again. So I stopped drinking and I started working on my own version of the program. It was through the people I know that I heard about you and your company.'

We were coming to the point of all this, I saw, though I couldn't guess what it was. 'What is it exactly that you heard?' I asked.

'I know that you were in contention to be appointed as Spectrum's advertising agency. People thought highly of you. You learned how Spectrum works. You understand the markets the company operates in. From what I understand Carpe Diem came up with some very innovative and creative ideas.'

'If you know all that, you must also be aware that the account went to KCM,' I pointed out.

'Of course. I wouldn't be here otherwise.'

'So why *are* you here exactly?' I asked.

'As I said, I want to hire you. I need your talents, Mr Weston. And I have something which you need. Your company is in financial difficulty. I can help you.'

'This has something to do with the program you've been working on?' I guessed.

'Of course. Spectrum are planning to launch their program in three months' time. But this was my idea, Mr Weston, and my version is far superior to the one Morgan now owns. I want you to manage its marketing and distribution.'

Every time he breathed his chest sounded like an old bellows, and occasionally he'd break into a paroxysm of coughing that creased his face in pain. Now he slumped in his seat. He looked drained. As he'd talked I had begun to experience a sinking feeling in my gut as I saw that Spectrum Software had been a far bigger opportunity than I had ever imagined. If all of this was true, Morgan intended to invest millions of dollars advertising this new program. Tens of millions. Even as I absorbed this Hoffman was watching me, waiting for a response. I hardly knew how to begin to tell him the commercial realities of life.

'Mr Hoffman, let's assume for the moment that your program is superior to the one that Spectrum is planning to launch.'

'Morgan,' he corrected. 'Morgan Industries owns the company. Nelson Morgan is putting up the money. And it isn't just superior, my program makes his out of date before it even goes on sale. I may be sick, and I may have wasted my talent, but I do have talent, Mr Weston. If Morgan hadn't cheated me, if I hadn't begun drinking, I could have done great things with my life. Even he would agree that I am very, very good at what I do.'

'Okay,' I agreed to placate him. 'I have no reason to doubt that what you're saying is true. But the point is that having the better product isn't always what it's about. Letting people know about it, and persuading them to buy it costs a lot of money. There's packaging, distribution, administration sales, billing. You're talking about a company infrastructure, which Morgan has with Spectrum, and which you don't, unless I'm mistaken. That costs millions of dollars. And that's before you even consider marketing.'

I broke off with my crash course in business, because it was clear from his expression of bemused impatience that it wasn't needed. 'But then you know all this already don't you.'

'Of course. And everything you say is true,' Hoffman agreed. 'But it only applies if I want to compete with Morgan. That isn't what I want to do.'

'I'm sorry. I don't follow,' I admitted.

'Morgan will sell his version of the program for something like two hundred and fifty dollars a shot at retail. I plan to sell mine exclusively over the Internet, which takes care of packaging and distribution. Anyone who wants it can download it directly to their computer.' He paused and a sly expression crept into his eye. 'For five dollars.'

'Five dollars?' I echoed incredulously. I wondered how he thought he would make any money by selling it for that amount.

He took out a single sheet of paper from his inside jacket pocket which he passed over to me. I studied the columns of figures, which I saw represented a basic business plan, and my eye was drawn to a particular figure.

'Advertising budget three million dollars?'

'That's two million for media, and a million to cover your fees for creative input and managing marketing. The way I see it that should be more than enough in the first year. I think with some initial print ads and some selected links to websites that ought to cover it. Once the media hear about a great program anyone can download almost for nothing, you should get plenty of free publicity. The three million will be funded by the five dollar charge. After the first year the trust will pay Carpe Diem an annual fee of half a million dollars to continue to manage the process. Which will be money for very little work required. Remaining money will be donated to charity.'

'The trust?' I asked. My head was spinning as I tried to take in what he was saying, and I kept going back to what he'd said would be our fee. A million in the first year.

'I've set up a trust which owns the rights to my program.'

I looked again at the figures. I thought there had to be a flaw, but the more I studied them the more I was forced to conclude that Hoffman had thought it all out very carefully. My eye was drawn like a moth to a nightlight back to the one that interested me most. A million dollars in the first year. Enough to pay back what we owed. More than enough. It was so simple. That was the beauty of it. If Hoffman's program lived up to his claims, how could Morgan possibly compete with something that would be virtually given away? Only one question stuck in my mind.

'Why?' I asked.

He smiled as if the answer was self-evident. 'I'm dying, Mr Weston. Money is no use to me. I have no family. The last thing I can do with my life is to ensure Nelson Morgan doesn't profit again from my work.'

I nodded my understanding. Revenge. The oldest reason in the world.

CHAPTER THIRTEEN

I cancelled the staff meeting planned for that afternoon, and repeated everything Hoffman had told me to Marcus. I tried to keep my voice even, to sound sceptical but I think he picked up on something beneath all that; hope. A drowning man will clutch at any lifeline, he doesn't stop to analyse it too closely. Marcus studied the sheet of figures that Hoffman had left with me, and when he finally looked up his disbelief was apparent.

'This can't be true,' he said

'I don't know,' I answered honestly. I had come up with a hundred different reasons why I shouldn't believe him, but one thing I couldn't answer. Why make up a story like this? That I couldn't fathom.

'You think he's on the level?'

'I think we ought to consider that possibility.'

Hoffman had given me his address, and told me if we were there in the morning he would show us his program. When I told Marcus where Hoffman lived his scepticism deepened. I couldn't blame him for that. Genius software designers in California didn't live in places like San Leandro in East Oakland. They were more likely to own a big house with a tennis court and a pool in a fashionable suburb on the western side or up in the hills overlooking the Pacific ocean, and they drove expensive European cars. San Leandro was where you lived if you were the guy who cleaned the pool or whose job it was to polish those expensive cars on the lot before they were sold, that's if you even had a job.

'Are you serious?' Marcus said.

'Would you rather I tell those people out there they don't have jobs any more?' I asked, gesturing beyond his office. He considered that. 'Another day can't hurt. It might change everything.'

It was the thought of our employees more than anything else that made up his mind, though I think in the end it wouldn't have made any difference if Hoffman told us he lived in a box at the end of a disused alley. We would still have gone to meet him. What choice did we have?

In the morning we took my car and drove over the Oakland Bay Bridge. It was overcast, low cloud shrouding the Oakland hills. On days like this the surrounding area has little of the appeal and scenic attractiveness that has been captured in millions of tourist snaps. The container yards and the sprawl of industrial buildings on the east shore are as ugly as the dull grey waters of the bay. The urban sprawl is visible as concrete freeways and pale swathes on a barren landscape, noticeably devoid of trees. It's only when the sun is shining and the bay is all dressed up in her finest glittery blue, when the trees on the hills break the slash of development and soften it, when the skyscrapers gleam against a cloudless sky, that everything is seen in a fresh light.

Marcus had barely said a word since leaving the office. He was sunk in his seat, absorbed in his own thoughts.

'Did you talk to Alice about this yet?' I asked.

He looked over at me quickly, jerked from whatever he'd been thinking. 'Alice?'

'Yes. Did you tell her about Hoffman?'

'No.'

I thought that was strange. Sally and I had talked about

nothing else the whole evening. At least I'd talked, and Sally had mostly listened, though she'd picked up on my burgeoning hope and cautioned me not to get too carried away until I was certain that Hoffman wasn't some nut.

'Actually Alice moved out,' Marcus said.

I did a double take. I couldn't believe something like that had happened and I didn't know about it. 'When?'

'A couple of days ago. She's staying on the boat.'

I wanted to ask what had happened, but it was clear he didn't want to talk about it, at least not with me. He stared back out the windshield looking sullen and I wondered if somehow he blamed me for this too. I could imagine Alice's reaction when she heard we didn't get the Spectrum account. No doubt she'd reminded Marcus what an asshole I was and how she'd always warned him he shouldn't let me get away with the things he did. Secretly I wondered if perhaps once Alice had heard the news she'd decided Marcus was no longer a reliable meal ticket. Out loud though I said I was sorry.

'Is it permanent?' I ventured.

He glanced at me, and there was an odd look in his eye which I couldn't fathom. 'I don't know.'

I thought this was sudden, but then I realized it probably wasn't. It only seemed that way because I hadn't known about it. There had been a time once when he would have confided in me long before this. 'You know, if you want to talk,' I said tentatively, and let the rest hang in the air.

For a second something seemed to amuse him, then he looked away. 'Yeah.'

I knew I shouldn't hold my breath.

We took 580 south off the bridge and exited at Fruitvale. The address Hoffman had given us was a few streets back from the International Strip. Once this boulevard had such an unenviable reputation for drug gangs and shootings that it had been renamed East 14th street in an effort to erase the past. I had never even been to this area before. I mean, who would? We passed under the elevated freeway and the BART track. The concrete pillars were sprayed with gang graffiti and the dirt ground was littered with all kinds of garbage. Where once there had stood a notorious housing project which was the haunt of hookers and pushers and was the scene of daily episodes of violence both domestic and gang related, there now stood a new shopping mall. The old projects had been torn down in a plan to rejuvenate the area, but a block further on the pervading sense was of a neighbourhood that remained steeped in decay and deprivation. A lingering whiff of menace seeped from the cracks in the concrete, and from the faces both brown and white who stared at my shiny new convertible Saab as we drove by, from sidewalks and sagging porches of what I was certain were crack houses. I was glad I had the top up. But I wished we had brought Marcus's car.

We found the main strip, and turned off again following the directions Hoffman had given us. I felt as if I had trespassed into a foreign land. One I only knew from TV shows. An unfamiliar unease stirred in the pit of my gut as we passed pawnbrokers and dollar stores housed in beat up ugly buildings with garish signs over the door. Many of the stores had Spanish names and heavy iron grilles over the windows. El Pollo Loco jostled for space with Jack In The Box and the Supermarcardo. Street sellers had set up their carts outside Renta Centa selling corn and chilli pretzels. Liquor stores were on every corner, heavy grilles on the windows. We turned into a residential street. An old woman pushed a shopping cart loaded with junk. She was dressed in bright reds and yellows. A guy lay sleeping on a corner, one shoeless foot in the gutter. Piles of paper and rags, cardboard boxes and other crap littered the sidewalk and sometimes the street.

'Where to now?' I said at an intersection. I hoped this wasn't all a bad joke because I didn't like driving around here. I thought we'd been along this same street once already.

'Go left,' Marcus said, studying Hoffman's directions and a map. 'Then make a right two blocks down.'

A tall guy, black, maybe thirty or so watched us go by. His hand went to his pocket, perhaps reaching for a cigarette. Or maybe a gun. A car lot on the corner was full of bargains for under five grand. Rusting gas guzzlers or beat up Japanese compacts. A Honda passed in the opposite direction, gleaming black, gold trim and wheels, a low rider driven by a youth wearing a baseball cap on backwards, one hand nonchalantly on the wheel the other on his girlfriend's thigh, or maybe an Uzi he kept on the seat. The cars parked against the kerb were often missing a hubcap or two or else were marked by dents and scratches and bore the same overall look of neglect as their surroundings. My nine-month-old Saab convertible stood out like a beacon. It might as well have had a sign on the window that read STEAL ME.

We finally found Hoffman's building and pulled up behind a big green monster with fat wheels and darkened windows. Across the street three brown skinned Latino kids wearing baggy jailhouse trousers that rode on their hips stared sullenly at us. They eyed the way we were dressed and my car.

'There's going to be nothing left of this when we get out of here,' I said to Marcus.

'Give them money.'

'What?'

'To take care of it.'

'Great idea. And then they'll have my money as well as my CD player and wheels.'

'Maybe they're not as bad as you think.'

'Right,' I said. He was always prepared to see the best in people. 'They're probably just waiting for their applications to the police force to come through.'

He shrugged at my cynicism. 'It's your car.'

I decided to give his idea a shot since I didn't have a better one myself and when we crossed the street I went over to where they were lounging on the steps. A young woman walked by. She was perhaps eighteen or nineteen wearing a short skirt and a skin-tight top through which her nipples stood out like hard little cherries. She had long black hair and was pushing a baby stroller and as she went by the kids all made clicking noises at the back of their throats and spoke in soft Spanish undertones. I had no idea what they were saying but I doubted they were commenting on the likelihood of rain that day. The girl threw them a disdainful look and said something that came off her tongue like the rat-a-tat of a machine gun, then she tossed her hair and walked away, swaying her hips in an exaggerated fashion. This seemed to delight them and they whooped and cackled in high-pitched voices and one of them, the youngest who was perhaps fifteen or sixteen, stood up and grasped at his crutch and made thrusting movements in her direction, to which, when she glanced back, she responded with a sharply upthrust finger. This triggered more laughter. It was an ugly sound. Under the general merriment there was a dangerous edge born of boredom and deprivation. I felt exposed to a sub-culture that I normally only got a glimpse of on the evening news, where violence hung in the air like the stillness before a heavy electrical storm.

When the girl had gone the kids turned their attention

back to me. They seemed mildly curious by this totally foreign presence that had appeared unexpectedly among them and they were waiting to see if it had possible entertainment value. Or should they just squish it.

'Hey, how're you doing?' I said, knowing that I looked and sounded exactly like some white guy from across the bay trying to look as if I came to neighbourhoods like this one every day. They grinned back at me with amused contempt, flashing brilliant white teeth. I picked on the one who appeared to be the eldest and who I figured from the way he was sprawled with his legs out, leaning back on the top step, the others occupying positions just below him, was their *de facto* leader. He had short hair like the others, and a wisp of a moustache across his top lip that I was sure he was very proud of. It had probably taken him a year to cultivate it to that point. He was perhaps nineteen or twenty.

'I need to leave my car there for a little while. I thought you guys might like to take care of it for me.' I had already taken a fifty out of my wallet, which I let him see.

He looked beyond me to the car with a lazy gaze. 'Take care o' that, man? You fuckin' serious?'

His two buddies giggled, their bright eyes full of anticipation.

'We gotta lotta do. Got bui'ness to take care of. Can't hang round here takin' care some fuckin' car, man.'

'Right. Your time is precious. I know that,' I said with veiled sarcasm. 'I'll give you another twenty okay?'

His gaze flicked over me, taking in my designer jeans, the five-hundred-dollar jacket, and then he looked at Marcus who was hanging back by the corner. He affected a look of disdain mingled with boredom. 'Hunnerd, man. Tha's it.'

I gave him the fifty in my hand. 'Okay, you get the rest when I come out.' He slipped it in his pocket without a word. When I reached Marcus I said, 'I think I just paid some kids to steal my car.'

We found Hoffman's apartment on the second floor at the top of a flight of stairs that smelled of cat piss and other underlying odours I preferred not to contemplate. I knocked on the door and waited, while Marcus regarded me with a blank expression, though I could tell what he was thinking. Along the hallway a door opened a crack and a thin girl of seventeen or so put her head around the corner, looked at us for a moment then quietly closed it again. I knocked again and from inside we heard a hacking cough getting closer, then Hoffman opened the door. He looked worse than he had the day before. I introduced him to Marcus and he invited us in. He saw me looking at the chain and dead bolt which he didn't use.

'Aren't you afraid someone'll break in?' I said.

'Did you see three kids on the street outside?'

'Latino types? I paid them to take care of my car.'

'How much did you give them?'

'We settled on a hundred.'

He shrugged. 'A little high, but your car will be fine. When I moved here the eldest one, his name is Pepe, he stopped me in the street outside and told me this was a dangerous neighbourhood. Lots of burglaries, people on drugs. He told me I needed some insurance if I was going to live around here. I pay them a few dollars every week to make sure nobody bothers me.'

'A protection racket?' I said. 'They're only kids.'

'Protection, security, it's the same thing. And they may be young, but they're not kids.'

It occurred to me that the vague references Hoffman had made to his missed opportunities meant he'd spent a lot of his life living in places like this. He led us into his apartment. It was small. Just one bedroom and a living room with kitchen and bathroom. I think I half expected it to be full of piles of rubbish and empty liquor bottles, but in fact it was neat and clean. There wasn't much furniture to speak of. I glimpsed a narrow metal framed cot and a battered chest of drawers in the bedroom and in the bathroom I saw an array of pill bottles and other medication in a cupboard that had no door. The walls were bare, paper fraying and peeling, and the paintwork was faded and cracked, but I doubt if Hoffman even noticed. His living room was absolutely crammed full of electronic equipment. He had set up several long tables on which rested computer monitors, and scanners and so forth and one wall was covered in pencil scribblings, all kinds of symbols and numbers which to me were unintelligible but I imagined would make sense to another programmer. There were wires everywhere, and dismantled computer parts, circuit boards and other electronic junk.

'How familiar are you with this type of software?' Hoffman asked us as he sat in front of a screen.

'I know a little,' Marcus said.

'Sit down then.' Marcus drew up a chair as Hoffman started tapping the keyboard and the screen came alive. 'First I'll show you a version of the Spectrum program. This is a few months old but they won't have been able to change it much in that time. Then I'll show you my program.'

I looked around for somewhere else to sit, but every available surface held some piece of equipment or one of the piles of notebooks and manuals that cluttered up the room, so I wandered over to the window. It was up to Marcus to figure out whether Hoffman's program was as good as he claimed. When it came to markets, and distribution and so on I knew my stuff, but for practical knowledge Marcus was way ahead of me. I used my laptop for word processing and designing presentations, but for me that was about as far as it went. Unlike Marcus I hadn't yet been converted to the wonders of the Internet age. He used a computer at work loaded with design and graphics software, but he also had one at home to connect to all kinds of sites to buy products and services over the web, whereas I still preferred to do my banking in person and walk into a store if I wanted to buy something. Sally had tried doing the grocery shopping over the Internet for a while, but she found it clumsy and time consuming, and in the end she missed actually going out into the world among other people.

I had no doubt that computing power had revolutionized business. But at home I thought it was still a clunky tool. Whenever I used the Internet I found it so crowded with information it was practically impossible to find whatever I was searching for, and the vast majority of sites that I'd logged onto were so poorly designed anyway that I soon gave up trying. Of course that's all going to change. The personal computer will probably disappear and be replaced with some all-purpose TV device that enables people to do their banking and shopping as well as downloading movies and games or whatever. Companies will get better at delivering the services they offer, websites will become easier to navigate and more interesting and the whole experience will become a hell of a lot simpler than it is right now. Until then I was happy to continue with my Stone Age ways.

I went over to the window and looked down on the street where I could see my car. So far it appeared to have remained untouched. I glanced over at Hoffman as he explained something to Marcus. They were both intent on the screen. Marcus asked a question and Hoffman clicked on the icons, bringing up different applications. From what I could see of the graphics the program looked easy to use and was interesting to look at, and Marcus was apparently absorbed. I left them to it and wandered through into the kitchen. The cupboards were mostly bare, but I found coffee and some cups so I busied myself making coffee for us all. While I was at it I went into the bathroom and sneaked a look at the medicines in the cabinet. There was a whole array of pills and liquids, all of them with long complicated names that I couldn't get my mouth around. When I took the coffee through I watched Hoffman in front of the screen, surrounded by leads and manuals and notebooks, bathed in the faint light from the screen, and I pondered how he'd lived in this cheap apartment spending his final days working on his program. This act of revenge against his old partner had become the focus of his life. There was nothing in the apartment to indicate he thought of anything else. No other books, no music, no pictures.

Eventually, after they'd been at it for almost two hours, Marcus had seen enough. As they finished up Hoffman was seized with a coughing fit that made his eyes stream and his whole body convulse in pain. It came in spasms that left him weak and gasping, and we had to take him through to his bedroom and help him onto his bed. He kept a bottle of something on the bedside table which he glugged back that appeared to help.

'I think we should get a doctor,' Marcus said quietly as we stood just inside the room.

'No doctor,' Hoffman called hoarsely. He waved a hand weakly. 'I'll be all right in a little while.'

He didn't look it. He lay with his eyes closed, his breathing shallow. We retreated to the doorway and spoke quietly.

'I still think we ought to get him a doctor,' Marcus said.

'He doesn't want us to, and it's his decision. Besides,

I don't think anyone can do much for him.' I gestured back towards the living room where they had been working. 'So, what do you think?'

Marcus took off his glasses and started polishing them thoughtfully. 'As far as I know there isn't anything like this available. At least not in a package like this. It's easy to use, it has a lot of different applications for business and home use. I'd say that it's a good product.'

'How does it compare to the Spectrum program?'

'It's better,' Hoffman said from his bed. He had propped himself up against his pillow and was watching us.

I looked questioningly at Marcus who shrugged. 'He's right. It's easier to use and it has more applications.'

Then I asked the big question. 'But is there a market for it?'

'No question.'

When we got outside my car remained untouched across the street. I went over to the three kids who hadn't moved from their step and I gave the one Hoffman had called Pepe the other fifty.

'Thanks.'

The note vanished into his pocket. 'No pro'lem, man. You need anything else? Lil somethin' make you chill, he'p you relax, man?'

'I don't think so.'

He grinned. 'Well if you do, you know where we're at.'

I promised I'd remember that. As I pulled out from the kerb the three kids watched. They were skinny and faintly ridiculous in their oversize clothes. Put them in some middle class suburb, get rid of the amateurish tattoos they all wore and give them a football to throw around and they would be little more than children. But here in this environment they exuded an air of casual menace.

We hit the freeway again and headed back towards the bridge. Marcus hadn't spoken since leaving Hoffman's apartment. We had the address of a lawyer downtown who Hoffman told us had set up the trust that would retain ownership of his program, and who would draw up an agreement detailing the arrangement between Carpe Diem and the trust. He said he would call the lawyer's office and tell him to expect to hear from us.

Marcus appeared lost in thought. 'You don't look too happy about any of this.'

He came to. 'I don't know what to think.'

'Think about a million dollars, Marcus. This deal saves our lives.'

'Maybe it's what happens afterwards that I'm worried about.'

'What do you mean?'

'I mean if this works out, if we repay what we owe, get ourselves back on our feet. What happens then? How long before another Spectrum or OfficeLine comes along?'

I looked over at him. 'Marcus, we've been friends for a long time. I can't change what's already done, and you've got every right to think the way you do. But this isn't going to happen again. I swear. From here on in we don't do anything unless we both agree to it. I won't ever try to push you into something you don't want to do. I don't expect you to believe that right away, but I'd like it if you gave me a chance. I'd like it if we were friends again.'

I meant every word, and I hoped he knew that. I could see that at least part of him believed me, but I could also see doubts and reservations remained.

He pointed ahead to the sign for the bridge. 'You better switch lanes or you're going to miss it.'

In the morning we went to the offices of Brinkman, Kessler, Baker, the firm Hoffman had hired to draw up our agreement. They were a mid-sized firm specializing in corporate work, mainly contracts and advisory work for companies whose businesses involved them in complicated regulatory issues and so forth rather than litigation. They were housed on the twenty-eighth floor of a tower on Battery in the Financial District. At reception we were asked to wait and were offered coffee. The waiting area was furnished with leather couches and a table held a selection of business magazines. The atmosphere was clubby and expensive, which was a spectacular contrast from the apartment where Hoffman lived.

'Would you come through?' a woman who appeared asked us. 'Mr Brinkman is free now.'

His personal assistant showed us through to his office, which was in a corner with windows looking straight towards Pier 31 on the Embercadero and the Bay beyond. A tourist boat was heading out to Alcatraz which obliged the folks from Kansas by appearing rocky and grim. Brinkman rose from behind a massive desk made of some kind of dark richly polished wood and waited for us to cross the acres of carpet to reach him. We shook hands all round and he asked us to take a seat.

'Can I offer you anything. Coffee? Water?' We said we were fine. 'Thank you, Carol,' he said to his assistant, and she murmured something and left us to it.

Brinkman was in his fifties. He had a confident, distinguished manner, with greying hair and manicured nails. He wasn't fat, but he was well fed, though the impeccably cut dark suit he wore disguised it a little. There was no doubt that he enjoyed the good things in life. A bright red silk handkerchief was carelessly stuffed in the breast pocket of his jacket so that it overflowed like a flower bursting into bloom. It was a flamboyant and somehow telling note. His eye travelled quickly over the jeans and T-shirt Marcus wore and as he opened a file on his desk the merest suggestion of a frown creased his brow.

'Well, gentlemen, I believe that you're aware that my client, Mr Hoffman, engaged me to set up and administer a trust that is to retain ownership of certain intellectual property belonging to him,' he began. 'A computer software program to be precise.' He smiled and relaxed back in his chair, his hands clasped loosely over his stomach. 'It's a slightly unusual situation. You're aware of course that Mr Hoffman is not a well man.'

'I understand he has cancer,' I said.

'Yes. That's also my understanding. It's inoperable I believe. Very unfortunate.' Brinkman paused, looking suitably solemn, then he spread his hands in a helpless gesture. 'However, it comes to us all in the end.' He leaned forward and began leafing through some papers on his desk.

'Now, my instructions are that I'm to draw up an agreement between the trust and the company nominated by my client to manage the sale and promotion of his software program. That company is of course yours, which is called . . .' He searched among his notes.

'Carpe Diem,' I said helpfully.

'Yes, Carpe Diem.' He looked up and smiled affably. 'Interesting name. Now, the terms of the agreement are quite simple in essence. As I believe you know, your fee is to come from the total advertising budget of three million dollars, which in turn will be derived from sales of the program which are to be made via the medium of the Internet. The price charged for each program is to be the amount of five dollars.' He paused. 'Any excess funds are to be channelled into the trust for later distribution to charity. That's if there are any of course,' he added.

'I think you can pretty much count on it that there will be,' I said.

'Really?'

'You sound surprised.'

'Well, to be perfectly honest with you, I didn't know quite what to make of all this at first. I don't pretend to know a great deal about the type of program Mr Hoffman has devised, in fact he hasn't told me a great deal about it.'

'You haven't seen it then?'

'I'm completely in the dark. You, on the other hand, have had an opportunity to study it I presume?'

'We've seen enough to be convinced it lives up to your client's expectations,' I said. 'With two million dollars' worth of advertising behind it I think you can expect it to sell well in excess of a million copies in the first year. Perhaps a lot more.'

Brinkman absorbed this fact silently. 'You truly believe that?'

'I don't see why not.'

He shook his head slightly bemused. 'To be frank with you I wasn't certain that everything Mr Hoffman claimed about his program would be borne out in reality. He's an unusual character,' he added tactfully. It was clear that Brinkman had entertained the same initial misgivings as we had. 'It just goes to prove that we shouldn't judge by appearances,' he remarked. 'Nevertheless, isn't it true that this program competes directly with another? One that belongs to a company with, by comparison, almost infinite resources.'

'Spectrum Software are planning to sell their version for two hundred and fifty dollars. Against the five Hoffman is asking, that'd be a tough sell even if Hoffman's wasn't the better of the two.'

'And the one belonging to my client really is better in your opinion?'

'By a wide margin,' Marcus said, making his first contribution.

Brinkman digested that, appearing thoughtful. I had the impression that until now he hadn't taken any of this completely seriously.

Over the next half-hour he went through the main points the agreement would cover. It was pretty straight-forward and there was nothing there I didn't already know. He reiterated that our fee was fixed at a million in the first year and five hundred thousand thereafter which was all to come from sales, and that the remaining money would go to the trust for distribution to his client's nominated charity.

'Which charity?' I asked out of curiosity.

'Cancer research.'

When we were finished Brinkman rose from his desk and walked us to the door. 'By the way,' he mentioned casually. 'I meant to ask. I assume my client chose your company for this project because you've had previous dealings together?'

'No, but he knew we were involved with a bid for the Spectrum Software account recently,' I said. 'I guess that gave us an advantage.'

'I take it your bid wasn't successful then?'

'No. It went to KCM.'

'KCM? I've heard of them I think.'

'They handle all of Morgan Industries' business.'

'Really?' He held out his hand. 'Well, I'll see you again no doubt. If you leave the name of your lawyer with Carol I'll have something for him to look at in a few days.'

We shook hands and he opened the door for us. 'You know, it's really such a shame isn't it? If my client wasn't terminally ill he would soon be a very wealthy man. I mean if this program is as good as you say, and I'm sure you're right, he could have marketed it legitimately at a competitive price.'

'I suppose that's true,' I said.

'Still, I suppose that money isn't his motivation,' Brinkman mused.

Once we were in the elevator I thought about Brinkman, and though his manner was generally easy going and pleasant, I decided there was something about his seemingly casual questions that didn't ring quite true, and I made a mental note to tell our lawyer to check the agreement he received very carefully.

CHAPTER FOURTEEN

Nothing good lasts for ever, so they say, but I'd hoped for a little longer than a week. Copies of the contract that formed our agreement with Leonard Hoffman had been shuffling back and forth between the lawyers, both sides making alterations to the other's amendments and arguing about interpretation. They were doing their best to make a decent fee out of what amounted to a straight-forward deal, but nothing is ever easy once lawyers are involved. I spoke to Hoffman several times over the phone and he sounded as frustrated as I was.

'I told Brinkman I'm not going to live for ever,' he said one morning. He wanted to move things along, im-patient to see his program available on the Internet and the first stage of our advertising campaign up and run-ning so that he could confront Morgan.

'I want to see his face when I tell him I just cost him fifty million dollars,' he said with grim anticipation. He broke off then, coughing so badly I had to hold the phone away from my ear until he was finished. I winced as I imagined the damage being inflicted on his tattered lungs and when he came back on the line he sounded exhaus-ted. His voice had grown so weak I had to strain to hear him.

'I heard Spectrum are launching their program in August,' he said.

That was just a couple of months away. We needed to go

out around the same time to maximize the free amount of publicity we'd get on news websites devoted to this kind of thing, and hopefully that would lead to regular press coverage in the financial media. Time was getting short. We couldn't do a thing until we had a signed agreement to take to the bank so they would give us the short-term operating finance that we needed to cover our initial costs.

I was getting worried about Hoffman. Every time I spoke to him he sounded worse and sometimes I thought it was only his burning desire for revenge that kept him going. Finally our lawyer gave us the green light, and Brinkman's office called to set up a meeting for the morning when all parties would sign.

That night I called Sally and told her I would take care of dinner. On the way home I stopped by an Italian deli in North Beach and picked up a few ingredients. I planned to wilt some baby spinach leaves through linguine and then finish the dish off with the deli's own homemade pepperoni which I'd fry first in a little garlic and oil. To wash it down I splashed out on a bottle of '96 Australian Merlot.

'To us,' I said later, when Sally and I sat down to eat and we touched glasses.

'To us.'

When I went to refill her glass she covered it with her hand. 'Uh-uh. That's enough for me.'

'What's wrong? Don't you like it?'

She smiled a secretive smile. 'I just don't think I should.'

It took a moment for the penny to drop. 'You don't mean . . . ?'

She shook her head. 'No, I'm not pregnant. At least if I am I don't know it yet. But, well, we have been doing all the right things.'

I felt a lurch in my stomach, but if it showed in my expression Sally didn't notice. I reasoned to myself that it was a natural reaction, the small shock of coming to terms with the reality that if it hadn't happened yet, sooner or later it would. As Sally said herself, we'd been doing all the right things. I looked at her across the table. She appeared happy, her skin glowing in the soft light. I hadn't seen her this content in a long time. As I cleaned up after our meal, I thought to myself why shouldn't it happen right now? We were ready to sign the deal with Hoffman in the morning. Everything was coming together.

When I went upstairs Sally was wearing a nightdress, sitting in front of the mirror brushing her hair. I watched her as I got undressed and she smiled at me when our eyes met in the mirror.

'You're beautiful, you know that.'

I went over and kissed the back of her neck. She put down her brush and closed her eyes, smiling to herself. When I took her arms she stood and I lifted her nightdress over her head. From behind I laid my hands on her belly while she leaned back into me and we looked at our reflection. My hands strayed to her breasts.

'I guess we should have another go.'

'Do we have to?' she asked with mock resignation.

'Oh yes,' I said, pressing my erection against her buttocks. 'We do.'

She grinned. 'Well, since you insist.'

Our meeting was at ten-thirty in the morning, and by ten-forty everybody was assembled in Brinkman's office except for Leonard Hoffman. Brinkman checked his watch again and asked us for the third time if we had any questions about the contract. We didn't. Our lawyer had gone over it with us and we both had copies.

We had coffee while we waited, and as time dragged on Marcus got up and went over to a bookcase to examine Brinkman's library. Brinkman watched him as he took out a volume and started flicking through it. Marcus had dressed for the meeting in an old grey T-shirt and faded khaki cargo trousers.

'They're all law books I'm afraid,' Brinkman said with a faintly patronizing air. Light flashed on Marcus's glasses and he put the book back, then went on to examine some prints on the wall.

'I hope my client hasn't had a change of heart,' Brinkman joked.

Even though he hadn't been serious I thought it was an odd comment. 'Why would he do that?' I asked.

'No reason,' Brinkman said, but he quickly looked away. Marcus glanced at me from across the room, a little puzzled. I didn't say anything, and in the silence Brinkman smiled nervously. 'I did suggest he reconsider some of the terms he stipulated,' he confessed.

'Oh?'

'Nothing that directly affected your position,' he added hastily. 'But after our last meeting I did some research. It seems to me that if my client's program is as good as you believe it to be, then to sell it for five dollars is ridiculous. I suggested he might like to reconsider.'

'What did he say?'

Brinkman frowned. 'He wasn't enthusiastic.'

I wasn't surprised. Hoffman would give the program away for nothing if he could. The five dollar tag was only to cover advertising costs. 'You have to remember,' I pointed out, 'he's not interested in making money. He wants as many people as possible to know about his program so they'll download his instead of buying Morgan's. He wants revenge.'

'Yes, that's what he said,' Brinkman mused.

He took a sip of coffee from the china cup that was part of the service his assistant had served us from, then he got up and went to the window and gazed out over the streets below.

'Can I ask you something?' he said suddenly. There was a distinctly casual note in his tone that sounded entirely artificial. As if he wanted to give the impression that something he'd been considering for some time had only just occurred to him. 'What do you make of Leonard Hoffman?'

'Make of him?'

'His . . . state of mind?'

'He seems rational,' I said cautiously. I wondered where Brinkman was going with this.

'He's very ill, as you know.'

'He has lung cancer. As far as I know that doesn't affect a person's brain.'

'No. Well, perhaps not the disease itself. But the medication? I don't know. You have to admit what he's doing is a little unusual.'

'Perhaps.'

'Did you know that Morgan Industries paid forty million dollars for Spectrum Software?'

'Yes, I knew that.'

'Interesting man, Nelson Morgan. You know that of all the companies he's bought, their value has increased by an average three hundred and fifty per cent during the first five years. Of course one of the things Morgan does is bring investment funds to cash-starved companies, but it's his ability to spot potential that's remarkable.'

I wondered what Brinkman was leading up to. Even Marcus was listening now, and he came back over and sat down.

'Of course you know quite a lot about Spectrum don't you?' Brinkman said. 'How much, in your opinion, do you think they will spend marketing their program?'

'I don't know exactly,' I answered.

'A guess.'

'Ten million perhaps. Based on what Morgan paid for the company, he must be prepared to invest at least that much.'

'Yes,' Brinkman agreed thoughtfully. 'You know I did some rough calculations, just for interest. Morgan will invest fifty million dollars, let's say, all told. If his expectations for Spectrum are in line with past history, he must be expecting this program to reach sales of anything upwards of a hundred and fifty million dollars.' He paused, smiling. 'Remarkable.'

'What is exactly?' Marcus asked.

Brinkman shrugged. 'I was referring to my client's motivation, I suppose. Revenge as Mr Weston pointed out. It struck me that this only goes to prove that we're not always a logical species.'

'Is that why you mentioned the medication Mr Hoffman is taking?' Marcus questioned. 'You're wondering if what he's doing is logical?'

'Perhaps rational is the term I would use.'

'He's dying,' Marcus said. 'Revenge isn't an unusual motive for anything and never has been. The only difference here is the way it's applied. Your client has no use for money. It seems rational enough to me.'

'Yes. Of course, you have no reason to question his actions do you?'

I didn't like what he was implying. 'Meaning?'

'I understand that this contract comes at an opportune time for you.'

I wondered how much research he had done, and what exactly he knew. Before I could ask him his phone rang and he picked it up and listened for a moment. When he put it down he said his assistant had tried Hoffman's number but there was no answer.

'He must be on his way,' Brinkman said. He shot his sleeve and looked at his watch. 'Unfortunately I have another appointment. I'm afraid I'm going to have to leave you with Carol for a little while, but by the time I'm done, he ought to have arrived.'

'That's fine,' I said, getting to my feet. 'But actually we have another meeting of our own, so what we might do is come back in say an hour?'

'Of course. That's probably a good idea,' Brinkman said.

Marcus shot me a puzzled look but had the sense to know I must have a reason for inventing another meeting and he waited until we were in the elevator before he said anything.

'What meeting?'

'There's no meeting, I just have a feeling that something's wrong.' I looked at my watch and then took out my cell phone and tried Hoffman's apartment, but I got no answer.

'What was he angling at in there do you think?'

'Brinkman? I don't know. But I don't trust him.' I thought for a moment then I said, 'I think we should go out to Hoffman's apartment and make sure everything's okay. This time of day we can be there in thirty minutes.'

'What if he turns up here?'

'If we don't find him, we'll call and see if he's arrived and say we're on our way. No harm done.'

Ten minutes later we were heading towards the bridge. I drove as fast as I dared without running the risk of getting stopped by the traffic cops on the way out to San Leandro. On the way I had a little time to think ahead and I parked several blocks away from Hoffman's apartment building. Marcus shot me a puzzled look.

'Why are we stopping here?'

I had my reasons, but I didn't give them. Instead I said something about not wanting to have to pay those hoodlums a hundred bucks not to steal my car.

We passed plenty of people on the way to the building but nobody paid us any special attention. Marcus's dress code fitted right in with the area, and I didn't look too out of place in black jeans and a white polo shirt. When we reached the corner I saw the steps where Pepe and the other two Latino kids had lounged on our previous visit were empty. As we entered the building I checked to see if anyone had noticed us, but it appeared that nobody had. When we reached the second floor I knocked several times, but there was no answer. Along the hall a door opened a crack, and then closed again. I supposed it was the nosy girl neighbour we'd seen before but I didn't think she could have got more than a glimpse at us, and it was gloomy on the landing. I tried the door one more time, then I took out a Swiss Army Knife and opened the biggest blade. Marcus stared at it.

'I keep it in the car,' I said casually. 'I've always thought it would be useful one day.'

'You're going to break in?' he said.

'Unless you want to do it?'

He didn't answer, so I went ahead and worked the blade into the space between the doorjamb and the door, then slid it down to the lock. I don't know what I expected to happen, except that in the movies it looked easy. But nothing happened except that the blade met solid resistance. I worked away at it for several minutes while Marcus looked on wearing a disapproving frown, until finally I acknowledged that it wasn't going to work. I opened up all the tools on the knife, and there was one that was a long spike of steel. I'd often wondered what it was for. Whatever its real purpose, it worked well as a lock pick. It took me fifteen seconds of wiggling and fiddling to trip the lock, and a moment later we were inside the apartment. I closed the door quietly behind us.

I think by then Marcus had figured out what I was thinking, and the moment we were inside we both knew I was right.

'Christ!'

He covered his mouth and nose with his sleeve, and I did the same. The weather had been warm over the past few days, and the smell of disease and death was thick in the air. Out on the landing the sulphurous stench of animal urine mingled with the heavier cloying smells of cooking, not that I ever wanted to taste whatever ingredients combined to produce such a stink, but inside the apartment the air was steadily putrefying. I breathed through my mouth as we went along the passage and paused at the bedroom door. The window that opened onto the alley was open a little, enough to let in the flies that had been attracted to the corpse. Perhaps a dozen of them, big fat and black, took to the air and buzzed lazily. One of them smacked drunkenly into my face and careered off as I slapped at it in disgusted horror.

Hoffman lay face up on the bed, his face caved in, a brown stain on the bedspread and rug which I assumed was some bloody mess he'd coughed up. The medicine bottle he'd freely glugged from lay on its side on the floor in the corner where I suppose it must have rolled. The flies we'd briefly disturbed returned to their feast and one walked across an open eye. Something tiny wriggled near the corner of his open mouth and I looked away and stepping back pulled the door to.

I took a deep breath. Marcus looked white. We all know that we're going to die some day, and all we can hope for is that when we do we've lived a long and satisfying life and that we haven't caused too much misery to others along the way. To be faced with what we will become, just rotting meat to feed the maggots and foul the air is an unpalatable truth.

Marcus started towards the living room and I went after him. I went into the kitchen and repeatedly rinsed out a cup. I wouldn't drink from it until I was certain I had sluiced it thoroughly as if I feared death was a communicable disease. When I returned to the living room Marcus was just about to pick up the phone.

'What are you doing?'

'Calling an ambulance.'

I went over and disconnected the line and then took the receiver off him and replaced it. 'He doesn't need an ambulance.'

'We have to tell someone,' Marcus protested. I looked around at all the equipment in the room and then we stared at each other. He knew what I was thinking.

'Why?' I said.

CHAPTER FIFTEEN

'Dead?' Sally echoed when I told her that night about Hoffman. 'Oh that's terrible. How?'

'His cancer I guess.'

I tossed a salad while Sally paused in the act of serving broiled chicken stuffed with goat's cheese. She looked at the food on the table, the open bottle of wine.

'It doesn't seem right somehow does it? I know it's silly. People are dying all the time, but still . . .'

I knew what she meant. I assumed Brinkman would have become worried about his client and by then Hoffman would have been discovered. He was probably lying in cold storage somewhere, a hollowed cadaver with a toe tag, and we were about to sit down and eat. The endless rhythm of life. Babies are born, people die and for the living the world turns just the same. We remain consumed with the trivia of our existence. The lawn still needs mowing, the car washing, and so on and so on. When we're gone we leave an empty space and nobody even notices. Unless we have children to carry our genes forward into new generations. Is that what it's all about I wondered?

'Nick?' Sally said, giving me a strange look.

'I was just thinking about what you said.' I shrugged and carried on with what I was doing. It was only then that Sally started thinking about the implications of Hoffman's demise for Carpe Diem.

'Wait a second, you were signing the contract this morning . . .'

'Didn't happen,' I completed the thought. 'He'd been dead a day or two. Apparently.'

'What does that mean?' Sally asked. She hadn't begun eating yet, though a combination of hunger and the need to do something distracting made me take a bite of the chicken. It was good.

'I guess the trust Hoffman's lawyer set up owns the program now. Which Brinkman administers.'

'So, as far as Carpe Diem's concerned nothing's changed,' Sally reasoned, relief creeping into her voice.

'In theory.' I forked more chicken into my mouth.

'You don't sound sure.'

'That's because I'm not.' I told her about the conversation that took place in Brinkman's office while we were waiting for Hoffman to show up. 'He'd been digging around for information about us. And I didn't like what he was inferring about Hoffman's state of mind.'

'What are you saying?'

'I don't trust him, Sally. Think about it. Here's a lawyer in a downtown firm who has a client who wants to give away a fortune, which is what this amounts to. That program is worth a lot of money, and Brinkman knows it. What Hoffman had planned goes against Brinkman's natural instinct.'

'But surely he has to do what Hoffman wanted. Won't that be in the terms of the trust?'

'I don't know exactly what the trust stipulates, but my guess is that it lays out Hoffman's intent, not the mechanics. I don't think there will be anything in there that requires Brinkman to use Carpe Diem, for example. That part was a separate contract.'

'You mean he could use another agency? But why would he want to do that?'

I stopped eating and put down my knife and fork. I wanted to explain this carefully because it was important that Sally go along with my reasoning. 'What if he wanted to change the whole deal? Maybe he decided to claim that Hoffman was mentally unfit to reach the kind of decisions he was making. He might want to try to alter the terms of the trust, and he might decide it was a good idea to appoint himself in some kind of consulting role to work with the agency. I don't know. I'm just saying that I think Brinkman never liked this deal in the first place, but now that Hoffman is dead he'll try to find a way to change it so that he benefits in some way. In which case it's almost certain he'll find an excuse to cut Carpe Diem out. He'll probably claim we were not the best choice. That we're financially unstable. He'll think of something so he can appoint people who don't have any preconceived notions about Hoffman's original intent. That way he has more control, and nobody to dispute whatever he does.'

I had figured all of this out between leaving Brinkman's office and driving back to the city from San Leandro. Much of it out loud with Marcus, so I'd had practice as well as time to hone my rationale. I'd been persuasive enough to get Marcus to agree not to say anything to anybody until the morning at least, though he'd acceded only reluctantly in the end. The hard part with Sally was coming, and I still hadn't figured out a way to tell her what so far I had left out.

She considered what I'd said. I started eating again, though she still hadn't touched either her meal or the glass of wine she'd allowed herself. Her brow was creased as she thought through what I'd said.

'Surely if Brinkman did try to do any of these things, you could challenge him in court,' she said at length.

'Possibly,' I said, sounding patently unconvinced. 'But

he's a lawyer, Sally. He knows what he's doing. I don't even know what the terms of the trust state for sure, and maybe nobody else does. Who's to say he wouldn't just alter it and nobody would be the wiser.'

Now it was Sally's turn to be sceptical. 'Isn't that being slightly paranoid? I know how important that contract is to you, but you're making Brinkman sound like some kind of crooked small-time attorney.'

'Just because a guy has a downtown office and wears a thousand-dollar suit doesn't automatically mean he's honest. The biggest crooks of all are lawyers, they just use words to steal money instead of guns. And a lot less of them get caught.'

I set down my cutlery, and refilled my wine glass. 'The chicken was great.'

Sally looked at her own untouched plate then back at mine. 'You're taking all this very calmly,' she remarked, sounding puzzled.

'Am I?'

'Yes. If you're so concerned that Brinkman might try something that cuts you out, how come you can sit there and talk it over this way?'

I avoided her eye. 'You can see it's a possibility?'

She didn't answer right away and when she did she sounded suspicious. 'Is there something I don't know? What did Brinkman say when you found out Hoffman was dead anyway?'

'He didn't say anything.'

'Nothing?'

'I mean I haven't spoken to him since then.'

'I don't understand.'

'Brinkman doesn't even know that we're aware that Hoffman died,' I said. 'When he didn't turn up for our meeting Marcus and I left. We were supposed to go back later but I called and left a message to say that something had come up and we'd be in touch in the morning.'

Sally appeared baffled. 'But I assumed it was Brinkman that told you. If it wasn't him, then how did you know . . . ?'

'That Hoffman was dead? We went to his apartment. It was Marcus and I who found him.'

'But didn't you tell Brinkman after you reported it? I don't understand, Nick. What are you trying to tell me?'

'I'm saying that we found Hoffman dead, and we thought the best thing to do was not let anyone know we'd been to his apartment.'

'You mean you found him and you left again . . . ?But how did you get inside if he was dead? Nick, what did you do?' Sally stared at me. 'For God's sake, will you please tell me what's going on?'

I took a breath, and I related how we'd driven over to San Leandro and how we'd broken into Hoffman's apartment when nobody answered the door. 'I thought he might be hurt and couldn't come to the door or something.'

'But he was dead?'

'Yes. And the reason we didn't call the authorities is because we had just been talking to Brinkman. You have to understand, Sally. I don't trust him. I knew if we didn't do something he would find a way not to sign the agreement. Without this deal Carpe Diem is finished. The bank isn't going to wait around while Brinkman ties us up in legal knots and takes his time. I couldn't take that chance.'

Sally stared at me as all this sunk in, then she said, 'What did you do, Nick?'

I took a deep breath. 'We took the program. Marcus copied it onto a disc and erased the original off the hard-drive on Hoffman's computer.'

Her eyes widened. 'You stole it?'

224

'No.' I shook my head. 'We took it into safe keeping.'

'Please, at least have the honesty to call it what it is. You stole it, Nick.'

'No,' I insisted. 'Hoffman wanted his program on the net, and he wanted us to make sure people knew about it. He didn't care about money, all he cared about was getting his revenge on Morgan. But do you honestly believe Brinkman is going to think the same way? There isn't a chance. You weren't there today, you didn't see the way he was talking, how he'd figured out that Morgan was expecting to make sales of a hundred and fifty million dollars or more from the Spectrum program. There's no way he's going to let an opportunity like this slip by without trying to figure a way of making money from it.'

'But you don't even know that any of that is true. You have no idea what Brinkman will do.'

'But what if I'm right? At least if I have the program we have some negotiating power.'

'And what if Brinkman insists you hand it over? If the trust is the legal owner he's entitled to do that isn't he?'

'Maybe. I don't know. I haven't thought that through yet.'

'Don't you see, even if you're completely right about Brinkman, it doesn't matter. There's nothing you can do. You can't just go ahead without a contract. The bank won't give you the finance you need without it. And Brinkman will find out anyway. He'll stop you. You could go to jail.'

She was right. Marcus had come up with the same arguments. But even so I knew we weren't completely lost. 'So long as we have the program, we have the upper hand,' I said. 'We can negotiate. You know what they say. Possession is nine tenths of the law.'

Sally looked at me and I could see she wasn't buying it. I knew what she was thinking, I could see it in her eyes as clearly as if it was written there. She was afraid the fragile dream she'd entertained that from now on everything would be okay, that our lives would become normal, was beginning to disintegrate.

She pushed aside her meal. 'I'm not hungry.'

CHAPTER SIXTEEN

Brinkman called the next morning to give me the news. 'Leonard Hoffman is dead,' he said, after Stacey put him through.

'Dead? That's terrible,' I said, affecting disbelief. 'I knew he was sick of course, but still . . .' I was lost for words. 'When did it happen?'

'A few days ago apparently. Obviously that's why he failed to arrive for our meeting yesterday.'

'That would explain it,' I agreed.

Brinkman paused, a silent censure of my inappropriate humour. He went on, 'When I didn't hear from him I contacted the authorities. He died in his apartment.'

'Really?'

'Yes.' There was a long pause, then he said, 'Incidentally, my secretary told me you called to say you couldn't make it back yesterday. She said you wanted to reschedule.'

He tried to make his remark sound casual. Difficult in the circumstances, but especially when he couldn't conceal the hint of suspicion in his voice.

'Yes. Something came up.'

'It must have been important.'

'It was.' I decided it was time to move our conversation on. 'You're still the executor of Hoffman's trust I suppose?'

'Yes.'

'I mean what's happened is terrible, but Hoffman knew he was dying. I assume we sign the contract with you and everything goes ahead as planned.'

In the silence that followed I imagined Brinkman sitting at his desk across town, trying to figure out all the angles. 'Well, of course this is all unexpected. I'll need to look at exactly what the provisions of the trust are,' he answered evasively. 'In the meantime I think we ought to delay putting any plans in place. I assume you have a copy of the program at your office?'

Of course he knew Hoffman would never have given us a copy before a contract had been signed, so was he just fishing or did he already suspect something? I wasn't sure, but I wasn't ready to admit anything until I had a better idea of what he intended to do.

'So, how long will that take, for you to look into the trust provisions?' I asked.

'That depends,' he answered. 'These matters aren't always straightforward.'

'But you drew up the trust yourself didn't you? And nothing's really changed except that Hoffman died sooner than he expected to.'

'There may be some legal issues to explore.'

I wasn't sure if he was delaying because he didn't want to admit the program was missing, or if it was because I'd been right about him, that if he got his hands on the program we could kiss goodbye to the original deal. Probably any deal.

There was a short silence. 'Actually there may be a problem,' he admitted finally.

'A problem?'

'There's some uncertainty as to where exactly the program is.'

I counted to four, as if I was absorbing the implications of this. 'I don't follow.'

'I mean,' he said, his voice tightly controlled, 'that it's missing. The police think that somebody may have broken into Hoffman's apartment before his body was discovered.'

I allowed a pause, then I said, 'Are you telling me somebody stole it?' I tried to sound incredulous.

'That's the way it looks.'

'I can't believe this. Who would do that? Who else knew about it? It's not something Hoffman would have made general knowledge.'

'A good question.' Brinkman made it sound loaded with meaning. So, he did suspect it was me, I thought.

I waited. I thought about the neighbour who'd opened her door and who must have seen Marcus and me in the hall. Though it was gloomy and she couldn't have had more than a fleeting impression of us, she might have recognized us from our previous visit. But if she'd already told this to the police I doubted we would be having this conversation over the phone. More likely a squad of cops with Brinkman looking on would have descended on us in the early hours of the morning.

'So, what happens now?' I asked.

'Well, assuming that somebody is in possession of the program, it won't do them any good,' Brinkman said. 'Anyone trying to sell it will find themselves arrested and charged.'

He allowed a pause, to be certain I absorbed what he was telling me.

'Of course, once the program is recovered, we can proceed with the contract as planned.'

'I thought you needed to look at the provisions of the trust,' I reminded him.

'That's true. But I'm sure if there are any details that need to be adjusted they will be minor ones.'

It seemed clear to me that Brinkman had strong

suspicions, but the problem I was beginning to see, was that if I admitted that he was right, and I used that fact to hold him to signing any kind of deal there was nothing stopping him from reneging straight away. No contract entered into under those circumstances would ever stand scrutiny in court. He could alter the trust, make any kind of claim and not only sue us but have us charged with stealing, as well as maybe adding extortion, blackmail and fraud which were all federal crimes. Enough to land Marcus and me in jail for fifty years anyway. We were at an impasse. I didn't see how I could possibly admit anything until I'd had a chance to think this through.

I told Brinkman to let me know if there were any developments. He seemed surprised when it was clear I was going to hang up.

Sally was home before me, and as soon as I walked through the door I knew she'd been thinking all day about what I'd done. She asked if I'd spoken to Brinkman, and when I said that I had she appeared to steel herself a little.

'What happened?'

I told her what he'd said. 'I still don't trust him.'

'So, you didn't tell him you had the program?'

'No.'

Her mouth tightened. 'What are you going to do?' she asked sharply.

'I thought this was something we should all discuss. I asked Marcus to come round later.' I thought she'd be pleased that I wasn't planning to do anything without everyone else agreeing and having their say first. Instead her expression was clouded by all kinds of emotions I couldn't interpret. I knew she was angry, disappointed in me even, but it seemed there was more than that.

'I need to get changed.' She turned and fled the room.

I went after her but when I reached the bedroom she went into the bathroom and closed the door. A moment later I heard the shower turned on. I got changed myself and by the time I was ready she hadn't come out so I went to the bathroom door but paused before I went in. I didn't know what I would say to her. Perhaps it would be better, I thought, to wait for Marcus to arrive, so that all of us could discuss what we should do.

I went downstairs and opened a bottle of wine and took some glasses into the living room. When Sally came down it was almost eight. She gave an edgy smile.

I went over. 'We're just going to talk,' I said. I leaned to kiss her, but she moved and my lips brushed her cheek instead of her mouth.

'I think I heard a car.'

'Right.'

I went to the door to let Marcus in and was surprised to find he wasn't alone. Alice offered me a thin smile. She was dressed in jeans that clung to her long legs and a fitted white T-shirt. As she stepped past, ignoring my evident surprise she offered me a look that would have frozen an Eskimo.

'You're back together?' I said quietly to Marcus.

He hesitated, then shook his head. I could only assume that he imagined they would be, however, at some point, and had therefore decided she had as much right to be involved as any of us. I didn't like it, especially as I saw Alice wouldn't make the job of persuading the others round to my way of thinking any easier, but I could see I didn't have a choice.

Sally was waiting in the living room, a glass of wine already in her hand. She forced a brief smile and for a second or two we made an uncomfortable foursome. This was the first time we'd all been together since the night of the exhibition. Alice emanated coldness and the tension between her and Marcus was palpable. Add to that how things were between Sally and me and between Marcus and me and it seemed like everybody was doing their best to avoid looking directly at anybody else. The room was charged with invisible currents.

I poured wine and passed the glasses around and when I reached Alice she accepted hers with a curl of her lip.

'What are we celebrating? Or is this a wake? That must be it. We can drink to Mr Hoffman and to the demise of Carpe Diem at the same time.' She looked at each of us with a sardonic gleam in her eye. 'Isn't this nice. All of us together again.' She raised her glass in an ironic toast. 'To the great Nick Weston. Entrepreneur extraordinaire.'

'This isn't helpful,' I said. 'We have things to discuss.'

'Oh really? I'm sorry, is that why we're here? And what things exactly do we have to discuss?' She gave me a caustic smile. 'I knew it was all too good to be true. I told Marcus you would end up ruining us all and I was right.'

'Alice . . .' Marcus said.

'No, let her say what's on her mind.' I figured we may as well get it out of the way.

'You mean I have your permission to speak?' she said with heavy sarcasm. 'I'm so grateful.'

'If it's going to make you feel any better,' I told her.

'Don't patronize me! It's because of you we're here in the first place remember. I knew as soon as I heard all about this Hoffman character that it would be another one of your schemes that ends in disaster. And I was right. It's all turned to dust and what's going to happen now? I'll tell you, the bank is going to call in your loan and that will be the end of Carpe Diem, not to mention that none of us will have anywhere to live. Congratulations, Nick Weston strikes again!'

Both Marcus and Sally were looking on apprehensively, uncertain what to expect. I'd had enough of Alice. Even if what she was saying was partly true I didn't have to listen to her rub my face in it.

'You know, I don't even know why I should have to take this crap from you,' I said. 'I don't even know what it has to do with you anyway.'

'What the hell does that mean? It has as much to do with me as it does Sally,' she said.

'Sally and I are married. We've been together for almost nine years. You didn't even know Marcus when we started Carpe Diem. Not that you let that get in the way of having your say whenever you felt like it.'

'And why shouldn't I have a say? Maybe you could walk all over Marcus but you can't do it to me. You just hate that don't you? You like to have things all your own way. You make all the decisions and Marcus has to go along whether he agrees with you or not. Because you know best. Isn't that so, Nick? You've always resented me because I tried to get him to stand up to you.'

'I resented you?' I said in disbelief. 'That's rich. You know what your trouble is, Alice. You hate it that I make a living from something as low and detestable as advertising, while you with your precious fucking art scratch around to make a few hundred dollars here and there. That's what this is all about. Plain and simple. And now you're pissed off because you're going to lose the comfortable lifestyle you've been enjoying over there in Sausalito. The cozy house, your studio, all of it paid for by Marcus.'

My voice was raised, and I was enjoying every second of this. I was finally getting off my chest some of the stuff I'd always felt.

'But of course,' I added, snapping my fingers as if I'd just remembered something. 'You're not living in the house right now are you? What happened, Alice? See the writing on the wall and figure you might as well leave since the pot is about all empty?'

Her hand shot out with incredible speed. I saw a blur and then felt the resounding impact as she slapped my face. 'You really are an odious bastard.'

There was a shocked silence, apart from the ringing in my ears. My face was stinging painfully. It felt like everyone was holding their breath. A voice in my head said I should let it go, but I didn't listen. I grinned.

'What's the matter, Alice? Truth hurt?'

Suddenly she became calm, and smiled menacingly. 'The truth? Would you like to hear the truth, Nick?'

I was struck by the taunting note in her voice, the sly cadence that made me think of the way a cat plays with a mouse before dispatching it with a careless flick of sharp claws. For a second the room seemed to vibrate with something she was implying.

'I thought we were supposed to be here to decide what to do about Hoffman's program,' Marcus asked suddenly, breaking the silence.

'You're right,' I said.

'The program?' Alice echoed, looking at Marcus.

'I was going to tell you on the way over here.'

I gathered he hadn't got the chance. No doubt they had been fighting all the way from Sausalito. He explained how we'd come to have it, and for once I saw Alice was thrown and she fell silent as she pondered this new information.

'You have to give the program to Brinkman,' Sally said after a moment.

'If we do that, he's going to cut us out of the deal,' I countered.

'You don't know that.'

I went through it all again, so we all understood how things were. I repeated my conversation with Brinkman, explaining again my reasons for not trusting him, and why if we tried to do a deal with him he could renege

234

the moment he had the program and have us arrested.

'This is all pure guesswork,' Sally argued.

'Perhaps. But you heard him too, Marcus,' I appealed. 'Perhaps I've got all this wrong. Maybe Brinkman is really a stand-up guy and he gives half his salary to charity. But I could be right, and what if I am? Are we prepared to take a chance over this? Once we admit we have the program, the ball is in Brinkman's court. We're at his mercy. That's a chance I'm personally not prepared to take.'

'A chance you're not prepared to take, Nick?' Sally echoed. 'I thought this was a decision we should take together.'

'I meant us.'

'No, you didn't.' She shook her head. 'You've already decided in your own mind haven't you?'

Alice made a snorting sound of derision, as if this was no surprise to her. She said, 'Brinkman must know you have the program anyway. Somebody must have seen you go to Hoffman's apartment.'

'He might suspect, but he doesn't know for sure,' I said. 'If he did the police would have been all over us by now. I parked a few blocks away to make sure we weren't seen.'

Sally stared at me. 'You mean you planned this?' Her voice became leaden with understanding. 'You knew he was dead.'

'I didn't know. When he didn't show up to sign the contract I thought there was a chance, that's all.'

'No. You had this all figured out,' Sally said. 'You went there because you knew Hoffman was dead and you intended to steal that program.'

There was silence while everyone, it appeared, contemplated the depths to which I was prepared to plunge. Was it true, I asked myself? Perhaps. Partly. In so much as I was already suspicious of Brinkman, and maybe it had occurred to me that Hoffman was dead. He was a sick man. I looked at the others, who were all staring at me.

'For chrissakes,' I protested. 'It isn't like I killed him. You think that what Brinkman would do if he gets his hands on that program is any better? He'll steal it from us. Without that deal Carpe Diem is finished. We're broke. Is that what we all want?' I appealed to Sally. 'Is that what you want? We'll lose this house, everything. We'll have to start all over. I don't even know if I could get a job in this town now.' I discounted Dexter's offer, which was beyond contemplation. 'Do you really want that to happen, Sally, right now when everything is going well for us again?' The implication was clear. The family she wanted, our future happiness, it was all at stake.

I could see she was thinking about it, but there was a look of faint condemnation in her eye. She seemed to resent what I was saying, as if she thought I was using a not very subtle form of blackmail. I might as well have waved one of those baby magazines she was always reading in her face.

'Hoffman chose us to market his program,' I said, calmly, reasonably. 'Let's not forget that. He didn't know he was going to die before he signed the contract. We're not actually doing anything morally wrong here. Technically maybe we are, and Brinkman would argue that for sure, but who believes lawyers are the moral guardians of the truth?'

There was a short silence, then Marcus spoke.

'Aren't we forgetting something here. Even if we kept the program, what can we do with it? Brinkman would know we stole it.'

I was conscious of them all looking at me, but mostly Sally who was staring as it dawned on her that I hadn't brought them all together without having an answer to this very obvious and problematic question. I avoided her eye. 'It's true there's no way we can sell the program the way Hoffman intended. If we do Brinkman will jump on us. But the fact is if we hand it over, we get nothing, but Brinkman will make damn sure he profits from it. That can't be right can it?'

I wanted them to agree, so at least they were partly on my side but they just stared back waiting for me to get on with it.

'So, I think we ought to sell the program to the one other person who will want to buy it.' I paused. 'Nelson Morgan.'

There was silence in the room for several seconds as they each thought about what I was suggesting.

'Hear me out,' I went on. 'If the deal had gone ahead as planned, who was going to be the big loser? Spectrum Software, which is in effect Morgan Industries. It would cost them millions of dollars. Tens of millions. Their stock would take a beating. Which of course is exactly what Hoffman intended. So, think about what Morgan would pay to prevent that happening. What would you pay if you were him?'

Abruptly Sally turned and started for the door. 'I don't want to hear any more of this.'

'Wait a minute. Shouldn't we at least discuss this before anyone makes up their mind. That can't hurt can it?'

She stopped and looked back at me. 'For God's sake, Nick. You were talking about what was right and wrong before. You claimed there was nothing morally wrong in taking the program. But now you're suggesting doing something that is the exact opposite of what Hoffman intended.'

'I know that,' I said. 'And if there was a way we could go along with the original deal, I would. But that isn't an option.'

'Would you?' she asked me, her eyes searching mine. 'Is that really true?'

'Of course,' I replied but I could see she didn't believe me. 'Look, if you think about it Hoffman's plan wasn't exactly born of altruism. The man was bitter and twisted. What he intended would have damaged Morgan's stock and probably been the end of Spectrum. People would lose their jobs, and investors would lose their money. Not just Morgan but the little stock holders as well. The innocent guy on the street who plays the market with his savings. How can that be such a great thing?'

'I can't believe I'm hearing this. You're trying to justify yourself. You're turning things around to suit you. It doesn't matter what Hoffman wanted, or that Morgan would be ruined, or that you couldn't trust Brinkman. This is about you, Nick. It's about what you want.'

I always knew that trying to convince Sally on the moral front was going to be a long shot, so I abandoned that idea. 'The fact is we have a choice here. Either we take our chances with Brinkman, and I believe if we do that we lose everything, or we sell the program to Morgan. That's what I want, and why not? You think Brinkman is such an upright citizen, or that Hoffman was a terrific person, or that Morgan would care about the ethics? This is about saving everything we have, and it isn't going to hurt anybody. So why not?'

'Because it doesn't belong to us.'

And there it was, a dividing line which separated us. For Sally it all came down to that one simple fact, unsullied by whatever muddy waters my rhetoric stirred up. She looked at me with silent appeal. I envied her in a way, because she could cut through all the pros and cons and see to the heart of the issue. I knew deep inside that she was right, but I simply couldn't accept it. Several seconds passed.

'This isn't about me,' I said finally. 'Whatever we do, it has to be something we agree on, a majority decision.'

'And if we decide against it?' Sally asked.

I hesitated, but I knew this was the only way I could hang onto whatever respect she still had for me. 'I'll go along with it,' I agreed.

She turned to Marcus, and suddenly the pressure was entirely on him. 'What do you think?' she asked.

As I waited for Marcus to answer I knew I was lost. I didn't even consider Alice. Her vote was certain to be against anything I was for. I suddenly wondered why I'd ever thought I could persuade them.

But it was Alice who spoke first, not Marcus.

'How much do you think Morgan will pay?'

It's not an exaggeration to say that the change in the atmosphere was immediate and electric. The implication of that one question and the strange intensity with which she looked at me was clear to us all.

'It's hard to say,' I managed to answer at last.

'You've thought about this, Nick. You must have some idea.'

And she was right. I did. 'Morgan Industries stock is valued at almost a billion dollars,' I said at last. 'He paid forty million for Spectrum, and I figure he expects to get that back five fold.' I took a breath. 'I guess he wouldn't mind paying another, say, thirty million dollars to protect his investment.'

Nobody spoke, nobody breathed. It was Alice who finally broke the silence.

'I think Marcus and I need to talk alone.'

We gave them five minutes, which is all it took. Sally and I waited in the kitchen where she gazed out the window and refused to look at me. I tried talking to her, but when she refused to reply I gave up. When we went back through it was Alice who did the talking.

'Marcus and I agree that we should do as you suggest, Nick,' she said calmly.

I thought it was a joke. I looked at Marcus but he wore a heavily resigned expression as if he had switched off from what was happening.

Only Sally, when I looked at her, showed no surprise.

CHAPTER SEVENTEEN

Nelson Morgan lived on the peninsula near Woodside in the hills above Palo Alto, in a house from where I gathered he spent much of his time running his empire. Getting to see him proved to be about as easy as making an appointment with the President. It took several calls to Morgan Industries' headquarters before I was finally able to persuade somebody to give me the number of one of Morgan's assistants, and then it took several more calls after that to get through to the keeper of his diary. I imagined that was her title: Keeper Of The Diary. Like some handmaiden to a god. When I spoke to her she sounded like somebody whose last job was with the security police in some totalitarian state. I envisaged an über efficient assistant, with severe unsmiling features. She demanded to know my business and when I told her it was of a personal and confidential nature she curtly informed me that Mr Morgan was unavailable.

'Then I'll leave a message,' I said. I told her that I had something belonging to Leonard Hoffman that I was certain would be of interest to her boss, and gave her my name and number. She called back within the hour and gave me an address where she said I would be expected the following morning at ten. Then abruptly she hung up.

The following day I took the 280 freeway to Woodside, and then headed towards La Honda until I found the turnoff that led up through canyons of tall trees and wound in meandering curves through the hills. Every now and then the woods gave way to broad open vistas of the ocean on my right, the distant sea cobalt blue in the sunshine. I passed the occasional turnoff which invariably led to a gate set back from the road a discreet distance and flanked by a fence on either side. This was real estate for the seriously rich, many of them people who'd made their money in Silicon Valley. As I slowed down, looking for 2026 Ocean View Road, I wondered about the people who lived up here in their mansions that lay tucked away among the trees, hidden from prying eyes, with the views of the ocean and the wooded hills all around. The suburbs and the freeways that were clogged with traffic during the early and late commuter rushes belonged to another world. These people lived lives completely foreign to the rest of us. I tried to comprehend how it would feel to never have to think about money again. For most of us balancing the budget to pay the mortgage, household bills, taxes, insurances, vacations, the kids' education and all the hundred and one other expenses that suck up every cent we earn is a lifelong struggle. It never ends, and making the money to cover it all occupies the greater part of our waking hours. There is almost nothing that we do, or think about doing, or wish that we could do, that is not affected by our ability to pay for it. But the people who lived up here were free from all of that.

I drove slowly, both because I didn't want to miss Morgan's house and because I was caught up in my own thoughts. At one point I glanced in the mirror and saw a car on my tail about a quarter of a mile back. As I rounded the next bend I started looking for a place to pull over to let it pass. I stopped and waited, but the car didn't appear, so I figured it must have turned into one of the gates. The road to the bend behind me remained empty, so after a couple of minutes I started off again.

My thoughts drifted back to money and what it really is. Freedom from everyday financial constraint is a difficult concept to grasp until you really start to think about it. I wasn't under the illusion that money automatically makes people happy, but I did believe it releases us from a hell of a lot of the strains and pressures and frustrations of everyday life that are a hindrance to happiness. I likened it to for ever climbing a hill, and the going is tough. Sometimes you come across a part where the slope isn't as steep, and you can even take a moment to enjoy the view, but a lot of the time you're breathing hard and your head is down watching where you put your feet in case you stumble and fall, and sometimes the cloud gathers around and the wind gets up and tries to whip you off the hillside altogether and the rain lashes down. Then you get through that and the cloud parts and you're in a patch of sunshine for a while and the going is a little easier. And so it goes, our lives an endless struggle upwards with brief interludes of sunshine. But for the very rich things are different. They have reached the top, clambered over the ridge, and they find themselves suddenly in a for ever sunny meadow filled with wildflowers and humming insects and pleasant breezes, and they can stop and look around, enjoy, wander aimlessly, lie down and take a nap beneath a shady tree.

Rounding another bend in the twisting road I found myself on a ridge where the road straightened out for perhaps three quarters of a mile. Halfway along I glanced in the mirror and there was a car behind me again. I wondered if I should pull over, but it appeared not to be getting any closer, even though I was crawling along at no more than twenty miles an hour. I didn't have time to be more than mildly curious about this because a hundred yards ahead of me a broad turnoff led to a massive pair of double gates set thirty yards back among the trees. A discreet sign announced I'd reached 2026 Ocean View Road. I pulled in and got out of the car. A security camera was fixed on the wall above an intercom device. I pressed the button and waited. The air was still and quiet. Beyond the gate a road vanished among the trees through which far below glimpses of the ocean were visible. From here I could be back on the freeway within twenty minutes, and in downtown San Francisco in less than an hour, quicker into San Jose, but it could all have been a million miles away. The intercom crackled into life.

'Yes?'

I announced myself, and was asked to wait for a moment, then I heard an electronic whirring and when I looked up the camera pointed at me. It was disconcerting to look into the lens and see nothing but my own reflection in miniature, knowing that I was being scrutinized. It was like looking back at somebody wearing dark mirrored shades. Maybe Morgan was there, getting a first look at me. I returned its stare without blinking, and after a few seconds the electronic lock buzzed and the gates started to swing smoothly open.

As I went back to my Saab I heard the sound of an approaching car back on the road. As it got closer it slowed, and I expected it to pass by, but when it didn't I realized it must have stopped. I could hear the low rumble of the motor, the dull bass of a supercharged monster. It was an odd sensation, listening to this vaguely menacing sound that seemed so foreign in these otherwise tranquil surroundings. The hairs on my arms stood up on end as if a cool breeze had come up from the sea. Then suddenly, without warning the beast roared and rubber squealed like a herd of pigs at slaughter. It went on and on, a loud protesting scream and a hazy cloud of blue smoke drifted along the section of road I could see. The air was tainted with the sharp unpleasant smell of burning rubber, then the tyres found purchase on the asphalt and the din of the motor began to fade as the car sped back the way it had come.

When once again it was quiet I allowed myself a smile. Even the very rich weren't immune from the draggers looking for somewhere to go at night. I'd read in the papers how they travelled in packs like marauding wolves to some new spot where they could drink beer and race their machines along a piece of straight road away from the eyes of the cops.

I drove through the gates, which closed smoothly behind me, and followed the private road which led down the hillside, curving through the woods until it emerged in a broad open parkland studded with trees. A large house dominated the foreground, and beyond it lay brown hills and glimpses of the ocean. I'd been prepared for something extravagant but this exceeded my expectations. Until that moment a part of me had felt like a burglar. It was partly because Sally's moral stand pitched what I was doing in stark relief, but it was a lot more than that. We're conditioned from a very young age to believe that we should work hard, and that the rewards we get in life are directly linked to the level of effort we put in. But that isn't true, and probably never has been. People get rich for all kinds of reasons. Some do work incredibly hard, relying on tenacity and talent to make their mark, but others are just plain lucky, or dishonest, or they are born with advantages that ensure they live out their lives in a world closeted by privilege and power.

Take the guy in the factory who does a ten-hour shift five or six days a week for forty-five years and raises a family and lives in a modest house in a sprawling suburb on the edge of a big city. Does he work any less hard than somebody who sits in front of a screen and pushes numbers around the money markets, or buys and sells stocks? One makes a million a year, the other thirty or forty thousand. Maybe the guy on Wall Street is smarter, but that's just luck. But maybe he isn't. Could be if the guy from the factory had a better education, different opportunities, he could have made a fortune on Wall Street as well, or if he had an idea for a dot.com perhaps he too would live in a house like the one before me. There were people in Silicon Valley making obscene fortunes, often on shaky foundations. We're talking hundreds of millions. Sometimes they're still in their twenties.

I thought about my dad who had worked hard all his life, believing in fair play and the notion that people ought to be rewarded for their own efforts. Then a big corporation decided to increase their share in the local market. Some junior executive in an office tower across the country looked over a few numbers on a report and sent out a memo before he went to lunch, no doubt feeling he'd done a good day's work. And the end result? My dad ended up broke. His dreams shattered to the extent that he believed putting the barrel of a gun to his head was preferable to another day in this world.

Looking at Morgan's house I didn't feel like a burglar any more. It's all a lottery, and it will never be fair. Communism was meant to be the great leveller, but it didn't work because it goes against human nature. Instead of making everybody equally rich, it made everybody equally poor and unhappy. As a species we're designed by nature to scramble to the top of the pile. It's an evolutionary absolute and we adapt to the prevailing conditions. In our world the ability to make money is the modern equivalent of being adept at smashing in a rival's skull with a club or fending off wild animals.

The house was huge, built of stone, with a wing on each side and a circular drive out front that met wide steps leading to massive double doors. It was a mixture of baronial European and American kitsch, pure Californian gothic. The door was answered by a man in a dark suit who I gathered was Morgan's butler. He showed me across a hallway dominated by a staircase that swept up to the first floor, from which I expected Scarlet O'Hara to appear at any moment. He opened the door to a large sitting room-cum-library where he asked me to wait. The room was probably forty feet long, and at one end windows looked out over the garden towards the ocean. Beyond a broad stone terrace was a swimming pool and tennis courts. Somebody was practising using a ball machine on one of the courts. The faint repetitive pop of the machine firing balls across the net was followed by the whump of the racket as it made contact.

I saw that it was a woman and while I waited I watched her. Though she was fifty yards away I could tell that she was beautiful. She had long dark hair and tanned, smoothly muscled legs. She moved about the court with supple ease and from the way she swung a racket she seemed to know what she was doing. Somehow the scene was so completely appropriate it was almost a cliché.

'Mr Weston?'

I turned at the sound of a voice. I recognized Morgan from pictures I'd seen of him. His greying hair was combed back, emphasizing sharpish features and intelligent blue eyes. He wore light tan trousers and a button-down blue shirt with no tie.

'I'm Nelson Morgan.'

We shook hands. His grip was firm, his demeanour polite but cool as we weighed one another up. He appeared confident and utterly relaxed, but I sensed the steel behind his eyes. I was curious about him. I knew a little from what I'd read, that he was private, supposedly a tough man to work for who expected high standards from those around him, and that his business acumen was matched only by his ruthlessness. But none of that revealed anything about him really. I only knew what everyone did, that he had made more money than most people could even conceive of.

He glanced out of the window towards the tennis courts. Most people would have made some remark, asked if I played, said something about the woman perhaps, even commented on the view, but Morgan made a brusque gesture towards some chairs across the room.

We sat down, and he crossed his legs and fixed his gaze on me. 'My assistant said that you have something belonging to Leonard Hoffman that I might be interested in.'

Evidently he believed in getting down to it, but I wasn't going to be hurried. I was curious about the relationship between Morgan and his old partner and I wanted to know more. 'You're aware that he died recently?'

He raised his eyebrows slightly and tilted his head a fraction. 'No, I didn't know that.'

I waited for him to ask how it had happened, but he didn't and I saw that he wasn't going to. He wore no expression. No pretence that he was cut up about it. I was irritated by his lack of reaction. 'I believe you and he used to be partners.'

'A long time ago.'

'You were friends as well I understand.'

He studied me for a second or two, and then he said, 'I'm a very busy man. What is it that you want, Mr Weston?'

I understood a little better how this man had achieved so much. He knew how to seize the initiative and remain in control. But I wasn't fooled. If he didn't want to know what I had to say I wouldn't have been sitting there. I let a few moments pass, long enough to make my own point.

'I run an advertising agency,' I told him.

'Carpe Diem, yes I know.'

I was taken aback, which was his intention, though I reasoned that I shouldn't be surprised since I'd left my name with his assistant, and our office number.

'You were recently involved in a bid against KCM for the advertising account of one of my companies. Spectrum Software,' he went on with the suggestion of a faintly arrogant smile.

'You know a lot about me,' I said, figuring he probably had one of his assistants call Larry Dexter, who no doubt had been happy to fill in the blanks. I guessed Morgan probably thought he knew pretty much all there was to know. I decided that I didn't like him very much. 'Did you also know that Leonard Hoffman worked for Spectrum Software before you bought the company?'

Nothing more than a slight twitch in the corner of his eye betrayed a reaction. But it was there. 'Really?'

I stood up, and wandered to a table where I picked up a heavy polished paperweight and examined it. 'Really. In fact that's how I met him. He knew I'd had dealings with Spectrum, so he thought Carpe Diem might be able to help him with something he was working on.' I smiled and put the paperweight down. 'You know, Mr Hoffman didn't like you much, Mr Morgan.'

Morgan steepled his fingers beneath his chin and regarded me silently. 'He told me an interesting story actually. He said the two of you were once partners.' I paused, and the silence extended. I felt as if I was playing some kind of mind chess and in a way I was enjoying myself. Finally Morgan conceded the next move.

'He told you the truth. We were partners once, briefly. A long time ago.'

'He also said that after your business venture failed and you both went your separate ways, that you got started again by selling a software program that he'd written.'

'I assume there is some point to all of this,' Morgan remarked.

'You assume correctly. Mr Hoffman said that without the money you got for his program you wouldn't have been able to start your own company again. But he claimed that you never paid him his share. He said you cheated him.'

Morgan's expression was implacable, though behind his eyes the machinery in his mind moved with calculating precision. Eventually he smiled, as if he'd decided that for now anyway he should be nice to me.

'Mr Weston, how well did you know Leonard?'

I shrugged. 'We only met a few times before he died. He was sick. It was cancer by the way, in case you're interested.'

'I'm sorry to hear that,' he said, sounding not at all sorry.

'I could let you know the funeral details if you felt like sending flowers,' I said.

He hesitated before commenting wryly, 'Obviously you empathized with Leonard's story.'

'Are you saying it wasn't true?'

'Truth and fiction have a way of becoming mixed over time, in my experience. I'm sure Leonard believed his version of events to be accurate.'

'But that's not how it happened?'

'When Leonard and I started our first company we were both very young. We thought we would make a fortune.' He spread his hands. 'That proved not to be the case, and for all sorts of reasons. After our company failed I decided to start again. I offered him the chance to come in with me, but he refused.'

I was surprised and it must have showed. Morgan smiled ruefully. 'No doubt Leonard neglected to tell you that. You see Leonard was a very clever software designer, but he wasn't a businessman. It takes a certain resilience to succeed in anything. It also takes determination, self-belief, and you have to be willing to take risks. Frankly, those were all qualities Leonard lacked. When I offered him a second partnership I insisted on different terms. I wanted him to be responsible for the technical aspects, but he was to leave the business issues to me. He chose to refuse.'

'But you still used software he wrote to start your company.'

'He had relinquished any claim to it. Although I'm sure he convinced himself over the years that he didn't. It was only when he discovered that I was successful that he decided I owed him money. But the truth is that the money I made from that software was convenient, but it wasn't essential. I would have succeeded without it. Leonard didn't understand that.'

Although I suspected that Morgan's version of what had happened might be closer to the truth than the one Hoffman had told me, there remained something cold about the way Morgan rationalized his actions.

'Whatever happened, you could have paid him off when he came to you years ago,' I said. 'That's all he wanted. After all you could afford it.'

'I saw no point. Leonard was also an alcoholic. Throughout his life he destroyed whatever opportunities came his way. His relationships failed. His career suffered. Even though he was brilliant in his way, he was flawed, Mr Weston. Whatever he told you has to be considered in that light. If I'd given him the money he asked for it wouldn't have made any difference to his life.'

Interesting. There are fourteen thousand homeless

people on the streets of San Francisco, a city with a population of little more than three quarters of a million. The prevailing wisdom is that you shouldn't give them money, and the logic that's generally espoused is the same one Morgan used in relation to his old partner: Basically that they'll only waste it. It's a very morally superior stance, so automatically suspect. Personally I give the panhandlers with the best lines a buck or two. 'Can you help me with a down payment on a cheeseburger?' Or how about, 'Could you spare some money for whisky?' Or a sign I read that said, 'WWW. Got any change dot.com.' Irony is alive and well even among the homeless.

To Morgan I said, 'You don't know that for sure.'

'True. But it's what I thought at the time.'

I could see that Morgan was comfortable with the decision he'd made. But then why had the mention of Hoffman's name gotten me into see him? And why for that matter had Hoffman carried such a burning enmity for his old partner for so long? This had all happened a lot of years ago after all. Intuitively I guessed there was more to this.

'Leonard Hoffman approached you more than once didn't he?' I asked.

'As a matter of fact he did,' Morgan conceded after a slight hesitation. 'He came to me regularly over the years. Usually he was in some kind of fix. He wanted money. Always he said I owed him.'

'But you didn't agree?'

A flicker of defensiveness showed in his eye. 'I didn't feel I owed him anything. And as I said, he was a drunk. I didn't believe giving him money would help.'

But he could have helped, I thought, if he'd really wanted to. He could have gotten Hoffman into a clinic. There were a lot of things he could have done. Maybe he didn't have to, but that wasn't the point. Perhaps until then I hadn't actually been certain I would go ahead with what I planned. But now I had no qualms.

'I think you made the wrong decision.'

'Oh?'

'As I said earlier, Mr Hoffman was working for Spectrum, at least until a year or so ago. He had stopped drinking and was getting his life together. He came up with an idea for a software program that he thought the company should develop, a program that he thought had huge potential. Sam Mendez thought so too, but he didn't have the money to develop the idea, so he started looking for investment capital.'

Morgan listened without comment. He knew I was getting down to the reason for this meeting.

'When he heard that Morgan Industries was negotiating to buy Spectrum, Mr Hoffman quit,' I went on. 'He told me he couldn't bear the idea that you would profit from his work again. So, for the last year he's been developing his own version of the idea he came up with. I've seen both programs by the way, and his is much better.'

Morgan absorbed all of this, and then got up and went to the window where he stood with his back to me gazing out towards the tennis court. I could still hear the sound of the woman practising out there. I let Morgan think about what I'd told him. Finally he turned around.

'And how does this involve you, Mr Weston?'

'Mr Hoffman came to us for help. He wanted to put his program on the Internet, so that it would be available virtually free to anyone who wanted to download it. He needed us to manage that process and make sure that people knew about it. Unfortunately he died before his plans were realized.'

'I see.'

'I wonder if you really do. I should explain a couple

of things,' I continued. 'Mr Hoffman, whether justifiably or not, bore you a considerable degree of enmity. He knew he was dying and his sole purpose in all of this was to make sure you didn't benefit from his work again. Obviously you won't want to take my word that his program is superior. I have a sample here. Just enough to prove my point.' I took out a disc onto which parts of Hoffman's program had been copied and I put it on the table.

'I know the investment you have in all of this,' I said. 'Spectrum Software wouldn't sell a single copy of their program if this one was released onto the Net.'

'And you have this program?' Morgan said after a moment, and now he did, I think, really begin to see.

'That's right. Although technically it belongs to a trust that Mr Hoffman set up to ensure his wishes are carried out after his death.'

Morgan stared at me thoughtfully. 'So, as Leonard is now dead, you naturally thought you would steal this program and use it as a means to extort money.'

I smiled. 'I prefer to think of it as a business transaction. I'm offering you the opportunity to purchase something that is worth a great deal of money to you to ensure it never finds its way back into the hands of the trustees.'

He considered that, his eyes never leaving me. 'Assuming the program is everything you say it is, how much are you expecting me to pay for it?'

I took my time answering. My gaze never once wavered from his. I wanted him to know I'd thought about this carefully, that it wasn't just some figure I'd plucked out of the ether. From outside came the steady rhythmic pop and whump of the woman practising on the tennis court. I wondered if she was Morgan's wife. She appeared to be a lot younger than him. His daughter? Girlfriend? I was aware of the dimensions of the room I was in, and of this big house protected from the outside world. I think I smiled a little when I answered him.

'Forty million dollars,' I said, upping the ante another ten from my original figure. 'A mixture of cash and stock would be acceptable.'

He betrayed almost no reaction at all, apart from a slight tic in the corner of his eye.

Less than fifteen minutes later the gates at the end of the drive swung smoothly open as I approached, and I turned onto the road and headed back the way I'd come. I almost laughed out loud. I couldn't believe that it had all been so simple. How long had I been at Morgan's house? I looked at my watch. Less than half an hour. I worked it out, forty million divided by thirty, that's one point three million a minute. Plus change. It was incredible, it seemed almost unbelievable. But I did believe it because I knew that it happens more than most of us think, and not to people who put in sixty hours a week for all their working lives, but to people who manipulate the system. They tap away on keyboards, shifting fortunes around the globe with a stroke of the key, or they raise venture capital for some new Internet business that will probably never make a dime, or they star in a movie, or they get a call from somebody in the know about a merger about to be announced and they buy up stock which they sell on a few weeks later and make enough money to buy a small country. So why shouldn't it happen to me? No reason. All it took was an opportunity, the nerve to take it, and someone willing to pay. For once I had all three.

I passed a gate on my left and slowed down when I glimpsed a house through the trees. It was a three-storey modern design, constructed of steel and glass, built on a knoll that allowed views of the surrounding hills and the ocean. It didn't have as much land as Morgan's house, and it certainly wasn't built on anything like the same scale, but for a family, say a couple with two or three children for instance, it would be perfect. I wondered how much a house like that would cost. It was expensive real estate here, but I figured further south towards Monterey I should be able to pick up something that would suit Sally and me for between three and five million. I knew she didn't like any of this, but she would come round.

I was considering this when I came around the curve and saw a car pulled over on the side of the road with the hood up. The doors were open and as I passed I glanced over. It was a Ford I thought, maybe an old Mustang with darkened windows and a jacked up rear end. I remembered the dragger I'd heard earlier and when I glanced in the mirror I could see several people bent over the engine. I don't know why but something about the scene jarred with me. I couldn't put my finger on what it was, but it was there in the back of my mind like an itch I couldn't scratch. I was still thinking about it when I hit the freeway.

CHAPTER EIGHTEEN

Leonard Hoffman was laid to his final rest in Fairlawns Cemetery which lay thirty miles east of the Bay. Aside from myself there were no other mourners. On a nice day it would be a pleasant spot, the cemetery was well kept with plenty of shade trees growing among the gravestones, where relatives could come and sit out of the sun on the seats provided and contemplate the peaceful surroundings while they remembered their loved ones. But on this, the day after my meeting with Nelson Morgan, I stood underneath an elm sheltering from the pouring rain. The sky was leaden and the ground underfoot soggy. The rain fell in slanting grey sheets making the world appear shot in monochrome. Thirty feet away a hole in the earth contained Hoffman's casket. The priest had left as soon as he'd delivered his brief eulogy, his black garments flapping wetly as he scuttled off among the gravestones looking like a drenched crow. A pile of mud waited to fill the hole, a roll of turf beside it like a bedspread. The two men whose job it was to do the filling stood further away, sheltering under another tree. I could barely make them out as they stared out morosely and waited for the rain to stop.

I was wearing a coat, my shoulders hunched, with the collar up and my hands in my pockets. It wasn't cold but heavy drips of water splashed from the branches above. I looked down at my shoes, the soles of which were caked with heavy reddish mud. The rain wasn't about to end anytime soon, and I decided I'd done my duty, but as I made to leave I saw somebody approaching along the path. He too was wearing a long dark coat, and when he saw me he hesitated then came over to join me.

'I didn't think you were coming,' I said to Brinkman.

'I had a meeting,' he said curtly. He mopped the rain from his face with a handkerchief and squinted up at the tree, disappointed it seemed by the scant protection it offered.

'Nobody else came,' I observed.

Brinkman glanced towards the grave. 'He didn't have any relatives.'

'He was married a few times wasn't he?'

'I informed his most recent wife of his death. She asked if he'd left her anything and when I said no she hung up.'

I'd wondered if Morgan might show up. I hadn't told him about the funeral arrangements which Hoffman had made himself, apparently some time ago, but I assumed it would've been easy enough for him to find out. I wasn't surprised that he hadn't come. Morgan didn't strike me as the sentimental type. Apart from the fact that he and Hoffman hadn't been friends for many years, Hoffman's last act on earth was going to cost Morgan a great deal of money.

I had only been to one other funeral in my life. It had rained the day my dad was buried too, though not heavily like this. Unlike Hoffman my dad knew a lot of people and he was respected, if not exactly seen as the life and soul of the party. He was always a quiet type, a little introverted. All the men who had worked for him came along, even though they had all lost their jobs when his business failed. And a dozen or so from the street where we lived turned up as well, plus my dad's sister and mother who was still alive then. That had been a desolate enough occasion I thought, but this was worse. To be buried without anybody to mourn his passing as Hoffman had been was a sad testament to his time on earth I thought.

'Why did you come?' Brinkman asked suddenly and I realized he'd been watching me. I was surprised by his question and I had to think for a moment.

'I don't know. I didn't know him very well. I felt sorry for him I suppose.'

'Sorry for him? Why?'

I shrugged. 'He was clever. He had a particular talent for something that in this age of technology makes people like him wealthy. But look how he ended up. He died with hardly a cent to his name.'

'Don't tell me,' Brinkman said, 'that you have a sentimental attachment to the underdog.'

I noted the cynicism in his tone. 'Not one you share obviously.'

'Whatever talent he had, he wasted it. He drowned it in the bottom of a bottle.'

'He stopped drinking at the end,' I pointed out. 'He was sober for his last year.'

'And how did he spend that time? He devoted himself to a plan for taking revenge on his old partner. Hardly a proud epitaph.'

'He had his reasons.'

Brinkman smiled coldly. 'Which of course you feel should be honoured.'

I didn't say anything. The rain showed no signs of letting up. Water was running past my collar and trickling down my back. The ground was turning into a swamp, every dip and hollow turning into a miniature muddy reservoir. Brinkman and I started walking back towards the parking lot, our feet splashing through puddles.

'Did the program turn up yet?' I asked him.

'No.'

'So there's no contract.'

'Obviously.'

We reached the lot and stood between our cars. 'And you have no idea who took it?'

He didn't say anything for a moment, then he smiled thinly. 'Oh, I wouldn't say that exactly.' Then he turned and went back to his car.

I thought about our conversation as I drove back to the city. Brinkman had asked why I'd gone to the funeral, and my answer had been vague. The truth was, I admitted to myself, that I felt guilty. I'd argued to Sally that Hoffman's motives weren't exactly laudable, but that was no justification for what I was doing. Sally knew that. I thought Brinkman suspected that was why I was there. His parting comment made me certain he knew I had the program, though I couldn't figure out why he didn't come out and openly accuse me. On reflection he seemed too sure of himself for my liking. If I had been him I would have been making more threatening noises, trying to scare me into handing over the program and the fact that he hadn't done that seemed to me somehow wrong.

When I reached the office I asked Stacey if there were any messages for me.

'Just the one.' She handed me a message slip with a number on it which I didn't recognize, but no name.

'Who's it from?'

'He didn't give his name. All he said was that you should call him about the matter you discussed yesterday.'

'Mysterious,' I joked.

'Actually he was kind of rude. He gave me that number and hung up.'

It had to be Morgan. I thanked Stacey and went through to my office and while I took off my damp jacket I punched in the number. It turned out to be his private line and was answered by somebody I assumed was the butler. I gave my name and asked for Mr Morgan and was told to wait. A minute later he was on the line.

'Mr Weston?'

'Yes.'

'I've had time to have a look at the item you left me. It seems to be everything you claim.'

Morgan paused, and I waited, my heart rate climbing rapidly. After I'd left his house I'd been on a high, but my euphoria had gradually faded and left me feeling anxious more than anything else. I wasn't quite able to convince myself that what was happening was real, that Morgan really would pay what I'd asked for the program. Attending Hoffman's dismal funeral had added to my uncertainty.

'Thirty million.'

I heard the words, but it took a few moments to accept them.

'Ten in cash, the rest in stock,' Morgan added.

'Thirty-five. Twenty in cash, fifteen in stock,' I countered and held my breath.

Finally he answered. 'All right. I'll need a few days to make the arrangements. I'll be in touch.'

The line went dead and slowly I replaced the receiver and sat down. My wildly beating heart gradually subsided. After a couple of minutes I got up and went into the conference room, and after I'd shut the door and drawn the blinds I opened the wall safe where we'd put the disc that held the program. I just needed to reassure myself that it was still there. Thirty-five million dollars. I could hardly believe it. I closed the safe again and went to look for Marcus. I passed Karen who threw me a quizzical look.

'You're in a good mood,' she said.

I grinned. 'Never better.'

*　　*　　*

I wanted to celebrate, so I booked a table at Marios for the following evening. When I told Marcus he wasn't exactly enthusiastic about the idea.

'This is a lot of money, Marcus,' I said, in case he hadn't got the point. 'I think we're entitled to be happy about it.'

'Are we?'

I spread my hands. 'What is it with you? You agreed we should do this.'

'Yes,' he admitted, avoiding my eye. 'I did.'

'Is this still about Spectrum?' I asked. 'Are you going to hold that against me for ever?'

He looked at me. 'It's not that. Not exactly.'

'Not exactly? What exactly is it then? Because I don't understand the way you're acting. This is what you wanted right?'

But whatever he was thinking he wouldn't tell me. He said something about being busy and went back to his office. I kept thinking about the scene in my living room, and I wondered again, not for the first time, what Alice had said to persuade Marcus to go along with this. For once, however, I was glad that she had that kind of influence over him, no matter how she managed it.

When I got home and broke the news to Sally, she too was less than overjoyed, but at least I had expected it from her and I understood it.

'A celebration?'

We were in the kitchen. Sally was cutting up tomatoes for a salad while I opened a bottle of Chablis that had been chilling in the refrigerator.

'Why not?'

She pursed her lips. 'Did you mention this to Marcus?'

'Yes.'

'And?'

'He looked as if he'd as soon slash his wrists.'

Sally kept her eyes down on the board she was using. 'Perhaps he just doesn't think it's a good idea, the way things are between him and Alice right now.'

I hadn't thought of that. 'Maybe this could be a chance for them to get together and work out their differences.'

'They're hardly going to do that in front of us.'

'But at least it gets them together. It might help.'

'Maybe they don't want your help.'

Sally had already chopped the tomatoes into quarters but now she started chopping again, using the flat of her hand on the back of the knife as she see-sawed the blade back and forth.

'You're not making sauce,' I commented.

She stopped, realizing what she'd done, and pushed the board aside, with an angry gesture. 'I don't think Marios is a good idea, Nick.'

'Why not? Look I know how you feel, but think about it. This is a new start. For all of us.'

'I don't know, everything has changed.'

Perhaps it was still the funeral that was bothering me. The combination of the rain and the mud had made the wrapping up of Hoffman's life seem bleak and depressing. I wanted to wipe that image out. Perhaps it made me doubly certain that you had to take your chances as and when they came about and in whatever form, and I wanted Sally to recognize that fact too. Between her and Marcus I was beginning to feel like I was banging my head against a brick wall. I poured a glass of wine.

'You know what, you're right,' I said. 'Something has changed, and you know what it is? We're about to be thirty-five million dollars richer, that's what! I don't understand why everyone is so fucking depressed about that. It's a good thing isn't it? The bank doesn't shut us down. We don't have to sell the house. You can quit working and get pregnant like you wanted to. With that

263

kind of money if we use it carefully we never have to worry about anything again. That sounds to me like we all get to live happily ever after. I just wish somebody would explain to me why that is so terrible because I don't understand it.'

'Maybe it's because this is what you've always wanted, what you've thought about ever since your dad died and so you're forgetting something. This isn't some great deal you've pulled off. Some business coup that you can be proud of and tell our children about one day. When you sell that program to Morgan you're selling something that doesn't belong to you. It isn't yours to sell. In fact you can't even call it selling, what you're doing amounts to blackmail.'

'Come on, Sally, we've been through all this. There's no clear right and wrong here, the boundaries are all blurred. What we're doing is no worse than what Brinkman would've done and nobody should feel sorry for Morgan. It's a business transaction, nothing more.'

'No, Nick, it isn't. And that's the problem. You can't even see that. Or you don't want to.'

'Aren't you forgetting something here? This isn't only about me,' I reminded her. 'I didn't make this decision all by myself. This was a majority vote. Marcus and Alice both agreed to do this.' Even though, I added silently to myself, Marcus must have had his own reasons for doing so.

That seemed to stop her almost like a physical blow. 'Yes,' she said heavily, 'I know.'

I went over and placed my hands on her shoulders. 'I know how you feel. You're a good person. But you'll forget about it in time. Once we have the money we can start again. We'll have kids, Sally. Three or four, as many as you want. And we'll never have to worry that anything bad will happen. We'll be happy.'

She looked into my eyes. 'Will we, Nick?'

'Yes. We will. So why don't we go out tomorrow and celebrate.'

She went back to preparing the salad, but I could see she was thinking. After a while she stopped what she was doing and said, 'All right. We'll go to Marios, but after this I don't want to be involved. I don't want to know about the money.'

'Okay,' I agreed. 'If that's what you want.'

'It is. And Nick.' She laid her hand on my arm. 'Don't expect things to be the way they were. With Marcus I mean. Some things you can't change back. And let him and Alice work out their problems alone.'

She let go of my arm and turned away.

The following evening I decided to chance the weather and put the top down in the car while I waited for Sally. It was one of those nights when the air feels like warm breath against the skin, faintly moist and cloying. It was cloudy, not a star in sight, and the breeze was coming from the south. It would rain later but for now it just felt close. When Sally came out of the house she was wearing a black dress that ended at mid-thigh and emphasized the beginning of a summer tan. Her hair shone and her scent reminded me of tropical flowers. I couldn't take my eyes off her.

'What is it?' she said, catching me looking at her as we drove along Mountain Road.

'You. You're stunning, you know that?'

I meant it. She looked different in some way. There was a glow to her skin that I hadn't seen before, some indefinable aura of sexiness. My comment melted a little of the reserve that had remained in her eyes since we had talked the night before, but only a little. She gazed out of the windshield, her thoughts lost to me. I didn't hurry. I slipped a disc into the player and we listened to Madonna doing the old Don Maclean song 'American Pie'. There was hardly any traffic on the road. Once I glanced in the mirror and I saw a car coming up behind us fast but then when I looked again it had dropped back and stayed several hundred yards in our rear.

It was dusk as we wound our way up the hill towards the restaurant. As we approached the intersection where I had to turn off Skyline Boulevard, I checked the mirror and the headlights of the car behind were getting closer again. I slowed and as I did I heard the rumble of twelve cylinders and then an amplified growl as the driver put his foot on the gas.

I stopped at the intersection and made sure nothing was coming. The car behind was getting closer, the noise of the engine getting louder. Sally heard it too and looked over her shoulder, then at me, her brow furrowed.

'What's he doing?'

When I looked in the mirror he was coming up quickly.

'Probably kids,' I said.

All the same I looked to see if I could make the turn but there was a steady stream of half a dozen vehicles passing, all of them stuck behind a beat up old truck. The car behind kept on coming and now the engine sounded like a series of rapid explosions.

'Nick . . .' Sally looked really worried, her voice sharply edged with concern.

I looked from the road to the mirror. It was coming up way too fast, and I knew it was some idiot game.

'It's not going to stop.' Alarm sounded in Sally's voice.

I knew then if I didn't move he was going to plough right into the back of me. I wanted to make a right turn but there was another car no more than fifty yards away coming from my left and if I pulled out in front of him he was going to have to hit his brakes hard, but I couldn't sit there either. I looked one more time in the mirror and the headlights were right there. In a split second I made my choice and floored the gas pedal as I spun the wheel. I heard an outraged honking as the driver I'd cut in front of hit his brakes and horn at the same time, then as I sped away and looked in the mirror I could see the driver right on my tail mouthing curses. Just behind, probably no more than a foot from his rear a blurred shape flew over the intersection without even slowing, in an explosion of sound. I registered darkened windows and green paintwork and then it was gone. The driver in the car behind looked slack jawed in his mirror wondering what the hell just happened.

'Shit. Crazy bastards,' I said.

'What were they doing?' Sally sounded shaken.

'I don't know. Just kids playing chicken I guess.'

But for the rest of the drive I kept thinking about the sound of the engine and the glimpse I'd had of the car. It looked like the same one that I'd seen the day I went to Morgan's house.

When we arrived, Alice and Marcus were already there. Mario greeted us like long lost friends, and he too appeared to notice something about Sally. He took her hands and looked her up and down and for once was almost lost for words.

'I hope you know how lucky you are, Nick.'

I made some light hearted reply, and he led us to the table where with great attention he pulled out Sally's chair, and unfolded her napkin.

I had to admit that Alice too looked stunning, though in a different way. She wore high heels to emphasize her already considerable height and a long blood-red dress that hugged every curve of her body like a soft sheath. If she was wearing anything underneath, I couldn't see evidence of it. Her dark blonde hair was swept back from her face, highlighting her cheekbones. Marcus wore jeans with a shirt and tie and looked distinctly uncomfortable. Something had altered in the way they related to one another. Alice was slightly cool when we arrived but she was poised, while Marcus appeared on edge. It seemed for a moment that none of us knew how to behave towards each other. I made the first move, and went to kiss Alice on the cheek.

'Great dress.'

'Thank you, I bought it today.' She glanced at Marcus. 'And these too.' She touched the diamond earrings she was wearing.

For a moment it was as if she had broken some rule of etiquette with this oblique reference to the money and nobody knew quite what to say or do, though Alice remained unabashed. Then I laughed.

'Good for you,' I said quietly. Her eyes flashed in ironic acknowledgment.

I decided to follow her example and I ordered the most expensive wine on the list and a bottle of Krug to start that was priced at five hundred dollars. It was an absolutely outrageous extravagance and something that I wouldn't ordinarily have done no matter how much money I had. Sally shot me a reproving look.

'This is a celebration,' I said. 'We can afford it, and tonight we should indulge ourselves.'

I thought the champagne might loosen everybody up. When it came I filled everyone's glass myself and raised my own in a toast.

'To success.'

'Success.' Alice clinked our glasses together with a smile.

But it seemed that only we had any real enthusiasm. Both Marcus and Sally went through the motions, but neither of them looked happy. After a glass or two I didn't care.

'So, what will you do now, Alice?' I asked. 'Will you still paint?'

'Of course. But I'll build myself a new studio with a view of the bay. And you know what? If nobody likes my pictures, the hell with them.'

I laughed. 'Here's to a new start.' I raised my glass again. 'But why stop at just a studio. The two of you can build a whole house if you want to.' Marcus glanced at Alice then looked away, and a faint frown creased her temples.

'We will see,' she said.

There was some unspoken subtext going on between them, but I didn't know what. Maybe they wouldn't get back together again, but I figured she would get half of Marcus's share of the money anyway. Who knows, I thought, maybe she was entitled. Without her I was sure Marcus would never have agreed to any of this. In fact I felt in a generous mood towards her all of a sudden.

'You know, Alice, you and I haven't always seen eye to eye, but maybe this is a good time to bury the hatchet.'

'I'll drink to that,' she agreed, and added with a sly laugh, 'Maybe you're not such a bastard as I thought.'

'And you're not such a lousy painter.'

We eyed each other across the table. I quite liked that there was an edge beneath our light sparring. We were like inert chemicals which when mixed had a tendency to explode. Maybe we would never be great friends, but maybe we wouldn't be enemies any more either. Money has a way of easing tensions.

Over dinner I raised the subject of Carpe Diem. I'd been thinking about it, and I wasn't sure I wanted to work in advertising any longer. The agency had been a means to an end, the skills Marcus and I possessed individually had dovetailed neatly, but now I could afford to consider doing something else with my time. 'As it is the business still runs at a loss,' I pointed out. 'Perhaps we should think about selling.'

I'd expected Marcus to be surprised, and maybe to even disagree. He'd always enjoyed the creative side of the business, but he looked up quickly and then said, 'What do you think we'd get for it?'

'I don't know. The truth is we owe more than it's worth.'

He hesitated and suddenly I knew what was coming. 'Then how about I pay off our debts, and you sign over your share?'

I saw this wasn't a spur of the moment decision. It was something he'd thought about and if I hadn't suggested selling, he would have offered to take over my share anyway. I knew then that Sally was right, nothing would ever be the same again. I felt a mixture of sadness and hurt, but I tried not to let it show. 'Sure,' I agreed. 'If that's what you want.'

He appeared to suddenly realize how hasty he must have seemed. 'I mean, I don't know what else I'd do anyway.'

'It's a good idea.' I filled everyone's glasses. 'To the new sole owner of Carpe Diem.'

I could see how it would probably work out. Marcus had the creative talent, and I guess Karen could fill my role. She was bright enough and hard working. With slight bitterness I acknowledged that he would probably do pretty well without me. I met Sally's eye and from her expression it was obvious that she knew what I was thinking. Our smiles were forced as we touched glasses. Across the table even Alice gave me an oddly sympathetic look.

I'd probably drunk two hundred dollars' worth of Krug and it had settled sourly in my stomach. My good spirits evaporated like the gas in the wine. Over our meal conversation was stilted, filled with uncomfortable pauses. I wondered what the hell I'd been thinking of when I suggested we do this. Sally was reserved, Marcus and Alice barely spoke except when Alice made some comment directed at him that seemed barbed with an inflection only they understood. She seemed to be enjoying herself, but chiefly because of Marcus's discomfort.

'This was such a good idea, Nick,' she beamed as I refilled her glass. 'I always wanted to know what it felt like to be rich.'

Marcus glanced at her sourly but didn't say anything. By the time we'd eaten dessert I needed a cigarette though I hadn't smoked for years so I excused myself and went back to the machine outside the washrooms and bought a packet. I lit up out on the terrace. I was standing in the shadows thrown by the lamps beneath the bougainvillea that grew along the overhead trellis. There had been a shower earlier and out in the lot vapour rose in steaming wisps from the tarmac. The air felt closer than ever, and my palms were damp. It was going to rain anytime, a real deluge.

'Care for some company?'

I turned and was surprised to find Alice there.

'I went to the bathroom. I saw you standing out here.' I offered her a cigarette and she took one and leaned over when I lit it for her, the flame highlighting her eyes in the flare of light.

'I never expected this,' I said.

She raised her eyebrows. 'Meaning?'

'You and I as allies, I guess. It seems we're the only ones happy about this money. That's kind of ironic don't you think?'

She stared off into the lot. I couldn't see her eyes or tell what she was thinking. 'I suppose it is.' She turned back to me. 'You were surprised when Marcus said he'd take over the agency weren't you?'

'Yes.'

'Because he'd thought it out?'

'Partly,' I admitted. 'I suppose I hoped that everything would go back to the way it used to be. Sally warned me not to expect it would.'

'Did she?' Alice didn't say anything for a while, then she said, 'Why did you think everything would be the same again?'

'We've been friends for a long time. At least I always thought that we were.'

'But you don't now?'

'In the past? I don't know. I always thought I was doing the right thing. I never meant to deceive Marcus exactly, or push him into anything.'

'Oh?'

'Well, maybe I did in a way. But only because I thought it was the only way to go forward. Don't get me wrong, I've always thought Marcus is talented. I just think he can be a little conservative when it comes to business decisions.'

'Unlike you.'

I looked at her, expecting to see a familiar sarcasm taint her features, but to my surprise it wasn't there. I suppose that allowed me to say what I did next. 'Maybe you were right about me all along,' I mused.

'In what way?'

'You never thought I was much of a friend did you?'

'Well, I thought a lot of things.'

I wondered what she meant by that. I watched her as she smoked her cigarette. She'd sounded slightly bitter, which I assumed had something to do with what was going on between her and Marcus. 'You can tell me to mind my own business if you like, but will you and Marcus get back together?'

'No,' she said without a moment's thought, and without looking at me.

'I'm sorry.' I hesitated before asking my next question. 'Did this have anything to do with me?'

She turned to face me again and I could tell she was thinking about how to reply. 'In a way,' she said at last. 'But it wasn't your fault if that's what you're wondering.' She put out her cigarette. 'It's going to rain.'

'Yes,' I agreed, looking up at the night sky. I gathered she didn't want to talk any more. I felt we'd torn down some of the old barriers between us, but it would take a little time before we could really feel comfortable with each other. However, there was one question I needed to ask. As we turned to go back inside I stopped her. 'One more thing?'

'What?'

'The other night. What did you say to convince Marcus to agree to sell the program to Morgan? I didn't think he would.'

She smiled enigmatically. 'You're right. He wouldn't have.'

Then she went inside without answering my question.

As we threaded our way back to our table I saw a man talking to Sally and Marcus. He had his back to us, but as we drew nearer something about him was instantly familiar.

'What is it?' Alice said, seeing my expression.

Sally saw me just then, and picking up on that the man turned around. He smiled, that mocking smile I hated so much, as if he always knew more than anybody else, and his eye travelled quickly and lasciviously over Alice's tight fitting dress and what it hinted of beneath.

'Nick. What a coincidence meeting you here like this.'

'Dexter,' I said without enthusiasm. 'What the hell do you want?'

He blinked and adopted a look of exaggerated hurt.

'That's no way to greet an old friend and colleague.' He turned his attention to Alice who looked puzzled. 'Nick and I once worked together. I suppose we were rivals in a way. Nick takes these things to heart. I'm Larry Dexter by the way.'

He held out his hand, which Alice automatically took. He was impeccably dressed as usual, wearing a charcoal suit with a white silk open-neck shirt. It was the first time I had ever seen him without a tie.

'Nick, where are your manners? Marcus here has introduced me to your lovely wife by the way.'

Sally was looking at me with an odd expression. Both she and Marcus appeared to be silently trying to tell me something.

'Alice,' I said. 'Dexter here works for KCM. He's the sonofabitch that was responsible for making sure we didn't get the Spectrum Software account.'

'Me?' Dexter said with theatrical affront. 'That's hardly fair now is it? You make it sound personal. We were competitors, Nick. Somebody had to lose after all.'

'The only reason we lost is because you bad mouthed Carpe Diem to Mendez, and you know it. Otherwise you wouldn't have had a chance.'

Dexter laughed unpleasantly. 'All I did was point out one or two facts that you had omitted to let anyone know about, Nick, that's all. The rest had nothing to do with me. Admit it, you bit off more than you could chew that time.'

I shook my head, struck all at once by the absurdity of this conversation. Dexter had always had the ability to get to me. It was the combination of his smug superiority along with his willingness to go to almost any lengths to get ahead that I detested. But I reminded myself that maybe Dexter thought he'd won, but if he knew the truth his victory would be a hollow one. I smiled, genuinely amused.

'Dexter, get out of here.'

I brushed him off, and walked around him as if he wasn't there, and held Alice's seat out. As I sat down myself Dexter hadn't moved and he still had the mocking look in his eye. Once again I saw that something was bothering Sally and Marcus. They stared at me but didn't seem to know what to say.

'Celebrating I see,' Dexter said, picking up the empty bottle of Krug from the ice bucket. 'You must have had a change in fortune, Nick.'

'Dexter,' I said again wearily. 'I've tried to be polite, but my patience is wearing thin. Why don't you do yourself a favour and get the fuck out of here.'

I fixed him with a look that was meant to signal that I was serious, but he seemed unaffected.

'I wonder if it has anything to do with Leonard Hoffman? This change of fortune?' he said casually.

I reacted, even though I hadn't meant to. Some flicker of shock registered in my expression and Dexter saw it. Silence had fallen like a hammer over the table and I knew now what Sally and Marcus had been trying to tell me. As casually as I could I reached out for my glass and took a sip of wine, but it was an act and Dexter knew it without a shadow of doubt.

'Cat got your tongue?'

'What about Leonard Hoffman?' My mind was working overtime, wheels spinning within wheels. It wasn't inconceivable that he could know about Hoffman. I didn't know how. Maybe from someone in Morgan Industries. Even from Morgan himself for all I knew. But it didn't mean he knew anything else. But why would Morgan tell Dexter about Hoffman? He wouldn't was the answer, unless I was missing something. Thoughts spun around and around but I couldn't grasp anything for long enough to think straight. I don't think I betrayed any of

275

what I was thinking outwardly, but Dexter looked on with amusement as if he knew exactly what was going on in my head.

'Perhaps this isn't the time to discuss business. Tell you what, I'll call you.' He started to turn away, then stopped. 'By the way. Enjoy the rest of your evening.'

I could hear him laugh softly to himself as he strode towards the door. An idea struck me and without saying anything I went to the window to see what Dexter was driving. But of course he didn't get into any green gas guzzling monster. He went to a blue Mercedes, and a second later he pulled smoothly out of the lot.

CHAPTER NINETEEN

Dexter's unexpected visit put an end to our celebration, such as it was. I went back to the table and sat down.

'He knows,' Marcus said.

'He knows about Hoffman.'

Sally stared at me as if she wasn't certain she understood what I meant. 'Nick, he knows everything.'

'We can't be sure of that.'

'Then what was all that about?' she said incredulously.

'What do you mean?'

'I can't believe this. He didn't need to spell it out.'

'Spell what out? So Dexter knows about Hoffman. So what?'

'He came here for a reason, he was taunting you. He wants you to sweat.'

Of course I knew she was right, I just didn't want to think about it right then.

'I don't understand,' Alice said. 'This Dexter, he works for KCM? So if he does know about the program it was Nelson Morgan who told him?'

I shook my head. 'I doubt if they've even met, and why would Morgan tell him anything anyway? Why would he tell anyone? The last thing he wants is for more people to know about this. All Morgan wants is to make sure that program never sees the light of day.'

'Then Dexter must have found out about Hoffman from someone at Spectrum,' Marcus reasoned. 'And he must know that Hoffman came to us. Which means he must know about the program.'

It seemed the most likely answer, I had to admit, and I couldn't argue against his logic. 'So he knows Hoffman designed his own program and wanted us to help him sell it. It doesn't change anything.'

'You can't still be thinking of going ahead with this?' Sally said.

'Why not?'

'You can't be serious,' Marcus said, the two of them allying themselves against me. 'Sally's right. Dexter was enjoying himself. He wanted to rattle us. Why the hell else did he come here? He's probably thinking about us having this conversation right now and laughing to himself. If he found out about Hoffman he knows everything.'

I thought about the look on Dexter's face, the sly innuendo when he'd asked if we were celebrating and I knew that they were right. It worried me, but I wasn't about to give up thirty-five million dollars because Dexter had succeeded in making us jumpy. I tried to reason with them, talking in measured tones. 'Let's just say for argument's sake that he's somehow figured out about the program, he can't know for sure we have it, he's only guessing. What can he do about it?'

'He could go to the police.'

'And tell them what? He has no proof. Besides, if that's what he was planning he would have done it by now.'

'Then what does he want?' Marcus said.

'Just as Sally said. He's trying to rattle us, see what happens. But if we don't react, if we stay calm, he can't do a thing.'

'And what if you're wrong?' Sally demanded.

'I'm not. And I don't think we ought to start thinking about changing our plans because of this.'

Sally shook her head. 'As long as nobody knew what you intended I thought maybe you could actually get away with this, even if I didn't agree with it. But Dexter knows, and maybe he isn't the only one. Face it, Nick. You can't go through with this now. It's started to go wrong, stop it before things get any worse. Call Brinkman, try to reach an agreement with him. I don't want to spend the rest of my life looking over my shoulder.'

'That isn't going to happen,' I insisted. I reached for the wine bottle again and as I did I fumbled and knocked it over, spilling wine across the table. Sally pushed back her chair, dabbing at the patch on her dress.

'I'm sorry.'

She stared at me, and shook her head. 'It doesn't matter.'

I felt pressured by their arguments, all the more because in part at least they were right. I appealed to Alice, hoping for some support.

'What do you think?'

I sensed the change around the table immediately. A sudden charge in the air. We all waited for her to answer, but a kind of slack acceptance of what was coming was foreshadowed in Marcus's eyes. Alice looked directly at him before she spoke.

'I think Nick is right. Even if this Dexter thinks we have the program, what can he do? I say we go ahead. If there's something we haven't thought of, he'll come back, and if he does we can decide what to do then.'

'So, that's two for going ahead,' I said, counting myself as well. 'Sally?'

She looked trapped, her eyes darting around the table, and then she settled on me with a mute appeal. For the barest instant I wavered. But then it passed, and Sally dropped her gaze.

'Against.'

We all looked at Marcus. Seconds went by, then looking down he quietly said, 'We go ahead.'

Sally stood up. 'I want to go home.'

I couldn't sleep. Sally and I had barely exchanged two words on the way home. The tension in the car seemed to suck the oxygen from the air and threatened to smother us. Sally stared out of the window, and once when I heard her sniff I thought she was crying but when I reached out she shrugged me off. As soon as I stopped outside the house she climbed out and slammed the door shut behind her. When I went inside she had just come down the stairs and I saw her in her robe go through to the kitchen. By the time I'd locked up she was back again, sweeping past me without a word towards our room. I lingered for a while in the kitchen drinking a scotch with a cube of ice, trying to convince myself that she would calm down by morning. Eventually I went up to our room. It was dark, Sally was already in bed. When I slipped in beside her and reached out a tentative hand she shrugged me off. As I lay on my back staring into the darkness I heard her breathing slowly grow regular until eventually I knew she was asleep.

I drifted off now and then into light dreaming slumber. My mind was full of images, a whole kaleidoscope that whirled and flashed before my inner eye without apparent connection. I saw Dexter as he'd appeared at our table that night, but I also saw myself as a child riding a bicycle along a sunny sidewalk, my dad running behind to make sure I didn't fall off. I must have been very young, learning to manage without training wheels for the first time. It was a fragment of memory that held no meaning. Another image was of Sally, the day we met on campus, as she walked across the grass under a lowering sky, and then later on a boat in the bay not long after we'd moved to San Francisco, and there were other disjointed snippets of her, like flicking through a photograph album. I also saw my dad lying on the floor in his office where he'd fallen after he shot himself. He was behind the old battered desk he used, the top scarred by years of use. A pool of dark blood spread around his head, seeping into the cracks between the wooden boards, his eyes were open, vacant and staring. But this image was a false memory, a figment of my imagination. I was at school the day he shot himself. By the time I got home, my mom was there, her eyes reddened with grief and my dad's body had been taken away.

I woke with a start, aware of everything around me. As my eyes adjusted to the darkness I listened to the undisturbed rhythm of Sally's breathing as she slept, but otherwise the house was silent. My fragmented dreams vanished, and as I lay there I wondered what had made me wake so suddenly. The clock at the side of the bed told me that it was only one a.m. It felt later than that. The last thing I'd dreamed of was the disc containing the program lying in the safe at the office, and Dexter stealthily creeping towards it. I knew it was only a manifestation of my subconscious fears. Very few people even knew of the existence of the safe, besides which there was no way to get past the locks and the security systems for the building and office without setting off enough alarms to alert every cop in the city.

For a while reason battled with paranoia, but in the end I knew there wasn't a hope I would be able to sleep again that night. Paranoia took a grip and I began to imagine a fire at the office or a gas explosion and other equally unlikely events. Finally I decided to get up and go downstairs and watch TV to take my mind off it, but the second I swung my feet out of bed I changed my mind. Gathering jeans and a shirt in the darkness I crept from the room, pausing at the door to reassure myself that Sally was still asleep, and satisfied I went downstairs to dress.

A thin stream of late night traffic inhabited the freeway heading both in and out of town, but it was a straight drive in. When I reached our building I turned off the street and raised the grille to the basement car park. As I drove down the ramp a red lamp on the wall at the bottom cast an eerie glow that made me think of a glowing furnace. I parked in my usual place and went back up to the side entrance off the courtyard beyond the street. My footsteps echoed against the high walls. I paused in the recess by the door, buried in deep shadows and searched for the right key. I heard the sound of a vehicle turning at the intersection outside, the engine slowing, and I remembered the car that had played chicken with me on the way to the restaurant earlier. This one, however, lacked the characteristic deep throated rumble, and I relaxed as I put the key in the lock.

The key turned, and then I froze. Something was wrong, but it took me a moment to figure what it was. It was quiet, but it shouldn't have been. The car I'd heard turn at the intersection should have driven past the front of the building, but it hadn't. I wondered if it hadn't registered, but I wasn't convinced. Then I thought; so it had stopped, so what? But why stop on a deserted street in this part of town at this time of night? The apartments close by all had their own parking areas. I looked around the courtyard. The walls and the corners were thick with shadows. I had been in and out of this building at all times of night and day, and had never given it a thought. It was a familiar landscape I hardly registered even in the dark. But now I was edgy. The silence was menacing. I knew it was just the workings of my mind. I was like a child who pulls the bedclothes over his head and conjures monsters from his imagination far worse than could possibly be real. A bedroom that by day is comforting and full of familiar playthings is transformed in an instant to a perilous nightmarish landscape of dark corners, hiding places where THEY are waiting.

'Get a grip,' I told myself, slightly comforted by the sound of my own voice.

I turned the key and stepping inside closed the door behind me as I groped for the light switches. I only turned a couple of them on, enough to see by but not enough to attract the attention of a passing security patrol, then I punched in the security code. In the dim light the inside of the building with its metal perimeter walkways and flights of stairs resembled a prison more than ever. The darkened stores and offices like rows of cells. My footsteps clanked on the metal tread of the stairs and echoed hollowly in the gloomy space. I unlocked the office door and punched in the code then went straight to Marcus's office which had a window overlooking the street. Without turning on the light I went over and peered outside. At first I thought the street was empty, but then, right below the window, I saw a car pulled up against the sidewalk. Because of the angle and the fact that it was shadowed by the wall I couldn't make out anything except the roof and the hood. A dark shape, the colour indeterminate. I watched for a little while, looking for some sign of movement, but there was nothing. What now, I thought? I imagined stepping back out into the courtyard with the disc in my pocket, waiting for someone to jump me.

While I was thinking about it, out in reception the phone began to ring.

The sound startled me. For a moment I was rooted to the spot then I went out front as the ringing stopped and the answering machine cut in. I heard Stacey's voice announcing our office hours and inviting callers to leave a message, and then the tone, but whoever was there didn't speak, but neither did they hang up. Any second the machine would cut in and hang up automatically, and at last I leaned over the desk and picked up the receiver.

'Yes?'

'Time we had a little talk I think, Nick.'

It was Dexter. 'Where are you?'

'Outside.'

I hesitated, then said, 'Come to the door.'

He looked around as I led him through to my office. Of course he'd never been there before. He wore an expression of slightly amused disdain as he took in the modern furniture, the pale blonde wooden floors and the curving glass wall that stretched around the central work space. It was very different from the corporate bland image that KCM projected. He paused when his eye fell on the chrome scaffolding against the wall, his mouth curling in a derisory sneer.

We went into my office and he swept his gaze around. I imagined his own was several times the size of this one, with views of downtown and the bay. He went over to the pictures on my bookcase and picked up the one of me with Sally.

'This is your wife isn't it? Very nice.'

'How about you tell me what you're doing here, Dexter,' I said.

'Plenty of time for that.' He picked up the other picture, of me and my dad. 'That's you? So who's the guy, your father?'

He peered close, as if he wanted to see if there was a resemblance. His condescending manner bothered me. It was as if everything he saw amused him. I went over and took the picture from him.

'You probably had one of those yourself, though maybe your mother didn't remember his name.'

He stared at me, his expression suddenly hardening in anger.

'My parents were married for twenty-five years, asshole. Right up until my dad died when I was fifteen.'

The anger faded, and he regained control of himself. The mocking light I was familiar with returned to his eyes.

'How did you know I was here?'

'I followed you, of course.' He grinned. 'What's the problem, Nick, couldn't sleep?'

I was irritated that he had read me so well. 'Well now that you're here, what do you want?'

He sat down, and crossed his legs, ignoring my question. 'You know how my father made his living?'

I started to think of some caustic reply, but I changed my mind and sat down, thinking the sooner I let him have his say the sooner he would leave. 'I expect you're going to tell me.'

Dexter ignored my tone. 'He worked in a food warehouse his whole life. He was a picker, though you probably don't know what that is. He went around the bins on the shelving and picked out orders from a sheet, which he hauled onto a pallet on the front of a forklift truck. He had to stack them up there until he had the whole order. A lot of the time he would be down on his hands and knees so he could crawl back into the shelving to haul out boxes of canned peaches or whatever. Sometimes the big catering packs can weigh eighty or ninety pounds. Can you imagine how hard that is? The strain on a person's back when they're doing it day in day out for years on end. I remember he'd come home at the end of his shift and the pain in his back was so bad my mother would massage him and I'd be sent to another room so

I wouldn't see how much he was hurting. For that he got fourteen dollars an hour. It killed him in the end. He had a heart attack one day when he was trying to lift a crate of cherries down from a high rack.'

As he sat there talking in my dimly lit office, Dexter's expression was masked by shadows, but he sounded bitter.

'Why are you telling me this?' I asked.

He didn't reply for a moment, and then he made a dismissive gesture. 'You wouldn't understand.'

But I was intrigued. 'Try me.'

He stared at me, then I saw the gleam of his sardonic smile. 'Don't try to analyse me, Weston.'

'Hey, you're the one that started this conversation,' I reminded him. 'Does this have something to do with why you're such an unpleasant prick, Dexter? Is it why you hate everyone? Because you do don't you? You walk around with that look in your eye like you're so much smarter than everyone else.'

'That's because I am. I proved I was better than any of you.'

'Is that what you're about? Proving you're better? Why? Because your dad worked all his life in a lousy job?'

'You know, I remember the day you came to work at KCM. You were just like all those other slick assholes. All with your college degrees, the bullshit way you talk, and the way you dress in your designer jeans and T-shirts. You know what I thought? I thought here comes another fucking phony like the rest of them.'

I was taken aback by the strength of his feeling. 'Jesus, Dexter. If you hated everyone so much why did you stay?'

'Because I wanted to show you all who was really the smart one. You just walked into that job without a thought, as if it was something you were owed, but you know how long I'd been at KCM when you started? Five years, that's how long. I started out in the mail room and making coffee for a bunch of shitheads like you who didn't even notice I was alive. But you know what? I told myself I'd keep my head down, listen and learn, and one day I'd be telling them what to do.'

I understood something about Dexter then. I'd always had him pegged as simply highly ambitious, one of those people who are determined to get to the top, and he wasn't too fussy about whose face he stepped in on the way up, but there was more to him than that. He was walking around with a chip on his shoulder the size of Texas.

'My God, this is about jealousy isn't it?' I said. 'You think you had it tough and everyone else had it easy. That's what you hate.'

'What the hell would you know? You probably grew up in some well to do suburb. Big house, nice school. Mom at home, your dad making a hundred thousand a year to put you through some fancy college where you probably spent half your time going to parties and fucking your brains out. Well let me tell you something, I had to work my way through college. While people like you were having such a great time I was up to my armpits in greasy water washing pans in the back of a restaurant. Only I couldn't finish my last year because my mother got sick and somebody had to take care of her. Do you have any idea how hard it was to get hired by a company like KCM without a degree? Do you know about all the shitty fucking jobs I had to do before anyone would even take me seriously? Yet asswipes like you just walked through the goddamn door and got hired like that.' He snapped his fingers in the air.

I glanced at the picture of myself as a kid with my dad. I almost wanted to tell Dexter how wrong he was about me, but I realized it didn't really matter. There were plenty of people in the world who didn't have college degrees, who had nevertheless done well. Whatever had made Dexter feel so bitter and insecure had happened a long time ago. The same set of circumstances might have made someone else equally as ambitious, but Dexter's genes and his own peculiar interpretation of the world had made him into a shithead with it. He didn't fit in, because that's what he believed, but I thought he liked it that way. The truth was he saw himself as struggling against the odds and it gave him an excuse to be the asshole that he was and enjoyed being. The rest was just a smoke screen.

He took my silence, however, as tacit acknowledgment that he was right. His eyes mocked me.

'But I proved I was better than any of you. Look at me now. Vice President for one of the biggest agencies on the coast. And look at you. Sitting here in your fancy designer office, running this rinky-dink outfit without a pot to piss in.'

Finally I thought I saw the answer to a question that had long puzzled me, and I laughed.

'What's so funny?'

'You Dexter. When I decided to leave KCM, I thought you'd be pleased to get rid of the competition, but I remember thinking you acted like you resented me more than ever. Now I know why. It's this isn't it?' I gestured around. 'Maybe it's rinky-dink, maybe we don't have a pot to piss in, but you hate it that I have something you never did.'

'This? You don't have anything. I know you're in deep shit remember. Your clients are leaving you quicker than rats off a sinking ship.'

'But what about before that, Dexter? It must have been eating you up the last few years, hoping like hell Carpe Diem didn't do well.'

'Are you serious? Do you have any idea what I earn?'

'But you could get fired. And all the time you were climbing that greasy corporate pole I bet you hated it that I didn't have to kiss ass to get ahead the way you always have. There's always somebody one step above whose cock you have to suck isn't there? No matter how much money you make or what fancy title they nail on your door, you're still somebody's errand boy.'

He stared at me in silence, and I knew I'd hit home. I could feel his anger grinding away inside. When he spoke his voice was full of venom.

'You're wrong. Why would I want anything you have? You're a loser. You always were. Even when you get something handed to you on a plate, you still fuck it up. Did you think you were going to get away with it?' He shook his head and clicked his tongue reprovingly.

'Get away with what?'

'Please, don't insult my intelligence. You didn't drive down here in the middle of the night to catch up on paperwork did you? Where is it?' He looked around and when I didn't say anything he sighed theatrically. 'The program, Nick. The one you stole from Hoffman's apartment. I know you were there. You found his body and you took the program. You see I know it all. I know about the deal you made with Hoffman, and I know he died before he signed the contract. How am I doing so far?'

When I didn't say anything Dexter just smiled and went on.

'You knew you couldn't do anything with it. Hoffman's lawyer would have seen to that so you decided to sell it to the one person who has a vested interest in ensuring it never sees the light of day. Nelson Morgan. You went to his house.' Dexter spread his hands. 'Do I have to go on?'

I no longer had any doubt that he knew everything, and suddenly I knew how. There was only one way he could have known in such detail. 'Brinkman.'

He didn't bother to deny it. 'Of course.'

'Let me guess. When Brinkman saw what Hoffman planned to give away, he couldn't bear the thought of it slipping through his fingers.'

'Something like that,' Dexter conceded. 'Brinkman's a lawyer, you shouldn't expect too much of him. Hoffman was dying, his state of mind was suspect.'

'So, how did you come into it?'

'Brinkman came to me when he learned that KCM represented Morgan Industries.'

Recalling my first conversation in Brinkman's office I realized it must have in fact been me that put him on to Dexter. Life was full of ironies these days. 'So what would have happened if I hadn't taken the program after Hoffman died?' I asked, figuring there was no point in denying any of it.

'Brinkman would have stalled, then found a way to alter the terms of the trust.'

'And the two of you would have set up a company to market it,' I guessed.

Dexter laughed. 'You see, Nick, that's your problem. You're not quick enough. We were never going to set up any company.'

For a second I didn't follow, and then the light went on. 'You were going to sell the program to Morgan.'

'Of course.'

I saw that though I had underestimated Brinkman's duplicity I had at least been right not to trust him. 'So what now?' I said after a while. 'What's stopping me from going ahead and selling it? You can't prove I have it, and Morgan isn't going to say anything.'

'True,' he admitted. 'But consider this. If you suddenly come into a lot of money, Brinkman will file a suit against you on behalf of the trust. How're you going to explain your new-found wealth? That's if you ever get any money.

Once Morgan hears the courts are going to be involved he'll never pay over a cent. He wouldn't want to risk getting caught up in a damaging law suit, and anyway he could afford to wait and see what happened. The case could drag on for years and meanwhile he continues selling his own program, and by the time it's all resolved the market has moved on.' Dexter spread his hands. 'Face it, Nick. You're screwed.'

He was right, and we both knew it. 'So what do you want?' I asked.

He didn't answer right away. He sat back, savouring the moment, aware of how much it stuck in my throat to have to admit he had the upper hand.

'Firstly, how much did Morgan agree to pay?'

I considered lying, but I knew he'd find out eventually. 'Thirty-five million. A mix of stocks and cash.'

'We split it,' Dexter said. 'I take thirty million, you and your friends get the other five.'

I was speechless. At first I thought I'd misheard him, but gradually it sank in that he was serious. 'Are you crazy? You can't believe I'd agree to that.'

'Another thing. Brinkman doesn't want to be involved personally, so I'll take care of him myself.'

I guessed what that would mean. Brinkman's share would amount to whatever Dexter decided to give him and he would never be the wiser.

'Forget it,' I said flatly. I made a fist with my right hand, sorely tempted to go over and knock Dexter on his ass.

'I don't think you understand the situation here. You don't have a choice,' he said. 'Let's not forget that without this money you're finished. Your business is broke, you're nothing but the loser you always were.'

He rose to his feet, smiling grimly. 'We're partners now, Nick. Partners shouldn't fight over money. Five million is still more money than you would have ever made yourself in a lifetime.'

I worked it out. Five million split two ways meant Sally and I got two and a half million. We could pay off the business debts and the house mortgage but we would have to start over. There was no sense in pretending Marcus and I could ever work together successfully again, he'd made it clear he wanted me out. So what would I do? Two and a half million dollars was a lot, but it wasn't close to what I really needed.

'I won't do it,' I said.

He shook his head. 'This isn't negotiable, Nick. You see I don't really need the money. I make more than I can spend now. But you do need it. The bank is going to close you down. You'll have nothing left. You should thank me really.'

'Thank you? What the hell do I have to thank you for, Dexter?'

'Because I'm tempted to let Brinkman sue you, and watch you lose everything. That's almost worth thirty million.' He grinned. 'Almost. But not quite.'

I wanted to tell him to go and screw himself. I wanted to retain that much pride, but the fact was he had me and we both knew that I had no choice.

'Last chance,' he said.

I swallowed hard. 'All right.' The fight and anger went out of me. Maybe Dexter was right, maybe I was a loser. Everything I touched turned to dust in my hands. Perhaps it was a family trait.

'Very sensible.' His eyes were alight with triumph. 'A person should understand their own limitations.'

I followed him out to reception where I unlocked the door and we stepped out onto the landing at the top of the steps.

'You know what your trouble is, Nick,' Dexter said,

turning towards me. 'You know why I always come out on top when I'm up against you?' He grinned. 'It's simple. You don't have it. You don't have that killer instinct. You dress in your designer clothes, and you talk the good talk, but in the end you're like all the rest. You know what makes the really successful stand out from the common herd? I'll tell you. We do whatever it takes to get ahead. It's the difference that sets us apart. And you, Nick, you don't have it. In the end you're another loser punching the clock. And you know what else? If it wasn't for me, you'd screw up this deal too somewhere along the way. It's a certainty. You ought to thank me for saving your skin.'

I should have hated him for rubbing my nose in it, and part of me did. But I had no energy for verbal boxing. I consoled myself with the knowledge that at heart Dexter would always be a sad figure, weighed down by his malevolent spite against a world he believed had treated him wrongly. Even though I imagined thirty million dollars would help him to get over it.

He laughed quietly and turned away. But as he did he stumbled. Perhaps it was the dim light that made him miss his footing. I was behind him as his hand flew out and grabbed the rail but somehow his fingers slid free and he twisted around towards me. For a second he teetered on the edge of the step, both arms held out high and away from his body in a precarious act of balance. It had happened in a second, even less than that. It was only then, at that moment as we faced each other, that his expression really changed. Panic and fear flashed in his eyes with the understanding that the slightest movement could cause him to overbalance. He was poised absolutely at the furthest limit of his centre of gravity. A millimetre, a sudden breath, would be enough to tip him over. His mouth gaped, his eyes widened in a silent plea, his outstretched fingers twitched infinitesimally as if clawing the air for purchase. I could have reached out and without the slightest effort helped him. But I hesitated.

Comprehension and accusation flooded his expression. And then he was gone.

He didn't scream, or even cry out, though I heard an exhalation that sounded like acceptance. 'Oh.'

He fell away, succumbing to gravity. He hit the steps and momentum carried his heels over his head. I saw the soles of his expensive shoes flash in front of my eyes and he did a backward roll and fell again, half standing on the way. I think he was still all right at that point. Bruised, and winded no doubt, but when he went over again there was a sound like an unripe melon being dropped from height onto a hard surface. It started as a thud but ended with a pulpy softness. I think I looked away. There were more thuds and soft bumps and a clatter which must have been his heels on the metal tread. Then silence. Total, utter, silence.

When I looked, he was sprawled on his back, legs and arms akimbo, half on the steps, half on the metal landing below. I couldn't tell if there was any blood, but he made no audible sound and he didn't move at all.

CHAPTER TWENTY

I don't know how long I stood at the top of the steps looking down at Dexter. Probably it was no more than half a minute at most. I kept thinking about that split second before he fell, when I could have saved him and I didn't, and the mute accusation I'd glimpsed in his eyes. Why hadn't I reached out? Was it because I froze, my reactions just not fast enough? Or had I made a deliberate decision not to help him? It happened so fast I told myself, that I would never know for sure, but I wasn't convinced. The instinct to reach out should have been automatic, not requiring conscious thought. I might even have started to move, the impulse that originated in my brain firing off electrical messages to nerve receptors in my muscles, but even as my hand twitched my brain had sent another message that said, wait up!

Let's think about this for a moment.

What if he fell? What then?

And that was as far as it got because by then my hand had been stayed and he was gone.

I went back into the office, leaving Dexter lying where he'd fallen. I poured myself a stiff scotch which I drank quickly, and then another which I took my time over. At one point I picked up the picture of myself and my dad, wondering what he would have made of all this. But when my eye fell on the one of Sally I didn't have to ask myself the same question. For perhaps half an hour I sat in the darkness. It occurred to me eventually that Dexter might still be alive, though he'd looked dead enough from where I stood. But still, he could be critically injured and every minute that passed might lessen his chances. I thought I ought to pick up the phone and call for an ambulance, but I didn't move.

When my mind began to function again, I considered the position I was in. To all intents and purposes I was home asleep next to Sally. Nobody knew I'd driven to the office in the middle of the night and I assumed nobody knew Dexter was there either, since it wasn't something he'd planned. Following on from that I reasoned that if he wasn't found there, I wouldn't have to answer a lot of awkward questions about what happened. The best thing would be to move him. Let him be discovered someplace where it looked as if he'd had some kind of accident. I saw right away that the problem with that idea was there was no way I could do it alone. His car was outside. Maybe I could get him to it, and drive him somewhere, but then I would have to get back without being seen to retrieve my own car and get home before Sally woke in the morning. I looked at my watch. It was already two-thirty. There was no time.

It didn't take long to run through my head the people I knew who might be willing to help me dispose of a dead body. There was Marcus, who I rejected straight away. Even if I explained that it was an accident he would tell me to go to the police. It wouldn't do any good to point out that if questions started being asked, which they undoubtedly would, sooner or later Brinkman was going to get scared and come forward and then the whole deal with Morgan and the money would come out. Marcus might even wonder if Dexter's death was really an accident. Perhaps there had been a time when that possibility wouldn't have occurred to him, but back then Dexter wouldn't have fallen anyway, because I would have reached out and stopped him.

After Marcus I thought of Sally. For about a second and a half. And that was the end of the list.

And then it came to me, and the irony actually made me smile. I thought I needed a friend, but sometimes friendship isn't called for, it's something else entirely. Understanding was what I needed, and there was only one person who would understand what I planned to do. I picked up the phone and punched in a number.

'Hello?' a sleep-filled voice asked after I let the phone ring a dozen times.

'Alice, it's Nick,' I said. 'I need your help.'

Alice listened to what I had to say without interrupting. I imagined her sitting up in bed on the boat, suddenly wide awake. When I had finished there was a long pause which lasted perhaps four or five seconds. All kinds of possibilities probably occurred to her, including that this was some kind of joke, or even a bad dream, but finally she understood that it was real and that I was serious. I let her work it through in her own time, though five seconds is a very long time when you've just asked somebody to help you move a dead body. In the end she only asked me one question.

'Are you sure he's dead?' Though she was clearly shaken, there was a certain cool logic to the way her mind worked which I wasn't sure what to make of but it was reassuring to think she wouldn't become hysterical before the job was finished.

'I think so,' I said

'I'll be there as quickly as I can.'

'Come to the side door, and park off the street. And, Alice?'

'Yes?'

'Thanks.'

I hung up. My mind was working normally again, and I started to consider what had to be done. I pondered the question Alice had asked and I figured the first thing was to check that Dexter was really dead. As I went back out onto the walkway I remembered the awful sounds I'd heard as his skull struck the steps and how still he'd been when he hit the next landing. There seemed little doubt that he couldn't have survived. But when I looked down at where his body should have been, he was gone.

My heart almost stopped. The thing that struck me was that though he was obviously alive he had to be in a bad way. And I had left him there without summoning help. He must have come around and known that.

I ran down the steps and looked both ways along the landing. I expected him to be close by, lying where he'd collapsed after managing to crawl a few feet. But there was no sign of him. In both directions the metal walkway vanished into the shadows. Panic and fear rose in my chest. It was quiet, and suddenly spooky. I turned around, struck by the sudden notion that Dexter was behind me, one outstretched bloody hand groping towards me. There was nothing there, but my foot slid in something wet and when I looked down I saw the dark sticky pool I was standing in. And then I saw the smear where Dexter had dragged himself away and then another smear on the handrail where he must have raised himself to his feet. I started following the footprints he'd made after stepping in his own blood. The prints became fainter, but there were smudges on the handrail where he must have staggered along, clutching for support. My horror was tinged with amazement that he could walk. He had been making for the next flight of steps down to the ground floor. I started to run. My steps clattered loudly.

At the top of the stairs I paused. Below me I heard a

thump and then a groan and I peered into the gloom. I saw him then, on his knees at the bottom. He must have heard me coming and in his haste to get away he'd fallen again. Even as I watched he started shuffling across the floor on his hands and knees. I took the steps two at a time. He really was in a bad way. When I hit the floor he collapsed on his belly and pushed himself up with one arm to roll over. I froze as I reached him and bent over.

'Get away from me,' he said. The way it actually sounded was more like gegh ayee. The words were clogged in his throat and blood leaked from the side of his mouth.

I was horrified by his appearance. One entire side of his head was caked with wet blood and his skull seemed oddly flattened. Something sharp and hard appeared to move of its own volition beneath a patch of matted hair, as if something was trying to escape from inside his head. His face was smeared with gore but though he looked and sounded terrible it was his expression that hit me most. This was no longer the Dexter I'd always reviled. The smarmy, oily, ruthless bastard. It wasn't the man who'd sat in my office half an hour ago telling me I was a loser and I should be glad he was running things because I would be sure to screw it up, who looked at me with undisguised contempt. This was a damaged, terrified, pathetic and gruesome parody of what he'd been. He tried to inch away from me which was obviously and pathetically futile.

'Don't move,' I said.

'Geaghyrumph.'

I had no idea what he was saying. His words were completely unintelligible. I didn't know somebody could leak so much blood and still be alive. I pressed his shoulders to the ground.

'Stay still. You shouldn't move.'

His eyes practically bugged out of his skull and he tried to raise one feeble hand against my chest. I could feel the other somewhere underneath me flapping around like a stranded fish. I was partly lying over him, trying to stop him from moving around and hurting himself any more.

'Sshh,' I said ridiculously, attempting to sound soothing. 'You shouldn't try to talk.'

'Eeaaaagh.'

I shifted more of my weight over him and cradled his head against my chest. I thought he might stay still that way. His hand still flapped around underneath me, the other scrabbling weakly against my chest.

'It'll be all right. Help's coming.'

I thought he might feel better if I told him that. I couldn't see his face any more. As I held him I tried not to think about the sponginess beneath my fingers.

'You had a fall. Don't worry. You'll be fine. Few days in hospital. Good as new.'

His hand flickered. He twitched and struggled weakly. I held him tighter until he stopped moving altogether.

I sat with him in the semi-darkness for a few minutes. There was a lot of blood on the floor, and more on the steps and up on the landing which I had to clean up. Eventually I let Dexter go and laid him back down. For some reason I expected him to look peaceful, that's how dead people are often described, but Dexter looked anything but peaceful. Aside from the gore his eyes bugged and his expression was contorted in terror.

I took off my shoes and socks so I didn't make any more bloody footprints and then I went to the washroom and cleaned the soles of my shoes. The water from the tap ran clear into the basin, then briefly red before turning a brownish hue. When it was clear again I dried my shoes with a paper towel and put them back on, then I took off my shirt which was covered with blood and pieces of tissue and hair and I rinsed that out too. My jeans were stained around the thighs, but relatively dry so I figured it was safe to leave them on and dispose of them later. I went to the cleaning supplies room and filled a mop bucket with hot soapy water, then I went back out to where Dexter lay and turned on the lights. I started working as fast as I could, beginning on the stairs and working upwards. The last thing I wanted was some security guard stopping to see who had turned the lights on. I didn't look at Dexter, though now and then I caught sight of him in the periphery of my vision as I turned to wring out the mop. Working quickly but not hastily, I scrutinized each step and every inch of the handrail before I moved on. I knew that I couldn't hope to erase every microscopic trace of blood, and that if the building was subjected to a proper forensic examination in the near future I was finished. But I was relying on that never happening. So long as I removed all the visible evidence there was no reason for anyone to suspect Dexter had ever been there. I planned to get rid of him a long way from there.

Most of the blood was at the bottom of both flights of stairs, along with footprints and smears on the walkway where Dexter had originally fallen. Cleaning up didn't take too long and by the time I did a final check the lights had been on for only twenty minutes. There was still the body and the blood around it to deal with, but I decided to wait for Alice to arrive until I tackled that part. In the meantime I turned out the main lights again, emptied the bucket and filled it with fresh water. Then I sat down to wait and think.

Less than five minutes later I heard a knock at the door and when I went over I heard Alice speak in a low urgent voice.

'Nick? Are you there?'

I opened the door to let her in and after taking a quick look around outside I closed it behind her. We looked at each other.

'You're all wet,' she observed.

'I had to do some cleaning up.'

She peered beyond me at the dark shape lying on the floor, and then she took a visible breath as we went over. Belatedly I wished that I'd covered Dexter's head with something so that she didn't have to see the worst of the damage, but it was too late for that. When she looked at him her gaze was pulled inexorably to his face and she blanched. I reached out a steadying hand.

'You okay?' She had gone very pale and I was worried she would faint. After a while she managed to nod.

She looked at the steps and her eye travelled up to the walkway and along to the second flight of steps that led to the second landing. 'I thought you said he fell outside your office.'

'He did.'

She took a moment to absorb that, and then she looked back at me and didn't ask any more questions.

'I've cleaned everywhere except here. I'll do that when we've moved him,' I said. I'd used the few minutes' time I had to think before Alice had arrived to formulate a plan. I explained that I'd bring Dexter's car around to the door from the street and we'd put him in the trunk and drive along the coast and dump him over a cliff into the ocean.

'We have to hurry, we don't have a lot of time.'

Alice started to say something, then stopped. I think she was having trouble taking it all in. Her mind couldn't keep up with it. Her mouth kind of hung open as if she was in a state of mild shock which I could understand. I'd already been through that stage and now I was running on nervous energy. I couldn't pause or allow myself to think too hard about what I was doing. I gripped her arm.

'I need to know you're not going to give out on me, Alice.'

She swallowed, then nodded.

'Good, let's get to it.' I looked at Dexter, then bent down and went through his pockets until I found his keys.

It took forty minutes to get the body in the car and clean up the rest of the blood. I made sure the bucket was rinsed and the mop and cloth I'd used too, and did a final check before I reset the building alarm and locked the outside door. First we took both my car and Alice's and parked hers a couple of blocks away, then we went back to fetch Dexter's Mercedes. It was almost four in the morning by the time we headed for Daly City and then onto Highway One through Pacifica and beyond to the coast. I drove Dexter's car, and Alice followed in mine. We drove into the hills past Point San Pedro, where the road cuts through carved out rock and twists and turns treacherously as it dips and rises. I knew a spot where in the winter when it rains heavily the hill turns into a muddy slide blocking the road and tumbling down to the ocean. It was the perfect place for what I had in mind and wasn't too far, which was important because in less than an hour it would begin to get light and I still had to get home before Sally woke.

I drove carefully and Alice kept close behind all the way. Thankfully we didn't even see another car, which wasn't unusual at that time of night. Eventually I slowed because I knew we were getting close. I had the window down and I could hear the surge and restless growl of the ocean as it slapped at the rocks far below. The headlights picked out an approaching bend and as I came through it there was a pull over on my left and just before my lights dipped as the road fell away they picked out the shape of an old World War Two battlement. I put on my indicator and pulled over, and Alice followed me.

'Turn out your lights,' I said when I went over. She killed the engine too, and suddenly we were pitched in blackness. The noise of the ocean was louder now.

'Where are we?' Alice said.

'It's called Devil's Slide.' I motioned for her to follow me. We crossed the road and walked over the soft earth to the edge of the cliff. 'Don't get too close,' I warned. The edge was crumbling and unsafe. Down below the ocean surged restlessly. I could just about make out the pale foam, and faint streaking on the rocks picked out by the pale moonlight which struggled to penetrate thin cloud.

'Pelicans nest down there,' I said, seeing Alice looking at the streaks. 'This cliff is maybe two hundred feet straight down. There are rocks at the bottom, but the water off them is quite deep.'

We looked back towards Dexter's car. I was tense now. I wanted this over with. All the way there I'd thought about a hundred different things that could go wrong. That we be seen was the most obvious, but even if we weren't questions were going to be asked when Dexter's car was found. Like what he was doing there, how he came to drive off the cliff, and once an autopsy was carried out and the car examined properly it wouldn't take the authorities long to figure out that there was a lot that didn't add up. Such as why there were blood traces in the trunk and no doubt there would be dozens of post-mortem details that didn't sit with Dexter having decided to drive over a cliff for no good reason. I had read my share of Patricia Cornwell novels. But there was no time to come up with a better plan. I was relying on the hope that nobody had any reason to tie me to Dexter's death no matter how suspicious it appeared, and with any luck the ocean and the fall would do a good job of obliterating, or at least clouding, much of the evidence anyway. Plus if I got home in time I had the best possible alibi inasmuch as I was home in bed all night with my wife.

Alice too had been thinking and she looked worried. I was getting concerned about the time.

'We put Dexter behind the wheel and send the car over the edge,' I said. 'By the time he's found nobody is going to know what happened. Okay?'

Alice nodded. I checked back along the road. It was dark but that didn't mean a car couldn't come along at any moment.

'Let's get it over with.'

I drove the Mercedes close to the edge of the cliff at what I remembered was the steepest spot and we hauled Dexter out of the trunk and sat him in behind the wheel. Then, with the door open and the motor running I put my foot on the brake and slipped the car into drive. For a second I hesitated, wondering if there was anything else I could do. Dexter slumped over the seat, and seemed to be looking back at me with that same accusing stare he'd worn as he fell.

'Looks like you were wrong about me,' I said quietly.

I wasn't gloating, and I wasn't proud of myself, but what was done was done and there was no going back. I took my foot off the brake and touched the gas. That was all it took. The car rolled forward and slid over the edge into the darkness as smoothly as a ship launched on her maiden voyage. It vanished into the void, and for several seconds there was silence before we heard the sound of splintering glass and grating metal as it hit the rocks, then that too was swallowed in the roar of the sea. I looked over and could see nothing of the wreck. Alice stepped up beside me and gripped my arm.

We looked at each other, then wordlessly went back to my car.

CHAPTER TWENTY-ONE

Alice and I didn't speak much as we drove back into town. A couple of times I looked over at her and she was staring impassively into the night. She was pale, her jaw was clamped tight, the tremor of a muscle below her cheek betraying her inner tension. I noticed a stain on the shirt she was wearing over her jeans.

'You better get rid of those clothes when you get home,' I said.

She blinked and looked at me uncomprehendingly, then glanced down at her front. She touched her fingers to the stain which had turned a rust colour, and then let her hand drop.

'Wash them first, but then cut them up and dump them in the trash somewhere away from the boat.'

Perhaps I was being a little over cautious but I planned to do the same with what I was wearing. She nodded her silent agreement.

'Are you going to be okay?' I asked.

She gazed back at me. 'I'll be fine.'

For some reason I believed her. She was undoubtedly affected by what we'd done, but when I'd called her she could have refused. She'd had time to reconsider before she reached the office, but though she knew what she was getting into, she hadn't changed her mind. Even after that there had been ample time for her to stop it but she had chosen not to.

We drove in silence for a little while, and then she said, 'What happened?'

'I don't know exactly. He slipped. It happened so fast.'

She shook her head. 'No. I mean why was he there?'

'Oh.' I explained how I couldn't sleep and started worrying about the program. 'Dexter followed me.'

'Where is it now?'

'The program? Still in the safe.' It was funny, but now it seemed like the best place. I told Alice about my conversation with Dexter. When I told her what he'd demanded her eyes widened.

'What did you say?'

'What could I say?'

She looked across at me and I guessed what she was thinking. 'I didn't push him, Alice. He fell.'

'I know.' She touched my arm reassuringly, but all the same there remained a shadow of doubt in her eye. She was probably wondering about how he managed to finish up where he did, looking the way he did, if he only fell. As we drove on I was conscious that every now and then she glanced over at me, her expression deeply thoughtful.

'What is it?' I asked eventually, beginning to feel uncomfortable.

'Nothing.'

'You're surprised by all of this? By me, is that it?' I guessed.

'Actually no,' she answered after a minute. 'That's what I was thinking. I ought to be surprised, or shocked or something. But I'm not.'

There was no inflection of condemnation in her tone, but nevertheless she had put me off balance. I wasn't sure I relished the fact that she should find my actions that night within the bounds of her expectations of me.

'Do you remember the picture of mine you bought?' she asked suddenly.

'The meadow? Of course.'

'You asked where it was.'

I remembered. 'You said it wasn't anywhere in particular.'

'It wasn't. I copied it.'

I looked at her, surprised by her admission. I suppose in the back of my mind I'd had this idea that she had grown up dirt poor in the rust belt of the mid-west or something and that the house in the picture was her childhood home. She offered a wry smile as if she knew what I was thinking.

'Before I met Marcus, before I came here, to California, I was living in Seattle. I met a man there who I lived with for a year. He was quite wealthy. He was nice enough. He owned a factory that made parts for other factories. He worked very hard, and he was honest and decent and he wanted to marry me. He was older than me, fifteen years older, and I found him physically unattractive. But I stayed with him until I couldn't bear it any longer.'

Her expression became very intense. 'I couldn't bear what I had become. I used to look at myself in the mirror and think the only reason I was with this man was because he had money.'

'Where did the picture come in?'

'It was in the bedroom on the wall opposite the bed. I could see it when he was making love to me. He would be lying on top of me and I would imagine I wasn't there. I imagined I was in that picture, walking across that meadow.'

She fell silent and I considered her story. In essence I supposed she was telling me that she didn't intend to sell herself again. She didn't sound sorry for herself, or expect me to feel sorry for her. It wasn't as if she'd escaped from some terrible past that hadn't been of her choosing. It was more like she was telling me that I shouldn't feel too badly about what I'd done. We both had our reasons.

'What about Brinkman?' she asked a couple of minutes later.

'I don't think he has any idea what Dexter was doing tonight.'

'But he knows about the program. Won't he be suspicious when Dexter's found?'

'With any luck by the time anyone finds him we'll have the money. If it comes to it and Brinkman looks like being trouble, we'll deal with him.' Alice gave me a funny look when I said that. 'I mean we'll pay him off if we have to,' I added.

When we reached her car I let her out. We agreed that neither Marcus nor Sally should ever know about this. Marcus was no problem since Alice was staying on the boat, but she asked what I would tell Sally about where I'd been.

'She was asleep when I left. I should be back before she wakes, she'll never know I was gone.'

I thought she was going to say something else about Sally, but she changed her mind.

'Don't forget about your clothes.'

She promised she'd take care of it, and when she was gone I drove home.

By the time I turned into our street it was five-forty and the sky was beginning to lighten. I turned off my lights and coasted into the driveway so as not to draw attention to myself. None of the surrounding houses had lights showing in their windows and when I let myself in the front door everything was quiet. I went through into the laundry and stripped off my clothes and shoved them in the washer, even my trainers, and set it to a fast cycle, then I went upstairs to the bedroom. I listened outside the door, which was open a crack. The room was in darkness and I couldn't hear anything, so I crept in and made my way towards the bed.

I registered the sliver of light escaping from the closed bathroom door at the same time as the toilet flushed and the door opened. Sally was in the act of reaching for the light switch when she saw me and for a second we stared at each other in mutual surprise.

'What is it?' she asked.

I realized how I must look, frozen in mid-step like a burglar caught in the act. I recovered as quickly as I could and managed an unconvincing laugh.

'You startled me, that's all.' I got back into bed. 'I didn't know you were in there.'

'Where were you?'

'I went downstairs for some juice.' It was the first thing that entered my head. 'I was thirsty.'

She gave me a faintly puzzled look but didn't say anything, then she turned out the light and came back to bed. She lay with her back to me as I wondered how long she'd been awake. I waited for her to say something, expecting a rush of questions any second, but they didn't come. It struck me that she'd looked sleepy, her eyes half hooded, and after a few minutes I could tell from her breathing that she was asleep again.

I stayed in bed until seven, and then I got up and made enough noise to make sure that Sally woke too. I took a shower and when I came out of the bathroom I went over and sat on the edge of the bed beside her, and bent to kiss her cheek.

'I'm sorry about last night. I don't want us to fight.'

She looked up at me, her eyes searching mine. I found her hand and held it, and though she didn't respond she didn't resist either. I had never needed her more than I did right then. It came over me in a wave of feeling, a swelling rush of emotion. She was the best thing in my life, and right then she felt like an antidote to the horror of the things I'd done only hours before. I thought of our marriage as a safe harbour, a place of refuge from the storms of the world. She didn't like what I was doing, but once this was all behind us she would get over it. Things would be the way they used to be. I wanted to hold her, breathe in her sleepy scent, feel the softness of her breasts against my chest, but perhaps she saw something of my intent because I sensed her reluctance.

'Nick . . .' she began.

'Don't say anything.' I put my finger against her lips. It was suddenly important that I stop her. 'I know how you feel. But it'll be okay. I promise. Leave it to me. You said you didn't want to be involved and I think that's a good idea.'

'It isn't just . . .'

'Please, Sally,' I said, quickly talking over her and cutting her off. 'I love you. Everything will be the way it used to be. Give it a little time.'

She gave in, but when I leaned to kiss her she didn't respond. While I got dressed she went into the bathroom and a second later I heard the shower being turned on. When I got downstairs the washing machine had finished its cycle so I took out the wad of clothes and stuffed them into a plastic bag which I took out to the car. By the time Sally came down I'd made coffee and cut some grapefruit. We sat down and I turned on the TV and tuned to KTVU to catch the morning news because I wanted to see if there was anything about Dexter's car, though I wasn't expecting it would have been found so soon. The mayor, Willie Brown, looking as dapper as ever, was giving his views on how San Francisco was going to cope with the insatiable demand for office space in the city which was creating chronic shortages and crazily escalating rents. Last year in the Financial District the rate was forty dollars a square foot. Now try eighty-five. A Berkeley professor came on to warn that in three years' time eighty per cent of the dot.com companies in existence who had created this boom would be gone. Tell that to the investment houses making multi-millionaires out of college kids, I thought. I switched channels looking for something about Dexter, but there was nothing.

Sally and I didn't speak much. When I left she was resting her elbows on the table, nursing her cup as she stared over the rim, steam drifting like clouds before her face.

Instead of going straight into town I went to the pool and swam for forty minutes. By the time I got out my arms felt like lead and my chest ached and it was all I could do to haul myself out of the water. The burn of the exercise and the water itself was like some kind of cleansing ritual. I was trying to sluice off the events of the night as if they were an outer skin I could discard to emerge made new again. It didn't work though. I felt physically drained and I knew some inner part of me was for ever corrupt. In the changing room I looked in the mirror to see if my appearance had changed. Still the deep lines around my eyes, and dark smudges, and more grey hairs at my temples but otherwise no different. I leaned close and peered deep into my eyes and I could see, or thought I could, a faint desperation, or was it the look of a haunted man? Whatever happened for the rest of my life I would have to carry around the knowledge of what I'd done. I had discovered I was capable of acts I wouldn't have thought possible a few weeks ago. I could never tell Sally, never unburden myself and I wondered how something like this would affect us. Would I ever be able to put it out my mind or would I always be tempted to tell her out of desire for some kind of absolution? An absolution that I knew I'd never receive.

As I left I glanced back through to the pool, and there

they were, the old people serenely ploughing their watery furrow in the slow lanes. For once I envied them.

It was almost ten by the time I arrived at the office. I parked in my normal spot and went through the door out of which only hours earlier Alice and I had struggled to carry Dexter to his car. Inside the building everything looked the same as it always did. The stores were open, the coffee stand was busy and people went to and fro about their business. My eye was drawn to the place at the bottom of the steps where Dexter had come to rest. A couple of young women wearing fitted black suits were drinking coffee and chatting. One of them had bright pink lipstick that matched her nails and at her feet lay an ultra-slim Italian leather case. The other had a sheaf of documents in her hand and was talking animatedly. I moved closer, studying the area around their feet until I realized they had stopped talking and were watching me curiously.

'Hi. Thought I dropped something.'

They looked down automatically and shifted their feet. 'What was it?' the one with pink lipstick asked.

'Nothing. It's okay. My mistake.'

I knew that my behaviour was a little odd. I imagined the police questioning people and how the two women would snap their fingers.

'Hey, remember that guy the other day? Doesn't he work in the agency on the second floor, well he was acting really strangely when we were having coffee.'

'That's right. He was staring at the floor with this really weird look in his eye.'

'Is that so?' the cop would ask. 'Could you show me where you were standing at the time.'

Jesus. Get a grip I told myself. Behind me the two women had resumed their conversation. I examined the stairs on my way up, taking care this time not to appear conspicuous. I paid special attention at the foot of the steps on the next landing but I needn't have worried. My cleaning had been thorough and there was nothing incriminating for the naked eye to see.

Stacey smiled brightly when I went through the door. 'Good morning.'

'Hi. Any messages?'

She handed me a couple of slips but there was nothing from the police requesting me to call back urgently. Stacey went back to tapping her keyboard, her eyes intent on the screen in front of her. As I went to my office Karen stopped to ask me about a presentation she was doing that afternoon.

'What do you think?'

I took a look at the notes she handed me without taking in a word. 'Looks great.'

'You think so?'

'Of course.'

'Okay. Thanks.' She smiled and went on her way.

Everything had a surreal edge, as if I was in a waking dream. Neil and Susan, a couple of our creative people, were arguing over colours on a graphic as I passed them. Susan shook her head vigorously as she drank from a coffee cup.

'That's bullshit, Neil!' She caught my eye. 'Hey, Nick. Take a look at this.'

I paused to pass my eye over it.

'What do you think?'

I remembered it didn't matter what I thought because pretty soon Marcus would be the sole owner of Carpe Diem, and anyway I had other things on my mind. I said it looked bright.

'You see!' Susan exclaimed.

I left them arguing and sidled away to my office. I knew Marcus was around somewhere because his car was in his slot but I hadn't seen him. Inside I closed the door behind me and found myself staring at the seat Dexter had occupied not too long ago, when he'd still been among the living. I tried to reconcile that thought with the fact that he now rested somewhere under the surf at the foot of a rocky cliff. The churning water would wash the blood away. I imagined his normally immaculate hair floating like seaweed tendrils. What I was experiencing was probably the disorienting effect of mild shock. A mixture of fear, nerves and adrenaline had carried me through the night but now that had worn off and the enormity of what had happened was hitting home, filling my mind with strange thoughts and images. It was difficult to accept that life continued as normal. People went about their day, showed me their work, asked my opinion on the colours for an ad, greeted me without recoiling in horror. The world continued to turn. The only changes were in my perception.

Except of course for Dexter. The changes for him were slightly more permanent.

Gradually throughout the morning I managed to function. By the time Marcus looked in I had shut my guilt away and padlocked the door with heavy chains.

'I thought we ought to talk,' he said, coming into my office. He sat where Dexter had.

'About what?'

'About what happened last night.'

I looked at him blankly. 'What do you mean?'

'He knows. Nick. Remember? Dexter knows for chrissakes! Or did you forget about that? Nothing would surprise me any more.'

'Forget about him. He's not going to be a problem.'

Marcus's brow furrowed. 'How can you be so certain. Did you speak to him again?'

'I don't need to. If he really knew anything we would

have heard by now. He was just trying to make us jump. He was fishing.'

'I don't believe this. You really intend to carry on as if nothing happened don't you?'

'Of course. Because nothing has happened, Marcus. Nothing's changed. And what the hell is this all about anyway? This was decided last night. You agreed if I remember.'

He looked uncomfortable at being reminded of the fact. 'Well, I've been thinking about that.'

'Does Alice know you're having second thoughts?'

His head snapped up. 'What is that supposed to mean?'

'I don't know, Marcus,' I said honestly. What the hell was going on between them I wondered?

'I just think if Dexter does know we ought to think about this more carefully,' he said in a slightly more conciliatory tone. 'You think he's going to sit back and do nothing? We could go to prison for this.'

'Nobody's going to prison, Marcus.' I felt remarkably calm in the face of his agitation. The moment he'd walked into my office I knew one thing with absolute certainty. There was no turning back now. I intended to see this through to the end. He picked up my resolve and he slumped back in his chair.

'It doesn't matter what I think does it? You've already made up your mind and there's nothing I can do about it.'

'We all agreed,' I reminded him again.

'So we just pretend Dexter doesn't exist.'

Of course I knew we could do exactly that, and without pretending anything. But I couldn't tell Marcus that. I said nothing and my silence spoke volumes.

Marcus got up and went to the door. He paused and looked back at me. 'You know I wish we'd never heard of this program. I don't think I know you any more. I don't think I ever did.'

I had heard that a few times over recent weeks, and now it occurred to me it was a sentiment I might echo myself. I remained impassive, and Marcus hesitated uncertainly as if he expected me to say something. But what was there to say?

When he was gone I went to the safe and removed the program. I took it back to my office and closed the door, then I got out the old cigar box where I kept my dad's gun and I put the disc inside. I caught sight of my dad's writing on the note he left me, and his image swam into my mind. Not the photograph, but the way he'd been the last time I saw him. He knew what he was going to do that day. He smiled at me as I left the house, and told me to have a good day. Don't think badly of me, son, he said. I thought it was a strange thing to say, but I promised him I wouldn't.

Well, I kept my promise, Dad. So now don't you think badly of me.

CHAPTER TWENTY-TWO

The weekend arrived and there were still no reports of Dexter's car being found. Three days had passed, and the waiting was making me tense. I was having trouble sleeping and there seemed to be a knot of bunched muscle in the back of my neck that was giving me headaches. Part of me wanted it to happen and get it out in the open, another part began to entertain the hope that Dexter wouldn't be found for a very long time. Maybe out of sheer luck I'd chosen a place on the cliffs where the water below was deep. I was even tempted to drive out there and take a look though I knew at once that it was the worst possible thing to do. I understood why criminals are said to return to the scene of the crime. It's a kind of superstition. Not only did I want to see for myself in daylight where I'd sent Dexter's car over the edge, but I thought by going there I was somehow challenging fate and that if I got away with it I would be strengthened by the experience.

I resisted the urge by keeping busy. On Saturday I started on the back yard, going at it with a rake and spade, digging up the weeds and cutting back the overgrown tangle of bushes. It was a warm day, and by midmorning I had taken off my shirt and I was streaked with dirt and sweat. The work was hard, but at least for a while I hadn't thought about Dexter at all. I took a break and went to the house for a drink. Sally was in the kitchen on her knees, emptying out the cupboards. She was dressed in an old pair of denim shorts with one of my old shirts knotted around her middle, her hair held back with a bright red band.

'What are you doing?' I asked.

She looked up, her gaze a little vacant. 'I haven't cleaned in here in an age.'

I looked at the inside of the empty cupboard she was working on. The sauces and tins that were normally kept there were piled up behind her, and the cupboard itself was spotlessly clean. I didn't say anything, but when I went back outside again she had her head down and was working away again with her wipe. I paused, wondering if she too felt the need to occupy her mind.

The plant that Frank had obliquely advised me to spray looked the worse for neglect. The leaves were spotted with rusty marks, and tiny aphids were clustered all over. I gave it a rigorous soaking with a solution I found in the garage that I seemed to remember was for taking care of aphids among other things, though the print on the pack was so faded I couldn't be sure. When I'd done the leaves glistened wetly with chemical residue. I didn't know what the rusty marks were. For all I knew my haphazard remedy was both too late and imprecise and I had only made the situation worse.

Around lunch time Sally came out and said that she was going shopping. She asked me if I needed anything. She was wearing hipsters and a T-shirt that exposed her midriff, and her hair was newly washed. I couldn't think of anything, so she left, saying she'd be back later. I took a break for a sandwich then I went back to my work until around mid-afternoon I was too tired to continue. When I stood back it seemed that my efforts had made a little difference, but not much, but at least I knew I'd sleep well that night. I was tired and my back ached from bending over so much. I was also hot and thirsty and I had a sudden craving for a cold beer. There was none in the house, since I'm not much of a beer drinker usually so I got changed and drove down to the store in Hillsborough to buy a cold six-pack. As I walked back across the lot outside the mall I saw Sally's car and I changed direction when I realized she was sitting inside. She was talking on her cell phone. I stopped and watched her speaking and simultaneously shaking her head. She seemed agitated, then she listened for a while and rested her head against her hand with her eyes closed in an attitude that struck me as intensely weary. I wondered who she was speaking to. It seemed as if it was a pretty intense conversation. In the end I felt conspicuous and I turned to leave before she saw me.

By the time she came home I had finished four of my beers. I noticed she wasn't carrying any packages, and she kept her sunglasses on when she came in the house.

'Hi,' I said cheerily. 'How was your afternoon?'

'Fine.'

'Didn't find anything you liked?'

She looked down as if noticing for the first time her hands were empty. 'Oh. No. Not really.'

'Where'd you go?'

'Into San Francisco.'

I smiled and nodded. 'Want one of these?' I offered her a beer.

'No thanks. I'm going to take a bath I think.'

'Okay.'

When she'd gone I went over to her bag and found her phone. I pressed the redial button but the battery warning bleep sounded and the phone went dead. I figured she must have been talking for a long time.

On Monday I spoke to Morgan, and he told me that he had to go to New York for a couple of days but when he got back the money would be ready. I wanted to share the good news with somebody, but I wasn't sure who. In the end it was Alice that I called. She picked up after half a dozen rings.

'Hello?' she said cautiously.

'It's me,' I said.

'Has something happened? I watched the news earlier but there was nothing . . .'

'I'm not calling about that,' I cut in. 'I haven't heard anything either.'

'Oh.' She sounded relieved and disappointed at the same time and I imagined her weekend had been no easier than my own. 'What is it then? You sound different.'

I told her about my conversation with Morgan. 'He'll be back from New York in a couple of days, then we'll have the money. It's all going to work out, Alice.'

She took a moment to absorb what I was saying. I think she could only now begin to believe it. She asked if I'd heard anything from Brinkman.

'Nothing.'

'Don't you think that's strange?'

I did, although I had no idea what arrangement he had made with Dexter. But I told Alice not to worry about him. We talked for a little while and then I hung up after promising I'd call her if I heard anything.

I left work early that day and on impulse instead of going straight home when I came off the freeway I continued down into the village. At the flower shop I asked the girl who helped me for a dozen red roses.

'Make it two dozen,' I said, again on impulse.

She raised her eyebrows. 'Must be for somebody special.'

'My wife.'

She grinned and started arranging the flowers for me.

'Is it an occasion or a peace offering? I tell you, if everybody suddenly started getting along together, I'd be out
of business in a week.'

'Little of both.'

'Well, hope it does the trick. That'll be thirty-seven
eighty.'

I gave her fifty and told her to keep the change.

'Thanks,' she said with a surprised smile, and as I left
she called after me. 'If she throws you out, I'm single
myself you know.'

I grinned and waved back at her.

As I turned into the street where I lived the roses were
on the seat next to me along with a bottle of champagne
I'd picked up from the wine store. I'd had the idea that
we should go to Europe for a while. Take a long vacation.
I had never been there, and yet the more I thought about
it the more it seemed like exactly the right thing to do.
We would go to Paris and Rome and maybe we'd rent
an old farmhouse near Florence or somewhere romantic
where we could sit on a terrace drinking wine and watch
the sun go down over the vineyards and olive groves. We
could take our time, be away for months. We would forget
about everything that had happened.

As I drove past our neighbours' houses with their well
kept lawns and gardens, the houses set back, freshly
painted, I thought that it wasn't so bad there. I regretted
in a way that I didn't know the people around us better,
but there hadn't been time, I was always working. I
decided that after we returned from Europe, when we'd
moved, I'd join a local tennis club, maybe buy a yacht if
we lived near the coast and get involved with people. It
would be good for the kids, and Sally would like it. That
was what she'd always wanted. A family environment,
belonging to a community.

When I pulled into our driveway I didn't notice the dark coloured Ford parked outside. I gathered up the flowers I'd bought in one hand, and the champagne in the other and I was struggling to get my key in the lock when the door swung open and Sally stood there.

'Thanks.' I grinned holding up my offerings and when I placed the roses in her arms she clasped them automatically. 'I've got good news.'

It was only then that I registered her expression. She looked shaken.

'What is it?' I asked. Even as I spoke I noticed the stranger standing in our hallway behind her. He was in his fifties and wore an ill fitting suit with a cheap tie. Sally stood aside.

'Nick, this is Detective Morello.'

My insides turned to liquid and a lump formed in my throat. My heart started beating wildly like a trapped bird. I felt as if I'd lost all feeling in my face and my features arranged themselves into a slack look of surprised fear instead of the mildly inquisitive smile I intended.

'Detective?'

'San Mateo County Sheriff's department, Mr Weston. Hi, how are you?' He came towards me with outstretched hand, which I took automatically. 'I'm sorry to drop by like this and interrupt your celebration.'

'Celebration?' I remembered the champagne and flowers which I suddenly wished would just vanish. 'Oh, right. That's okay.'

I all but snatched the flowers back from Sally and went on through to the kitchen where I put them on the bench with the champagne before closing the door and going back to the hall. It must have seemed odd behaviour but to me they were like a smoking gun. I felt as if I had the word murderer tattooed across my forehead. Morello gave me a strange look.

I tried hard to appear normal 'So, is there a problem?'

He looked towards the living-room door he'd emerged from. 'Could we sit down? Your wife is a little upset.'

'Of course.' I took Sally's arm. 'Are you okay?' I asked her. I kept my back to Morello hoping she would give me some clue as to what the hell was going on.

'I think so.'

She looked dazed rather than upset. We went back into the living room and when Sally was sitting down Morello said, 'I was explaining to Mrs Weston before you arrived that the body of a man I believe you know was found yesterday. A Mr Dexter. Larry Dexter.'

'Yesterday?' I said.

'That's right. Looks like his car went over a cliff into the ocean near Montara.'

'I didn't see anything on the news.' Before the words were out of my mouth I knew it was dumb, but my brain wasn't functioning properly. Morello, however, didn't seem to notice.

'No, it wasn't reported,' he said casually.

I realized there was no reason it should be. People died all the time. Murders happened every day. A car going over the cliff was no big deal. From the corner of my eye I noticed Sally looking at me with a vaguely puzzled frown.

I shook my head as if the news was only just penetrating. 'Larry dead? Sorry, it's hard to believe.'

To my own ears I sounded patently insincere. My mind was in two places at once, slowly starting to grind into action. On the one hand I was trying to pay attention to what the detective was saying, and figure out the appropriate response, and on the other I was trying to beat down my rising panic and think clearly. Morello wasn't acting as if he was there to arrest me. In fact he appeared a little bored, as if this was routine. He opened a notebook.

'The thing is I'm trying to establish Mr Dexter's movements so we can figure out what exactly happened.'

'We really didn't know him that well,' I said.

He looked up at that, and his eye flicked to Sally. For a second he looked as though he was trying to reconcile what I'd said with our reactions.

'Your wife tells me he was a business associate.'

'I wouldn't say that exactly. We both work in advertising, but not together.'

'Yeah. Mr Dexter worked for KCM I understand. And you have your own firm. Carp Deem?'

'Carpe Diem.'

'What is that, French?'

'Latin. It means Seize The Day.'

'Latin huh?' He sounded unimpressed, as if he wondered who the hell spoke Latin anyway. 'So, you and Mr Dexter were competitors?'

I hesitated, unsure if I liked the direction he was heading. 'I suppose. Strictly speaking.'

Morello looked up. 'Strictly speaking?'

I shrugged. 'I never thought of it that way.' My mind was working feverishly. If Morello was trying to figure out what happened to Dexter, why was he here? What did he know? I wondered if he was playing some kind of game, trying to slip me up. How the hell had he connected me to Dexter anyway? Hundreds of people in the business knew him, why pick on me? Morello took some gum out of his pocket and put a piece in his mouth and started chewing.

'I quit smoking,' he explained, and offered the pack.

'No thanks.'

'So, your wife tells me the last time you saw Mr Dexter was about five nights ago. At a restaurant called Marios? You were there with friends?'

Christ! I looked at Sally wondering what else she'd told

him. 'That's right. We did now that you mention it.'

'He stopped by your table?'

'Yes. We talked for a minute, and then he left.'

Morello made a note. His pen made a scratching sound as he wrote, and he stopped to give it a shake, then frowned and tried again. I tried to appear calm but my heart was beating way too fast and my palms were sweating. I would have given anything to know exactly what Sally had already told Morello so I could anticipate where this was all leading to. He knew Dexter had talked to us. Did he know what about? Had Dexter told someone what he had planned that night. Brinkman maybe?

Morello looked up. 'What did you talk about?'

I fought the impulse to look to Sally for a hint. 'Nothing in particular. He just stopped to say hello when he saw us.'

'Did you happen to notice if he was with anyone?'

I made a show of thinking. 'I don't think so. But I'm not sure.' I tried to make it look natural when I glanced at Sally for confirmation. She shook her head. I couldn't fathom what was going on in her mind but something in the way she was looking at me sent alarm bells ringing in my head.

Morello didn't appear to notice. 'Okay. Your wife didn't remember anyone either. I've already checked with the restaurant and they thought he was alone, though he didn't eat. Somebody remembered him talking to you, which is how come I'm here, by the way. I'm going to need to talk with the people you were with.'

'Of course.' I gave him Marcus's and Alice's names which he wrote down.

'Mr Dexter didn't happen to mention if he was meeting anyone or maybe say anything about where he was going that night did he?'

'Not that I remember.'

'What kind of mood would you say he was in?'

'Mood?'

'Yeah. I mean did he seem upset or worried about anything?'

It struck me that Morello was hinting that maybe Dexter killed himself, which I supposed wasn't out of the question when somebody drove their car over a cliff. 'No more than usual.' I tried to make it sound as loaded as possible.

'You mean other times he gave that impression?'

'I mean Larry was very intense. Sometimes I got the feeling he let things get to him.' I was making this up on the hoof. I imagined Morello would ask other people who knew Dexter if they went along with the things I said, so I couldn't lay it on too thickly. 'He was sort of a loner. He didn't have a lot of friends in the business.' I shrugged. 'I mean who knows what goes on inside someone's head.'

It was at least enough to make him think suicide was a possibility. Morello scribbled notes, and when he was finished he looked thoughtful. 'Well, that's about it. I guess I'll leave you alone.' He stood up. 'Sorry again to bust up your celebration. Good news huh?'

'Sorry?'

'I couldn't help overhearing when you arrived with those flowers. They were beautiful roses by the way. I should buy flowers for my wife sometimes.' He looked at Sally and smiled. 'Anyway, it's none of my business. Thanks again for your time. Thanks to you too, Mrs Weston. Sorry to bring such terrible news.'

I showed Morello to the door. There were a lot of things I wanted to ask him, but I didn't want to draw attention to myself.

'Your wife took the news of Mr Dexter's death badly,' Morello said quietly as he left. 'It happens with some people like that, even if the deceased isn't a close friend or a relative or anything. Better take care of her, Mr Weston.'

'Yes I will,' I assured him. 'By the way. I gather from what you were saying that you think Larry might have driven over that cliff deliberately?'

'Well, we're not sure it was an accident.'

'Really?' I willed him to tell me more.

'It's kind of hard to say for sure at this point. Devil's Slide is a bad stretch of road. Perhaps he'd been drinking. He'd been in the water over the weekend, probably since the night he was at the restaurant. That's the last place anybody seems to have seen him anyway. Actually that's kind of strange.'

'What is?'

'Well I only knew he was there because of a match book that was found in his car. But the restaurant said they didn't know him, so he wasn't a regular, and he didn't go there to eat. It's kind of out of the way up there. Not the sort of place you just drop in. So what was he doing there?' He pondered that for a second, then shrugged. 'Well, we'll know more when we get a full ME report. Anyway, thanks again for your help.'

'Anytime. Sorry I couldn't tell you more.'

'That's okay. Call me if you think of anything.' He handed me a card. 'And if you could ask the friends you were with to give me a call in the morning, that would be great.'

'I'll do that.'

'Okay. Have a nice evening.'

'You too, Detective.'

I closed the door, and took a deep breath to calm myself. A feeling of dread settled sourly in the pit of my stomach. I waited until I heard the sound of his car before I went back into the living room, but Sally wasn't there.

I found her in the kitchen looking out through the window into the yard with her back to me. She must have heard me come in but she didn't turn around.

'He's gone,' I said eventually.

She turned to face me and she searched my expression with an intensity that I couldn't entirely fathom, but it made me uncomfortable none the less.

'Hard to believe, isn't it?' I went to a cupboard and took out a glass. 'I think I need a drink. How about you?'

She shook her head in response.

'You sure? You look pretty shaken up.' I busied myself getting ice and fetching the scotch bottle, talking all the time, uncomfortably aware of Sally's continued scrutiny. 'I'm not going to pretend I ever liked Dexter, but it's still kind of a shock to hear that somebody you know is dead, isn't it? Makes you think about our own mortality or something I guess.' I was trying to affect the right mixture of surprise with a hint of regret. I didn't want to overdo it but I didn't want to sound callous either. I wished Sally would say something instead of staring the way she did. I took a mouthful of scotch and it tasted good enough that I had to restrain myself from gulping down the entire glass. At least my hand wasn't shaking.

'You sure you don't want one of these?'

She shook her head mutely again.

'You know I hate to say it, but this actually removes a problem for us.' My glance fell on the champagne and flowers on the bench. I put the champagne away in the refrigerator. I could feel Sally watching me but she didn't ask what the good news was that I'd intended us to celebrate. When she did speak at last her tone was flat.

'I heard that detective say they think it wasn't an accident.'

I took another mouthful of scotch. 'What?'

'At the door.'

I tried to treat it lightly. 'Well, he said they didn't know for sure. I think he was just covering the bases.'

'You asked if Dexter had deliberately driven his car off a cliff.'

'That's what I thought he was suggesting.'

'And you let him think . . .' She stopped, her brow furrowed as she thought back trying to remember exactly what had been said. 'You said he was intense. What were the words? He let things get to him? A loner.' She peered at me as if she was seeing me through a fog, trying hard to make me out.

I spread my hands. 'Sally, what is this? I was trying to help.'

'But you know he wouldn't have killed himself. He wasn't depressed or unhappy when we saw him.'

'I couldn't tell Morello that, could I?'

'But you encouraged him to think Dexter might have killed himself.'

'I just told him what Dexter was like. Who knows what goes on in somebody's mind.'

But Sally wasn't really listening. Her brow creased deeper in thought. 'He said the last time anyone saw him was at the restaurant.'

'Well I don't think they know that either, it's as far as they've been able to trace his movements so far.' I didn't like all these questions or the way Sally appeared to be sifting things through her mind, looking for something that she knew was there. 'Sally, you're upset. It's a shock I know, but leave it to the police to figure it out. Anything could have happened. What was he doing down there on the coast in the middle of the night anyway? Perhaps he was robbed or something.'

'The middle of the night?'

'What?'

'That's what you said. But Detective Morello didn't

mention anything about it happening in the middle of the night.'

'Are you sure? I don't know. I just assumed . . . Look, can we just drop it?' I said, feeling suddenly exasperated. I desperately wanted another drink but I couldn't look away. I felt like I had to hold her gaze. She didn't say anything for a second.

'You went white when you saw that detective,' she said at last.

'Of course I did. Gave me a hell of a scare. I wasn't expecting to find a cop in the house.'

Silence. A moment passed, and then another. 'You said it wasn't on the news.'

'What wasn't?'

'Dexter. You said it wasn't on the news. Why did you say that?'

'I did? I don't remember.'

'I thought it was odd. Detective Morello said Dexter's car went over the cliff and you said you didn't see it on the news. As if you expected that you would.'

I spread my hands. 'I don't know what you mean.'

There was another silence, and when Sally began to speak again I could almost see fragments of incidents tumbling into her mind. 'That night, after we got home from the restaurant. I woke up and you weren't there.'

My insides lurched but I didn't give it away. 'I probably went to the bathroom.'

She shook her head. Our eyes remained locked, but she was thinking back, trying to remember. 'No, the light was off, I remember that because I looked and the door was open.'

'So I went downstairs. Jesus, Sally what difference does it make? I probably just went for a drink or something. What does this have to do with anything?'

'You were gone for a while. I remember now,' she went

on, ignoring me. 'I couldn't get back to sleep.' She looked as if there was something gnawing at the back of her mind which she couldn't quite get a hold of.

'Look, I still don't know what this has to do with . . .'

Suddenly it came to her. 'You weren't there in the morning when I woke up. I went to the bathroom and your side of the bed was empty.'

'What are you talking about? I came in when you were coming out of the bathroom remember?'

And it was evident that she did. 'Yes. You looked surprised. No, it was more than that. When I came out of the bathroom you froze. Like, I don't know, like you'd been caught out.'

'Sally . . .'

'The bed was cold.' Her entire expression altered. Instead of looking puzzled, worrying at a problem she couldn't quite solve, insight flooded her eyes.

'What are you talking about?'

'I remember thinking your side of the bed was cold.'

Silence again. This time I broke it. I wanted her to know my patience was running out, that I'd had enough of this crap. 'What is it you're trying to say?' I wanted her to stop, to realize this was crazy.

But she paid no attention. 'That morning, you used the washing machine. After you'd gone to work I went to take out my dress. I'd put it in the night before because I got wine over it at the restaurant. But it wasn't there. I remember thinking I must have taken it out but the setting had been changed and I realized you must have used it. I meant to ask you about it, but I forgot.'

I stared at her wordlessly. The damn dress must have gotten tangled up with my own clothes. Black dress, black jeans. Easy enough. When I took them out I didn't even look, just bundled them into a bag and ditched the lot in a dumpster near the pool that morning.

'Why did you do that, Nick? You never wash your own clothes.'

I broke her gaze and went to the refrigerator for more ice. I needed a drink badly, but Sally came after me.

'Look at me!' she demanded.

I turned on her when I'd poured a stiff scotch. 'What the hell are you getting at? What do you want me to say?'

'You went out that night didn't you?'

'You're letting your imagination run away here, Sally.'

'DIDN'T YOU?'

'NO,' I shouted. I took a deep breath. My heart was thumping like a drum. I went on in a calmer, quieter tone. 'I was here all night. I was in bed. Asleep.'

'What about the washing machine?'

'I don't know anything about the fucking washing machine, Sally. I don't know what hell you're driving at. Why don't you come out with it? Say it. You think I went out, and what?'

She stared at me. I could see her mind working, I could see what she thought, how she was trying to put it together. Waking up and finding me gone. The bed cold. The washing machine. But she couldn't bring herself to say it, to actually put into words what she suspected. Her expression dissolved into confusion. She shook her head.

'I don't know what to think any more.'

I took the scotch bottle into my study, where I sat in my armchair hunched over my glass. Sally had fled from the kitchen. She didn't want to look at me, and when I instinctively reached out to try and stop her she recoiled as if I were some hideous creature. I flicked on the TV for a while and flipped through the news programmes, but there was nothing about Dexter so I turned it off again. For several hours I sat there, steadily drinking, my thoughts spinning first one way then another. The way Sally had looked at me, the silent accusation in her eyes which she couldn't bring herself to speak out loud was burned into my brain. I looked down at my hands and wondered how things had come to this. Now and then I thought about Detective Morello, trying to remember everything he'd said, his questions and my answers, analysing every nuance of tone, every gesture he and I had made, attempting to second guess what conclusions he had drawn. But it was hopeless. He hadn't appeared to be suspicious, but maybe that was what he wanted me to think. I knew I should call Alice, and Marcus too, but I couldn't bring myself to talk to anyone and Morello had asked me to have them call him so it wasn't likely he was planning on paying them a visit.

It grew dark, the shadows in the corner of the room creeping outward and up the walls. I didn't turn on the light. As the scotch took hold of my brain and I started to nod off I fell into a dream. A nightmare that consisted of fractured images. Dexter in my office that night, his twisted smirk as he'd left, and then his mute appeal when he'd lost his footing on the steps. In my dream I reached out to save him and caught his jacket and as relief flooded his expression I gave him a shove and he went cartwheeling backwards into space. Then I saw him crawling on his hands and knees, making pitiful unintelligible sounds as I advanced on him, my shadow falling over him like some great dark insect as I descended to smother the remnants of his life.

I woke with a start, crying out in horror. I spilled my drink and got up to turn on the light, and only then did my heart slow down. It was pounding so hard in my chest I thought it would explode, that I would collapse and die of a coronary.

After a while I made my way upstairs, not knowing what I would say to Sally, only knowing that I needed her. A part of me wanted to throw myself on her mercy and beg her to understand. It was an accident. I hadn't meant for Dexter to fall, and I hadn't meant to smother him. I didn't know what I was doing. It was all so confusing. But I knew I couldn't ever admit to Sally what I'd done. In fact if I wanted to have any hope of keeping her I had to convince her that she was wrong to suspect me. Outside our bedroom I paused, my hand on the door trying to think what I'd say. From inside I heard the muffled murmur of her voice and I knew she was talking on the phone. I pressed my ear to the door and listened.

'. . . can't go on like this. I need to see you.'

There was a long pause. She said something I couldn't distinguish then I caught a fragment of a sentence.

'. . . don't know what I'll do if he comes . . . Oh God . . .'

She broke off into sobbing. I didn't need to guess who she was talking to. It was Garrison Hunt, standing in the wings ready and waiting with a shoulder for her to cry on. Her knight in shining armour. My anger flared and burned out like a spent match. Suddenly I was exhausted. I went back downstairs and sat down in my chair and eventually I fell into a deep and drink-sodden, dreamless sleep.

CHAPTER TWENTY-THREE

In the morning I crept into our room and found Sally in a deep sleep. Her face was red splotched from crying, especially about her eyes. I figured she wouldn't wake for hours, and there were things I needed to do so I grabbed some clothes and showered and dressed downstairs.

My head was thumping painfully. Breakfast consisted of painkillers with a cup of coffee before I drove into the office. I was the first to arrive. I picked up my phone and called Alice to tell her about Morello's visit, but she got in first.

'Nick, I was just going to call you. It's on the news, they found Dexter's car.'

I asked her which channel then said I'd call her back and I went through to the conference room and turned on the TV. The item was brief. They used a still shot of the road at Devil's Slide which meant it hadn't merited sending out a camera crew to get some live footage, which I supposed made sense as by then the car was already gone.

'A car was found at the bottom of the cliffs below a dangerous stretch of road on Highway One south of Point Pedro on Sunday,' the woman said. 'Apparently it had been there for several days, submerged in fifteen feet of water beyond the surf. Police have released the name of the male occupant discovered in the car. He was Larry Dexter, an advertising executive from Fillmore. He was thirty-nine years old and unmarried. Police are speculating at the moment that Mr Dexter's car was driven over the edge of the cliff several days ago. A medical examination will take place today to establish the exact cause of death. Sources within the San Mateo County Sheriff's department suggest that Mr Dexter's death may not have been accidental, though we understand suicide has not yet been ruled out.'

That was about it. The traffic report came on, and a piece raising speculation once again that another bridge might be built linking the East Bay with the Peninsula to ease congestion. Brilliant. Encourage more cars onto the roads. That'll fix it. With grim humour I noted that from now on there would be one less Mercedes to worry about anyway. I channel hopped to see if I could find anything else but when there was nothing I called Alice back. She picked up on the first ring and I told her about Morello.

'Oh my God. Do you think he knows anything?'

The truthful answer to that was I didn't know, but I didn't want to worry her any more than necessary. 'He's just doing the basics. Figuring out Dexter's movements. We don't have anything to worry about.'

She thought about that. 'But if he knows we spoke to Dexter at the restaurant he's got a connection.'

'But that's all he knows. From his point of view Dexter saw some people and stopped by at their table to say hello and that's it. He doesn't have any reason to think any of us saw him again after that.'

'Unless he knows about the program.'

'He doesn't,' I said, sure of that much. 'If he did he would have mentioned it.'

I gave her Morello's number and told her to call him, adding that if he was suspicious at all he would at least want to speak to her and Marcus in person, which, when I thought about it, made sense and I wondered why it hadn't occurred to me before. It went a long way to reassuring me that for now anyway we were in the clear. What really bothered me was how long that would last once Morello received the coroner's report. Then he would really start digging.

Alice asked how Sally had taken the news, and I told her she'd been a little shocked but was otherwise fine.

'Then she doesn't suspect anything?'

'She doesn't know a thing,' I lied, because I didn't want her to panic. I knew I had to do something about Sally. I just didn't know what.

'Have you heard from Marcus?' I asked. I thought he might have seen the news reports and called her, but she hadn't spoken to him. 'Okay, well I have to tell him,' I said. 'He should be here soon. Call me back when you've spoken to Morello.'

We hung up, and I sat down to think. I wasn't expecting Marcus to be a problem. He would be surprised to hear about Dexter, but he didn't have any reason to think I had anything to do with it, at least not unless he talked to Sally.

Sally. What the hell was I going to do about her? One thing was certain, I had lost her unless I could somehow convince her that she had made a huge mistake. A terrible mistake. I just didn't have any ideas about how I was going to do that.

Apart from Sally the only other person who could be a problem was Brinkman I thought. Over the past few days I'd put him out of my mind. I'd convinced myself that the best way to deal with him was to do nothing, wait until he came to me, if he ever did, but I saw now I couldn't take the chance and wait for that to happen. What if Morello made a connection to Brinkman and then the detective found out about the program? What if Brinkman heard about Dexter and called the police himself? I decided to play it safe and arrange a meeting with him. At least that way I'd find out if he suspected anything and I could figure out how to handle him. I called his office at nine, and was put through to his assistant, whose name I remembered was Carol.

'Carol, hello, this is Nick Weston,' I said cheerily. 'From Carpe Diem? I was trying to reach your boss, is he around?'

'Mr Weston, yes. Good morning. No, I'm afraid Mr Brinkman isn't here.'

'Perhaps I'll call back later. What time do you expect him?'

There was a pause before she answered. 'Actually I'm not sure. Mr Brinkman didn't come into the office yesterday. In fact I don't know where he is. It's very unusual. He's missed several appointments and I haven't heard anything from him at all.'

'Well, could you tell him I called. And I'll try again later.'

I hung up. She had sounded a little worried. It was kind of a coincidence that amidst everything that was going on Brinkman had apparently vanished, though I couldn't imagine there was any connection. I made a mental note to try again later. I hadn't seen Marcus arrive yet, so I went out to reception to ask Stacey if she'd heard from him. She said he'd called to say he would be late. I wondered if he'd seen the reports about Dexter on TV already.

'Did he say anything else,' I asked casually. 'Like when he'd be in?'

'He said he'd call later.'

'He sound okay?'

Stacey looked puzzled. 'Sure. I think so. Why?'

'You don't sound certain.'

'Well, it's just, I don't know, he was kind of distracted or something. Maybe he was in traffic.'

'Okay, thanks. If you hear from him again, put him through to me will you?'

I went back to my office and tried his cell phone, but he had it switched off, so I left a message for him to call me. The more I thought about it, the more I figured he had heard about Dexter. I wondered where he'd gone. I called his phone a couple more times over the next half-hour but it remained switched off. It occurred to me in the end that he might have gone to see Alice, but when I called I got her answering machine. I told myself that if she had seen him and anything was wrong she would have let me know anyway. I tried to think where else he might have gone. Finally I called Sally's office. I knew I couldn't put off talking to her for any longer, but I was told she'd called in sick, which didn't surprise me. I called home and waited tensely as I listened to the ringing tone. The machine kicked in and I tried to sound as normal as possible.

'Sally? Are you there? Pick up if you are, okay? I need to talk to you.'

Nothing. I hung up and tried again and went through the same routine. Now I started to get worried. Either she wasn't picking up, or she wasn't there. I tried her cell phone but it was turned off. A disturbing possibility occurred to me. I grabbed my phone and told Stacey that if she heard from Marcus she was to tell him I needed to talk to him.

'Tell him it's important.'

'When will you be back?' she called out as I went out the door.

'I'm not sure.'

It took me forty minutes to get home, and even as I pulled in the driveway I knew what I'd find. Sally's car wasn't in the garage. Inside the house I went up the stairs calling her name. I found her closet almost empty, her drawers stripped and her make-up and toilet things were missing from the bathroom. I went right through the house but she hadn't left a note. The flowers I'd brought home the day before lay where I'd left them on the bench. The petals were already curling, their colour fading from lack of water.

Sally had gone.

Part Three

CHAPTER TWENTY-FOUR

I have no recollection as to what I thought about when I drove to Oregon that night. I made one stop on the way through the city to go to the office where I pulled the blinds and closed the door before I unlocked the drawer where I kept the old cigar box that contained my dad's gun. I took out the disc with the program on it and locked that back in the drawer, but the box went with me. I kept it on the passenger seat of the car as I drove north on the interstate past Sacramento and then on up to the state line. As it grew dark I became weary. The oncoming lights blurred now and then and a couple of times I pulled over to snatch twenty minutes sleep, and once I reached Oregon I stopped for an hour. After that I was fine.

It wasn't until I started again that I began to give consideration to what my intentions were. Until that point the driving and staying awake had been enough to occupy my mind and keep me from thinking about anything much. I finally pulled over at a stop where I bought some coffee and stood outside to drink it in the early light, breathing the cool air beneath a grey sky. When I was done I tossed the cup in a trash can and found a public phone where I called information and asked for the listed number of a Garrison Hunt in White Falls.

'I have a listing at Cedar Drive. Thirteen thirty-three.'

'That's the one,' I said and I wrote it down.

I went back to my car and drove on until I reached the next exit, and then I followed the highway inland until I hit the turnoff for the county road to White Falls. By ten o'clock I was only a couple of miles away. I passed by a diner and half a mile on I slowed and swung around and I went back and sat in a booth with a cup of coffee and a pack of cigarettes I'd bought. I took the cigar box inside with me and left it on the table. When the waitress wasn't about I opened it and slipped out my dad's note. I read it through once, even though I knew it by heart. At first I didn't know what any of it had to do with me being where I was or what answers I hoped to find there.

My dad took his own life because the intricate machinery of his mind was more finely tuned than is the case for most of us. It required less to upset the balance. The failure of his business was the collapse of everything he'd worked for all his life. He'd always had faith in the idea that if a man worked hard and honestly, and provided he was suited to the work he did and could do it at least as well as the next man, then he would be fairly rewarded for his labours. But he learned that isn't true. When he was forced out of business, it wasn't just his livelihood that he lost, it was his identity. Everything he believed in, that had made him who he was, was taken away. In one fell swoop he understood that hard work and honesty count for little in an age when big is best and the little guy can be shoved aside in an instant on the whim of some faceless executive a thousand miles away. He felt like his whole life had been ground into the dust then tossed aside like so much worthless scrap. The delicate spinning cogs and wheels inside his brain seized up and a black veil fell over him. Another person might have picked themselves up and started again, got a job somewhere. But not my dad. He couldn't face the disintegration of his universe and so he took the .38 and blew out his brains.

The past remains with us for all our lives. The years of our childhood are like the heat of the forge, the hammer blows of the blacksmith the accumulated experiences that shape us as people as surely as a lump of metal is transformed into something useful. I grew up keenly missing my dad's presence. He left me at an age when I needed him most, when I needed him to guide me through the transitional years from boy to man. All the occasions when the changes his death brought on our lives made me feel excluded or separate or simply confused were in themselves of little consequence. But collectively they were filtered through an idea my dad's note had planted in my mind, that when you get down to the line it's the little guy against the world and if you want to survive and keep control of your life you better make money. The more the better. This seed was fed and watered abundantly by experience as I grew older. Everywhere I turned was the proof that money governs all. Like it or not, there's no escaping it. Even when I met the woman I fell in love with and married I couldn't forget, because if I ever did Sally's mother was there waiting to remind me.

I had no guilt about selling Leonard Hoffman's program to Morgan. It didn't matter to Hoffman, and Morgan had cheated his partner to make his fortune so I wasn't about to feel sorry for him. Even after he'd paid me off he would still have more money than he could spend in a lifetime. Dexter was a different matter, but he was no angel either. I would have to live with what had happened. But it was all worth nothing without Sally. She was the one thing that was pure and good in my life. I loved her as much as I ever had, perhaps more. What was the point in having done the things I had to wrestle control of my life from indiscriminate forces if Sally was gone? And in case I should have any doubts about any of this, where had she gone? She'd run away to be with Garrison Hunt who had grown up rich and never knew what it was like to be like the rest of us, prey to the whims of our boss, or some scheming bastard like Dexter. It seemed to be one irony too many for me to take.

I got up at last and tucked the cigar box under my arm as I paid for my coffee. The waitress gave me a smile and wished me a good day, but she sounded as if she meant it. She was in her late thirties and wore a wedding band. The skin of her hands was roughened and wrinkled from her work. She chatted to her customers and brought them their food and was on her feet all day. I expect she had a husband at home and a couple of kids and by the time she went to bed every night she was exhausted. I'd parked next to a rusting six-year-old Toyota in the lot which perhaps belonged to her. She and her husband probably struggled to pay their bills every month. Maybe he worked in a local factory that could close down any time because somebody a thousand miles away decided to buy it up and move production somewhere more convenient, or because doing so might earn him a few points against some rival in the corporate structure. I tipped her and she called me back holding up the bill.

'Hey, I think you made a mistake this is a ten.'

'No mistake,' I said.

She smiled. 'Thanks. Have a good day.'

Well, perhaps I would.

It didn't take long to reach White Falls, the town where Sally had grown up. I knew if I turned right at the gas station and passed through the centre of town I'd soon find myself at the house where Ellen and Frank still lived. At a store I asked the way to Cedar Drive and wrote down the directions. It turned out to be a road that led out of town which began with houses on either side, which petered out until a couple of miles further on there were hardly any. I found the address I'd written down, where Garrison Hunt lived. The house had been there for generations, set in acres of land and announced by a driveway barred by a white wooden gate, beyond which it led back through the woods. The gate was open, so I turned off the road and drove on through. It took several minutes to reach the house. Unlike the massive tasteless pile where Nelson Morgan lived, this was imposing but much more refined. It was built on three floors, a rectangular shape in English Georgian style with symmetrically placed tall windows in rows and a sloping slate roof. The outside was rendered plaster painted an off-white shade, and the garden and grounds that surrounded it were planted with mature trees that had probably been established for a hundred years or more. The entire place, surrounded by woods and fields as it was, spoke of old money, family money that Garrison Hunt and his forebears had made from land over several generations. Out front was parked a four wheel drive, and in a building the size of a family house that was evidently the garage the back of another car was visible, though it wasn't Sally's.

After I'd stopped I put my dad's gun in my pocket and went to the front door. While I waited a dog barked from out back somewhere, and then the door was opened. I recognized Garrison right away. I'd only met him once when I was dating Sally, but he hadn't changed a lot. His hair remained thick, his smooth good looks were unblemished and he had the healthy glow of those who live in the outdoors. Unlike me he wasn't showing any grey. He was wearing blue jeans and boots and a worn cotton shirt. Behind him was a cavernous entrance hall with doors leading to rooms on either side and a wide carpeted staircase. The floor was made of wood parquet which years of use had rendered slightly battered and scratched. Rock music filtered down from an upper floor.

'Hi,' Garrison said with slightly quizzical intonation.

I gave him a moment, waiting for the inevitable flash of recognition. Though he and Sally weren't aware that I knew about them, and so wouldn't be expecting me to turn up on their doorstep quite this soon, I figured the penny would drop. It didn't, however, which seemed like an added insult.

'You don't know who I am do you?' I said at last.

His pleasant smile faltered. 'I'm sorry, I'm not sure that I do.' He peered more closely but still couldn't place me.

My hand closed around the handle of the .38 in my pocket and I wondered if I brought it out it might jog his memory. 'Where's Sally?' I demanded.

He was distracted as I spoke because at that moment a dog came bounding through the hall. It rushed towards the door, some big hairy breed with a gruff deep bark like a bear. I stepped back in alarm.

'Jenny, get this dog out of here,' Garrison hollered as he seized it by the collar and dragged it back across the floor. A teenage girl appeared.

'Sorry,' she said and took hold of the dog's collar. 'Come on, Harry. Get back here.' She started dragging the unwilling beast away even though it was big enough to bowl her over with just one swipe of its dinner-plate sized paws.

'My niece,' Garrison explained when he turned back to me. 'Look, why don't you come inside? We can talk somewhere we won't be disturbed.'

I didn't argue, but followed him across the hall and into a large room filled with comfortable, if slightly worn furniture. The fabric on the couches was faded and even frayed here and there. Rugs that were thrown on the floor looked as if they had once been luxurious and expensive but that was in the dim and distant past. Now they were well used and the patterns were melting away.

Garrison stood by the fireplace, and though he invited me to sit I didn't. I could see from the way he was looking at me that he felt as if he should know me, but no matter how hard he tried he couldn't fit a name to the face. I didn't help him out. At one end of the room, by the window there was a pile of children's toys scattered on the floor. Upstairs the sound of rock music got suddenly louder then abruptly faded when a woman's voice shouted for it to be turned down.

'My sister and her family are staying with us right now,' Garrison offered in explanation. 'It's kind of a mad house here today.' He smiled disarmingly, and then held out his arms in a gesture of defeat. 'Look I'm sorry, you obviously know me, but I'm afraid I can't place you.'

I hadn't expected this. I'd thought he might try and stop me from seeing Sally, but not this. The only thing I could figure was that they had seen me drive up and decided to try playing it dumb.

'I want to see her,' I said flatly.

'See who?'

My hand closed around the gun again. I thought this would be so much quicker if I pointed it at him, but for the moment I refrained. 'Let's drop this façade shall we, Garrison. Where's Sally?'

'Sally?'

Either he was a brilliant actor, or he was telling the truth, because for a second or two he looked blank, then at last a glimmer of memory stirred.

'Wait a minute.' He snapped his fingers. 'Yes! You're Nick Weston aren't you? You married Sally Johnson.' He looked totally surprised and a little bewildered. 'Are you here visiting?'

'I came to see Sally,' I told him, but by now my

befuddled brain was clearing and a faint unease was stirring.

His bewilderment increased and then the door behind me opened and a woman's voice said, 'Oh. Sorry, I didn't know anyone was in here.'

I turned to find an attractive woman with tousled blonde hair in the doorway. She looked from me to Garrison with an expression of mild inquiry.

'This is . . .' Garrison paused for a fraction. 'Nick Weston. Nick married an old friend of mine from town. Sally Johnson, as she was then. You know, Frank and Ellen Johnson?'

The woman smiled and came forward with out-stretched hand, though behind the smile she looked vaguely uncertain. There was a mirror on the wall by the door, and I caught sight of my own reflection in it. I was unshaven and there was a kind of wild look in my eye and I saw how I must appear to them.

'My wife, Kate,' Garrison said.

I shook her hand in numb response as the blood drained from my face and I felt the world spinning out of kilter. Kate Hunt smiled pleasantly and said hello, but when she looked towards her husband I saw his quick shrug of incomprehension. She handled the moment smoothly.

'Pleasure to meet you, Nick. Can I offer you some coffee or something? You'll have to excuse the state we're in. Did Garrison tell you we have people staying with us? Four children as well as our own three.' She raised her eyes heavenward. 'Do you have children of your own?'

I managed to shake my head.

'Well, take it from me, even in a place this size, seven kids have about the same effect as a herd of wild elephants.'

As if to underscore her words the ceiling suddenly shook with the sound of running, pounding feet. She gave me a look that said, see what I mean?

I knew at once that Garrison hadn't been putting on an act, and that somehow I had got all of this completely and utterly wrong. The phone calls, Sally's odd behaviour, none of it had anything to do with him. My first impulse was that I should get out of there, mumble whatever excuse I could come up with and hightail it away from White Falls as fast as I could.

'Did you say you came to see Sally?' Garrison said before I could organize my thoughts into action. 'Is she staying with her parents then?'

I seized on that as an excuse. 'Yes, that's right. She came up for a couple of days.'

'I used to see her around now and then when she was in town,' Garrison said. 'Though I haven't for a while. Actually I almost ran into her in San Francisco the other week. I met her dad.'

'Frank?'

'Yes. He was waiting for Sally and her mother to meet him after they'd been shopping. Pity I missed them.'

Now I understood why Sally hadn't mentioned meeting Garrison. It was because she hadn't. I saw with horrible clarity that when Frank had told me about bumping into Garrison he hadn't meant anything by it, there had been no hidden implication.

There was a pause, as Garrison pondered that he still didn't know how any of this had brought me to his door, or how it explained my strange appearance and what must have seemed like threatening behaviour.

'Looks as if I've made a mistake,' I said apologetically. 'Sally went out earlier and I thought she said she was coming to visit you. I must have misunderstood.'

'I see,' Garrison said, obviously unconvinced. 'No, she

353

didn't come here. I didn't even know she was in town. What about you, Kate, you haven't seen her have you?'

'I'm afraid we've never actually met. Though I've heard Garrison mention her of course, and I know her parents a little.'

'Like I said, I obviously misunderstood. Well, sorry to disturb you. I'll get out of your hair.'

'You wouldn't like to stay for coffee?'

'Thanks, but I should be going.' I shook Garrison's hand, and then his wife's and apologized again for barging in. I could already see the questions and bafflement in their eyes. But they were pleasant well bred people and they didn't say anything.

'You and Sally should come around for dinner. How long are you in town for?' Garrison said at the door.

'Oh, couple of days. That'd be great. I'll tell Sally and we can call you.'

'I'd love to meet her,' Kate said.

I raised a hand and went back to my car, then waved again and called goodbye before I drove away. When I looked in the mirror they were standing at the door watching me. I could almost hear Kate asking her husband, 'Who was that nut? Did he really think his wife was here? Sounded a little fishy to me.' They exchanged glances and turned and went back inside.

When I reached the road I pulled over and leaned my head against the wheel with my eyes closed. I kept seeing the Hunts' bemused expressions, and I wondered how I could have made such a horrendous mistake. It was lucky that I hadn't pulled a gun, or by then I would have been trying to explain myself to the county sheriff. I trawled back in my mind through all the incidents that had led me to believe that Sally was involved with Garrison, and the fact was I saw that it was all pretty much supposition

354

on my part. If Frank hadn't ever mentioned Garrison's name I never would have even thought of him. But that didn't change the calls I'd overheard, and her other suspicious behaviour. Could I have misread all of that as well? Had those things all been innocent?

I couldn't think straight. My mind was sluggish. Nothing made any sense any more and I didn't know what the truth was. All I knew was that I had to find Sally. It was only then that I saw what I should have seen right away, that if anyone would know where she was, it was Ellen. In fact once that thought took hold I slapped my hand on the wheel and cursed myself for being such a moron. The chances were that's where Sally was. Where else would she go?

I drove straight to their house. There was no sign of Sally's car, but if she was there I reasoned that she'd probably flown into Portland. However, I wasn't about to make the same mistake I had at the Hunts'. I did the best I could to straighten my appearance, though it didn't help much. The old house was just the same, a little more faded, a little more of its lustre lost in the signs of peeling paintwork around the window frames, and the chimneys were in need of repointing. Even Frank's glasshouses that I glimpsed at the back of the house as I got out of my car looked as though they were sinking into the ground, and I noticed the odd pane of missing glass. They should have sold the place a long time ago when it was clear they couldn't afford the upkeep, but I guess Ellen would rather live in a crumbling dump than move into an ordinary house like everyone else.

At the door I hesitated before ringing the bell. I hoped Garrison Hunt hadn't called ahead of me. A lot of emotions see-sawed back and forth in my mind. Footsteps approached on the other side, and then the door opened and Ellen stood before me. She was surprised to see me, but only briefly. The merest hint of a gloating smile that flickered in her eyes told me that she knew Sally had left me and she wasn't completely taken aback to see me there.

'Hello, Ellen,' I said in as civil a tone as I could muster.

She took in the state of my appearance and I imagined I had at last confirmed everything she always thought about me. 'You better come inside, Nick.'

We went through to the kitchen where I sat down at the big scrubbed pine table. The wood burning stove was lit, though it wasn't cold outside. I guessed it was cheaper to use than electricity.

'Would you like some coffee,' Ellen asked. 'You look as if you could use some.'

'Thanks.'

'Frank's in the garden.' She said it in such a way that I gathered that what she meant was that we could talk freely, just her and I.

'Is she here?'

Ellen looked at me over the rim of her cup then set it down on the table. 'No.'

I believed her. If Sally had been in the house I don't think I would ever have crossed the threshold. 'But you know where she is?' I ventured.

'I have a phone number for her. But she doesn't want anyone to know where she is.'

'By anyone you mean me specifically.'

'Yes, Nick. I mean you.'

I drank my coffee and wondered what Sally had told her mother. I doubted whether she'd said anything. Not about the money or Dexter.

'I'd like to talk to her, Ellen. I need that number.'

'I can't give it to you. Sally expressly said that if I heard from you I shouldn't. She doesn't want to talk to you.'

'She'll have to sooner or later.'

'Perhaps.'

There was something in her tone that belied her agreement, however. 'You don't think so?'

'I think you should face up to the fact that Sally has left you, Nick. Your marriage is over and this time she isn't going back.'

'This time. You make it sound as if this has happened before.'

'In a way it has. Several times when Sally was staying here she almost didn't go back to San Francisco.'

'I don't believe that.'

'Nevertheless it's true. I knew she was unhappy, that's why we came down to the city to see you. I wanted to convince her to come home. I think that's why she hadn't visited for a while, because she was afraid if she did she wouldn't go back again and Sally hadn't yet reached the point of making that step.'

'But she stayed,' I pointed out.

'Yes. But I warned her she was making a mistake.'

I wanted to ask if Sally was seeing somebody else, but I couldn't bring myself to. I couldn't bear the humiliation. Besides, if there was somebody and Ellen knew about it, I was certain she wouldn't have been able to resist telling me. It seemed that I was at an impasse. Ellen was never going to give me Sally's number unless I beat it out of her, and tempting as that notion was I hadn't yet sunk to that level.

'Sally wouldn't say what made her finally leave, but whatever has happened, this time she won't change her mind,' Ellen told me. 'When she called she was distraught.'

'When was that?' I asked, wondering if it was Ellen I'd overheard Sally speaking to.

'Yesterday morning.'

'Not the night before?'

'No,' she answered uncertainly. She got up and took our empty cups to the dishwasher. 'I always told you it would come to this.'

'You're enjoying this aren't you,' I said bitterly.

'You aren't right for each other, Nick, you never were.'

'No, Ellen, I wasn't right for you. Sally had nothing to do with it.' I wondered what she'd say if she knew about the program and Dexter. Maybe she was right, I thought.

I was wasting my time there so I stood up to leave. 'When you speak to her again, tell her I need to talk to her.' I tried to think of a message I could leave that Sally would find compelling. 'Just tell her she's got it all wrong.'

'It won't do any good,' Ellen replied, and I saw that it didn't matter what I said, she would never pass it on.

There was nothing left to say. I went to the front door and let myself out, and Ellen followed me and watched me go to my car. When I looked back she closed the door. I would have left then, but I saw Frank come out of one of his glasshouses and at the same time he looked over and saw me. He came over, obviously surprised, and we shook hands.

'Where's Sally?' he asked.

I realized he didn't know she'd left me. 'She didn't come, Frank. I was just passing through.'

He appeared puzzled, but stood back as I got in my car. 'You're leaving?'

'Yes. Take care, Frank.'

'You too,' he said, bewildered by all this.

I started the car and was about to pull away when he called something and I wound down the window. 'What was that?'

He smiled. 'I said did you spray those aphids yet?'

I laughed.

CHAPTER TWENTY-FIVE

I turned on my cell phone when I was half an hour from San Francisco. I called home first, but I wasn't surprised when I heard my own voice on the answering machine. I waited when the tone sounded, in case Sally was there, but even as I spoke her name I knew it was futile and I hung up. I called Alice next, and the urgency in her tone cut through my fatigue like a cold water plunge.

'Oh my God where have you been? I've been trying to reach you.'

I sidestepped the issue of what I'd been doing for the past thirty-six hours, my attention focused squarely back on Dexter. 'Has something happened?'

A note of panic sounded in her voice. 'I couldn't get hold of you. I've been going crazy here. Everything's going wrong.'

She wasn't making any sense yet but it was clear that events had moved on while I was gone. 'Slow down,' I told her, trying to remain calm myself. 'What are you talking about. Tell me everything. Slowly.'

I heard her take a breath as she struggled to get a grip on herself. When she started speaking again she sounded calmer, more in control. 'Marcus called me. I tried to get hold of you right away but there was no answer at your house and your cell phone was switched off. He was asking questions. Strange questions. First he wanted to know if I knew about Dexter, and then he asked if I'd talked to you. I said I had of course, and then he started cross-examining me. He wanted to know every word you'd said.'

So Marcus was suspicious too. That was bad but it wasn't catastrophic. So long as he hadn't said anything to the police. 'What did you say?'

'I acted dumb. He kept asking me if you'd said anything about seeing Dexter after the night at the restaurant.'

That was worse, I thought. 'Has he said anything to the police?'

'I don't think so. I would have heard from Morello if he had.'

'What else did Marcus say.'

'Nothing at first. After I spoke to him I kept trying to reach you but nobody knew where you were. I couldn't get an answer at your house. Then Marcus called again and said he thought you might have had something to do with what happened to Dexter. He wanted to know what I thought we should do.'

'What did you say?'

'I told him he was wrong of course. I said he was crazy. And then we ended up fighting. He hung up in the end. I was sick with worry. I didn't know what he was going to do. I couldn't sleep at all so yesterday when I still couldn't find you I tried to call Marcus back to see what was going on but I couldn't get hold of him. All kinds of things have been going through my mind. I thought he must have gone to the police, that you'd been arrested or something. Every time the phone rang or somebody came near the boat I practically had a heart attack.'

My head was reeling as I tried to take all this in.

'Where have you been?' Alice said again.

'I went to Oregon.'

'Oregon?'

'Sally left me. I had to talk to her.'

'She went to Oregon?'

'Her parents live there, and . . .' I started to explain about Garrison Hunt, but stopped. 'Look it doesn't matter. She wasn't there.'

For several seconds Alice didn't say anything. I was trying to figure out how Marcus knew about Dexter until the answer was clear, that Sally must have told him.

'Sally knows doesn't she?' Alice cut into my thoughts. 'She knows about Dexter.'

'Yes,' I admitted. 'That's part of the reason I was trying to find her, to talk to her.' Alice made a groaning sound. 'What is it?'

'Oh, Nick. You still don't know, do you?'

And then in a flash of insight I did know. I knew exactly what she would say next and it was as if I had been stumbling around like a man lost in dense fog and suddenly a wind comes up and the fog lifts and the view is clear for miles.

'Sally is with Marcus,' she said.

I had no feeling inside but my grip involuntarily tightened on the phone. It was several seconds before I could trust myself to speak. 'How long has it been going on?'

'I'm not sure. I figured it out a while ago.'

Things started tumbling into place like the pieces of a puzzle. It was all suddenly so obvious. All the charged looks and tension when the four of us were together made sense as I imagined Sally and Marcus terrified their secret would come out.

'That's why you went to live on the boat?'

'Yes. After you came back from Mendocino I thought it was over between them. Marcus told me it was. He said that Sally and you were going to make a go of it. I would have said something if I'd thought they were seeing each other again. I didn't know. I'm sorry.'

How could I have been so blind I wondered? How

could I not have seen what now was so obvious. A hundred fleeting moments came back to me. Looks Sally and Marcus had exchanged. The odd tension I'd sensed between her and Alice the night we'd met to talk about the program. How the hell could I have been so stupid when it was right there before my eyes the whole time?

'That's why Marcus agreed to sell the program to Morgan isn't it?'

'Yes. I threatened to tell you about him and Sally if he didn't.'

'And at Marios. When he agreed to carry on with our plan after Dexter turned up. Damn it!' I pounded my fist on the wheel. How could I have been so fucking blind?

But if I thought nothing worse could happen I was wrong.

'Nick, I have to see you,' Alice said. 'We need to talk. There's more.'

'More?' I echoed dumbly. I didn't know how there could be.

'Brinkman's dead,' she said. 'It's in the paper.'

The boat where Alice was living was moored in the marina at Sausalito. It was in one of the last basins north of the town. I knew where to find it because I'd been there often enough. Before Alice had arrived on the scene we would go out regularly for the day or the weekend. Sometimes Marcus would have a girlfriend along, other times it was just the three of us. It was a forty-two foot launch called *Temptation*, equipped with a powerful engine and a comfortable interior fitted out with soft leather seating and ingenious hidden cupboards and folding tables designed to maximize the space. There were three cabins below deck, and two steering stations, one inside and another up top on the flying bridge. Marcus had always owned boats. He compromised the house he lived in to afford the drain on his finances, since they are an expensive hobby, what with mooring fees, gas and maintenance. But we'd had some good times. Swimming at night in some secluded cove where we'd dropped anchor. Barbecuing on the beach, eating fish we'd caught ourselves the same day, getting drunk beneath a velvet sky and lying on the sand staring up at the stars waxing philosophically about life and love and the meaning of it all.

I thought about those times we'd had as I walked along the dock, and my new-found knowledge curdled my memories. Everything would be that way from now on, I realized. Anything that reminded me of Marcus and Sally would be tainted, and since our lives had been so entwined for such a long time that was going to be almost everything. A fleetingly remembered image came back to me. One summer a few years back the three of us had gone away for a couple of days. We anchored in a bay down the coast near San Simeon and sat around on the stern deck drinking cold beers from the bottle and eating from a big platter of spaghetti and clam sauce.

It had been a hot muggy night and we were chugging through the beers. We were in good spirits, and Marcus brought out a little pack of grass and we passed around a couple of joints. It was mild stuff. Sally got the giggles the way she always did when she smoked, and we looked on in a benevolent fuzz when she decided we should all go for a swim. She said she wanted to go skinny dipping, which was something we never did. She often sunbathed topless, but she still retained enough of her small-town upbringing to think that was as far as it ought to go. All at once she stood up and shucked off her top and unzipped her skirt and stepped out of it then quickly peeled off her panties. She looked terrific. Her breasts were tanned, the slope of her belly smooth and taut. It was a pleasantly, languid, sensuous moment, helped of course by the effects of the dope. I thought she was beautiful and I was proud of her and overcome with a kind of warmth that I could feel so comfortable with Marcus that I didn't mind him seeing my wife naked.

We watched as she went to the edge of the boat and dived smoothly into the water. I'd always thought of that night as something intimate shared by friends. In a way asexual. But now I wondered what Marcus had been thinking. Was that when he'd first begun harbouring a secret lust for her? The memory was suddenly sordid and I banished it from my thoughts.

Alice was waiting anxiously for me on the deck when I arrived. She looked as if she hadn't slept much and worry lines were etched in her normally smooth features. Her usually cool eyes darted nervously beyond as if any moment she expected squad cars to screech to a halt at the end of the dock. There was nobody around. A lot of the yachts and launches here were barely used from one year to the next. The parking lot was empty save for my own and three other vehicles and a line of boats parked on trailers. It was sunny and the bay across to Raccoon Strait between Tiburon and Angel Island was ruffled with whitecaps from a stiff breeze. Gulls strutted up and down the dock, and others screeched in the wind. We went below out of sight, and she gave me that morning's *Examiner* where Brinkman's demise had made the inside front page with a quarter page piece that included a photograph of him that must have been taken a few years ago. In it he looked younger and considerably slimmer than I remembered.

Alice hadn't told me much on the phone, but the way she'd sounded had left me in no doubt that she was worried out of her mind. Once I read the article I knew why. Brinkman lived in a leafy residential street on the slopes of Cow Hollow bordering Pacific Heights. The report stated that he was divorced and lived alone, and that his two kids lived in the Sacramento area, presumably with his ex-wife. A neighbour had discovered his body in the garage of his house when he had called by to return something that he'd borrowed. Brinkman had been tied to a chair with electrical cord, and he'd been tortured with a power drill. The exact cause of death hadn't been established at the time of going to press, according to the report, which made me wonder what kind of damage had been inflicted while Brinkman was still alive that made that difficult to ascertain. Neither had a motive for the killing been established, though first reports suggested he'd been dead for a couple of days and the time of death was estimated as being sometime around Tuesday morning.

'Jesus Christ,' I breathed when I'd finished reading. I dropped the paper. Though the details given by the police were sketchy there was enough for a vivid picture of Brinkman to flower in my mind. Fuelled by images from a lifetime of witnessing extreme forms of violence portrayed in movies and on TV I imagined his sagging body held in place by its bonds, his head lolling against the chest, a dirty rag stuffed in his mouth to stifle his screams, and blood running across his torso from wounds in his face and chest and groin, pooling around his feet. The household drill would be lying on the floor carelessly discarded.

Alice and I stared at each other. I was no doubt now as pale as she was. Neither one of us wanted to voice the fear that had sprung to both our minds, but Alice had the advantage of having had longer to think about this.

'You don't think it has anything to do with . . . ?'

I finished the sentence for her. 'The program?' I wanted to tell her no. It was just a gruesome coincidence, but my capacity to accept coincidence had become vastly diminished of late. Instead I went to the TV and turned it on, and flicked through the channels until I found the news. I was turning over what we knew at the same time.

'The report says no motive has been established,' I reasoned. 'That means it probably wasn't a robbery because they'd know that right away. But there's no reason to believe there's any connection with us.'

'What if Brinkman told somebody,' Alice said.

'Why would he do that?'

'I don't know. But we don't know that he didn't.'

'What if he did?' I countered. 'That doesn't mean whoever he told would want to kill him.'

She thought about that, biting her lower lip nervously. 'I suppose.'

Neither of us were convinced, however. Deep down we both knew that Brinkman's death was inescapably connected with the program and therefore us. We just didn't want to face it yet.

'Look at what's happening to my nerves.' Alice held out her hand, and there was a barely perceptible tremor. 'I need a drink.' She looked questioningly at me.

It was still early in the morning, but I didn't hesitate. I had an insatiable craving for strong liquor. She went to a concealed cabinet and poured out a couple of half tumblers of vodka, which isn't normally my drink but on this occasion I wasn't about to be picky. I tossed off half of mine in one swallow. It burned all the way down my throat and I waited for the accompanying glow in the pit of my stomach. Alice watched me, then knocked off a good slug of her own. I still had one eye on the TV when something caught my eye. Brinkman's face, the same picture that the paper had used, stared back at me from the screen. I turned up the sound as the anchorwoman talked to the reporter at the scene.

The shot changed to show a typical three-storey house

with basement garage and bay windows on the first floor. The kind of place that typically goes for anything up to a couple of million or more in Cow Hollow these days. The garage door was open but it had been screened with black plastic, and crime scene tape encircled the property to keep back a mob of reporters and curious onlookers. The reporter regurgitated the facts we'd read in the paper, adding little more except some extra detail about Brinkman himself. It was clear he didn't know much more so they filled the piece in with an interview with a neighbour who lived along the street, who also didn't add much of interest but talked as if he had been Brinkman's best buddy in the world. He was enjoying his moment in the spotlight. Brinkman, it seemed, had been a model citizen. The neighbour couldn't understand why anyone would want to hurt such a terrific guy, let alone torture him. They were animals, he said, whoever had done this. He hoped when they were caught the s.o.b.'s got the death penalty. He only wished he could be the one to throw the switch because as far as he was concerned murderers had no place in the world.

Alice glanced at me when he said that, and I knew what she was thinking. He was talking about me too. It hadn't occurred to me before then but if I was caught and tried for Dexter's murder that guy might be talking about me. San Quentin was less than a fifteen minute drive from where I was sitting. An image of the massive ugly squat building that lies on a spit of land in sight of the Richmond Bridge filled my inner eye. How often had I passed it, eyed its forbidding presence, never dreaming that one day I might be a resident.

The anchorwoman asked a couple of questions of the reporter, trying to establish motive and more details about the nature of Brinkman's death, but the police were keeping a lid on what they knew. However, one piece of information at the end of the report made me sit up with a start.

'Do the police have any clue whatsoever about who the perpetrators might be, Alan?' the anchorwoman asked.

'Well, Trish, at the moment the police don't appear to have any solid leads to go on. They're still going over the scene with a forensic team and I guess they'll be waiting to see what they can learn from the results of that analysis. However, they are still conducting interviews with local residents to see if anyone saw or heard anything over the weekend that might be helpful, and so far the police have told us they are interested in tracking down a vehicle that was seen in the area. Right now they're not certain of the make or model, but a dark green car, possibly a mid-eighties Ford Mustang, was seen parked along the street on Saturday morning which is around the time they think Mr Brinkman may have been killed. Eyewitnesses said the vehicle was noticeable because it had wide wheels and darkened windows, and I guess that isn't the kind of car that you normally find in an area like this.'

I froze in the act of raising my glass. I thought back to the car that I'd seen the day I went to see Morgan. That had been green too. And the one that played chicken with Sally and me on the way to Marios that night. I glanced at Alice, but her eye was glued to the screen. Of course I hadn't mentioned the car before, because it hadn't seemed important. But now I wasn't so sure. Another coincidence? I told myself the police didn't even know this car was connected to Brinkman's death, and even if it was, there were millions of green cars on the road. But ones with wide wheels and darkened windows? That was stretching credibility a little too far. The report ended, and Alice turned off the set.

'What is it?' she said, suddenly noticing the way I looked.

I finished my drink. 'Nothing.' I couldn't see any point in worrying her unduly.

She looked at me quizzically, but before she could ask me anything else her cell phone suddenly rang. We stared at each other, then she picked it up.

'Hello?' she said cautiously. She listened for a second, then turned to me and mouthed the word Marcus. I got up and took the phone from her.

'Where's my wife you bastard?' I demanded.

CHAPTER TWENTY-SIX

Marcus was surprised when he heard my voice. While he struggled to gather his thoughts I let fly with a stream of threats and recriminations. I thought about all the times I'd felt guilty over the damage I'd done to our friendship. I thought that I had betrayed him, and all the time he'd been screwing my wife. The more I cursed him the angrier I became. I was losing control, practically shaking with fury. I was tired and strung out from everything that had happened over the last few days. The only thing that mattered to me at that moment was confronting Sally and Marcus together. I demanded repeatedly that he tell me where they were. I don't know what I planned to do. I don't think I had a plan. Through it all Alice hung back. I think she was a little afraid of me.

But in the end I fell silent. I was spent. Lack of sleep as much as anything overcame me with numbing fatigue. I sat down heavily.

'I want to see her,' I said at last, heavily, into the phone.

'Nick . . .' Marcus began hesitantly, and faltered. Then he gathered resolve. 'She doesn't want to see you.'

'Just tell me where you are.' I didn't sound angry any more, only beaten, almost pleading.

'Nick . . .'

'You owe me that much dammit! She's my wife. I want to talk to her.'

He was taken aback by the abrupt change in my tone.

'Wait a second,' he said, and in the ensuing silence I gathered he was repeating my request to Sally. He came back on the line after a few moments.

'Okay, but not now. Later. Tonight. You're tired, you need to rest. And we'll come to you.'

How the hell did he know I was tired I wondered, but of course Sally must have spoken to her mother by then and she would know I'd been to Oregon. No doubt Ellen had given a vivid description of the state I was in. I wanted to argue, but he second guessed me.

'Tonight, Nick. And don't try to find us. You won't.'

'Where?'

'The boat. We'll come to the marina.'

Before I could say anything else he hung up. I told Alice what he'd said and she offered me a sympathetic look.

'Why don't you get some rest. You look beat.'

I started to protest that I wouldn't be able to sleep, and besides I needed to think, but even as I spoke I knew that if I was going to think clearly rest was exactly what I needed. My eyes felt grainy, and I was a little light headed. The slight motion of the boat on the water made it worse.

'Why don't you take a shower and I'll wash your clothes. You'll find everything you need in the bathroom,' Alice suggested.

I gave in. 'But wake me in a couple of hours.'

She promised she would so I went back through to one of the cabins where I undressed and found a towel to wrap myself in. I stood under the hot jet of water in the shower for a long time, leaning my head against the wall and letting it run off my back. I heard Alice come into the bathroom and when I was finished I found she'd left me out a razor and a toothbrush. I felt a lot better when I was done, but when I looked at my reflection the gaunt character who stared back with red and bleary eyes came as a slight shock. When I went back through to the cabin my clothes were gone, and the curtain was drawn so that the room was dim, the bed turned back. The sight of fresh clean sheets was suddenly incredibly inviting. Alice appeared in the doorway.

'I'll take your clothes to the laundromat and then I'll be right back.'

I sat down on the edge of the bed and nodded.

'You'll feel better when you've slept,' she told me.

She looked tired herself, the strain showing in her face. I knew she had to be worried. 'It'll be okay, Alice. When I wake up we'll figure out what to do. It's going to work out.' I told her that I'd call Morgan later who would be back from New York. We both needed something positive to hang onto, and the money was all there was.

She attempted a smile. 'Go to sleep.'

After she closed the door I lay down. My head hit the pillow and in seconds I was gone.

I woke with a start. I was immediately alert, though it took a moment before I remembered where I was. I'd been dreaming, but as the images fled from my mind I couldn't remember what they were and I didn't try to hang onto them. The cabin was darker than when I'd lain down and I knew it must be late in the day. I started to get up, looking for my watch beside the bed.

'You're awake.'

It was Alice. She was sitting in a chair near the door, her legs curled up underneath her. I had the impression she'd fallen asleep there.

'What time is it?' I asked.

'About six.'

I found my watch and saw that it was twenty after. I'd

been asleep for almost nine hours. 'I told you to wake me,' I said.

'I didn't see any point. You were in such a deep sleep I figured you were exhausted. I thought the best thing was to leave you alone.'

She was probably right, I acknowledged. 'How long have you been there?'

'A couple of hours. I must have dozed off.' She anticipated my next question before I asked it. 'I've been listening to the news all day. There's been nothing else about Brinkman.'

I wasn't sure if I should be relieved about that or not, since it meant whoever killed him was still out there. 'Has anyone called?'

'Marcus. I told him you were still sleeping. I didn't know when you'd wake so he said they would come later, around ten.'

'Did he say anything else?'

'He asked if I knew about Brinkman. He sounded worried.' She knew what I really wanted to know though, and she added, 'He didn't mention Sally.'

I didn't say anything, and after a moment Alice got up and came over to sit on the edge of the bed.

'You love her a lot don't you?'

I wasn't sure of the answer to that any more. Before I knew about Sally and Marcus I would have answered without hesitation, but then I never would have believed she could do what she had. When I thought she was having an affair with Garrison Hunt I felt partly responsible, and if I blamed anyone other than myself it was him. But Marcus, that was different. I blamed them both for betraying me. What the hell could Marcus give her that I couldn't?

'It's funny in a way don't you think?' Alice said when I didn't answer.

'What is?'

'Perhaps funny isn't the right word. Ironic then. You and I ending up here like this. Perhaps we're more alike than we realized.'

'Alike?'

'Don't you think so? We both want the same thing in the end don't we? I used to resent you because Marcus wouldn't stand up to you. I was afraid you'd destroy the business and then where would I be? A failed artist, painting pictures nobody wants to buy. I know what it's like not to have any money, and I didn't want to be in that position again.' She paused. 'You were right about me. I was jealous of you in a way.'

'We've got something in common then,' I said, at which she looked puzzled. 'You were right about me too. I did wreck the business.'

She smiled. 'That makes us even then.'

'How long have you known about Sally and Marcus?' I asked.

'I suspected he was seeing somebody months ago. But I didn't know for sure who it was.'

'How did you find out?'

'I saw them together.'

'Where?'

'Here. When I confronted Marcus he said there was nothing between them, that they were just friends. He claimed they were both worried about you.'

'So they thought it might help if they started screwing each other,' I said bitterly. I imagined them lying naked in bed together. Maybe even the bed I was lying in. Consoling each other with tales of what an asshole I had become. Alice looked away, and I wondered what she was thinking. 'Did you believe him?'

She took a moment to answer. 'I wanted to. I suppose I was afraid of what it meant, where I would go. And I loved him.'

To hear her claim that she loved Marcus surprised me, though I wasn't sure why. Perhaps because I'd always assumed the worst of her. But now I saw that she too had been hurt and was angry, only she'd had longer to deal with it.

'Why didn't you tell me?' I asked.

'I almost did. A couple of times I called your house.'

I remembered the occasions when I'd picked up the phone and nobody had answered.

'But I thought if I did then you might leave Sally.'

'And then she and Marcus would have each other . . .'

'Something like that,' she admitted. 'Then after you went to Mendocino, Marcus said that Sally had decided to give your marriage another chance.'

'But you moved here to the boat?'

'Yes.' She looked me in the eye. 'I realized then how Marcus felt about her.'

I think that hurt me more than anything. I thought about what Alice had said. Perhaps she was right. She and I were alike. It was Alice who'd gone along with my scheme to sell the program to Morgan, and it was her that I'd turned to when I needed somebody to help me get rid of Dexter's body, and now it was Alice who was my ally. Maybe we deserved each other.

In that moment of understanding, what happened next seemed inevitable. I reached out to touch her face. She didn't move at first, though our eyes were locked together. She'd asked if I loved Sally, and despite everything I did, but nothing was the same any more. I was a different person. I had killed a man, and Sally would always revile me for that. I wasn't proud of it myself, and I wished it hadn't happened, but it had and there was nothing I could do about it. Alice understood that. Right then we needed each other.

I drew her onto the bed and we kissed. What started

tentatively became quickly passionate. We were driven by the need to forget, for reassurance, for blind physical satisfaction. Revenge even. Who knows? A lot of things we probably were only dimly aware of. The sheets fell away. I was already naked. I pulled and tugged at Alice's clothing in my haste to undress her. She lay beneath me, eyes half closed, lips partly open, her breathing heavy. She stared up at me. Lovemaking with Sally had always been a slow sensuous affair. It was the caress of her hand through my hair as I kissed the hollow of her neck that thrilled me. The whisper of her breath against my cheek when I entered her, the soft murmurs we exchanged as we moved together in an almost languid embrace. But as I looked down on Alice I felt a different need. She was beautiful, in a pale almost too perfect way, and I desired her. But I wanted something from her. I wanted to possess her, I wanted to fuck her and take something for myself, sate some vengeful lust, and I knew she wanted the same from me.

I knelt between her thighs gazing at her breasts and the pale hair below her belly. She was so unlike Sally physically and that excited me. She reached out and drew me towards her, locking her legs around my back as she thrust her hips upwards. I uttered a groan as I pushed myself hard into her. We clung to one another, our movements urgent and demanding. In the heat of the enclosed cabin our bodies made sucking sounds as we slid together in our combined sweat, panting from our efforts. Alice screwed her eyes closed, her expression intense with concentration. I moved faster and harder like a runner sprinting for the line and sensing that I was reaching the end Alice bucked her hips upwards furiously, uttering savage animal-like grunts. Our coupling was almost painful. We slammed our flesh together, each of us desperate to reach our own end regardless of the other. I looked down as

Alice's eyes flew open and she glared at me, then abruptly shifted herself sideways with a violent motion uttering a guttural exclamation of impatience as she did so. Then as she thrust upwards to meet me one more time she suddenly stiffened and gasped. Her teeth were clenched, eyes screwed tight as if she was suffering intense pain, and she gasped in shuddering breaths. I continued pounding into her even though she tried to still me, and then when I thought my strength would give out, that my lungs would burst, I climaxed and we collapsed in a sweating tangle of limbs.

Twenty minutes later I was showered and Alice was in the bathroom. She had folded my freshly laundered clothes on a chair, and when I dressed I found my dad's gun placed underneath my jeans. I picked it up, wondering what she'd thought when she found it. After I'd checked that it was still loaded I tucked it into the back of my jeans and covered it with my shirt.

I was making a call when Alice emerged, fully dressed again. She hesitated, then came over and kissed my cheek, her eyes questioning. I slipped my arm around her hip. It seemed we had made some kind of pact, the nature of which was uncertain, but Alice was satisfied with my response.

'Who are you calling?'

'Morgan,' I said.

She sat down to watch and listen. We understood this much about each other. Whatever else happened, we were going to get the money because now there was nothing else left. The phone was answered by a man and I asked to speak to Morgan and gave my name. I waited for a while and then the same voice came on the line again.

'Mr Morgan isn't available at the moment I'm afraid.'

There was something about this I didn't like, though I wasn't sure exactly what it was. 'He's back from New York isn't he?'

There was a pause before he answered. 'Mr Morgan has guests this evening. He wondered if you might call again tomorrow.'

It was a reasonable enough request. What difference did it make whether I talked to him then or in the morning, and yet a sixth sense warned me that something didn't feel right. I thought about the pause before he'd answered, and I suspected that Morgan was in the room, listening to the conversation, though if that was so I couldn't figure out why he didn't want to talk to me.

In the end, because I didn't know what to make of it I agreed to call again in the morning and I hung up.

'What is it?' Alice asked.

'Nothing. At least I think it's nothing.' I told her what had happened.

'You think something's wrong?'

I shook my head, dismissing my suspicions. 'No. Everything's fine.'

All the same, I decided it was time I had the program where I could keep an eye on it. There was time to go to the office and fetch it before Sally and Marcus arrived.

Traffic was light into the city, and it didn't take me very long to reach the office. I parked in the basement and let myself in the building. It gave me the shivers to be in there alone, bringing back as it did unwelcome thoughts of Dexter. It took me just a couple of minutes to retrieve the disc and lock up again.

When I was done I headed back towards the basement. I hadn't noticed before how quiet it was. Then I heard the unmistakable sound of a car turning the corner onto the street outside and then it slowed. The beam of its headlights lit the wall by the entrance to the courtyard' and stayed there, and above the faint background sounds of city traffic ten blocks away I heard the low idling of a motor. Instinctively I took a step back merging into the shadows beneath the high brick walls. My heartbeat grew faster, and sweat prickled my palms. I waited, counting to twenty, and nothing happened. It could be anyone out there, I told myself, it didn't mean anything, but an unbidden image of Brinkman flashed in my mind, tied up and tortured to death, and I recalled that the police were looking for a green car with darkened windows.

I felt suddenly vulnerable and exposed so I made my way along the wall and quickly slipped down the ramp into the car park. For a second I wondered if what I was doing was such a great idea. The red glow of the lamp on the wall created an eerie light at the bottom of the ramp, but further back the basement was pitch black and all at once forbidding. Nevertheless I didn't have a lot of choice since my car was down there so I hurried to where I'd left it and fumbled for my keys. The darkness was like a physical thing, closing around me. It was suddenly deathly quiet, or perhaps it had been before only I hadn't noticed. Somebody could have stood six feet away and I wouldn't have seen them. I managed to get the key in the lock, and as I opened the door the interior light came on, creating a dim oasis of welcome light, then I climbed in, closed the door and the light winked out. I turned the key and the engine started and I felt a sudden rush of relief, but it only lasted a second.

At the bottom of the entrance ramp a light bounced off the walls and grew brighter and I knew that a car was coming down.

For a moment I stared in frozen fascination then adrenaline kicked in and my mind was off and running. I put the car in reverse and without turning on the lights I backed up and swung around a pillar where I came to a halt. I had a clear line now to the ramp, though I'd need to do a sharp left at the bottom. I figured as the other car came down and swung to the right I'd have a couple of moments before I was seen and in that time I planned to hit the gas and be up the ramp and heading onto the street. I gripped the wheel tightly, my heart pumping as the car came into view.

As it started to turn the corner I put my foot down and the Saab shot forward with a squeal of rubber. At the same time I saw the roof lights and the door insignia and I realized the car ahead of me wasn't some crazed killer come after me like he had Brinkman, but in fact was a security patrol. The driver gunned his engine but when I hit the brake he did the same and slid around to a halt. A searchlight blinked on and hit me in the face. I tried for a friendly grin and showed my hands.

'Hi,' I called out. 'You gave me a scare there.'

The light continued shining in my face, dazzling me as it was surely meant to while the driver looked me over.

'I came into the office to pick up something I forgot. I work here,' I said.

I heard a car door open. 'Stay where you are, sir,' a courteous but firm voice said. He sounded young. I pictured some hot-shot who'd failed the police exam and this was going to be his big chance. He probably wanted me to be a burglar.

'Please identify yourself,' he said from the darkness. I still couldn't see him.

'Nick Weston. I run an advertising firm in this building. Carpe Diem.'

'Carp what?'

'Diem.' I spelled it out for him. There was a short silence and I imagined he was checking a list.

'What's your code, sir?'

Every business in the building was assigned a code,

which, in the event of a problem, the security company would request as verification of a person's entitlement to be on the premises after hours.

'Sixteen seventy-two,' I said.

He seemed satisfied with this because a moment later the searchlight was turned off. Though, as he came towards me he shone a torch at me just in case. His right hand rested on his holstered weapon which looked a lot bigger than the .38 I still had tucked in my jeans.

'Do you have any identification on you, sir?' he asked.

'Sure.' I started to reach for my driver's licence, and as I moved I saw him tense. I held up my licence and he took a look. He was indeed young, as I'd thought. Maybe in his mid-twenties. He had broad features and red hair. Without the uniform he would have looked at home tending a pumpkin patch around Half Moon Bay. A glimmer of disappointment showed in his eye, then he relaxed.

'I saw the grill was open when I came by on patrol,' he said.

'Right. Well, it's just me. So if everything's okay with you, I'll get going.'

'You left something behind you said?' he asked quickly.

'That's right.'

I think he was waiting for me to elaborate. Either some instinct made him suspicious or else he was just doing his job thoroughly, but I didn't offer any more information.

'Well, goodnight,' I said pointedly.

He took the hint and stepped back a little. 'Goodnight.'

He watched me leave. I hit the ramp and went out underneath the grill, then I was across the courtyard and out into the street. As I hit the intersection I slowed and made a right, and as I did a set of headlights hit my rear-view mirror and a car settled back several lengths behind me. I figured it was the security guard, though he must have moved fast to catch up so quickly. As I headed along the Embercadero towards the bridge I imagined him on the radio to a dispatcher, perhaps running a check on my licence plates. I didn't know if they could do that, but I guessed they probably could. Anyway I drove calmly and kept to the limit, and signalled before every turn as if he was a cop, and when I reached the approach to the bridge I lost sight of the headlights among so many others in four lanes of traffic. I guessed that he had probably given up by then anyway and turned around.

It was a little before nine when I reached the marina. The basin where *Temptation* was moored was quiet at that time of night. Closer to town there were the usual milling crowds of people heading for the various waterfront bars and restaurants but the noise didn't carry this far. The only sound was the rattle of rigging against the masts of yachts and the gentle slap of water against the hulls, and the only light was from a single high lamp in the middle of the parking lot which created a pool of yellow that faded towards the lot's edges and created deep wedges of shadow alongside the boat trailers.

Alice was waiting for me on the stern deck. She had a glass of something on the table in front of her and was smoking a cigarette. I held up the disc as I approached.

'No problem,' I said and went inside to put it away in a compartment she'd showed me earlier.

'What are you drinking?' I asked when I went back outside.

'I bought some bourbon. Would you like some?'

'Thanks.'

Then I sat down to wait for Sally and Marcus, wondering what would happen next.

CHAPTER TWENTY-SEVEN

Marcus arrived five minutes early. I saw the lights of his car as he drove down towards the lot and swung in through the open gate. The lights were extinguished and then a few minutes later I saw him coming along the dock. He was alone. I watched from the stern deck as he approached. Seeing him face to face put a renewed glow to the embers of my anger.

'Where's Sally?' I said when he drew close.

He stopped uncertainly, and glanced from me to Alice who stood in the shadows behind me, though what he ascertained from the subtle vibrations in the air I don't know.

'She wouldn't come,' he said finally.

'Where is she?'

He shook his head. 'That doesn't matter right now. I'm not here because of Sally.'

I took a slow deep breath. I didn't trust myself to speak. Marcus peered at me in the faint light that came from inside the cabin behind me. He was trying to read my expression, gauge my mood as if I had become something unpredictable. He kind of sighed, as if he didn't understand how any of this could have happened. As if he was weighed down by a heavy burden.

'It doesn't matter?' I said.

'I mean there are other things we need to think about.'

'It doesn't matter?'

That's all I could say. I was incredulous that he could imagine he could just push the fact that he'd been sleeping with my wife to one side. If that had been his intention, he evidently decided that it was a vain hope.

'Look, Nick, I don't expect you to believe this but I . . . we . . . never intended for this to happen.'

'Does it matter what I believe?'

'Believe it or not, it does.' He saw, as he must have known, that this wasn't going to be easy. He looked a little edgy, wary like a fox as if he didn't know what I might do. 'We need to talk.'

For a second I didn't answer, then I said, 'Come aboard. It's your boat after all.' I held out my hand to help him up, though he could've done it himself as easily. He looked at my hand and our eyes met. My expression offered him no clue as to what he should do. In the end he reached out as I'd known he would. We clasped hands and I pulled him aboard and when his feet hit the deck I hit him with a blow that caught the side of his head and knocked him sideways. He staggered and I released his hand and hit him again and this time he hit the deck, landing on all fours with a grunt of pain.

As I stood over him he took a deep breath, his head down, and a drop of blood hit the deck, followed by another. He picked up his glasses and put them back on. When he looked up his eyes were shining and his nose was bloody. He dabbed at his face with his T-shirt and rose unsteadily to his feet.

For some reason even though he'd deserved what I'd done, hitting him hadn't made me feel any better.

'I thought we were friends,' I said, part in accusation, part justification.

He looked at me sharply. 'That's a little rich isn't it?'

'How could you do it? Both of you. The lies, the cheating.'

'Right. And you never did any of those things.'

'Maybe I kept things from you sometimes, and maybe I should've listened to you more, but that isn't the same as sleeping with my wife you asshole.'

'Look, I'm not proud of this. Neither of us are. We didn't plan for it to happen.' He glanced at Alice, and I saw he was telling her this as much as me but she had heard it before and she looked away.

'But the fact is, Nick,' he said, turning his attention back to me. 'You're as much to blame for this as we are.'

I shook my head slowly. 'Don't try to do this. Don't try to make this my fault. Nobody forced you two together. Nobody made you fuck my wife! How long have you been thinking about it? I bet it was a long time. I bet you dreamed about it for years.'

I was just talking, spewing out whatever came into my mind because I didn't want to hear what he was saying, but I saw a reaction I hadn't expected, a lowering of his eye and in a flash of insight I knew that it was actually true.

Alice stared at him, and she too saw what I had. 'Bastard,' she said quietly.

'Whatever you think, nothing happened. Nothing ever happened. Not at first.'

'How long?'

'Does it matter?'

'Yes, it fucking matters,' I said.

'We used to meet to talk. We both felt like we didn't know you any more. I didn't feel like I could trust you. Sally thought you'd changed.'

'Is that right? Is that what Sally thought. And I bet you agreed with her didn't you? What else did you tell her, Marcus? Did you tell her that if she left me the two of you could set up house together and have a bunch of kids?'

'It wasn't like that.'

But I didn't believe him. I thought it had been exactly like that.

'Even after we knew we felt something for each other we tried not to let anything happen,' Marcus went on. 'Believe it or not when you went to Mendocino and Sally said you were going to make a go of it, I was happy for you. For both of you.'

I remembered the phone call I'd overheard Sally make from our room in the inn. 'That's big of you, Marcus.'

'Believe what you want, but it's true. Sally really wanted it to work between you. But after Hoffman died she knew it was the money that was important to you. More than anything else. Including her. You ought to think about that before you blame everyone else, Nick.'

But I didn't want to hear any more. 'I don't even know why I'm listening to this. I should be talking to Sally not you.'

'She doesn't want to talk to you. She doesn't want to see you again. Ever.'

'That's a lie.'

'It's true. She doesn't know who you are any more. Neither of us do. She's frightened of what you've become.'

'Frightened?' I echoed incredulously. 'That's bullshit. Why should Sally be frightened of me?'

Marcus stared at me. 'You need to ask that? Really? For chrissakes, Nick, you killed him. You killed Dexter didn't you? Sally knows you were out that night. You washed your clothes. Was that because you had Dexter's blood on you? Detective Morello left a message for me to contact him today.'

I reacted to the sound of the detective's name. I'd almost forgotten about him.

'You know what he said when I called him?' Marcus

went on. 'He told me Dexter was asphyxiated. Somebody bashed in his skull and then smothered him before they put him in his car and shoved it over a cliff to try and make it look like an accident. He said it happened the same night Dexter stopped by at our table in Marios. He was asking questions about you, Nick. He'd heard you and Dexter didn't like each other and that made him wonder.'

'Plenty of people didn't like Dexter. Why pick on me?'

'That's what he doesn't know. But he's digging. How long do you think it will be before he finds out about Hoffman and that's going to lead him to Brinkman.'

I supposed it was true, it was only a matter of time before he figured it out. But it was all circumstantial. Unless he had forensic evidence to tie Dexter's death to me, it was all just guess work, and I thought the ocean would have obliterated anything there might have been. And since there was no way he could figure where Dexter had died, there wasn't much chance of him finding any.

'And let's not forget Brinkman,' Marcus said. 'Somebody killed him too.'

It took me a second to realize what he was implying. 'You think I killed Brinkman too? I was in Oregon looking for my wife you prick.'

He blinked, realizing that was true, but then something else occurred to him. 'So you're admitting that you killed Dexter?'

I saw that until that moment he hadn't really believed it. Not completely. Perhaps Sally felt the same way. They must have talked it over endlessly, half convincing themselves that it couldn't be true. But in that second Marcus saw in my face that it was.

'It didn't happen the way you think. It was an accident. And Morello can't prove I had anything to do with it.'

'Then who killed Brinkman?'

'I don't know. It probably had nothing to do with any of this.'

But Marcus shook his head in disbelief. 'You know that can't be true. It's too much of a coincidence. It must have something to do with the program. You were prepared to kill for it. What makes you think somebody else isn't thinking the same way. Maybe it's Morgan himself.'

The same thing had occurred to me though somehow I couldn't see Morgan as a killer. Why take the risk when he could afford not to, apart from anything else. 'All I know for sure,' I said. 'Is that I still have the program and Morgan is going to pay to get his hands on it. Once we have the money Alice and I are going to get as far away from here as we can.'

The idea just came to me, but when I looked at Alice she met my eye and I knew she'd agree. Marcus stared from one to the other of us and understanding dawned.

'You knew about Dexter didn't you?' he said to Alice. 'You helped him.' He sounded as if he could barely take it in. This was something he hadn't expected. 'Don't you understand? Two people are dead. This has to end. Now.'

He appealed to us both as if we might come to our senses. I didn't know what he meant, that it had to end. Then he turned and climbed back down to the dock.

'Where are you going?'

'Where am I going? You didn't really believe we could go along with this any more did you? I'm going to get Sally and then we're going to the police. The reason I came here was to find out for sure if you killed Dexter. I suppose I hoped you'd convince me we were wrong, and we could all go to Morello together. You still could. If it really was an accident.'

'The police?' I echoed. 'Are you crazy?'

'You're the one who's crazy, Nick. Both of you.'

He turned and started walking away. I looked at Alice.

I wanted her to tell me he wasn't serious, but she stared back at me with a stunned expression. Seconds passed, and Marcus was already nearing the end of the dock.

'We have to stop him,' Alice said.

She was right. I leapt down from the boat and ran after him and I caught up with him on the edge of the parking lot. It was darker there away from the light and the trailers threw deep shadowy places.

'Marcus!' I shouted when I was ten feet away. He stopped and turned. I could hear Alice running after us. 'I can't let you do this.'

'Go to the police? How are you going to stop me, Nick? Are you going to kill me as well?'

Alice reached my side and appealed to him. 'You can't do this. You can't throw away thirty-five million dollars.'

He shook his head. 'You don't get it do you? Either of you. The money doesn't matter any more.'

He began to turn away.

'Marcus!'

He stopped. My hand went to the gun in the back of my jeans. I gripped the butt, but I didn't draw it. Alice saw what I was doing, and our eyes met. A second passed. Then another.

'Do it,' she urged quietly.

I didn't move. I saw something deep in her eyes, the knowledge of what she was capable of. Perhaps it was a reflection of myself. That moment of hesitation was like the beginning of waking from a bad dream. My grip slackened. Marcus didn't understand what was going on. His brow creased in a puzzled frown. Beyond him I saw his car at the edge of the lot, and then something else registered. In the corner, parked up close to a big launch on a trailer, where it was dark, was another vehicle. The faint light from the lamp in the middle of the lot gleamed off the hood and the darkened windows. I wondered if I was imagining things or if the car really was green.

What happened next seemed to occur in slow motion. Marcus began to turn away as three figures emerged from the shadows where they must have been listening to every word. One of them raised his arm and he was holding something that he pointed at Marcus who suddenly saw them and stopped in surprise. Then there was a popping sound and the back of his head disintegrated.

His head snapped back and as he crumpled I felt wet splashes on my skin. Alice looked down at the glistening pattern of blood and tissue on her white shirt. She opened her mouth to scream but a hand flew from nowhere and gave her a back-handed slap in the face that stifled the sound before it was formed. A singsong voice accompanied the aftermath of silence, managing to sound merry and chilling at the same time.

'Next time you gonna be one dead fuckin' bitch unnerstan'?'

CHAPTER TWENTY-EIGHT

There were three of them, all Latinos, aged somewhere between their late teens and early twenties. They wore oversized T-shirts and baggy trousers with the crotch hanging almost to their knees and the bottoms of the legs gathered over their Nike trainers. The eldest of them wore a thick gold chain around his neck and several gold hoops in both ears. His face was baby smooth, and might almost have been handsome when he smiled and flashed white teeth, except for his eyes. His eyes were reptilian. Black and soulless. The glitter in them was drug induced. They were all boosted on something and they acted like high-spirited kids one moment, giggling and hand slapping, full of machismo swagger, the next they were edgy and malevolent, looking for some way to expend some energy. They kept looking at Alice and licking their lips.

They all had guns shoved in the waistbands of their trousers. They made me help them drag Marcus's body back to the boat, where they dumped him inside the door from the stern deck. Alice was shoved roughly onto a seat in the corner. Her face was white and her eyes kept drifting irresistibly to where Marcus lay. Blood had continued to leak from his ruined head to soak into the carpet.

It took me a while to remember the name of the eldest kid. Pepe. That was what Hoffman had called him the day I paid these three to take care of my car. He was the one who'd shot Marcus, and who now brandished his gun with careless ease in my direction.

'Where's the disc at, man?' he asked in heavily accented street Hispanic.

'What disc?' I said.

I needed to slow everything down. Pepe appeared to attach about the same significance to killing Marcus as someone else might to putting out a cigarette. I understood that whatever he and his buddies were on made them unpredictable, but I needed time to think, to kick-start my brain again.

His tone changed instantly. 'The disc, man, where da fuck's it at?'

His eyes narrowed to slits and he shoved the gun into my stomach for emphasis. One of the others laughed in a high-pitched nervous giggle, almost like a girl. Abruptly Pepe's expression slackened into a grin and he removed the gun from my stomach.

'Fuck. I can't kill you, man. Never getta disc if I do that.' His grin became huge as if this was a terrific joke we were sharing, but I was looking into his eyes and there was nothing funny about what I saw there.

I was starting to think. The .38 was still in the back of my trousers. It hadn't occurred to them that I might have a gun. 'I know where I've seen you before,' I said. 'It was outside Hoffman's apartment building.'

I pictured the green car in the lot. I'd seen it before that same day when Marcus and I had gone to San Leandro. The same car I now realized that had followed me when I went to Morgan's house, that had played chicken with me the night Sally and I drove to Marios. It was these three who must have killed Brinkman though I didn't know why.

But Pepe wasn't listening to me. He swaggered over to the galley and started rooting through drawers. I glanced at the other two. They both stood just feet away, their guns held loosely at their sides. I calculated my chances of shooting all three of them if I tried to get my gun, and figured they were about nil. I had never even pointed a gun at another person in my life, in fact I didn't know if the .38 even worked. It had been lying unused for a long time. But mainly what stopped me was Marcus lying dead on the floor with the back of his head missing. In their drugged state these kids had no fear and I could count on them to react without hesitation if I moved. Even if I got my hand to my gun, if I fumbled for even a fraction of a second I was dead.

My brain was working now, racing at full speed, but my limbs felt leaden and frozen. Pepe found what he was looking for. He turned around and held up a kitchen knife with about a six inch blade and dread plucked at my insides. He tucked his gun inside his trousers and picked up a towel and I knew what was about to happen. The reports of Brinkman's death came back to me in vivid Technicolor. I doubt that he'd been a particularly brave man. He probably told them what they wanted to know before they ever used the drill on him, but they'd gone ahead anyway. I couldn't take my eyes off that blade and I knew right then I'd rather be shot than be sliced into pieces.

But it wasn't me Pepe had in mind. Alice realized at the same time I did that he was looking at her and when he moved towards her she shrank back against the wall and opened her mouth to scream but he was too fast for her. With one hand he slammed her head against the wall.

'Getter arms.'

The two younger kids held her while Pepe stuffed the towel in her mouth. Her eyes bugged and thinking she must be about to choke she struggled violently. It happened in a second.

'Wait!' I yelled.

But it was useless. Pepe wanted to make a point and he ignored me. The blade went up and flashed down again and pierced Alice's shoulder. Her eyes locked on mine in a silent plea as the initial shock and pain registered. I heard her muffled cry and tears sprang into her eyes.

Pepe looked over at me and remarked, 'You got about a second 'fore I stick her eye and affer that I'm gonna cut her fuckin' tits off, man.'

I didn't doubt for an instant that he would do it and I pointed to where the concealed cupboard was. 'It's in there.'

They let Alice go and she slumped back ashen faced, her hand going to the wound in her shoulder. Dark red blood welled through her fingers and seeped in a widening stain across her shirt. Pepe didn't even glance at her. He found the cupboard and when he retrieved the disc he looked at it for a moment, his head cocked to one side as if it intrigued him for some reason. Then he shook his head and clucked his tongue and put it inside one of his voluminous pockets.

'You know howta drive this thing?' he said to me.

Pepe stood beside me with his gun pressed into my ribs as I steered the launch out of the harbour and underneath the Golden Gate. Alice and the others remained below. The last I'd seen of them they were rummaging around for food, one of them complaining that they should have stopped at the McDonald's they'd passed earlier. I was worried about Alice. She'd been bleeding badly and was in a lot of pain though she'd had the sense to take the towel Pepe had shoved in her mouth and press it against her wound. Before I'd come up top she was slumped across her seat, looking pale and dazed with shock. I knew she needed a doctor, but once we cleared the bridge Pepe told me to head out to sea and I was under no illusion about what our fate would be. He watched how I handled the boat, which he must have figured didn't look too difficult because after a couple of minutes he grinned.

'Jus' like a fuckin' car, man.'

I wondered how far out he would take us, and when he glanced back at the lights in our wake I guessed it wouldn't be too far. He wouldn't want to run the risk of losing sight of land and getting lost. I tried to get him talking, hoping to distract him enough to give me a chance to make a move. I thought I had a few minutes at most. Probably the last thing to happen would be he'd tell me to slow down and cut the motor. After that I thought I could count my life in seconds.

'Do you know what's on that disc in your pocket?' I asked him.

He grinned at me. 'Whattya think I am, man? You think I never heard of fuckin' computers or something? This is what you took from the old guy's apartment. Some kinda software shit or something he made up.'

'What are you going to do with it?'

'What you think? I'm gonna do the same as you were and sell it to that rich fuck, Morgan.' He leaned back a little, and the gun came out of my ribs and he started waving it around in emphasis. 'Think I'm gonna buy me some new wheels, man. Prob'ly gonna get some chicks and fuck my brains out for while first though. Have a party. Maybe I'll buy me a boat like this fucker some time.'

He was having a good time. It amused him to tell me what a terrific time he'd be having with all the money he was going to get while I was lying on the bottom of the sea feeding the crabs.

I tried to keep him talking. 'Why did you kill Brinkman?' I asked.

'That fat lawyer? 'Cause I needed him to tell me what the fuck was going down, man. He come aroun' asking questions after the ol' guy died, wanted to know if anybody seen anything. Course nobody tol' him shit, but then he came back with that other dude Dexter, and he wanted to know the same kinda stuff, on'y he was handing out hunnerd dollar bills, man. So I figure it's okay to tell him my sister saw couple guys busting inna the old guy's place. Dexter, man, he gave me five hunnerd so me and my sister go with him in his car and he pulls up outside this office downtown and we wait awhile. Then this guy comes out and Dexter says to me, "That the guy?" and I tol' him yeah, tha's one of 'em.' Pepe smirked. 'That was you, man.'

'And Dexter paid you to follow me?'

'Tha's right. On'y I didn't know what it was all 'bout, and didn't give a fuck either, long as he was paying me. Then suddenly I can't get hold of Dexter no more. He's just gone, man, and he owes me money so I figger I talk to that fat fuck of a lawyer instead, and he starts cryin' an shit and talkin' 'bout this fuckin' software shit, man, so then I persuade him to tell me everything.'

'And then you talked to Morgan,' I guessed.

Pepe pulled a face. 'Yeah. 'Cept I couldn't get near that dude, man. Jus' kep' talkin' to some fuckin' bitch on the phone.' His expression became sly. 'Then I had a idea. I called back an tol' her I was you.' He giggled. 'This is Nick Weston,' he said, doing a bad imitation of what he imagined I sounded like. It must have worked though, long enough to get him talking to Morgan anyway.

'And tonight? You followed me from my office didn't you?' I guessed, remembering the car that had swung in behind me which I'd thought was the security guard.

'Tha's right, man. Been waitin' for you to show up somewhere.'

As we talked I dropped my right hand which had rested on the throttle control and it now hung against my side. Pepe was on my left. He was leaning against the control panel, his gun held loosely in his hand. His eyes had taken on a vaguely dream-like quality, as if he was coming down from his high, though they remained fixed on me. There was something indolent in the way he half leaned, half stood. I wondered if I could reach around and get my hand on my gun before he noticed. I shifted my body a little, making it seem like I was simply adjusting my balance. I couldn't hear anything from below above the sound of the engine and the unfurling bow wave on either side of the boat. A deep white foaming wake marked our progress across the dark ocean. The swell was very slight, the night clear and calm and a pale moon looked over us.

My heart started beating faster. I rehearsed in my mind what I had to do. Grasp the gun. Slip my finger through the trigger guard as I brought the barrel to bear. Pull the trigger. I remembered from somewhere that you're supposed to aim for the middle of a target to increase your chances of hitting it, though I didn't see how I could miss at this distance. I knew once I started to move I was committed. I couldn't hesitate, not for an instant. Pull and shoot. No warning. No hands up. No drop your gun routine. If I gave him an instant I would be dead. And though I was nervous I thought I could do it. After that I would have to go down for the other two, which I thought might be harder. They would hear the shot and know something was up which gave me very little time to surprise them. I thought I could wait for them to come to me, but then there was Alice. They would use her to get to me, of that there was no doubt. The only plan I had was to get down there as quickly as I could. There would be no time for thought. No time to hesitate.

Shoot. Turn. Run for the stairs. I'd be there in three steps. Leap down and hope it all happened too fast for them to react. There was a certain sense of unreality about all of this, despite my very real fear. I felt like some bumbling idiot dropped among a cast of very bad characters. I had been led to this. I had crossed the line where decent ordinary people lived their lives and now I was way, way out of my depth.

Pepe was still watching me. Though he appeared relaxed, kind of loose limbed and floppy, I knew he could move quickly and he never took his eyes off me. I needed something to put him off balance. Just for a second. Think! I told myself. Think! Then I had an idea.

'How much did Morgan say he would pay you for the disc?' I said.

'A lot, man.'

'How much? Half a million.'

Pepe's eyes widened a little. 'Half a million?'

I almost laughed. All this for what? 'How much then? A couple of hundred thousand dollars? A hundred?' I could see I wasn't far off the mark. These hoods had tortured a man to death, and shot another in the head without a thought, and they planned to kill Alice and me and dump us in the ocean. All for a few hundred thousand dollars.

'You know what he was going to pay me?' I said.

'How much?' Pepe said suspiciously.

'Thirty-five million dollars.'

I saw two things at once. One was that he didn't believe me, and the other was that the reason he didn't was because thirty-five million dollars was an incomprehensible amount to him. He simply couldn't grasp that anybody would pay such an enormous sum of money for something that looked like an ordinary music disc. No matter what was on it. But it didn't matter whether he entirely believed me. What mattered was that he at least partly believed me, and he knew Morgan had planned to cheat him. For a second he was so outraged he took his focus off me. And it was then that I moved.

He was quick. Even quicker than I'd been afraid he would be. As I began to reach for the gun, twisting my body around as I did, his expression altered in a flash. His eyes narrowed and glittered as he tried to stand straight and swing his gun arm towards me at the same time. Even though it happened in the blink of an eye it was still frightening. He didn't delay for even the briefest time. I moved. He reacted. That was it. He didn't know I had a gun. He didn't know what I planned to do, but it didn't matter. He looked directly into my eye and in that instant I knew that whoever was fastest would be alive a second from now.

I panicked and fired early, before I had him dead centre, and it was lucky that I did. There was a loud report and the bullet hit him in the groin and doubled him over. He screamed and fell backwards and I think he fired a shot because I seemed to hear a faint popping, then his gun clattered across the deck somewhere. He ended up in the corner, leaning against the side, his legs apart and blood seeping through the hands that clasped his groin area. He wore a look of surprised horror.

There was no time to check if he was dead. I was already running for the steps. I leapt down to the stern deck and as I landed I glimpsed a shape move inside. Instinctively my eye followed the direction of the movement and I saw one of the hoods reaching for a gun on the counter with one hand while he clutched at his baggy trousers with the other. I fired twice in rapid succession and one of my shots took away half of his skull. A pink mist filled the air as he dropped but I was already looking for the other one. The youngest of them had his arm around Alice's neck. She was barely conscious as he tried to pull her in front of him. She still wore her blood soaked shirt but it was twisted up around her neck and she was otherwise naked. I was momentarily shocked by the sight of her pale thighs and pubic hair. Then shock became rage. The kid was perhaps sixteen. His pants were caught up around his ankles and I registered this fact along with his still half erect penis as he fought for purchase and scrabbled for his gun. He was the only one who looked scared before I shot him. The bullet hit him in the shoulder and he screamed and let go of Alice. The impact of the bullet threw him to one side. He started to scream again but seeing what they had done to Alice had made me cold to his pleas. My second shot hit him dead in the centre of his skinny chest and destroyed his heart. The light went out of his eyes as he crumpled. His gun was three feet away. Out of his reach.

In the aftermath of the shooting I crouched with Alice on the floor and held her in my arms as she drifted in and out of consciousness. Her eyes focused on me, and blurred with pain and shock though they were, she recognized me.

'It's okay,' I told her gently.

The fear melted away a degree or two. I had covered her with a sheet I'd hastily ripped from a bed in one of the cabins. The boat was quiet, and rocked gently on the swell. I must have shut down the engine when I made my move against Pepe, though I didn't remember doing so.

'I'll get you to a hospital. You're going to be fine,' I said. 'It's over.'

She understood what I was saying, and a pinprick of hope lit her eyes. She was badly hurt. The wound in her shoulder had hit a major artery judging by the amount of blood that soaked the carpet. I looked at the young hood I'd killed who was lying against the wall with his head on his chest and his now small limp penis curled against his thigh and I felt no pity for him. When Alice attempted to follow where I was looking I stopped her. I changed my position so I could cradle her head in my lap. She was very pale. I pressed a wadded towel into her shoulder but it wasn't bleeding much any more. Her pulse was faint and as I spoke words of comfort her eyelids fluttered and closed and the hand that held mine fell limp.

For some time I stayed with her. I felt for her pulse, but I knew she was dead. In the end I covered her and went up top where I got a bad case of the shakes and was violently ill over the side. Pepe remained where I'd left him, his staring eyes sightless but still full of horror at what had been done to him, which I got a closer look at when I went to retrieve the disc. It was broken into a handful of pieces. Shattered either by the bullet that had destroyed his manhood, or else when he'd fallen. Either way, it was useless. I stared at the remnants for a while, waiting to feel something, but by then I was beyond feeling.

I swam a hundred yards away from the boat before I stopped to look back. She was well alight by then. The surface of the sea reflected back the growing yellow and orange of the flames. I watched, treading water for five minutes or more. Then all at once there was an explosion as the cooking gas I'd turned on in the galley ignited and the launch became a giant flaming torch in the night. A mile or so away I could see the lights of a boat as it changed course to investigate. I turned and began swimming towards shore.

* * *

I figured it was about a mile and half back to the coast. The lights winked faintly in the distance, vanishing every now and then as I bobbed in the swell. The fire receded behind me, and as it did the night gathered me up and held me close. When I looked back the fire had died right down and the boat was sinking, though another had drawn near. I didn't know what would be found. Perhaps a body or two, and enough wreckage to piece together who the boat belonged to. Sooner or later Morello would get involved and he would talk to Morgan and Sally and some kind of theory would be worked out. But Marcus and Alice were dead. And as far as the world was concerned I had met the same fate and I knew there was no other way it could be. Assuming I ever made it ashore. I hadn't swum such a distance in a long time. The current was against me, and there seemed little incentive to try too hard. I went through the motions. My arms and legs doing the work while my mind drifted elsewhere.

I was tempted to give up. Turn face down and wait until my lungs were bursting then open my mouth and swallow the sea. What else was there for me? Ashore I would have no money, no home, no identity even. I would be like a walking ghost. But I couldn't bring myself to do it, and so I swam on and part of me hoped I couldn't make it. When I grew weary and my muscles began to burn with fatigue I remembered the old people who swam in the slow lanes at the pool. Maybe they knew something. My arms rose and fell so slowly it was only just enough to keep me afloat and moving. The rhythm took over. Up down. No thought, no conscious effort. I could do this for ever it seemed.

When my mind started to go blank and I wasn't even sure of my direction I simply went on. My arms curved and dipped, and every third stroke I breathed and the water flowed around and across me and soon I didn't know where I finished and the sea began. I started hallucinating, thinking that Alice and Marcus swam below me. I glimpsed ethereal shapes beckoning me down. I'm coming I told them. Just a little longer. Then I was sinking and weariness sapped the last fragments of my endurance. I gave myself up and embraced the sea but as I did my fingers scraped sand and I raised my head and breathed the air and I could smell the seaweed collected in the rock pools on the shore.

CHAPTER TWENTY-NINE

I passed through Oregon a year after I came ashore. I rode a freight train through the Pacific northwest from Seattle down to Portland where I spent a day in a camp with some other hobos like myself. We are a motley bunch. Nobody has a name, save the ones we give ourselves and by which we are known. There's a guy I run into now and then who calls himself Iron Man, and there're others like The Kid, Old Man, Princess and Runner, and one who is almost a legend that people call The Ghost. Most of the names are more colourful than the people to whom they belong. The latter day hobos, unlike the men and women who drifted across the country looking for work in the days of the depression, are for the most part misfits and escapees from society. They are the bag men and women of the open country, preferring a box car on the railroad and the camps that grow up near the sidings to a life on a street corner in some big city. Many are afraid of the city, and of each other. They should be too. A high proportion are either mentally ill or psychotic and killings happen more often than anybody knows or cares about. A lot, however, simply freeze to death in winter.

I don't have a name. I talk to no one, and people have learned to stay clear of me. They are wary of me, in case I'm one of those who might be a serial killer, since there are a few of that type around. I know they call me Nobody, which is appropriate. I don't exist.

Sally lives with her parents now. I went to the house in the spring and watched her for a while when she came outside with the baby. She looked good. Tired perhaps, but whether that was from the baby or the after effects of what happened I don't know. A little of both probably. I was standing in the trees, close enough to see the child's features. Hard to say who he looked like, but I think there was a little of me in him. Sally looked happy when she held him and kissed his cheek, though there were signs of tiredness around her eyes. Frank pottered in the garden, Sally and her baby sat on the grass in the warm sunlight. I wanted more than anything I have ever wanted in my life to go over and just be with them. Even for a little while. I wanted to hold the baby, have Sally put her arms around me. The pain of my emptiness was almost more than I could bear as I watched them. To be a part of that scene was worth more than all of the money in the world. I understood then that what I'd truly missed in my childhood was my dad after he died. It was that, nothing more. Money, security, none of that mattered. Tears fell unchecked across my cheeks.

After a while I turned and started away. I looked back and Sally stared towards the trees as if some movement caught her eye. For several long seconds I half hoped she would see me, that this loneliness would somehow end. But then she looked away again and I waited until she went back in the house before I went on my way.

I won't return, because it's too painful. Perhaps I won't last another winter anyway. A couple of times I nearly froze when I was caught in the open last year and the snow came.

I think that would be a good thing. Anything would be better than this.